the

ENTITLED

a duet

CASSANDRA
ROBBINS

Copyright © 2018
THE ENTITLED by Cassandra Robbins
ISBN-13: 978-1726446495
ISBN-10: 1726446492

Edited: Nikki Busch Editing
Cover design: Michele Catalano Creative
Cover Photo: Wander Aguiar Photography
Cover Model: Andrew Biernatt
Formatting: Elaine York, Allusion Graphics, LLC
www.allusiographics.com

the
ENTITLED

a duet

For my mother

Ob•ses•sion

1. the domination of one's thoughts or feelings by a persistent idea, image, desire, etc.

chapter 1

And in the end, we were all just humans,
drunk on the idea that love,
only love, could heal our brokenness.
— F. Scott Fitzgerald

REED

Present day – twenty-five years old
London, England

"Deeper... Yeah... that's it, suck me hard." Leaning my head back, I close my eyes. It's too bright for me. I should have made her turn off the lights. The warm mouth that's sucking makes me moan, distracting me. The woman squirms, her hands reaching for my tight balls. She definitely knows how to suck my cock. If I could keep her from talking, we would have a perfect relationship.

The fantasy that I need, crave, is there, waiting for me. Grabbing the back of her head, I shove myself down her throat.

"Yeah, that's it, suck... like that," I growl at her.

I'm way too large for her to take me comfortably. Roughly I hold her head, watching her brown eyes widen as she starts to gag. Staring at her, I wonder why women allow me to do this. I almost ask her, but that would require her to speak. She tries again to deep throat me, working her hardest to accommodate my size. My stomach muscles clench. Her smell fills my nose: arousal and flowers. Why does every woman wear so much perfume? Except one... one didn't. Vanilla. That's what I desperately need to smell. I should have lit some candles. It would have helped me, soothed me. Aggravated at the thought, I pull her even tighter.

"Fuck yeah, that's it. Breathe through your nose." Mascara and tears cover her cheeks, her nostrils flaring. Taking pity on her, I release her head. She sucks in air with a small gasp. Like a cat in heat, she frantically grabs at me. A smile is on her lips like she is pleased with herself. Scooting forward, she pumps my cock from root to tip, then spits the thick saliva that comes from the back of her throat, making it easier for her to stroke me. Starting slow, then almost savagely, she goes at it.

Pleasure fills me, taking me to that place. "I like that." Grunting, I lean my head back and my eyes close, blocking out all noise, everything but *her*. My fantasy, my soul, my greatest regret.

She starts to suck me again, and in my mind, I see her. Beautiful blue eyes stare up at me. Black long lashes sweep down, her brown hair like silk in my hands. Up and down, she sucks and strokes, *fuck if only*... If only.

"Like that baby?"

What the fuck? Her voice startles me back to the present.

My eyes snap open, the precious fantasy gone as I blink at the lights in my penthouse, reminding me where I am.

"Fuck." Roughly I pull her mouth off me with a loud pop. She reaches for my cock like I stole her lollipop. Grabbing her hair, holding her still, I give her a firm jerk, my desire to get off gone. Somewhat hurt, she whimpers, licking her lips, her brown eyes questioning.

My phone rings again. Absently my eyes drift to where I left it charging on the counter.

"I asked you not to talk. It shouldn't be that hard if you kept my cock in your mouth."

"Sorry, you're right." She whines, "Can I try again?" Her swollen lips almost make her look deformed with the amount of collagen she has pumped into them.

Pulling my pants up, I tuck my dick back in as she watches like an adoring, defeated puppy.

I shake my head. "Lay off the injections. You're starting to look like a duck."

Moving her aside, I stand to retrieve my cell phone but still flinch when it rings again. *It's probably a robocall.* I grimace, shaking off the uncomfortable feeling.

"But... I thought you liked a girl with big lips?"

Her question makes me freeze, and I turn toward her. "Why would you think that?"

She shrugs. "You mentioned it once, saying you had a thing for puffy lips." Looking over at the counter, I can't resist moving toward my phone. My glass penthouse, with its unending view of the stone-gray Thames, is cavernous and sparsely furnished. To a stranger, it would appear I recently moved in. Not that it matters; I've been here almost a year. But with the apartment's emptiness, every sound echoes off the white, unadorned walls.

"You must have misunderstood. I loathe fake lips," I say, needing to shut her down. Her eyes narrow as though she's deciding if she believes me. Shaking her long blond hair, she runs her hands through it. My eyes take in her appearance. She is every man's dream: fake boobs and a tan, fit body. Yet I don't want her no matter how hard I try.

She can't understand my need to be cruel. After all, it's not her fault I'm miserable, and fuck it, she looks absurd. Someone needs to tell her. "They're too big, Victoria. Also, I don't like your perfume. Please change it to something else."

Removing the charger, I glance at my phone. Three missed calls. My heart pounds.

Frowning at the screen, I say, "It's late. Get dressed, and I'll have my driver take you home."

"You okay?" She tries to touch my arm. Christ, when did she become so clingy? Pulling away from her, I walk into the other room. As I close my tired stinging eyes for a moment, I take a breath and brace myself for what's about to come—*my past*, threatening to take me over.

Pressing my finger on my brother's name, I glance at Victoria, relieved that she's dressed now. I'll need to be alone for this call, and I want to be sure she's on her way out.

Waiting for Jax to answer, my mind drifts to the last time I saw my twin.

"*Don't do this, Reed. Give her time—just give her time,*" he'd begged me. If only I had waited. If only.

"Reed." Jax's voice fills my head. I miss him. My eyes dart around my empty space while I try to compose my voice.

"Reed? You there?" Shit, it's bad. I can sense it through the wire.

"Yeah, I'm here..."

The ominous silence over the phone makes my skin prickle. Glancing down at my Rolex, it's 3:00 a.m. London time. Panic grips my chest... *Tess!*

No matter how many years go by, that's my first thought whenever a 212 area code shows up on my phone. Jax clears his throat.

Fuck! The past, it's like a python slowly choking me.

"Reed... sorry, I know its early." My brother sounds tired.

"What's wrong?" I demand.

"It's Grandfather Ian. He had a massive heart attack yesterday and didn't make it. You need to come home."

Guilt takes over as I puff out the air I didn't know I was holding.

The relief that this call has nothing to do with Tess makes me sink into the chair. *Jesus, I truly am a shit.*

"How's Dad holding up?" It's all I can think to say.

"I think everyone is in shock. One minute, Grandpa was laughing with a drink in his hand. The next, he's dead."

"I'll take the G5 Jet. Be there in ten hours or so."

A hand caresses my hair, startling me. Victoria leans close, her perfume almost choking me. "Should I pack too?"

How did I forget she was still here? The past! That's how. All my mistakes have conspired against me, dragging me back to my life before I became a monster.

Jax clears his throat again. "Should I warn everyone you're bringing someone?"

"No." My voice is harsh. "It will just be me."

"Good." Silence fills the phone. I should hang up, but I wait as if Jax is going to say something that will make it all better. *Make me better!*

"I miss you, man. Everyone does."

Staring numbly at my blank walls, I say softly, "Me too, brother, me too."

REED

Past – eight years old
New York, NY

"Boys? Come downstairs. They're here!" my mother yells from the bottom of the stairs. When I glance at Jax, he rolls his eyes.

"Keep going," I urge.

"Working on it." He frowns at the computer screen. We're in Jax's room since his computer is better than mine.

Clenching my fist, I shift from one foot to the other. "Come on. She's going to yell at us to come meet that stupid girl."

"Don't rush me. I have no idea what Dad's password is. It takes time," he says with a hiss.

"What takes time, boys?" I jump and turn to stare at my dad's green eyes. They're filled with suspicion.

"Nothing." I shrug, trying to play it casual.

"What are you two doing?" His face tightens as he stares at the screen. Thankfully, Jax has put on some educational stuff. He's a computer whiz. I smirk. Figures, he'd be ahead of Dad.

"It's for school," is all Jax says. I hold my breath.

Frowning at us, Dad says, "I don't know what you two are up to, but your mother's childhood friend is here with her husband and daughter."

Crossing his arms, he looks at us pointedly. "We expect you both to be *kind* and take her under your wing. She is the same age as you two and will be starting at your school in a couple of weeks."

Groaning, I say, "We know, Dad. Mom has been talking about this for a month."

"Good, come on then." He still eyes the computer screen, then gazes around the room.

Jax's room is super clean compared to mine. All his games, cars, planes, Legos, and marbles are put away in their proper place. Greens with greens, reds with reds. His need for order drives me crazy.

Although, he does have a bunch of Pokémon cards on the dresser. And a few of them have even fallen onto his thick blue rug.

My room is so much cooler. Our mom decorated both of ours the same way. But unlike Jax, I leave all my Legos out. I mean, it takes forever to put them together. Why tear them apart, right?

Plus, it's super fun and easy to make a mess, knowing someone will always clean it up for you.

Both of us start toward the door, but a warm hand on my shoulder stops me.

"Go ahead, Jax. I need to talk to Reed for a moment." My brother's blue eyes meet mine and he shifts his gaze to our dad.

Jax shrugs but leaves. I wiggle my shoulder free, already tuning out what I'm sure will be a long lecture. I look over at Spiderman, who's painted on one wall. Mom hated it as it didn't fit with her color scheme. I think it's cool. Spidey is swinging from a web like he is coming right at you. In my room, I have the Hulk smashing out of my wall. Hulk would kick Spidey's butt even with all of Spiderman's special powers.

7

"Reed Saddington!" I swing my gaze to my dad, who is shaking his head. "What are you doing, son? Are you even listening to anything I've said?"

"Sorry." No way am I admitting I wasn't paying attention. It's not my fault that Spiderman and the Hulk are way more interesting. Silence greets me. At last, I risk a look: he is standing with his feet apart and arms crossed.

"What? I thought we needed to hurry and meet *the special girl*," I taunt.

"Reed, for the second time, what do you have Jax doing on the computer?" He leans over to pick up the cards on the floor.

"I knew it," I say with a snort. "It's always me, right? Jax is perfect." I know full well that is not the way my parents feel, but it always throws them off when I say it.

"No, that is not what I said. Jax is far from perfect, but he would rather eat garbage than rat you out."

That makes me laugh. "Eat garbage, that's a good one, Dad." I slap my knee, trying to get him to smile.

"I wasn't trying to be funny, son." He glares at me. "I know you two are smart. But you're only eight, so if you guys need help with something, I hope you know that you can come to me."

"What fun would that be?" I mumble.

"What was that, Reed? You're still a little boy, who—"

"Dad, I have to pee, and we don't want to keep Mom waiting. Honestly... all Jax and I were doing was checking out a science site." My eyes lock with his. "Geez, you are always thinking we are doing bad things." Hopping on one leg, I act like I have to go.

My dad's eyes narrow on me. "Fine, go to the bathroom and go meet your mom's friend."

"Finally," I say, running into my bathroom.

"Remember to be nice to Tess, Reed." His voice is serious.

I barely hear the last part as I slam the door shut. I take a deep breath. That was close. Jax and I should know better. We were trying to get into our dad's passwords, so we could turn off the parental control and get access to the whole internet. Jax assures me he can do it, and I believe him. He's better at the computer than anyone. Looking down at the toilet, I'm amazed at how much pee is coming out. I had no idea I had to go.

Quickly, I make my way downstairs. Turning the corner, I run right into the skinniest woman I have ever seen.

"Sorry," I mumble, trying to get around her, but her clawlike hands grasp my shoulders.

"Caroline," she yells. "I found your other boy."

Obviously, this is my mother's friend. She's tall and has crazy blond hair. Her face is so thin, her lips look like big pink bubble gum balls. I'm not kidding—her lips take over her face. Wriggling out of her grasp, I try to go around her. After all, she looks scary, kind of like Olive Oyl, Popeye's girlfriend, but with blond hair and weird lips.

"Excuse me," I say, trying to be polite. My mom will freak if I'm not.

She grabs my chin and screams, "How are you going to keep the girls away? My God! Caroline! Your boys are gorgeous."

Thankfully my mother comes around the corner, laughing, carrying two large glasses of wine.

"Claire, you're the one who has to worry. Tess is exquisite." She gives Olive Oyl a wink.

"Lucky for you my boys will take care of her like she was their own, right Reed?"

"Ah... yeah, Mom."

"That would be nice. She seems to have problems making friends," Olive Oyl mumbles as she drags me into our vast living room. I turn and my mom smiles as she follows.

"Poor Tess. Well, she doesn't have to worry anymore, right Reed?"

"Ah, yeah, Mrs.... um... Mom, what's her name again?"

They both laugh, "Call me Auntie Claire." She lets go of my arm to tap my nose. "God, it's good to be back on the East Coast again. California is so fake." She sighs dramatically.

My mom hands her a wineglass. "To my best friend, coming home at last." They clink their glasses together. I use the clinking to move around them and spy my twin sitting next to a girl with lots of dark curls. Both of their heads are together. He's showing her one of our new Game Boys.

"Hey." I walk over.

"Hey," Jax responds, not lifting his head.

"Hi." The girl looks up. I almost stop breathing as I stare at the most beautiful face I have ever seen. Shyly, she stands. She's dressed in a bright pink dress that makes her look like she is ready to go out to dinner with my parents. I take another breath as I stare at the most incredible blue eyes. They look like the ocean. Shaking my head, I think, this girl cannot be from the skinny blond woman who is giggling with my mom. She is literally her polar opposite. Her mother has a long pointy nose; this girl has a small cute nose. Her mother's eyes are a dull blue. The girl's vibrant blue eyes turn up at the ends. Cat eyes. She's like a magnificent scared kitten. In fact, that's what I am going to call her: *Kitten*. Thank goodness her lips are normal. Well, they are puffy, but at least she doesn't look scary.

"Son? You okay?" My dad interrupts my fascination with the girl.

"Sure." I step closer to her. She smells like strawberry lip balm.

"I'm Reed," I say, flashing her a grin, showing off my dimples. Mom says girls like dimples. Lucky for my identical twin brother and me, we have them.

Jax realizes the girl is no longer paying attention to him and looks up at us. An evil grin escapes his lips as he stands up so I can sit down.

"Sit." I motion to the girl.

She does with a shy smile on her pretty lips. "My name is Tess Gallagher."

With a shrug, I tell her, "I'm going to call you Kitten."

Her big eyes widen and she nods. "Okay, Reed," she whispers.

"So, I guess you don't have to worry about Tess anymore. Reed seems to have claimed her." My dad laughs at the guy standing next to him who must be her father. Thankfully, she looks a lot like him. He has brown wavy hair and the same blue eyes as hers.

He frowns. "Yeah, it appears so."

"Oh, Robert, lighten up. They are eight for heaven's sake," Claire snaps. "He's never any fun anymore."

The room goes silent enough that Tess's small hand finds mine. I give it a tight squeeze, and she peers up at me.

My mom unexpectedly sits down on the other side of Tess, her hand stroking her long dark curls. "Reed, Jax, why don't you show Tess around? Maybe show her the playroom." She smiles at us.

"You're making a scene. Stop drinking now," Tess's dad hisses at Olive Oyl. All three of us look over at them. They're in the corner behind our grand piano. I wonder if they think it's hiding them? I glance back at Kitten—her eyes almost look too big for her head as she sucks on her bottom lip.

"Sure." I jump up, excited to get away from her parents since they seem to upset her.

Tess stands quickly too. She's wearing some type of shoes that are covered in glittering gold stuff. Jax has finally looked up from his Game Boy, noticing her shoes too.

"Wow, um... well, we can always play Nintendo or watch TV because in those shoes"—he shakes his head—"I don't think you'll be able to keep up with us." He grumbles as we start to show her the upstairs, where our rooms are located.

11

Her small face looks crushed. "What do you mean? You don't like my shoes?"

Jax stares at her. "I said you wouldn't be able to keep up wearing them." He points at the heels.

She looks at me as if I should tell her I like her shoes. I don't. Instead I tell her the truth. "Listen, Kitten, if you want to hang with us, you can't dress like this. First, it's stupid, and second, how are you going to be our partner in crime, wearing shoes like that? See, it just won't work."

"Oh... I don't have any other clothes than this." She motions to her ridiculous outfit. "This is all my mother lets me wear." She nibbles on her bottom lip as if that's going to help her.

"What? This is how you dress, *every day?*"

She nods her head yes and lets out a small sniffle as she looks at her stupid shoes.

"Reed, you're making her cry. I hate it when girls cry." Jax puts a friendly arm around her shoulders.

I stare at them, this weird tightening in my chest. Now that she is getting comfort from my brother, she is full-on crying. If I didn't want to kick my brother, I would be laughing at him—the look on his face is priceless.

"Enough with the baby tears. Jax, let go of her. She's fine."

He glares at me, as she weeps some more. "Way to go, dumbass." He pats her back.

I don't know why I'm angry. I mean, it's some girl I met moments ago. But I stomp over, grabbing her arm, and pull her to me. She buries her head in my shirt and sobs. My brother and I are super tall for being eight, so her head comes up to my chin.

"God, stop, Kitten." I sigh. "You can wear these stupid dresses if you want. I have to toughen you up."

She shudders and mumbles something about hating New York, her mother, father, and being alone.

"Hey, if you stop crying, we'll let you in our club. It's us against the world. But you can't be a crybaby, okay?" Tightening my arms around her, I notice she's awfully skinny. She must get that from her mom.

She looks up at me. I mean she's only a girl, but with her long dark eyelashes that are spiky with tears and her deep blue eyes, she's so pretty I almost look away. *Almost.* Before I can stop myself, I blurt, "You don't ever have to be alone again."

It's then that her big red puffy lips break into a smile and I smile back. "I like your dimples." She reaches up and pokes them. We both start giggling.

"Gross, come on. Are we going to have any fun? Or are you guys going to stare at each other all day?"

"Oh, we're going to have fun all right." I grab her small hand, pulling her with me.

chapter 3

TESS
Present day – twenty-five years old
Santa Monica, CA

Lifting my head, I squint at my phone, glaring at it like it's the phone's fault it displays 4:45 a.m. on the home screen.

I groan and lie back down. Tiredness bears down on me like a heavy cloak draped across my body. Fluffing my pillows, I turn onto my side and stare at my dark room. *What is wrong with me?* Something's not right. I never do this. All night, I've tossed and turned but can't fall into a deep sleep.

"God..." I murmur, laying a hand over my eyes. Whatever *this* is, I'm on edge. This is ridiculous. I have to get up in two hours. I rarely, if ever take Valium anymore. It is strictly for emergencies. Unfortunately, after tossing and turning all night I wish I had taken one.

Closing my eyes, I take measured, slow breaths in and out, visualizing I'm on a raft, and the peaceful ocean is all around me. The warm water soothes me; the waves gently rock me.

If only this nagging unease would go away, then sleep would come. Even an hour will help me get through the day, and I do need to get through the day.

At last, I start to drift. And then I hear it—my phone vibrates as if it has a life of its own.

Sitting up, I grip my sheet like a security blanket, the feeling of doom taking over my body. I know whoever awaits me on the other end of the line is what has kept me up all night.

I think about ignoring it. Prolonging my fate, my body in fight-or-flight mode. Slowly I reach for it, transfixed as it vibrates then stops.

Pulling my knees to my chest, I wait.

I have long ago given up on trying to make amends with myself. My pain pierces into me and I wonder if I will ever get over it. The decisions I made will haunt me, torture me. And I own it. I'm not the same scared girl anymore—I can't be.

The phone comes back to life in my hand and I jump. Blinking at the name on the screen, I don't hesitate this time. I answer it because I'm not running.

"Hello." My voice is gravelly and I try to clear it. I have a raspy voice to begin with; the morning makes it worse.

Silence. "Tess?"

"What's wrong?" I demand, barely able to swallow, my guilt threatening to pull me apart, my body starting to tremble.

"Oh, Tess," I hear him sigh. I can almost see him pinching his nose.

Dread snakes around me, almost crushing me. "What?" I snap. "What is it, Jax?"

"I'm tired." His voice cracks. Compassion floods me along with terror. Jax rarely admits weakness.

"What's wrong?" I'm trying to hide my panic, but I can sense the truth. My heart pounds so hard, I feel it in my temples.

He snorts. "Funny. That's exactly what *he* said." He chokes on a sob.

Holy shit, this is bad!

"Jax? You're scaring me." My own harsh breathing is audible. I swallow, trying to stop a panic attack from coming on.

"You need to come home, Tess," he sighs. Your time's up. I wish... shit, I don't even know what I wish."

"What are you talking about?" I almost scream, my throat tightening.

"Come home. It's time," he demands rather harshly. I must not respond because his next statement knocks the breath out of me.

"My grandfather died last night, and all hell's going to break loose."

I drop my phone.

chapter 4

TESS

Past – fourteen years old

My mother bursts into my room, right as I finish packing.

"Tess, come on. You know I need to get you over to Caroline's." Pleading, she presses her palms together at her chest. "I can't be late for this appointment—it took me three months to get this plastic surgeon."

"I'm almost ready." I try to smile at her. She looks so nervous, and without makeup, she almost looks normal... well as normal as she can.

"I swear to God, Tess Rose Gallagher, if you make me late." She's screeching now.

"Mom," I snap. "I'm ready. Jesus, you are getting *more* surgery. And I'm not coming home for weeks. I have to make sure I have everything."

I haven't spent the night at Reed's in probably a year. When we were little, I slept over at their penthouse all the time. Not so much as we got older and it became apparent that Reed and I were together.

"Don't take the Lord's name in vain." I stop for a moment. I can't help but laugh because *really*? My mom has a mouth like a truck driver! She glares at me.

"Why don't you have Alex drop me off?"

"Because I need Alex with me." She nervously pulls her bleached-blond hair into a messy bun on top of her head.

That's weird, but whatever—my mom is weird. We run out of the house. Alex is waiting and helps me with my Louis Vuitton duffel. It's my latest gift from my absent father.

He smiles, and his white teeth clash with his tan. It's so startling because no one is that tan in Manhattan.

The traffic is awful and Alex is swearing away. My mom doesn't scold him about his language. We sit in uncomfortable silence as I stare out the window. My mind is going a mile minute. I get at least two weeks with Reed. That means we get to spend twenty-four hours a day together. Just as I start to think about Reed's full lips and the hot way he kisses me, my mom decides to appease her guilt and talk.

"So, Tess..." I roll my eyes. "I know I said it would be a couple of weeks, but it might be more like three, is that all right, Kitten?"

I *hate* when my mom calls me Reed's nickname. It's his and only his. Shooting her my best disgusted look, I turn back to look out the window. It's gray as usual, and dirty, also as usual. We have lived in Manhattan for almost seven years now and I still hate it. If I didn't have Reed and Jax, I would seriously be depressed.

"Whatever, Mother. Take as long as you need," I mumble.

She sighs, fidgeting with her wedding ring. "Exactly, I mean I need to heal properly. Since your father is never home, you will be happier with Caroline and Brad."I turn to glance at her, and she looks small even though she is not a short woman. She's so skinny, she looks petite.

My father has been gone for months. He left one morning, claiming he had an urgent case in London, which makes no sense because I'm pretty sure he can't even practice law in England.

That was six months ago, and even though she hasn't said it, obviously they are having problems. As much as either one of them talks to me, they could be divorced and I would never know.

I snicker at the thought. My mom would rather swallow poison than divorce my father. It's one of her few joys, tossing around his name, spending his money. See, he is a famous lawyer, or at least as famous as you can get in the legal world. He has won so many high-profile cases that he's become a bit of a celebrity.

Yeah, they're not divorced. He simply can't stand her, and she won't ever give him up. *Pathetic!*

"Tess?" Her nasal voice makes me cringe. Reed constantly makes fun of my mom in general, but her voice... He loves to imitate her voice. Now any time she sounds nasal, I have to fight back the laughter. Today, I can't help but crack a smile.

"You know you will almost be on summer break when I'm healed." Biting my bottom lip, I try not to burst into laughter. So, I look out the window for a moment, then back at her.

"Yeah?" Giggling, I can't help it.

She tries to raise an eyebrow, but with all her Botox, it looks like her eyes are big. "Am I amusing?"

I shake my head no, not trusting myself to speak.

Staring at me for a second before continuing, she says, "Anyway, I was thinking we should go to Paris. You know, buy a whole new wardrobe. Maybe go to London and visit your father." Her eyes light up—it's the first real spark of interest I have seen in them in a while.

I'd rather take a bullet to my head than go to Paris with my mom. All right, that might be a bit dramatic. But there is no way in hell I'm spending time away from Reed. Also, why would I want to surprise my dad? If he wanted to see us, he would come home.

"No, thanks. Reed and I have plans." I smile, and her eyes narrow as much as her tight face allows.

"What does that mean, Tess?"

"It means I'm busy, Mom." I smirk at her. "And for the record, do you honestly think you should get more work done? You can barely smile as it is."

"What the hell does that mean?" She flings a hand in the air.

"Language, Mom," I remind her.

"Knock it off. I'm the mother, not you." Her face is turning red—a sure sign I'm getting to her. I snort in disgust at that comment.

"You know, Tess, I feel sorry for you." She's so fake, it makes my stomach hurt.

"What are you talking about?" I snip, not wanting to look at her when she gets ugly like this.

"I'm talking about *your boyfriend.*" She sneers. "He will leave you so fast. The first time you do something wrong, or you do something he does not approve of, he will drop you like you never existed." She snaps her skinny fingers in my face. "So, prepare yourself." Leaning back into the gray leather seat, she wears a disturbingly satisfied expression on her skinny face.

I'm taken aback. "Why would you say that to me? It's so mean." Shaking my head at her, I tell myself it doesn't matter what she says, but it does. Deep down, I feel it.

Suddenly, I desperately need Reed.

This time, she snorts. "Please, Tess, you need to grow up. I don't even recognize you anymore." Her eyes sweep up and down me. "You have completely changed since you've been with him." She crosses her arms over her fake boobs.

I can barely react. Once again, she has stripped me of all my self-confidence. *What is wrong with her? She's my mother. Shouldn't she be my biggest fan?*

"I guess I will take my chances," I choke out.

Alex clears his throat. My face heats up, and I'm embarrassed that he has heard every ugly thing. "Um... we're here." His deep voice is filled with sympathy.

"Thank God," I say, grabbing my purse.

Turning to my mother, I glare at her. "Good luck, Mother. Try not to die on the table."

The door opens, and I can't get out fast enough. Strong hands reach for me. I'm filled with relief as I stare into the most intense blue eyes with a ring of green around them.

"Hello, Kitten. I've been waiting for you." He flashes me his incredible dimples and my heart skips a few beats to the point that I absently wonder if I should have it checked out.

"Reed." I breathe in his fresh scent. We're standing on the curb. It's crowded with people, but all I see is him.

"You're fine, beautiful. I've got you." And just like that, I am fine. Those little words erase all the ugly things my mother said. She's right that I've changed—hopefully for the better. If I ended up like her, I don't know what I would do.

Bringing me close, he brushes my lips with his. There's that flutter again.

This time he smiles and holds my hand up to his strong heart. "Mine flipped too."

"I doubt that yours feels like a machine." I love Reed's heartbeat; I'm kind of obsessed with it.

He kisses my nose. "Come on," he says, lacing our fingers together as he pulls me toward his massive building.

"My mom is waiting for you. She's got some new rules." He winks.

Suddenly, I remember turning away from my mother. She's gone. "Great!"

What, if she does die on the plastic surgeon's table? And the last thing I said to her was "Good luck." Now I have guilt.

"What's wrong?" His dark brows arch at me.

"God, Reed, I told my mom to try and not die on the plastic surgeon's table." Putting my hands over my mouth, I swallow. "I'm the worst daughter ever."

He bursts out laughing as we zigzag through people. "Why the hell would you feel guilty about that? All you said was the truth."

See? I feel better. Reed is like a drug *I can't live without.*

"You think?"

"I know. You have to stop letting her crazy insecurities affect you. You're too strong for that. The only thing you need to worry about is how to sneak into my room tonight."

"Reed!" Slapping my free hand on his bicep, I wave hello to Thomas the doorman. He winks at me, causing Reed to glare at him.

"What do you mean sneak?" I glance around at the elegant lobby. It's pretty much all gray marble with giant mirrors.

"I always sleep with you whenever I stay the night," I whisper, so Thomas doesn't hear us.

"Yeah, that's part of the new rules Mom is going to talk to us about, I think." He slips my purse strap back on my shoulder, grinning. The sound of a ding makes us turn, and we enter the private elevator for the Saddington family's penthouse. It's the only one that can go from the ground floor to the top. Even making it work is a whole ordeal. He punches the code, then uses his thumbprint to start the thing, and... up we go. It's so smooth and fast, we are there before I can even comment.

The elevator opens to vast elegance and an incredible view of Manhattan. *Thank God, I'm not scared of heights.* Mozart's playing softly in the background.

Reed stops me, caging me in. "Kitten, Mom is going to try and guilt you. Do not let her!" He rubs my bottom lip with his thumb, and I quickly kiss it. My pulse speeds up.

"What is going on today? First my mom, now Caroline. You know I hate this kind of stuff."

When he cocks his head—*he's so hot!*—his blue eyes are filled with tenderness.

"You're mine. That's all you need to know. She's going to give us the 'we're too young' speech." He shakes his head, his eyes locked on mine. "I don't care, Tess. I will not have her dictate what is mine. *Especially,* when I get you for two whole weeks." His warm, clean breath caresses my lips. He rubs his nose on mine, and I can't help but smile.

"This is practice for when we get our place together." I nod. He grins and takes my hand, pulling me behind him. I love when he gets all possessive.

"I have no idea why we need rules, but she is insisting. So, let's get it over with, and we'll go to Zack's party."

"Maybe because we are only fourteen, Reed!" Okay, so we're almost fifteen. My birthday is in April, which is a month away, and the boys are early August. They're tall, so they look older. We walk into Caroline's award-winning living room. She actually won an award and a big spread in *Architectural Digest.* I love all of Reed's penthouse, but this room with the large windows and the panoramic view of Manhattan makes you feel like you are a king or queen ruling your empire. The celery-green walls and priceless art have a calming effect.

"You're so weird, Reed." I shake my head, teasing him.

His eyes turn a shade darker. "You love that about me."

And I do—I honestly do. Most people would feel insulted or insecure by someone thinking them weird. Reed. Does. Not. Care. I envy that. His self-confidence is amazing.

Also, I don't truly think he's weird. Brilliant, domineering, and intense yeah, but weird no. Maybe that is the definition of weird, I think, smirking. Whatever, I want him, and unfortunately, so does everyone else. It's like his *weirdness* makes him more desirable. His lack of conformity makes him a leader, which then makes everyone want to please him, including me.

"Sit," he commands. I do, sinking down onto one of Caroline's uncomfortable couches. I'm sure it cost a fortune, but it's the worst for your back.

"I'll go tell my mom you're here."

My eyes follow him as he leaves the room. Obviously, he is not worried about *The Rules*, so why should I be? Sucking on my bottom lip, I look around. It's perfect. Everything Caroline does is perfect. From the huge display of white orchids to the immense Andy Warhol hanging above the fireplace

Inhaling, I take a deep breath and remember the first time I was in this room. I found my soul mate in this room, my true love at eight years old. I start to pick at my manicure that I just got yesterday. Reed leaving the room makes my anxiety kick up a notch. Taking a breath, I chastise myself. I can't always have him with me twenty-four hours a day. I brush the pink chips of polish off my Diesel jeans. I have always been a nervous person and having my mom be the way she is doesn't help. When my parents informed me we were leaving Los Angeles and going to New York, I was terrified. Literally, I cried for a solid week. The thought of the plane crashing made my anxiety unbearable. So, my mom gave me my first Valium at age *eight*!

Manhattan, in general, upsets me. Too many people, which I hate. Only I hate being alone more! I despise that we go months without sunshine. Okay, the sun does shine in the summer. But who wants to be out in it with the humidity making it seem as though you can't breathe. I guess that's how I have always felt. Like I can't breathe, like I don't know who I am. Until I looked into a pair of turquoise eyes and suddenly I had oxygen!

Suddenly I knew who I was. *I am Kitten, and I belong to Reed!*

Yes, people judge me. My mom says that you can't fall in love at eight. But that's because other people haven't met their true mate yet. That's why people are so angry. They are constantly searching for their souls to be filled. I'm lucky because as soon as I found him, I knew I was never letting him go.

"Tess, sweetheart." Startled, I gasp.

"Sorry, I didn't mean to scare you." Caroline laughs. Reed sits down next to me on the couch, pulling me close.

"You know how jumpy I am," I say, laughing too.

"I do, honey." She frowns, and her face is the picture of seriousness. *Oh God, she seriously is going to set some rules! If Reed and Jax will never follow them, then I'm not going to follow them, and I'll have guilt!*

"Kitten, stop." Reed's hand is on my knee. I must have been bouncing it again. It calms me, but he would rather I lean on him if I get nervous. So, I do. I grab his hand and he leans back on the couch with me, completely relaxed. Caroline's hazel eyes dart back and forth from my face to Reed's, then to our hands.

Clearing her throat, she goes on. "Okay, here are the rules…"

"Shouldn't Jax be here?" Reed interrupts.

"No, this does not involve him." She starts to pace. "I need to have this conversation with you two. Also, I would like to speak privately with Tess."

"No," Reed states.

"No? Excuse me?" Her eyes are huge. "Reed Bradley Ian Saddington, you may be the star at your school, and you may have been blessed with good looks and a gifted brain, but I am your mother! I run the show in *my house!*" Her pretty face flushes.

He shrugs. "You can talk to Tess, but I will be with her."

Caroline stares at Reed as if he's grown two heads. "*No…* Reed, I will talk to her *alone.*" Her eyebrows lift in challenge. Feeling that I should help, I squeeze Reed's hand, hoping to keep him calm.

"It's all right, Reed. I would like to talk to Caroline alone anyway," I say, looking at her. I know he's shooting me daggers.

Silence fills the room and at last, I glance over at him. After all, his grip on my hand is becoming somewhat painful.

"What?" I look at him innocently.

His eyes are sparkling. He acts like he hates it when I stand up to him. But secretly, he loves it, *I think*. I start to shake my leg again, which must make him reconsider.

He pulls me closer and mumbles, "Fine."

Caroline paces again. "I've talked this through with Brad and Claire."

Both of us groan at the mention of my mom.

She stops and glares at us. "Knock it off, you two. Tess, we have *all* decided you can't sleep with Reed this time... I mean, in his bed, like you used to." We both must be staring at her as if she's insane because she starts to stutter, and her arms are getting animated. "You know what I mean."

"I have no idea what you mean, Mom." *God, Reed is such a smart-ass.*

Caroline gives him the mom stare. Her cheeks are still flushed. She's wearing a pale pink dress and her cheeks surpass it.

"Why now?" Reed's voice rises. "She has been sleeping with me since we were eight years old!"

"It was one thing when you were little. Tess had issues with her anxiety." Holding up a finger, she continues. "She is no longer eight, and neither are you! This time, she's staying for a couple weeks, maybe longer. She will sleep in her bed, in her room." Turning to me. "Tess, you're a smart girl. I don't think I need to get into details. You must know it's not appropriate." I can sense Reed's energy. He hates when anyone tells him no.

"Mom." Reed pulls me even closer. "Do you have any idea how jealous your friend is of Tess? Her own daughter!" He's getting angry, and I put a reassuring hand on his leg and squeeze. He glances down, then continues. "Every chance she gets, she tries to make her feel like shit. You know why? Because she can't stand that Tess is beautiful, inside and out." He shakes his head in disgust.

Taking a breath, I let it out, my eyes stinging with tears. If only I felt as beautiful as he sees me. Caroline doesn't move and looks down at her hands.

She sighs. "I know that Claire is not perfect, but she has been going through a rough time lately."

Reed jumps up. "Lately? How about Tess's whole life? I'm not going to allow her to do any more damage to Tess. You want to do something worthwhile, Mom? You should have Olive Oyl give you guardianship over Tess and call it a day."

Her head snaps up. "You know I can't do that, and there is nothing wrong with Tess."

Reed looks at the ceiling like it holds a secret message. "Of course there is nothing *wrong* with her, Mom. But thanks to your friend"—he points at her like it's her fault—"she suffers from anxiety and panic attacks. I'm the only one who calms her." He is literally the master of persuasion. I stare at him in awe.

"Reed, she is no longer a little girl. She's your girlfriend." Caroline, starts to sound unsure, then straightens her shoulders.

Shaking his head, he says, "Mom, you're making a big deal out of something that is nothing. All we do is sleep!" Silence is all we hear. I don't know when Mozart got turned off, but I wish he was still playing.

"Well," she says, clearing her throat, "as the adult, I can't allow this to go on. She will sleep in her room. Tess?" My eyes shoot up to hers. "Are you okay with that?"

Standing up, I'm completely horrified that Caroline thinks I'm a crazy person who can't sleep alone. Though, she is my mother's best friend, so God only knows what she's heard.

"Um, yes, I'm fine. You're right. We aren't kids anymore. I have no problem staying in my room. Thank you for taking care of me."

"Unbelievable, Mom." Reed throws his hands up in full protective mode. "I knew you would make her feel guilty. She gets enough of that with her own parents."

"Wow, good times in here, huh?" All of us turn to Jax. "How come I was not invited to this family gathering?" Tall and athletic, he walks into the room carrying a basketball. "I can hear you guys all the way down the hall." Tossing the ball on one of Caroline's priceless French chairs, he grins as she cringes.

He grabs my waist and pulls us both down onto the couch. "Don't worry, sis. I'll protect you."

"Jax," Reed warns, "get her off your lap." He turns to Caroline. "If it's anyone you should be lecturing, Mom, it's Jax. He has done *way* more than Tess and I have."

"*Nice*, brother, way to throw me under the bus." Jax stares at Reed.

Reed shrugs. "Whatever."

Jax eyeballs him and smirks. "Mom? If you need me to sleep with Tess, I will. That way I can report that nothing funny is going on with her and Reed in your house." His lips start to twitch. Reed looks like he wants to kill him.

"What? I'm only trying to be helpful." Laughter bursts out of him, and I can't help but giggle. Jax is ridiculous.

"Jax, I'm not kidding, *let Tess go* and never talk about sleeping in her bed again." Reed almost spits it out.

"That's enough." Caroline has her hands together as if she is praying—like that's going to stop them.

"Whoa... Mom, did you hear that? Reed, called *Tess*, Tess. He's mad."

"That's it." Reed lunges for Jax, who drops me onto the couch.

"Boys, stop. I swear to God, if you break anything," Caroline screams, holding her antique table in place, stopping her Tiffany lamp from being destroyed. "Stop it, you two! Tess, do something."

Taking pity on her, I jump up. "Reed, stop." They ignore me. "Reed, *please*, I... I need you!" It's the first thing that comes to mind.

That stops him. He looks up at me and our eyes connect. Stepping toward him, I notice how intense his eyes are. He needs me as much as I need him. This is how it is with us. Neither of us is complete without the other. He roughly shoves Jax away.

"Don't touch her, Jax." They're both out of breath. Reed keeps his hair longer than Jax, so his dark curls fall over his turquoise eyes.

The Saddington twins are drop-dead gorgeous. Both are tall, already over six feet. Both have dark curly hair, and both have a dimple on each cheek. *So hot!* And Reed is all mine.

I'm not going to lie—seeing him go crazy like that is such a turn-on. I stare greedily at his beautiful face. A small evil smirk appears on his full lips as if he knows what he does to me. I can't look away or hold back a smile.

"What am I going to do with you three?" Caroline is pissed, like really pissed. The last time I saw her like this was when we all snuck out, and a cop on a horse brought us back.

"You know what, Tess?" She points at me. "Come with me. Reed, Jax, knock yourselves out."

I have no choice but to follow her. Turning back, I see Jax wink at me and Reed smack him in the stomach, causing him to double over.

Caroline takes me upstairs to her bedroom and shuts the door. It's been years since I was in this room. Brad and Caroline's room has always been off-limits, which only made us want to sneak in. After numerous adventures of playing spies and never finding anything interesting, we quickly lost interest and moved on. Caroline must have redecorated because the walls are yellow instead of green. The ornate ceiling now has what looks to be gold inlay. And she has added a huge chandelier in the middle.

It's so elegant in here, I almost don't want to move in case I mess something up.

"God, I need a drink. I'm sorry, Tess, do you mind?" She doesn't wait for me to answer but pulls out a bottle that was in her underwear drawer and takes a swig.

"Wow, Caroline," I mumble as she takes another swig, closes it, and puts it back.

Holding up a manicured finger, she says, "You have to promise me, you will not tell anyone, especially the boys, that I have this in here."

When I stand there, mute, she adds, "I mean it. This bottle is ridiculously expensive. I don't want them getting their hands on it."

"Okay." This conversation is going to be awful if Caroline is drinking already.

She rolls her eyes. "Do not give me that innocent look. I know my sons steal bottles frequently."

Sitting down, she crosses her legs then pats the spot next to her.

"Please have a seat, Tess." Reluctantly I move to sit on a sofa that Napoleon once owned. Yes, this is my life. Caroline uncrosses her legs, then crosses them again.

God!

"Tess?"

"Yes?"

"I know what you and my son feel for each other is unique. I also see that you have developed into a woman." She motions with her hand. "You have breasts now and have started your period. I only wish I had your body."

She laughs, and I stare at her and start to bounce my knee again. Caroline notices, frowns, but continues.

"Anyway, you know I love you like a daughter. I need you to know that 'We'"—she uses air quotes—"meaning *women* hold the power."

Leaning over to me, she grabs my hands. "Never let Reed pressure you into doing something that you are not ready for. I know he believes you are his. But you have to start being smart, Tess. Do not give up your virginity easily." She gives my hands a squeeze and lets them go.

I almost fall off the sofa. *Holy shit!* She did not just say that.

Heat fills my cheeks and neck. I'm mortified, and all I want to do is grab Caroline's hidden bottle and take a sip. Maybe it's strong enough that I can forget we ever had this conversation. She must feel the same way because she jumps up and gets the bottle, taking a huge swig.

"Um... Caroline, Reed and I have only kissed. He doesn't pressure me at all." Hopefully I can assure her.

She looks at me. "Well, that will be changing faster than you know." Pointing the bottle at me, she says, "Be smart. You are such an incredibly exquisite girl. I know you love Reed. But, don't forget that there is a big world out there and settling down too soon..." Her voice trails off. She caps the bottle, setting it on her dresser.

Her eyes lock with mine. "Well, that would not be healthy for either one of you." Then she takes a deep breath. I find myself following, dreading what is going to come next.

"And when you do start having sex, please tell me, or your mother, so we can get you on the pill. The last thing any of us needs to deal with is an unwanted pregnancy!"

The look she gives me is like she just ate a lemon or something worse.

I so want to crawl under her Persian rug and die with shame. Instead I clear my scratchy throat. "Caroline, Reed and I are not having sex." I can barely say the word. "But... when we do, I will get on birth control." My face is on fire.

Caroline puffs out some air, then smiles. "Good. See? That wasn't so bad. So, no more sneaking in to sleep in Reed's room because if he is anything like his father—"

I stand up before she can continue. I don't want to hear or picture Brad and her having sex. Not because it's gross—I mean Brad is hot and Caroline is pretty—but it's something I don't want to think about.

"Do you have any questions about sex, Tess? I know the boys are obsessed with watching porn, so if you have questions..." She gives me a supportive smile.

"Wait, what? Reed watches porn? How do you know that?"

She looks like she's been caught stealing something. "Let's say Jax is a genius with the computer, but Brad is still one step ahead of him."

Shaking my head, I look at her bottle. *Is she drunk? What does that even mean?*

"No, I don't have any questions yet." I try to smile. At least she's trying, no matter how humiliating.

"Please don't worry, Caroline. I'll be sleeping in my bed from now on. Is there anything else?" I need to get out of this room and find Reed. I'm starting to feel claustrophobic.

"No, that's it." She slaps her legs. "I am so happy that's done. I'm going to call Brad and your mother and tell them I did it." She seems proud of herself.

"Okay... Do you want me to send in Reed or Jax?"

"No." She waves her hand as if dismissing me. "Now that I've talked to you, I don't need to worry about Reed and Jax. After all, boys will be boys." God, she has to be drunk. *Boys will be boys, seriously?*

I nod as if I understand her and thankfully escape. Shutting her door, I lean against it, closing my eyes. *What just happened?*

"That bad, huh?" Opening my eyes, I find Reed smiling at me, his hair wet, all of him smelling delicious. Perfect. He gets a relaxing shower while I get unwanted pregnancy talks.

Too confused at what I'm feeling to talk to him, I shoot him a death stare, turn, and walk straight to my room.

"Hey." He grabs my arm. "What happened? She had you in there a long time." His voice is so gentle, I almost soften. Almost!

"It was humiliating and enlightening all in one." Jerking my arm free, I ask, "Are you watching porn?" My eyes stare into his. I don't want to miss the truth.

God, I'm not even trying to hide my insecurities. Fuck it, this bothers me. It makes me feel inadequate like he's cheating on me.

I see it. The second he makes the decision, his eyes change. *Holy shit, he is going to lie to me.*

Dropping my arm, he cocks his head. "What did she say to you?"

"Whatever, Reed! That's a yes." Sneering, I breeze past him into my enormous lavender room. Throwing myself on the white lacey comforter, the bed squeaks with my dramatics. So, I toss the Euro pillows across the room to make sure he gets it. He stands there staring at me, his lack of control of this situation making his energy bounce off the walls. I turn my back on him, curling into a ball.

"Tess?" He's mad and going to try to turn this on me. I know him so well.

"Turn around. I'm talking to you." His voice is harsh.

Ignoring him, I bury my head in the down pillow.

"Fine. I'm not watching porn." *And there it is.*

My head snaps up. He must see the devastation in my eyes, for he takes a step back. I see a brief moment of remorse.

"Why would you care anyway," he snaps, the bed dipping as he sits down. "Kitten, come on, let's not fight. It's Jax who's into the porn." He takes my hand in his.

I pull away, scooting backward until the cold metal of the wrought iron headboard stops me. Reed's eyes look like they are going to bug out of his head. I have never pulled away from him *ever*. He's my lifeline.

Biting my lip, knowing I should keep quiet, I can't help myself—I want to hurt him. "I may not be as smart as you, Reed, but don't ever think I don't know when you're lying to me." Hot tears sting my eyes.

He stands up, facing me. "Wow... Okay, Tess... yeah, I watch porn! Is that what you want to hear?" Scrubbing his hands up and down his face, he keeps going. "Does that make you feel good knowing that I like to watch hot girls licking each other's pussies and *love it*? Do you want me to tell you how I get off watching threesomes too?"

I can't hold the tears back anymore. The image of Reed watching those girls makes me want to vomit.

"Get out of my room!" I scream at him. I must look serious because his face is red and he seems angry enough to strangle me.

"Fuck this." He holds his hands up and goes for the door.

Stopping, his hands open and close at his sides. "You know what, Tess? *This* is why I didn't want to tell you the truth. I knew you would act this way. *I knew it!*" He's panting.

"Every guy watches porn. And if they say they don't, they're lying. It's not a big deal, certainly not worth you getting hysterical."

"I'm not hysterical about the porn, you ass." *Well I am, but I'm sticking with him lying as the big deal.*

"I'm hysterical that you lied right to my face. Did you think I wouldn't be able to tell? Think again. Because if you *ever* lie to me again, we are over!"

I'm completely losing it, and he's looking at me like I'm insane. My pathetic hiccups are the only noise in the room.

At last, he shakes his head at me. "I can't deal with your insecurities today."

Tears blur my vision, and I can't even see him. But I hear my door slam and that about kills me.

REED

Barging into my brother's room, I practically punch the wall. Fighting with Tess has me wired.

"Let's get out of here."

Jax swivels his computer chair around. "What's up?

"What time's Zack's party tonight?" I kick his backpack a few inches across the floor.

Jax looks at the backpack then back at me. "Six."

Not being able to sit still, I pace, adrenaline pumping through me. *I fucking hate fighting with Tess!*

"Call Zack. Tell him we're coming over. I need to get away from here," I say, running my hands through my hair.

"Interesting. I take it Tess will not be joining us?"

Snorting, I look up at the white ceiling. "No, Tess will be crying herself to sleep, I'm sure."

Jax raises an eyebrow and closes his laptop.

"Fuck!" I glance around the room for something to punch.

"Don't even think of trashing my room. Go to your own." His tone is serious.

Looking at him, I need to get it together. He's right. Taking my anger out on him is wrong.

Slumping into a chair, I grab a basketball off the floor and throw it against the wall a few times. The loud thumps bring me some calm. I toss the ball to him. "Sorry about today. I did throw you under the bus. That was wrong."

He throws the ball up and catches it. "Are you sure you want to go out tonight? If you're fighting with Tess, it's only going to be ugly." He says it casually as if he's bored.

Leaning my elbows on my knees, I crack my knuckles. "Did you know that Mom knows we watch porn?"

Jax stops throwing the ball. "What?" He shakes his head. "There's no way. I cover our tracks."

"Well, obviously not well enough because she told Tess, and I had to lie." I lean back in the chair.

"You lied to Tess?"

Shame floods me. Tess's tears are already killing me. I don't need Jax judging me. "I didn't want to. She was looking at me with those fucking eyes of hers. You try telling your girlfriend that you watch naked women, and see how happy she is."

He shakes his head. "So, if you lied, why are you fighting?"

"Because... it's Tess. She knew I was lying as soon as I said the words."

Jax snorts. "See, *this shit*?" He motions with his hands. "This is why I don't want a girlfriend and why I'm going to get laid way before you."

"What the hell are you talking about?"

Jax smiles at me like I'm an idiot. "Getting laid! It's quite simple. You love Tess. You're not going to pressure her."

"Yeah... So?"

"So, while you wait for Tess, I will be getting all kinds of pussy."

I can't help but laugh. "I love how everybody thinks you're the good one."

He's right though; he is going to be having sex before me. Tess is not ready, and all our firsts will be together.

"Whatever, man, just figure out how Mom knows."

Not being able to sit still, I pace again, his blue walls closing in on me.

Jax is silent, and I can see the wheels turning. "Fuck!" he says. "You think they have cameras?"

I shake my head slowly as I think about it. "Mom wouldn't allow it." I can't accept that because I love my mom, and that would suck.

36

"I'll figure it out. I'll call Zack and let him know we are rolling over now." Reaching for his cell, he hesitates. "You sure you want to leave Tess tonight?"

"She's freaking out about porn, Jax. I can't deal with it. And don't look at me like that—it pisses me off."

"I want to have a good time. And when you and Tess are fighting, something always goes wrong."

He looks down at his phone as he starts texting. "Feel free to stay home and deal with your girlfriend."

"I'm telling Mom we're going," I say over my shoulder.

"Okay, but I don't want to hear you whine like a bitch as soon as you start drinking."

Not listening anymore, I slam his door. Gritting my teeth, I force myself to pass Tess's room. It's like she has some kind of voodoo spell on me. Always has. All I want to do is hold her and kiss away her tears.

Screw that. She needs to learn that she was completely crazy today.

I knock on my mom's door. My nerves are shot, and I want to erase this whole day from my memory. When Mom casually mentioned this morning that she was going to have some rules, I knew it would probably come up about Tess sleeping in my bed. Frankly, I was surprised it took them this long. I also thought I would be able to guilt my mom into relenting. I mean, she knows firsthand how bad Tess's anxiety can get. Now we're going to have to sneak, and if Jax is right and they have cameras...

"Come in."

A burst of citrus overpowers me. It's so strong my eyes water. "God, Mom! What's that smell?"

"My new detoxifying mask." The whole room is slightly foggy.

"Jesus." I grimace, resentful that she's the reason Tess and I are fighting. "It's burning my eyes! How can that be good for your face?" She's starting to do all sorts of pathetic things to keep herself looking like she's in her early thirties, rather than pushing forty, and it pisses me off.

"Reed? What is it?" she asks, pushing away the fresh oxygen machine. She sits up on her elbows.

"Seriously, what are you doing? What is that thing?"

"My oxygen machine. It blows fresh oxygen on my face, healing and energizing me." Her tone makes it sound like I should know that. "What do you need, honey?"

"Jax and I are going over to Zack's. We might stay the night. Thought I would let you know."

She lies down again, making sure her face is directly under her machine. "Absolutely not. No staying the night." She wiggles, making herself comfortable. "I just set the rules about Tess—you can't break them by staying at Zack's." She closes her eyes on me.

"Tess is staying home," I say, not disguising my bitterness. She opens one eye. "Why?"

"I think you have a pretty good idea, Mom. Thanks." Sarcasm drips from my voice.

"Reed." She sighs. "I did what I had to do. I love how I'm the bad guy."

"Whatever." I clench and unclench my teeth, getting angrier by the second, watching her pamper herself while I feel like someone has punched me in the chest.

"Fine. You guys can go, but have Jay drive you and please be home by midnight."

Laughing, I say, "That's not going to happen. It's Saturday, Mom. We'll be home when it's over."

"Reed!" She sits up to look at me, then waves her hand. "Just go," she grumbles.

Not waiting for her to change her mind, I hurry into my room. I change into jeans and a T-shirt. Then I raid my dad's liquor cabinet.

chapter 5

REED

Past – fourteen years old

I find Jax in the garage, waiting and laughing with Jay.

Jay has been one of our drivers and bodyguard for a couple of years now. He used to be a marine. So, he takes serious care of his body. Jax and I have started training with him in the mornings. He pushes hard, but I like making my body burn.

"Let's go. We're headed to Zack's," I say, sounding like an entitled prick even to myself.

He raises an eyebrow at me, his eyes scanning the garage. "Where's Tess?"

I'm gritting my teeth so hard my jaw twitches. I know Jay has a thing for Tess. I have no idea how much—I mean, he's in his midthirties. I also know he would never dare do anything unprofessional. But the way he looks at her makes me want to punch him and then destroy him. I always have him drive us, so I can watch him watch Tess.

Jax is convinced I have nothing to worry about with Jay and is always telling me to get over it, but I can't. With her long brown hair, puffy lips, and sapphire eyes, she puts any model or actress to shame. And her body. *Jesus,* her body keeps me up at night. She's tall at five eight, and skinny, super skinny, but with Olive Oyl as her mother, that's not surprising. She still has curves though: a tiny waist and incredible breasts. Not huge, but full, perky, with big nipples. Yeah, her nipples are mouthwatering. I almost came in my pants the first time she let me suck on them. Christ, now I have a hard-on and Jax is smirking at me.

"Tess is staying home tonight," I say at last as I climb into the back of our black Audi and shift my erection to the side, hoping it will deflate if I stop thinking about my girl.

"Everything okay?" Jay's brown eyes look at me in his mirror.

"Why wouldn't it be?" I sneer at him. Maybe Jax is right. I probably shouldn't go out tonight, seeing how I'm ready to kill Jay and all he did was ask where she was.

"Don't you say a word." I look over at Jax. He frowns at me.

Rolling his eyes, he grabs one of the bottles of bourbon I swiped and takes a swig. As I wait for him to pass it back to me, he looks out the window.

"Are you going to share?"

"Nah, I think you need to go slow tonight. I can already feel your anger. I don't want to have to call Dad tonight to bail us out of jail."

This makes me smile.

Zack's parents are out of town, so he has the entire apartment to himself. Zack comes from old money also. Not as old as my family's but old. My great-great-great-grandfather was a duke in England. He gave everything up and moved his family to America, and our fortune hasn't gotten any smaller. Every generation seems to expand the Saddington empire. I don't even know what we don't have a piece of.

Zack's parents' penthouse is a perfect place to let loose completely. His mom is into art deco crap or maybe it's modern. Whatever, it's easy to clean up. A lot of metal pieces with dark colors and ugly-but-sturdy furniture. I would probably take down some of the art. After all, a Jackson Pollock hangs across half the main wall, but hey, that's his deal.

Zack's older brother, Jason, is home this weekend from Yale. Hence the party.

I get along better with Jason, probably because his vocabulary consists of more than "damn" and "dude."

Music bounces off the walls so loud it pulses in my chest. We must not be that early because the place is surprisingly full of classmates. Most of them are carrying red plastic cups.

"Yeah, that's what I'm talking about." Zack gives me a bro hug and takes our bourbon. "Dude, since Tess isn't coming, we could..." I must look threatening because he holds his hands up.

"Damn, Reed, calm down." He shakes his head. "Jax mentioned it. I thought as the host, I'd give you a heads-up. Tiffany has been asking all kinds of questions." Thankfully the music is loud. Otherwise it would be uncomfortable.

Zack frowns. "You okay, man?"

"Yeah, I'm fine," I answer, forcing myself to chill. "Tess is sick—that's why she's not here."

Why the fuck did I say that? Looking over at the Pollock painting, I wish I could smoke some weed and spend the rest of the night staring at it.

Jax walks up and hands me a plastic cup filled with beer.

"Oh... dudes." Zack pats Jax on the chest. "Look at what my brother is bringing in."

Jason and his buddies are carrying another keg into the kitchen. A bunch of girls trail after them.

"Holy shit! Look at the tits on that redhead!" Zack is nearly drooling like a kid in a candy shop as he gawks at the college girls.

"Pull it together, man. They're just girls," I say with a snort before I drink half my beer.

Zack looks at me like I have two heads. "Dude, if I could get my hands anywhere near one of them, I would die a happy dude. Excuse me, 'host duty' calls." He air quotes and backs away to look for his brother's entourage.

I circle back to Jax, whose gaze is fixed on the redhead with large boobs. "Did you tell Zack that Tess and I had a fight?"

He looks at me, then back at the redhead, taking a sip of his beer.

"Did you?" I hiss.

"Reed... why did you come tonight?" Like I'm an annoyance. "You of all people know I don't discuss your shit with anyone. I'm starting to get pissed. This is not my fault that you lied to Tess." He drinks his beer.

I almost slap it out of his hand but control myself. "He said you *mentioned it*. What the fuck does that mean?"

"What is wrong with you? He asked me if Tess was coming. I said no. End of story." *That sounds like something Jax would say.*

"Hi, Reed. Hey, Jax." Tiffany slithers up to us. Her brown haircut is exactly like Tess's. Pathetic. I don't have the patience for her on a good day and certainly not tonight.

Groaning into my cup, I say, "What's up, Tiffany?"

"Where's Tess?" Her eyes are gleaming like she knows a secret.

"She's sick." *Fuck*, I never should have come without her.

"Oh... too bad. Well, at least you guys can have fun, huh?" The look in her eyes says she's trying to be seductive.

"Yeah, I'm going to get something stronger." I leave Jax to deal with her.

I almost want to play the twin game, where we fuck with everyone, telling them that we are each other. It works great at parties. Tess is the only one who can always tell us apart. We can even trick my parents sometimes.

Sauntering into the kitchen, I pour myself a cup of my dad's bourbon. I want to get shit-faced. The first bottle is already gone, and we just arrived.

"Can you make me one of those?" Looking over, I see a small pretty blonde smiling up at me. The way she holds herself indicates that she's with Zack's brother's group.

"Sure," I say, pouring some into a cup and handing it to her.

"What's your name?" She licks her lips before she takes a sip.

As I stare down at my drink, I smirk. She wants me. I should be flattered. Instead, my mind flashes to Tess and how if this situation were reversed, I would freak.

Quickly I down my shot, letting the burn subside before I answer her.

"Reed." My eyes sweep her body. In my defense, most of it is on display. Short skirt, short top, with boots.

"I'm Zoe."

The bourbon goes straight to work. I already feel that magical numbness. "Well, Zoe, have fun."

"Wait." She grabs my arm. "Do a shot with me," she says, licking her lips again. Her hand casually stays on my bicep. I need to get the fuck away from this one. Looking down at her, I make a bad decision and pour two more.

"I have a girlfriend." We clink our plastic cups.

Her eyes narrow as she slams the shot with barely a shudder. "That's too bad. Is she here?"

Ignoring her, I grab the bottle and make my way to the game room to play pool.

"I'm next," I inform David and Kyle, choosing a cue to chalk up.

"How about we play partners, Reed?" Zoe purrs, brushing her breasts against my arm. *Fuck*, why can't girls accept when I say I have a girlfriend, that means no?

43

"I thought I left you in the kitchen."

"Reed, you're such a dick." David steps over to Zoe like a pathetic puppy. She doesn't spare him a glance.

"Can't get rid of me that easily," she coos.

David's eyes are worshipping Zoe like she's a Victoria's Secret model.

Taking pity on him, I decide to give him some sound advice. "If you want girls to want you, you need to be a dick."

David coughs, his face turning pink. Zoe wrinkles her nose.

Whatever. I tried. "Zoe, this is David. He wants to be your white knight."

If possible, David's face turns even redder. God, I truly am a dick. I need to find Jax. It's obvious I shouldn't be on my own tonight.

"What if I want a dark knight?" Zoe hops onto the edge of the pool table, her short skirt riding up so that David and I have a perfect view of her red panties. Averting my eyes, I try to look at anything else. The last thing I need to happen is for someone to see this girl and mention it to Tess.

"I'll be back with my brother," I say, leaving before Zoe can stop me.

I find Jax upstairs with the redhead doing shots. *Great!*

"Jax," I yell over the music, "let's play pool."

He looks over, a wicked grin on his face. "Sure." Taking the redhead's hand, he follows me.

Zoe perks up as soon as I return, her eyes narrowing on Jax.

"Wow, there are two of you?" She's practically drooling. I want to tell her we don't turn fifteen for a couple months, just to fuck with her. I'm guessing she thinks we're older, but I won't. It would mess up Jax's chances of getting laid tonight. Instead, I take another shot and keep quiet.

The two girls are crap pool players. I have nothing to talk about except that I miss my girlfriend. Somehow, I think that might be a buzzkill. So, I spend the next couple of hours trying to keep Zoe's hands from wandering to places they shouldn't. Jax has disappeared with the redhead, and I'm completely drunk. Out of the corner of my eye, I try to focus on the girls from school. They're whispering and trying to act like they're not watching Zoe and me.

Zoe rubs her small body against me. "I want to fuck you," she slurs in my face, her hands grabbing my dick. Shit, this is getting out of hand.

"Listen Zoe..." I take her hand away. She pouts.

"I told you, I have a girlfriend. Maybe when my brother comes back, he can help you out."

"Right... the girlfriend!" She starts to giggle. "Although, I don't see no girlfriend." She leans into me, and her breasts brush my chest. "Unless you mean one of those girls over there." She frowns as she points in Tiffany's direction.

"Fuck no," I say quickly, putting her hand down. Comparing Tiffany to Tess is a slap in the face.

"She's not here tonight, but I don't cheat." *God, it's time to go home. I need Tess.* My eyes scan the room as if someone could save me.

"But I want you," she whines. "These high school girls have no idea how to fuck, but I do." Licking her lips, she gazes at me and winks. "I won't tell if you won't tell."

One more time, she tries to touch me. Grabbing her wrist roughly, I see her eyes dart to mine in surprise.

"I have a girlfriend!" I let her go, and she stumbles back, catching herself on the back of a chair. Her eyes are dilated. She should be pissed, but instead, she looks like she wants to drop to her knees and worship me.

"I'm out of here." I'm definitely regretting that last shot.

"Wait, Reed... At least give me a goodbye kiss. That's not against the rules."

I want to tell her it is, but she trips and falls into my arms. There's no choice but to hold on to her or let her face-plant. Her perfume permeates my nose, and it's all so wrong. This whole fucked-up day has been all wrong.

Hearing my brother's laugh, I search for where it's coming from. Finally, I locate him sitting in the corner, his whole body radiating confidence. It's obvious he talked the redhead into having sex with him.

His eyes wander up and down Zoe and me. "What are you doing, Reed?" Disapproval covers his face.

"This," I say, dumping Zoe into his arms. The redhead squeals as Zoe giggles. Hopefully he'll get lucky with both of them.

"I'll send Jay back for you as soon as I'm home," I yell over the music.

Trying to walk straight is a challenge. The apartment is packed with people, most of them drunk. I'm starting to feel mean and I need to piss. As I stumble into one of the numerous bathrooms, my hand goes up on the red-striped wall steadying me as I try to hit the toilet. Christ, I'm seeing double. Somehow my fingers work my zipper back up.

Opening the door, I fumble for my phone, not even looking up as I try to get the fuck out of here. I want my Kitten. Need to hear her voice. Tell her I'm coming home, that I love her.

There's a hand on my shoulder and I spin around. Aaron's stupid face swims in front of me.

"Damn, Reed, you and your brother are my heroes." He does some lame bowing at me.

"Now that you're banging college chicks, you don't mind if I ask Tess to—" And just like that, he's on the floor. I don't even remember my fists coming up. I do hear him screaming like the bitch he is, hands covering his face as blood gushes out of his nose.

Jax is pulling me off him and pushing me out the door. Jay is at our side, with the car doors open. As soon as we're in, he takes off, not questioning, only getting us away.

Panting, I look down at my fists. They're swollen and covered in Aaron's blood. Absently I open and close them. When I look over at Jax, he's texting.

"What did he say to you?"

My heart is racing, the rage still pumping through me. "He informed me that since I was banging college girls, he wanted Tess." My fist slams into the leather seat in front of me. Thankfully I'm on the passenger side.

"Cool down, Reed," Jay warns. "I get that you're amped up, but you need to breathe, man."

"How dare he think he can even look at Tess," I spit with rage.

Jax stops texting. "I'll take care of it." That's all he says as he goes back to his phone. At some point, I hear him talking. He is cleaning up my mess and I let him.

Jay pulls up to our apartment, and I stumble out. He and Jax stay in the car and pull back into traffic. I can't think straight. I'll deal with everything in the morning if Jax hasn't already fixed it. I'm on a mission—to Tess. Walking into our lavish lobby, I nod at the night doorman. I think his name is Tomas. He looks the other way as I enter my private elevator.

I'm still jacked up from Aaron. No doubt about it, I lost it tonight. *No one* will ever have Tess but me. If it were up to me, I would lock her up and only I would be able to see her, feed her, bathe her. Unfortunately, that can't happen, but it doesn't mean I have to like it.

Snickering at my drunken thoughts, I try to be quiet as I navigate in between my mom's elaborate furniture.

I head straight to Tess's room and lock the door quietly behind me. It's dark. The only light in the room is from the moon and the lights of Manhattan. Tess hates to be alone, so she always leaves the curtains open.

She's asleep, her long brown hair curling all over her pillow. Her even breathing alerts me. When I turn on the light, she doesn't even move. On the nightstand are her pills. Reaching for the bottle, I force my mind to focus on the arduous task of counting them. Twenty-seven. That means she only took one 5 mg of Valium. I hate that she needs it, but it seems to work the best for her. Doctors always want her to try other drugs that are less habit forming. Xanax did nothing for her and she is allergic to a lot of antianxiety and antidepressant meds. Seeing that she's a teenager, they don't want to mess with a bunch of stuff. So, they monitor her. It's unnecessary since I watch her, and she rarely takes one.

Right now, I feel like shit for numerous reasons, mainly that my girlfriend must have had a panic attack. I sit down next to her, watching her sleep.

I love to watch her. When she walks, she has the sexiest walk. When she laughs, she makes everyone laugh. When she smiles, she takes your breath away. And when she sleeps, she's like a beautiful angel. A sigh escapes her soft lips, and she turns toward me, her hand reaching for me in her sleep. Her black, sooty eyelashes move up and down. We stare at each other.

"You all right?" Her voice—God that voice—is raspy from sleep.

"Yeah, Kitten, I'm fine. Go back to sleep. I'll be right back." Caressing her hair, I turn off the light. After I use her bathroom to shower, I wrap a towel around my waist and walk down the dark hall to my room. As much as I would love to sleep with Tess naked, she's not ready. Plus, she might scream and alert the house I'm in her room. Pulling on some sweats, I'm almost ready to head back to Tess when I hear my mom.

"Reed?" She taps on my door.

"It's open." Pulling on a white tee quickly, I have no desire for her to see my knuckles, which are red and swollen.

"Have a good time?" she says, squinting at me. She glances at me from top to bottom.

"Yeah, sorry I woke you. Tess do okay tonight?"

"As far as I know. I checked on her around ten and she was already asleep. Just making sure you were okay, honey."

"I'm fine, Mom." She must feel guilty about Tess.

"Okay, well good night, sweetheart." She hesitates.

"What, Mom?"

Shaking her brown hair, she whispers, "I... I want you to know that I'm proud of you for following the rules. Also, you came home before midnight. You're still my wonderful boy no matter how big you get." She quietly shuts my door.

With a snort, her "wonderful boy" sneaks back into Tess's room and locks us in.

After I remove my shirt, I slip under the cool sheets, pulling Tess's warm body to mine. My nose snuggles into her hair and neck. Her vanilla scent wraps around me like a ribbon on a present. No more strawberries. I don't know when her skin morphed into smelling like vanilla or cookies, but it's her own scent, and I need it to live.

"Kitten," I whisper in her ear.

"Hmm? Reed? What are you doing? I thought we're not allowed to sleep together." Her voice makes me instantly hard.

My chest aches at how much I love her. "We're not breaking the rule," I murmur, pulling her even tighter. "Mom said for you not to sleep in my bed—nothing about me in yours." Kissing her neck, I want so badly to turn her over and take her mouth, but she's sleeping and I'm drunk. So, I close my eyes and allow her steady breathing and her scent to lull me to sleep.

chapter 6

TESS

My cell phone is ringing. Reed is wrapped around me like a boa constrictor squeezing its prey. I don't even try to reach for it. Thankfully it stops.

Closing my eyes again, I snuggle into his warmth and sigh at how good this feels. I never want to move. My eyes close right on the verge of sleep, and it starts up again.

Both of us groan. "Christ, Tess answer it, or I'm throwing it out the window." When I sit up, I'm somewhat disoriented. After I took the Valium last night, I passed out. I hardly ever take it, so when I do, I sleep soundly.

"Hello?" I say, not even bothering to open my eyes. Instead, I wiggle back down against Reed.

"Tess? Hello?" Loud giggles and squeals make my eyes pop open.

"Yeah?" I must sound completely out of it.

"How are you feeling?" A loud girl's voice rings in my ear.

"Who is this?" I try to sit up again, but Reed's not having it.

"Hang up," he grumbles, pulling me closer as he kisses my shoulder.

"Is that Reed?" The voice sounds way too happy. Screaming continues in the background, and I hold the phone away from my ear. *What the hell?*

"Listen, whoever this is. *Way* too early. Don't call back."

"Wait, Tess... Don't hang up. *Guys shut up...* Sorry, I just wanted to make sure you were feeling okay and that Reed was home. After he beat Aaron up, we were worried." Now I do sit up. Reed grumbles and opens one eye.

"Who is this?" I look at my phone as if it's magically going to tell me who I'm talking too.

"It's Tiffany!" Like I should know this. I think I've maybe talked to this girl twice.

"What time is it?" My bitchy voice is out.

"I don't know—early." I can feel her crazy, excited energy through the phone. Suddenly I'm cold. It's like I can feel doom infiltrating my veins. I want to hang up before she tells me what I know is going to ruin me.

"Anyway... we... I mean, I wanted to let you know that I was at Zack's party last night. And I couldn't help but see that Reed was into some skanky blond college girl. *I mean everyone saw them!* I know he said you were sick, but as your friend, I thought you should know... that she had her hands down his pants."

My brain is not allowing me to function. I should hang up or scream, anything but stare like a zombie, letting her continue.

"*Tess?*"

"What else?" I manage to choke out.

Reed's warm body stiffens, and his hand reaches for my phone. My brain eventually works and I turn sideways, my elbow preventing him.

"He probably didn't want you to hear about it, so he beat the crap out of Aaron. Broke his nose so badly he had to go to the hospital to get it put back properly. He also had to get stitches under his eye. As your friend, I thought you should know." Screams and laughter are going on the whole time she is talking.

All I can manage is a pathetic "I don't believe you" before I hang up.

I throw my cell phone away from me like it's been dipped in poison. Reed sits up, wariness in his turquoise eyes.

"Tess?" His voice is gentle like he's scared I'm going to bolt. I don't. I let him pull me to him.

"Nothing happened," he says, stroking my hair like he would a skittish kitten.

"So, you didn't break Aaron's nose?" Wow, I sound calm.

"Who called you, Tess?"

"Tiffany." I'm numb, or maybe I'm having an out-of-body experience.

"If what she says is true, I might start screaming and never stop." My mind fills with visions of Reed with some blonde touching him... putting her hands on what is mine!

Oh my God. My breath starts coming in small wheezing gasps. Yep, here comes the panic attack.

"Tess, look at me." *Are my teeth chattering?*

"Come on, baby." He shakes me slightly.

"Did you fuck the blonde who had her hand down your pants? Did you?" Staring at him, I give him a look that begs for him to tell me it's not true.

And he does. He shakes his head no.

"Thank God." My body melts into his.

"Kitten." His thumb strokes my lips. "You never have to worry about me cheating on you! It would never happen. You're all I want. You have to know that."

Reed hugs me so tightly it's hard to catch my breath. I was struggling with that anyway before he crushed me to his chest.

After what seems like an hour, he lifts my face to his, his warm mouth coming down on my cold lips.

He tastes like bourbon and Reed. He kisses me so hard, my mouth has to be swollen and bruised. With a groan, he sounds almost as if he is in pain. Opening my eyes, I find he's staring at me. I put my hands on his chest, right over that strong heart.

"What did you do?"

"I got fucked up and let a girl probably get the wrong idea. But I never touched her, kissed her, or thought about fucking her." His voice is sad.

"Everyone saw you?" Choking on the words, I lean my head against my hands where they're still pressed against his chest.

He shrugs and pulls me in tighter. His arms are like chains and yet I let him. See... I'm that pathetic. I need Reed to live. I need him to breathe! But he doesn't have to know that. I take an unsteady breath. "I need to take a shower, and I want to talk to Jax." Hurt is all over his pretty face.

Ignoring him, I lock myself in my bathroom. My hands are shaking as I turn on the water. "God..." When I gaze at my reflection on the glass shower door, the hot sting of tears burns my cheeks. This is the first time I have ever locked Reed out.

Overwrought, I push on all the buttons and water shoots from the top and sides. Undressing, I suck in a breath as the scalding water pounds my body almost relentlessly, reddening my skin. And then I let it go. I stay in the scorching shower crying, my imagination my worst enemy. Jealousy has taken hold of my mind, controlling me like the green-eyed monster she is. Finally, I turn the hot water to warm and force myself to get out. Breathing in the steam, I reach for a snow-white fluffy towel that is deliciously heated. I crack open the bathroom door and flip on the fan. I need to defog the mirror so I can see myself. I reach for my toothbrush, and like a robot, I clean my teeth. Watching the steam twist and swirl away, I pat on my moisturizer and take a long look at myself. As I lean forward against the sink, I watch the droplets of water slide down between my breasts. My hair is too long. I need to see my stylist soon. Sadness. Grief. Betrayal. That's what screams at me. My eyes are red and my lips are swollen.

"Great, Tess, you look like someone punched you." I'm tired and I just woke up. Squaring my shoulders back and peeking my head out, I search for Reed. He's gone. I'm not sure if I'm relieved or disappointed.

This is stupid! I throw open the bathroom door and march into my closet. I did nothing wrong. Reed's the bad guy—not me. Grabbing a pair of True Religion jeans, I jerk them on.

Mindlessly, I take stock of my numerous shoes and reach for my Tory Burch Reva flats. They're my favorites and I need comfort. Pulling open my lingerie drawer, I decide on a shimmery Calvin Klein black bra and a tight, sheer T-shirt. It's also black because I live in New York and I hate my life.

Screw makeup today. My cheeks are already flushed. I do add some MAC Ruby Woo red lipstick to my lips. Reed will hate it. He always complains that it reminds him of my mom's fake lips, but mine are real, so he can fuck off. *What is happening?* I never want Reed to fuck off!

How am I going to go to school on Monday? Everyone will be spreading different versions of what happened like a venereal disease. I groan thinking about all the shallow people at our school. Ninety-nine percent of them are followers, and it takes one bad rumor to fuck up your reputation. Not that I ever cared before. But this is different. This time, Reed and I are not united. It's uncharted territory and it terrifies me. When you go to one of the most expensive, exclusive high schools, you must accept the truth: it breeds shitty people.

Reaching for my new Prada bag and phone, I wish I could call my mom. For the first time since I was eight, I feel alone again. No one's here to talk to about what has happened to me. My best friend, my soul mate has gutted me. And my other best friend is his twin. I'm sad. I need to make a friend, my own friend! It's like an epiphany exploding in my head.

Leaving my room, I walk down the impossibly long Chinese runner and stop outside Jax's room. I can hear them.

"Reed, you're not listening. I get that you were drunk. But come on, you can't be delusional. No matter how many people we intimidate, someone was bound to tell Tess."

My pulse starts race. I should knock—it's the right thing to do.

"You know what blows?"

"What?" Reed's voice sounds pissed.

"That I begged you to stay home. I told you that you suck without her. But you *had* to go, knowing in the back of your head it was not a good idea. And now Tess is hurting."

Leaning hard on the door, I notice my hands are shaking.

"It makes me want to punch you. You know I hate when she cries." Jax's voice is so close I almost stop breathing.

"Jax! I need your support right now," Reed snaps. "And for the record, had you not been fucking the redhead, I would have pawned that girl off on you, saving me a lot of grief."

Jax snorts. "That's weak even for you. I'm not Tess. You think I'm going to let you blame me? A thank-you would be nice, seeing as I'm the one who cleaned up your shit."

"I did nothing wrong but get drunk!" Reeds voice is getting louder.

"Right? And I didn't have to pay Aaron off to keep his mouth shut?"

"That dick was asking for it. Everyone knows Tess is mine."

"Except everyone saw the blonde hanging all over you."

My stomach churns; I can't move. When was the last time I ate? Probably yesterday. Good thing because nothing is coming up as I stand frozen.

"*You* know I didn't touch her, right?"

"Yeah! I was watching. I'm kind of impressed. Let's be honest—not many guys would be able to refuse that girl." One of them sighs.

"I'm only sorry Tess is humiliated."

Collapsing against the wall behind me, my legs are shaky as relief floods me. Reed was telling me the truth.

"Tess will be fine," he mumbles, sounding like he's losing patience. "I know everyone thought that blonde was hot, but I didn't even want her. I might have a real problem." I can almost see Reed running his hands through his dark wavy hair.

"What are you talking about?" Jax sounds amused.

"I mean... I'm obsessed with Tess. I want to control her every move. The thought of anyone, even you, having her attention makes me crazy. Is that normal?"

Jax snorts. "I always said you were pussy-whipped."

"What's fucked up is that I told Tess the truth, and she didn't trust me. She wants to talk to you. It's making me kind of lose it, Jax."

"You love her, Reed."

"Yes! But it's more... I don't know how to describe it other than I'm obsessed."

"Wait until you and Tess start fucking! Talk about obsession. I'm not joking. It felt so good, I wanted to live inside that girl, and I don't even know her name. But if I loved someone, I can't even imagine how fucking intense it would be."

Holy shit, Jax had sex last night. My mind is spinning.

"When a girl comes, her pussy squeezes your dick."

My cheeks heat up at the image in my head. A bit guilty about spying on their private conversation, I rationalize it—this is what Reed has reduced me to. So, I lean closer staring at the dark ornate door.

Jax had sex, and he said it feels amazing. The first time Reed and I kissed was amazing. He took control and I had to hang on to him because it was like he was eating me alive. His lips were warm and full when he growled for me to open my mouth, and I did. His tongue took over. Wet and frantic and dizzy, as though I'd become a different person, I wanted more, never wanting him to stop. He finally did because I had no self-control. At that moment, I knew I would always give him anything. "You and I are going to have all our firsts together," he whispered.

Jerking back to the present, I make myself knock on Jax's door, and the room falls silent. When I knock again, Reed opens it. His eyes drift from the top of my head to my breasts and all the way to my flats then back again. He looks angry.

My stomach does a flip. He stands aside letting me in. Leaning against the wall, he crosses his arms, frowning.

He studies me. "Why do you have your purse?"

Usually I know what he is thinking, but right now, I'm somewhat unsure.

"I don't know. I guess I felt better having it with me." My voice is hoarse from crying. I hate my voice, but Reed loves it, so there's that I guess.

His eyes narrow like he's dissecting me. "Ask Jax what you need to know. Then you and I are going out." He pushes off the wall and leaves.

An awkward silence takes over Jax's room, and I can't look at anything but the shiny Tory Burch logo on my flats.

Jax sighs. "Come here." Taking my hand, he sits me down on his black couch. All his gaming stuff is neatly organized on shelves. As miserable as I am, I still can't help but smirk at how clean Jax's room is compared to Reed's. Jax pulls me onto his lap, allowing me to curl into him. "Just let it out, Tess."

Grabbing ahold of his T-shirt, which smells like Downy and Jax, I bawl into his chest. As the tears flow unstoppable, my hiccups are loud. I have no pride left. He says nothing and holds me and pets my hair. I love Jax's hugs. He is one of the most affectionate people. At least he is with me, and it drives Reed crazy, but Jax and I have a special bond. At last, I take a breath and wipe my nose on his shirt.

"Sorry about your shirt." My red lipstick is smeared on it. "That won't come out." Hiccupping again, I try to wipe the bright red stain.

"Doesn't matter. Feel better?"

"No. I've cried so much that everything on me hurts, especially here." I indicate my heart.

"All right, Tess, I'm going to tell you what happened, and I'm not going to sugarcoat it."

Shit, he is starting to scare me. Maybe I didn't hear the whole story.

"Yes." I clear my throat. *God* my voice is shot.

"We went to Zack's house. His brother Jason was home, and he brought some college buddies, including girls. I hooked up with one of them." He starts petting my hair again, and my anxiety returns with a jolt.

"Anyway, one of the girls decided to chase Reed. She is the one Tiffany was talking about." I grab his hand to stop petting me. I need to see his eyes.

"Reed was already on edge without you, so he was drinking. She figured that meant he was interested. Now remember, we all were pretty drunk."

"*So, what*? That makes it fine that my boyfriend allowed some college girl to give him a hand job? I'm supposed to look the other way because he was mad at me and drunk?" The wretched sting of tears hits me again.

"Stop it. That's not what happened. They were playing pool. Yes, her hands were roaming, but Reed—"

Jumping up, I say, "I can't hear this," and clutch my ears.

"Sit down, Tess. He didn't do anything with her! She was begging him to fuck her." Jax rips my hands off my ears.

"He said no, Tess! Because of *you*. He loves you, and you know it." I'm stunned at the fierce passion in Jax's voice.

"I love him too," I whisper.

"I know you do. What Tiffany told you this morning was because she's a jealous bitch."

"That's beside the point. Reed beat up Aaron. Now everyone thinks he slept with that girl, right?"

Jax's eyes sweep his room like he is looking for some way to escape.

"I'll take your silence as a big fat *yes!*"

"You shouldn't care what anyone thinks." He leans his head back like he has a headache.

"Perfect. So, tomorrow at school, Reed is going to be even more of a god. And I'll be pitied and humiliated."

Pulling away, I need to see Jax's face better. He rubs his hands over his face, and I want to kick him. When he does that, he looks so much like Reed.

"Probably, Tess. What do you want me to say? There are a lot of assholes at our school."

"Perfect." Standing up, I reach for my bag, but Jax grabs my wrist. "Tess, who cares? As long as you have us, believe me, no one is going to dare say anything to you."

Jerking free, I look toward his door. "I just want to hide, Jax."

He nods, turquoise eyes filled with compassion.

"You're strong, Tess. You'll get through this."

Snorting, I say, "I guess. I have no choice."

"Well, you could dump my brother and hook up with me." He winks.

"You wouldn't know how to handle me."

"I won't even try to deny that. You and Reed are pretty much destined to be together. You know he inherited that famous Saddington temper. He reacts before he thinks. And when it comes to you, he goes insane. So, forgive him." He swats my butt.

Reed clears his voice from the doorway "Are you two done?"

59

He's dressed in a black T-shirt and dark jeans. His wet dark hair is curling around his ears. I walk over to him and our eyes lock. Slowly, I run both my hands through his thick hair, trying to tame the untamable. God, I love him even when he hurts me. I need him to breathe, to function.

"According to your brother, I need to forgive you."

Snatching my hand, he pulls me with him. "We'll be back later," he says over his shoulder.

"You didn't need Jax to tell you that," he whispers.

"Reed?" I stop him before we get into the elevator.

"What, Kitten?" His voice is gentle as his eyes search my face.

"I hate feeling like this, and I hate that you did this to us. I'm scared you ruined us."

His thumb is on my bottom lip, rubbing it, and my stomach clenches. Why can't I stop wanting him so much? I'm doomed, and he knows it. His eyes are so deep, it's almost like I'm drowning in them.

"I'm going to make this better, Kitten. After today, you won't ever be scared again."

chapter 7

TESS

Jay is waiting for us. He gives me a grin as he opens the door. Sliding in, I'm hit with new car smell. The Saddingtons have so many vehicles, I lose track of them. Clearly this is a new one. Reed enters and I'm instantly on his lap. His warm hands cup my face. Slowly he leans down to kiss my puffy eyes and my nose. I shift so I'm closer as he kisses the side of my lips. When he gets excited, his turquoise eyes switch to green—they're green now.

I poke his dimples and his head falls back and a mischievous smile crosses his face. Bringing my finger to his lips, he sucks my pointer.

"I need you to forgive me."

Watching, I'm fascinated with his pink tongue as it circles my finger. "You promise you will never hurt me again?" I pull my finger away.

He sits up. "I won't. This never should have happened."

"Hey, Tess?" Jay interrupts us. "I need you to put your seat belt on, please."

Though I try to scoot off Reed's lap, he holds me tight. "Just drive, man. We're almost there."

Jay shakes his head. "Reed, you need to control that temper."

"Jay, this doesn't concern you." He glares at him and presses for the partition to zoom up.

"Reed!" My eyes open wide.

"Shh, I'm done talking about it. I fucked up. It will never happen again, and I don't need a lecture from Jay about my temper." He positions me so I'm straddling him.

"I only need this mouth." He pulls my head down into a deep kiss. Our tongues seek each other and tangle. I tentatively try rubbing myself against him.

"Yeah, that's it, Kitten." He grabs my ass, guiding me. I feel him. Like, I *feel* him. And he's hard and big. A warmth creeps up my belly straight to my chest. My nipples tighten.

"Jesus, Tess... that's so good. Tell me what it's like for you." He breathes into my mouth, stealing my very breath.

"It feels so good." My core moves against the thick bulge in his jeans.

The car slows down and stops. Suddenly the passenger side door opens for us. I almost tumble out. Thankfully Reed has strong arms.

"We're here." Jay's dry voice breaks us apart. "Jesus Christ, you two, come on. I can't have a teenage pregnancy on my watch." He rubs his neck, looking up and down the street.

"Jay? What's your deal?" Reed sneers, steadying me as I get out.

"Watch it, Saddington. You need me."

Reed rolls his eyes. Holding hands, we step onto the city street. New Yorkers are swarming, their busy lives making mine seem insignificant. Horns blow, cocooning us in a tunnel of racket. Faces pass so quickly, never slowing down enough to truly be seen. The scent of frying hot dogs invades my nose, making my stomach rumble. My appetite is back. A couple words, some kisses from Reed, and I'm starving.

As I clutch his hand, we all walk up to a dark gray building. There is no doorman, so Jay pushes the intercom. A loud buzz allows us in.

Jay has obviously been here before because he takes the dark stairs two at a time.

I look up at the steepness of them wondering how people don't kill themselves. "Wow, you would think if you are going to paint the stairs and walls black, you would at least put a light in here," I whisper.

Jay chuckles. "I think they like the ambience, Tess."

We stop at a large door. Jay raps his knuckles on it. After another buzz, he pushes the door open. My hand clutches Reed's tighter, and he winks at me. Entering, I stare at what appears to be a tattoo parlor. It's all dark purple, black, and red and smells like a hospital. Heavy metal music pours in from all sides.

Reed's mouth is at my ear. "This is one of your birthday presents. I think you need this one a little early." Taking a little bite of my neck, he makes me squeal. My eyes travel up to the ceiling. Half-dressed girls, mermaids, and Disney princesses with horns adorn it. *Interesting!*

A tall blond guy comes out of a room. A girl follows, wearing the shortest black dress I have ever seen. Literally her ass is hanging out. Maybe she wore it on purpose because when she bends over to get her wallet to pay, her bare ass is wrapped in Saran Wrap.

"That would be the last place I would get a tattoo." I sniff.

Reed grins. "Good, because I would never allow anyone but me to touch this anyway." He caresses my butt.

Turning toward him, I give him the warning eye. He laughs and wraps his arms around my waist, pulling me to his chest. Jay walks over to the blond guy who is assessing us.

"How are we going to get tattoos? We're not even fifteen yet."

"Money." Pushing my hair off my shoulder, he caresses my face with his eyes. "It can make me whatever age I need to be. And you're not getting a tattoo. I am."

"What? I thought you said it is *my* birthday present? I was kind of excited thinking I was getting one." I pout.

He laughs and leans down to suck on my bottom lip.

"Don't pout. I don't want this creamy skin marred. This is for you." He saunters over to Jay and the blond guy, who I'm guessing is the tattoo artist. Our pinkies are linked, so I follow.

"We ready?" Reed asks.

The blond guy turns and looks at us. I blink. *Holy shit, this guy is hot.*

He's covered in tattoos, like all the way up his neck covered, but his face is beyond cute. He looks like a young biker Brad Pitt. His eyes travel up and down my body. Biting my lip, I sneak a look at Reed to see if he's noticed, which is stupid—he notices everything, especially with me. Somewhere in the back of my head, I sense that sting of satisfaction. It's shitty to want my boyfriend to feel pain, but I do. After last night, a little reality slap is not uncalled for.

"The fuck?" he mumbles, his caveman energy vibrating off of him. He wraps his arms around my waist, pulling my back to his chest. "Property of Reed!" might as well be tattooed on my forehead. The inker smirks, crossing his arms.

"Reed, please..." I wanted him to feel a tiny bit of pain. But I'm too exhausted for more drama.

"Quiet, Tess." His eyes are still on Brad Pitt, who must decide he'd rather take our money than get into it with Reed. He backs off and turns to Jay, then plasters on a smile and opens one of the doors in the parlor.

Shocker. The room is large with black walls. A large purple velvet couch formed like a C sits in the back middle of the room, along with a black shiny coffee table. Piles of portfolio books lie on it.

"Is this your art on the walls?" My arms sweep the room, trying my best to lighten the tension. The paintings surround us. I love art. Some are quite impressive. It figures, most of them are naked girls. There are some beasts or monsters. On the far wall, almost like he's ashamed of them, are three oil paintings. One is Manhattan at night, her bright lights and the moon almost glowing. Another's of Coney Island. He's captured the colors of the restaurants and rides so clearly it almost looks like a photograph. And the last is of wildflowers blowing in the wind. Rain clouds are in the background as if to warn the viewer of trouble coming. This is the one that catches my attention.

Brad Pitt grabs a remote from a table and turns down the music, making it much easier to think.

"Did you paint these too?"

He looks over at me while he sits down on a swivel chair. I notice his eyes are a dark brown not blue like Brad Pitt's. He looks like he belongs in LA not Manhattan.

"Yeah, they're mine," he says gruffly, sounding defensive. "I started off as an artist, then discovered I could make much more money putting my art on people."

"These are amazing." I motion to the landscapes.

"Thanks. Someday I'll be able to just paint," he mumbles as he snaps on the rubber gloves.

Nodding, I sit on the velvet couch and reach for a book on the table. Reed is quiet, looking at the flower painting.

Placing his gloved hands on his knees, Brad Pitt asks, "Who's first?"

"Me. I'm the only one who's getting one." Reed pulls off his T-shirt, handing it to me. Unable able to stop, I let my eyes travel his chest. He loves to exercise—his body is lean and muscled.

Besides me, working out is probably Reed's second favorite thing. Which is why he is sporting a six-pack already. Licking my lips, I visualize what it would be like to lick those muscles.

His husky voice brings me back to him and where we are. "I want an arrow piercing my heart and I want the name Tess on it."

I gasp. Literally I might have even said his name because he turns and flashes me his incredible smile. I think I might die. *There goes my heart again.*

Brad Pitt is silent for a moment. "I like it. I can make it almost 3-D. It'll look like the arrow is almost injected into your heart." Grabbing his sketch pad, he starts to draw it.

Reed watches then shakes his head. "That's not right. I need the arrow in my heart. She pierced it when I was eight." His eyes never leave mine as he sits on the tattoo table, his long legs hanging. He's so gorgeous, my mind starts to twist things. I'm scared and jealous. It's like a poisonous pill that I don't want to take but do anyway.

Reed sits like a prince. What am I going to do when he's a full-grown man like Jay and Brad Pitt? What if I can't keep him? Or some girl tries to steal him from me? I hate when I torture myself with these morbid thoughts. He's mine. And I will do anything to keep him.

Suddenly the room is filled with a buzzing sound as Brad turns on the machine. He starts to outline the tattoo.

I'm mesmerized. Reed is branding me to him forever. We are truly soul mates. The buzzing of the machine calms me. With every drop of ink that enters Reed, he becomes mine more. I have to get one. His eyes narrow. *He knows.* Of course he does. I smile at him. He arches a dark brow at me, but he's smirking.

His tattoo takes a little over two hours. Brad is a perfectionist, adding details and shading until it looks exactly like an arrow has been shot into Reed's heart with my name on it. Reed sits still, acting like he is getting a haircut rather than a needle constantly piercing his beautiful body. No longer leafing through magazines, I sit quietly, staring at him, shifting every so often on the velvet couch. I have this feeling inside me that I can't explain. It's almost like we've shared something so intimate that I don't know how to process it.

Brad Pitt wraps it up. Not being able to contain my energy anymore I say, "I want one!"

All eyes turn toward me.

Jay frowns, Brad Pitt looks thrilled, and Reed looks... well, intense.

"What do you want, Kitten?"

I almost blurt out "you," but instead I walk up to him and hand him his shirt.

"It's a surprise. I need it. You need it."

He's silent; then he looks at Brad. "Whatever the birthday girl wants."

"Fuck yeah." Brad is excited, snapping on some fresh gloves. Reed shakes his head, pulls his shirt over his head. "Where do you want it, Tess?"

"Well I only want you to see it. So—"

"No."

"But... you don't even know what I was going to say." Adrenaline percolates through my veins.

"You are not piercing your heart, Tess." He walks up to me and wraps his hand in my thick hair and brings me close to his lips. "You would have to take off your shirt, and again, no one is ever going to see you naked but me." I huff because that's exactly what I wanted. But he's right. I would have to take off my shirt and my bra.

"Okay, I want the same arrow on my side aiming toward my heart with Reed's name on it." I stare at him.

"Pull up your shirt, Kitten."

67

I pull it up. His warm hand traces the area with his fingers. "Start here, have it travel to here." He motions right under my breast.

Brad is in his chair again, sketch pad waiting. "Yeah... that will work." His focus lands on me. "Do you want the arrow to be inserted like Reed's?"

"I want it making its way to my heart. Can you make it look like it's traveling?"

"Of course." He swivels around, getting everything ready.

Reed tucks my T-shirt into my bra and steps back. I move to the table and lie down on my side. Brad Pitt gets me a pillow. Reed stands toward my head giving Brad room to work.

"You ready?" I nod and bite my lip as I feel the gun start to outline. *Holy shit!*

"You okay, Kitten?" Reed caresses my cheek.

"Um... this hurts." But in a strange way, it's kind of empowering. Brad Pitt looks up at me and then at Reed and nods his head. "She's one of us now." A big smile spreads across his face.

Reed stares at him. "No, *she's only mine.*"

Brad looks at him for a moment then goes back to his work. It takes way over two hours. I'm almost begging him to not worry about another layer of shading and color. A sigh escapes me as the machine turns off at last. Brad peels off his gloves.

"I want to get a picture of this for my book. This looks better than I imagined."

My eyes meet Reed's. Today was more than a birthday present. It's his promise to me, and mine to him.

Brad comes back and happily snaps some photos, then wraps up my tattoo, explaining in detail how to take care of them. Reed's face is peaceful, and the awful night has been purged from us. I watch as he hands him a bunch of hundreds.

"Hey," Brad Pitt calls out to us, but his eyes are fixed on me. "You know where I am if you ever need me to fix any of that."

A slow smile appears on Reed's lips. "Good to know. Thanks, man." He laces our fingers together as we leave.

"Wow, I'm impressed. You must be relaxed—you didn't even engage."

Somewhat breathless at how a simple smile can undo me, I snuggle into him as he helps me down the dark stairs.

"I'm happy."

It's so honest, I stop breathing "Reed..."

Cocking his head at me, he says, "I don't care about that guy. I care about you. When that needle was engraving your name into my heart, I thought about my actions and how I almost destroyed the only thing I need to live." Cupping my cheeks, he keeps going. "It scared me."

Not even thinking about it, I launch myself into his arms, and thankfully, he catches me.

"How do you always catch me." I choke back a sob.

"I'll never drop you." We rub our noses together and he gently places my hand across his tattoo. "Happy Birthday, Kitten. I love you."

I feel like I'm glowing.

"You're beautiful."

"So are you."

As we open the door, the sun is blinding and I blink. Jay is waiting. A cigarette dangles from his mouth. He takes an inhale and tosses it to open our door.

"I'm starving. What do you want for dinner, Kitten?"

"How about pizza?" Resting my head on his shoulder, I nuzzle against him.

"Pizza it is. Jay, you hungry?" We both look at the back of his head.

"I could eat."

"Let's go to Joe's." I can't stop smiling as I bounce a little.

Jay says nothing, but I can feel his disapproving eyes in the mirror looking at me.

"What's wrong, Jay? You're so quiet," I tease.

"Just wondering what your parents are going to think when they find out their fourteen-year-old daughter tattooed Reed across her side."

Great, Jay.

"My dad pays you a shitload of money. Your job is pretty clear," Reed says calmly.

"You two are only kids. A lot will change as you get older." He stops at a red light and turns to face us. I want to stick my tongue out at him, but I'm turning fifteen in a week, so I don't.

"Jay, no one but I will ever see Tess's tattoo no matter how old we get." Reed's voice is dismissive.

"Really? Because when I was your age, I thought I was in love too. Until a year later, when I found someone else. Guess what? I'm still falling in love. Trust me—it doesn't last." He shakes his head in disgust.

I reach over and lace my fingers with Reed's because he looks like he wants to hurt Jay. Also, I was starting to feel better, and now Jay is bringing me down. I hate it. "Come on, Reed. Please focus on me. Tomorrow, I'm going to have to deal with all the crap at school. Tonight, I want to be with you. Don't you feel like... I don't know, like you and I have this big secret that no one else knows about?" I bat my eyelashes at him.

He stops giving Jay the kill stare and turns his focus on me. His hand caresses mine... eyes lock with mine, and I launch myself at him again. He catches me. Reed always catches me.

chapter 8

TESS

The next week of school is exhausting. Everyone talks behind my back but pretends they want to be my best friend. I show up Monday morning with Reed and Jax walking me everywhere. Reed has decided that if he kisses me all the time, everyone will stop talking about us. Sure enough, it only makes it worse. I know everyone thinks Reed slept with the blonde at the party. And I've worked hard to ignore it since I know the truth. Still, it hurts when I hear Tiffany and her posse giggling about how I have no self-esteem because I've stayed with him.

I'm over it today. My mother has risen from the dead. After three weeks of silence, she contacted me yesterday, informing me that she will pick me up tomorrow. This, along with all the other garbage in my life, makes me want to grab Reed and lock us in his room.

Is that too much to ask? It must be. Because here I sit, like a pathetic girlfriend who can't think for herself, waiting for her boyfriend. His football coach has called an emergency meeting after school. How annoying.

"Explain to me again why I can't go back to the penthouse?"

Reed leans over and kisses me. "I need you close."

I almost laugh. "Reed, that is ridiculous." My lips twitch. "Come on, I don't want to wait around while you and the other players get lectured about having personal trainers over the summer. Or what you're supposed to tell your chefs to prepare for you." I know I sound whiny, but sometimes it works with him, so I give it a shot.

He laughs and pulls me in for another kiss. This time, he tries to sneak in some tongue. I kiss him back for a moment because I can't stop myself until we hear catcalls from his teammates.

"Great. Exactly what I need—more people talking about me." Crossing my arms, I close myself off.

"Don't do that." He grabs my hands. "Fuck them." He motions at the team. "This is not going to take long, and then we'll go home together." His tone signals this is the end of the discussion.

Getting butterflies when he says 'home,' I know it's silly, but I can't wait until we're old enough to get our own place.

With a frustrated sigh, I say, "I hate this. I'm going to have to sit here with all of the football players' girlfriends. Pretend like I'm on the phone, so they don't talk to me, then watch them whisper behind my back about you." At least I see a flash of regret in his eyes.

"Tess, come on. I know this has been a shitty couple of weeks, but it's getting better. School is almost out. What will make you happy? Whatever my kitten wants, I will give her." He winks, *damn him.* "And we can't forget it's your birthday." He rubs my lips with his thumb, his eyes starting to change as I lightly suck the tip.

"Whatever." When I bite his thumb, he grins and I roll my eyes at him. "Why can't Jay take me home?"

He stiffens and pulls back. "He is not allowed to be alone with you," he says through his teeth.

"What is your problem with him?"

He glances in the direction of the guys filing into the locker room. "I have to go. I don't have a problem with Jay. But I don't trust him, especially with you."

"That is crazy—all he does is his job."

"Don't make excuses for him. I'll be back in an hour or so."

After I give him a dramatic sigh, I stomp up the bleachers, scooting into the corner.

Reed grins. "Perfect. Now stay there where no one can see you."

"That's the plan." Smiling sweetly, I wave to him. He stops and stares at me, then climbs the bleachers after me. I squeal as he grabs for me.

"Go, so we can get out of here." I laugh.

"One more kiss."

A loud whistle interrupts us. "Saddington, you plan on joining us, or are you going to keep groping your girlfriend?" Coach scowls and walks back into the locker room.

"Don't move, Kitten." He points at me and runs down the bleachers.

"You're so weird."

He grins, making my stomach flutter. I wish I could control myself more. Staring at his incredible ass as he takes the bleachers two at a time, I tear my eyes away to my backpack and pull out my history notes. I need to focus, concentrate. Reed sucks. He always distracts me. This gym always smells like sweat and feet and I hate it, I think, wrinkling my nose.

Leaning back, I try to keep my eyes from wandering. But I start to daydream about Reed. Somehow, I'm picturing if I want a train and a veil for my wedding or simply a veil. Groaning, I snap my notebook shut and it echoes in the almost-empty gym. I stretch and glance at the clock on top of the basketball hoops. "God, it's only been fifteen minutes."

Why, do I listen to Reed?

My attention is piqued when I see a guy come out of the coed bathroom. He is wearing a gray sweatshirt with the hood pulled over his head covering his face. He puts his hands in his pockets and slinks out of the gym. *Creepy.* It's hot and muggy out, so of course I start to visualize that the guy is a mass murderer or a terrorist. *What the hell is wrong with me?*

Standing up, I walk down the bleachers, noticing that most of the girls are outside. Apparently the cheer and dance squad members are having their own meeting today as well. Moving at a slow pace, I make my way over to the bathroom. I have no idea why I'm being so silly. The guy was probably working out or he likes sweatshirts. Either way, it's none of my business. Now that I'm almost at the bathroom, I might as well go pee. The gym bathrooms are coed for sporting events. The lights are off. Feeling around, I find the switch. And nearly trip over a body lying on the floor. I freeze. Blood is smeared all over the white tile, and a slim body is curled in a fetal position.

Shit, shit, shit! Oh my God! This poor guy is dead, and the creepy guy with the sweatshirt is a murderer!

Taking a breath, trying not to let my imagination take over, I yell, "Are you dead?" Frantically, I lean down to him and gently touch his cheek, thankful that he's warm.

"Don't worry. You're okay," I say, my voice soft. He starts to move and moan. I check his pulse; it seems normal.

Then, he opens his beautiful chocolate eyes and stares at me.

At first, I'm stunned. How have I never realized how striking this guy is? Blinking, I reach for my phone. "Don't worry. I'm calling 911 right now." I smile and stroke his cheek reassuringly.

He pushes up on his arms and sits up.

"Here let me help you." I help him scoot back, so he can use the wall to help him sit up.

"Don't call 911. Trust me, I'll be okay." His voice, which has a slight accent, sounds steady.

Shocked, I shake my head. "Don't be crazy. You need medical attention. You're bleeding... and you have a black eye."

"Fuck, I hit my head on the sink when that dick hit me in the eye."

God, what do I do? He's speaking clearly, and the bleeding seems to have stopped on his head wound.

"I'm so sorry you're stuck with me finding you." I give him a smile.

"I don't think I could have dreamt a better person to rescue me. Do you believe in fate, Pretty Girl?"

"Yes... I do."

"So do I." His pained eyes lock with mine, and it's like looking in a mirror. His loneliness and insecurities are all right before me.

Swallowing, I say, "You're sure you don't need an ambulance? I'm a terrible nurse."

He grunts. "I have been beaten way worse. I only hit my head. Anytime you hit your head it bleeds. Trust me, it looks worse than it is."

"If you say so." I take a shallow breath. The bathroom is clean, thank goodness, minus the blood. God, it's all over the white floor. *What do I do?*

As if he can read my mind, he interrupts my manic thoughts. "Here, Pretty. Help me to my feet."

Jumping at the chance to be useful, I let him grab hold of my hand. "Go slow and hold on to me." Puffing out some air, he seems steady. More than steady, he is stiff and angry.

"Can you walk?"

"I'll be fine. Give me a second." He's taller than me but almost as skinny. He's the most delicate boy I've ever seen. I mean Reed and Jax are beautiful, but they are big, tall, and masculine-looking. This boy is just plain pretty, with his black hair and dark eyes.

He smiles, and I see straight white teeth.

"Well, at least he didn't hit your mouth and mess up those pretty teeth." Can't help myself—he is that handsome.

He shrugs. "You saved me. I will be forever in your debt."

"Stop it. I hardly saved you. I almost tripped over you. By the way, you could have a concussion." I chew on my bottom lip.

"Don't worry. I have a whole team that will fix me up. Do you know who I am?"

"Kind of, I mean when you came here a couple months ago, I heard the rumors."

Nodding, he says, "Well, they are mostly true, so you can see why I don't want a hospital. But if I can use your phone? I should probably call one of my guys before I pass out." He rubs his wounded head.

I must be pale because the guy tells me to breathe.

"I'm kidding." He chuckles, gently taking my phone from my numb, cold hand.

He speaks what I think is Spanish into the phone, then hands it back to me.

He stares silently at me for a moment. "I'm Brance. My people are on the way."

"Good, that's good. Who did this to you?" Looking toward the door, I wonder if I should lock it. "Should we call the cops? I saw the guy leave here, but I didn't see his face."

"Fuck no, definitely no cops. I will have one of my dad's guys take care of him, *maybe*." He snorts as though disgusted. "He begs me to suck his cock and afterward freaks out because he loved it."

"Oh my God... that's well... I don't know what to say." I have my hands on my cheeks because they're on fire.

He smiles. "Come on, Pretty Girl, help your new friend to the curb. One of my bodyguards should be waiting."

"Oh... okay, are you sure I shouldn't go get them? I mean are you all right to walk?"

"I can make it."

I nod. "I'm Tess, by the way." Biting my bottom lip hard, I taste coppery blood.

"I know who you are."

We walk slowly as curious looks are thrown our way. But no one approaches us or asks if we need help. *Jesus, this school.* The rich are grotesque and that includes their offspring—our oh-so-elite student body. We make it outside and two men are waiting. One of them gently takes Brance, then turns toward me.

"Thank you," he says, getting into the driver's seat.

"Wait!" I call out, needing to make sure they take proper care of him. "Listen... he hit his head on a sink. Please make sure he doesn't have a concussion."

The man cocks his head at me confused and turns to listen to Brance from the back. His brown eyes take me in. "Mr. Martinez is inviting you over to his place. That way you can tell his physician exactly what you saw."

"Oh, well..." Hesitating, I look toward the gymnasium. "My boyfriend is inside," I say, pointing behind me. Reed will freak if I'm gone. But poor Brance needs me, and for the first time, the thought of having my very own friend, besides Reed and Jax, is almost too intoxicating. Without thinking of the consequences, I open the door to the limo and climb in, sitting opposite Brance.

He is leaning his head back, his eyes closed.

"So, you decided to be your own woman, huh?"

"I have no idea what you mean." Pulling my phone out, I text Reed. "Where are we going? I need to tell him."

He sits up and motions for me to give him my phone. I do. His graceful fingers glide over my phone, like a concert pianist as he texts Reed his address and phone number.

"There." He smirks. "He should only go slightly insane when he realizes that his *kitten* is with me. The son of one of the biggest Colombian drug lords."

"Oh," is all I can say. He is so right—Reed is going to go insane. "You shouldn't admit that about your father. People might take it the wrong way."

He snorts bitterly. "Pretty Girl, this is my life. Why lie?"

He surprises me with that. It's not often I hear blunt honesty. Needing to change the subject before I regret my rash decision, I ask, "How do you know Reed calls me Kitten?"

"*Everyone* knows. It's pretty obvious that he is obsessed with you. I hope he'll be cool about us being friends." He says this like it's a done deal. The contract has been signed in blood. In a way, it has: his blood.

"Well, he doesn't have a say. He has tons of friends, and I never say anything."

He simply looks at me, and I fidget with my nails.

"I am being honest, Tess."

I look up to find his face full of lonely sincerity. "My dad seriously is a drug lord in Colombia. And when you see where I live, it's a fortress rather than an apartment."

"Is that supposed to scare me?" I smile bravely. "We all have crazy parents."

"No, I hope it doesn't scare you." His dark eyes search my face as if looking for answers. "But it scares most people, that's all."

He closes his eyes again and leans his head back on the leather seat.

"Brance," I say firmly. "I'm not a doctor, but I'm pretty sure you're not supposed to go to sleep. As a matter of fact, that would probably be the worst thing you could do."

"I'm not asleep."

My phone starts ringing. I don't need to look down to tell me who it is. I can feel him.

"Reed, Don't frea—"

"Tess," he cuts me off, "what the fuck?"

"Reed, I'm fine." My voice remains steady as I try to calm him. "God... it's a long story. Anyway, I'm going to Brance's to help make sure he is okay. Can you guys pick me up?"

"Tess, that kid 'Brance' is Mateo Martinez! Do you have any idea what the hell his father does?" His breathing is harsh, and I hear him bark an order to Jay.

"Reed, stop it. He got beat up. I found him lying in his own blood in the gym bathroom. Thankfully, I was there to help."

"Listen to me, Tess. Jay and I are on our way. We'll be there soon."

"Reed, for once, trust me. He's hurt! I had to help him. I'm not in any danger with Brance. He told me right away who his dad is."

Glancing over at Brance, I make sure he hasn't passed out. His eyes are clear and he's watching me, a small smile on his lips.

Lowering the phone, I say, "Is it all right if I have Reed come to your apartment? I would love for you to meet him."

"Absolutely." He shrugs. "I will tell the guards to let him in."

"Are you shitting me, Tess?" Reed screams. "Did you even hear what he said? He has *guards!*"

"So, what? We have Jay! Look, I'm going to lose you. It looks like we are here. We're pulling into underground parking."

"Fine." He hangs up on me.

I force a smile at a very curious Brance Martinez. "He gets a little domineering at times."

"Of course he does. He's the Great Reed Saddington!" His voice is getting dramatic, and there's a spark of mischief in his eyes. "Heir to one of the biggest shipping companies in the world. He can have anything he wants, and he wants you, Tess."

"We're soul mates," I whisper.

"Are you always so submissive with him?" *What the hell? Is that what everyone thinks about me?*

He holds up a hand. "I'm not trying to be an ass. Look, if I had Reed Saddington as my boyfriend..."

The limo door opens, and our conversation is brought to an end, thankfully. A bald Hispanic man leans in to help him out, then pulls back a fraction to look at poor Brance. He's a mess: his clothes are covered in blood, his head looks awful, and his eye, which is seriously swollen and red, is rapidly changing to black.

"Jesus, Mateo, who did this?" Brance groans as the man helps him out. "I talked to your father. He wants me to see to it," he says quietly, looking over at me curiously.

"Thanks, Alejandro, but it's kind of my mess to clean up. This is my new best friend," he says, winking at me with his good eye. "Tess Gallagher. Her boyfriend will be arriving soon. Reed Saddington. Let him up." Brance kind of spits this out as he straightens himself up. Slowly, we walk into the building. "My apartment is the penthouse."

"Wait, this whole building is *yours*?" I turn to face him, which makes him sway a bit. "Sorry," I say, grabbing on to him. I'm used to extravagant wealth, but Brance has a giant building only for himself?

"Yeah, my dad is big on security, so all the guards and their families live here too."

The building is ultramodern. Gray is the main color theme, making the outside seem cold and unfriendly.

"So, you live all by yourself?" It's hard not to feel sorry for this guy. My life is not perfect, but at least I have Reed and Jax. Poor Brance has no one but staff and this building.

"Yeah. Miserable, huh?" Maybe he can feel my compassion. Because it's truly there. This place might be someone else's dream apartment, but my gut tells me it's his nightmare. A tomb making him an outcast. A lavish prison, secluding him from human touch.

He straightens up. "When I turn eighteen, I'm walking away from all this shit. Moving to LA. Starting fresh."

A man in a dark suit helps Brance into the elevator, and I follow. It's superfast, like Reed's, and opens to a sleek, white hallway. Orchids sit on a glass table. The whole idea of less is more applies to this building. It is almost too clean, too white, too perfect. He doesn't want to be perfect—how could he? Again, my heart swells with kinship for this stunning boy.

Yet another man is waiting for Brance. This one is apparently his doctor. My dislike of all this is new for me. Okay, I know I'm somewhat selfish, but this protective feeling I have toward Brance is startling. He has strength that I'm not used to.

No one says anything, so I perch myself on the edge of a red couch, one of the few things of color in this sterile tower. The doctor examines him with a detached, bored manner but seems to be thorough from what little I can see.

Clearing my throat, I pipe up, "Um, excuse me?"

Ignoring me, the doctor says something to Brance.

"Doctor?" I'm using my bitch voice. "He was out cold when I found him. I'm worried he may have a concussion." Again nothing. I'm beginning to wonder if I should call my doctor. This man might be insane.

At last, after Brance's ribs are taped and his head gets some stitches, the doctor turns to me. "He is fine."

That's it. Three words. Realizing this is what Brance is surrounded by makes me want to hug him.

"So, no concussion?"

"No," he snips. Turning back to Brance, he tells him to rest.

When I glance down, my phone is vibrating in my hand. *Thank God.*

"Hello?" I whisper, not sure why, except that the room is so quiet you could hear a pin drop.

"We're downstairs waiting for you." Reed's strong voice vibrates through the phone.

I can tell he is furious and I honestly don't need any more drama. I like Brance and want Reed to like him too. And, Brance is hurt and needs to sleep, I think, watching as his doctor hands him some pain pills.

"I'll be right down." Turning to Brance, I half smile apologetically. "I need to go. I will call you tonight. You gave Reed your number, right?" He looks disappointed but recovers quickly.

"Yeah, I gave him my number. I would love to talk later on. I never sleep well when I take pain medication. I'll probably be up all night." Nodding, I'm surprised at my connection with this guy.

"Well, if you are feeling better tomorrow, maybe we can hang out? My mom is picking me up in the morning at Reed's. She's recovering from another round of plastic surgery." Reaching over, I give him a hug. He clings to me for a moment then backs away.

"I would love that. Alejandro, please see Tess down." He grabs the remote as he slowly sits on the couch.

"Perfect." I wave at the scowling doctor as I walk by. The whole ride down in the elevator, I can't stop smiling. I've found my new best friend.

chapter 9

TESS

Past – fifteen years old

Today is my fifteenth birthday, and I wake to find my mother sobbing at the edge of my bed.

"Mom," I groan, barely opening my eyes, "what time is it?"

"We have to cancel your party!"

Sitting up, I blink away the sleep. "What are you talking about? It's only us, Reed, Jax, Brance, and Brad and Caroline." She continues to sob.

"What's wrong with you?" I'm getting aggravated until she raises her face, and I gasp in shock.

"*Holy shit*! What have you done to yourself?" Her left eye is literally drooping shut.

She wails again. "I went to get my monthly Botox and look what happened."

I'm horrified and genuinely sorry for her. She looks like she had a stroke!

Crawling over to her, I rub her back. "Mom?" I keep my voice calm, trying to be soothing. "Did you call the doctor? I mean... it won't stay like *that,* will it?" I have never understood my mother and her constant need to get plastic surgery, collagen, Botox, whatever new thing that comes out. She has made herself look like an embarrassment.

I don't even remember what she originally looked like. Her puffy red eye looks at me; the other, well...

"You don't understand, Tess. All I have ever wanted was to be beautiful." She throws her arms in the air. "I was always plain, and then I had you, and *you* really were beautiful. I wanted to be someone you could look up to." Throwing herself dramatically on my bed, she covers eyes with her arm.

"Okay, let's not panic." I jump up, trying to find my phone. My mom is whimpering on my down comforter.

"Mom!" I clap my hands to get her attention.

"Focus. We need Brance. I'm sure he can fix you."

Her face lights up at the mention of Brance. She has become a Brance groupie. From the moment I introduced him to my mother she *loved him*. He encourages it too. I think it's because Brance's mother died when he was five. So, he has basically moved in with us. He dresses me and picks out how I should wear my hair and makeup. It's like having my own personal stylist, and I love it. After he discovered that my mom was completely hopeless at making herself look good, he took it as a personal challenge to help her. We have done more shopping and spent more time together than I have ever spent with my mom before. I guess I have Brance to thank for that. Unfortunately, besides shopping and spa days, I have nothing in common with her.

At long last, I locate my phone at the bottom of my purse. Dialing his number, I try not to look at her.

"Pretty Girl." His gravelly voice indicates I've woken him up. "Happy Birthday."

"Thanks, Brance. I know it's early, but *we* need you. Mom got Botox yesterday and her left eye looks like she had a stroke." I wrinkle my nose as I look at her. She sees me and starts wailing.

Sitting up, she grabs the phone from me. "Brance! Oh God, I need you! When are you coming over? You will?" She sighs, her face relaxing, well, as much as her face can. "Okay... Okay, I will stay calm." Then she smiles, actually smiles. *Who is this person?*

"Absolutely... I will stay lying down until you get here." She hangs up, tossing the phone back to me.

"Well?" I demand. "What did he say?"

"He said he can fix me and it will get better each day. Nothing to worry about." Waving her hand, she looks like a queen.

My phone beeps, and I look down at my incoming text.

I don't know how you survived without me!

Love you, Pretty Girl.

Smiling, I shake my head. He's right. My life has become a whole different experience. Before, all I had was Reed and Jax, but now I have Brance. And he is all mine, loyal only to me. And I am loyal to him. We're like peanut butter and jelly.

Reed has been surprisingly good about sharing me. I think it's because Brance is gay. He is happy to let Brance take care of all the things he hates.

The doorbell rings. I glance over at my mom who has passed out on my bed. Obviously, she was up all night, hysterical about her face. Now that Brance is on his way, she seems at peace.

Grabbing one of Reed's sweatshirts, I pull it on over my black sleeping slip. When I call down to the front desk, I'm informed that there is a delivery guy with flowers.

Fighting my way past shiny balloons and decorations, I can't help but smile as I open the door. The delivery guy stands there with a flower arrangement that is almost as big as me. Well maybe not that big, but it's impressive. There are numerous long-stemmed red roses in the middle with white and pink hydrangeas surrounding the bottom. The vase alone probably cost as much as a cheap car. I hold out my hands for it and thank the delivery guy.

"Holy shit, *heavy!*" I say, barely making it past an onslaught of silver and gold streamers to place the vase on the table. My stomach has butterflies as I search for the card. *Hmmm, no card?* A knock at the door makes me jump. Skipping over to the door isn't easy when I'm swarmed by a jungle of ribbons hanging from balloons, but when I answer at last, I discover the frazzled-looking delivery guy, who stands holding a red card.

"Sorry. I have never had to deliver anything this expensive. My boss made me a nervous wreck. Here's your card." He shoves it at me.

"Oh, perfect I was looking for that." I laugh.

"Hold on." Grabbing my mom's purse, I pull out a hundred and hand it to him. "You deserve it."

He grins, handing it back. "I got a huge tip already."

He turns, then stops. "Wait, you're right. I do deserve this." He takes the hundred. "You have a great birthday. Someone *really* loves you," he says over his shoulder.

Shutting the door, I excitedly open the card.

Kitten, Happy Birthday!

You are my everything!

I love you, Reed.

I sigh and clutch the card to my chest. Best birthday ever! Well, aside from my mom's face. Twirling, I know two things: Reed has money and I love him. But at this moment, the emotion almost takes me to my knees. He is my everything. It's almost impossible to breathe as I run to my room for my phone. Glancing at my mom, who is still in the same position as earlier, I roll my eyes, and my hands slightly tremble as I push on Reed's name.

"Kitten." My stomach flip-flops at the sound of his rough morning voice.

"I love you," I blurt. "I love our tattoos. I love my flowers." I'm breathing rapidly, my eyes stinging with tears as I walk into the living room.

He chuckles. "That's a lot of love, birthday girl"

"It is." I smile. "When are you coming over?" I look around the room Brance and my mom have been redecorating. My mom's taste is far from elegant.

"Soon," I hear him groan as he stretches. I picture him all warm and hard, his dark curls a mess.

Which makes me remember my mom. "*Oh my God*, Reed!" I can't hide my excitement. "Mom got Botox yesterday. Her face looks like she had a stroke! You have to be nice though." A twinge of guilt swims over me. I shouldn't be happy at my mom's expense.

"Wait a minute... What?" He sounds distracted.

"Are you listening?" I demand. "She looks crazy! Just act like you don't notice it."

"You're kidding, right? What the hell is wrong with her? I thought you said she was looking better now that she has this sick codependence thing going on with Brance."

"Well he's not with her twenty-four hours a day. Although she is begging for him to move in." I twirl my hair around my finger.

"Well, he can't," he kind of grunts. "You don't have enough room for all his security." He's joking, I think. Ignoring his comment, I zero in on his breathing.

"Reed? What are you doing?" My core clenches and cheeks get hot.

"What do you think I'm doing?" I hear another harsh breath.

"Reed Saddington! Are you... *you know*." I check to make sure my mom hasn't materialized. I'm shy whenever I have to verbalize anything sexual.

He laughs. "Well, I was trying to rub one out listening to your sexy voice, but you ruined it with the visual of Olive Oyl and her stroke eye."

"I knew it." My voice sounds shaky. I should be chastising him. Instead I'm all tingly, thinking about him touching himself.

"Reed...?"

"Are you alone?" His voice is harsh.

Suddenly, I wish Brance wasn't on his way over. "Yes." It comes out like a whisper. Clearing my voice, I add, "But Brance will be here any minute."

Lately, all Reed has to do is say my name, and I start to flush. Trying to distract him and myself, I keep talking about my mom.

"She looks bad. I kind of feel sorry for her. She was crying, and I had to hear this whole speech about how she was always plain and I'm beautiful. It makes me feel bad for her... kind of," I say slowly, listening for any sounds indicating Reed is still masturbating.

He's silent for a moment. Then it sounds like he is moving around. I can't lie; I'm a little disappointed.

"Kitten, you are one of the kindest people I know." There's the sound of a door shutting. "Now, Olive Oyl, she's pathetic. Serves her right. She makes herself look like a freak."

"You have to stop calling her Olive Oyl." I bite my bottom lip so as not to laugh. He is right though. She does resemble the cartoon minus the black hair.

"It's my birthday. The whole place is decorated. She worked super hard on it, so try to be nice to her." Lying back on the couch, I picture Reed shirtless, his toned abs flexing down to that V that makes me drool.

"You're playing the birthday card today, huh? What will you give me if I'm on my best behavior? Actually, fuck that. Beyond good behavior. I'm talking major ass kissing." His voice is husky.

Bolting up, I ask, "What do you want?" sounding way too enthusiastic.

"I want to have you all to myself tonight. Me and my birthday girl." My heart races and my stomach flips again. As I rub my legs together, a ripple of pleasure zings straight to the inside of my legs. Reed and I have been doing some major make-out sessions. But he hasn't gone any further than my breasts. I wonder what he is going to do to me tonight. I hope he makes me come—I want him to.

"Deal," I whisper. My eyes dart around as I wait for my mother to explode into our sphere.

"What was that, Kitten?"

I smile into my phone. "You're such a brat... *deal, I can't wait!*"

"Neither can I. I'll be over around two. Claire still insisting we wear suits?"

"Yep!"

"Prepare yourself for prince charming. I love you," he says, his voice low and gravelly.

"Love you too." Hanging up, I literally start singing, not caring that my voice is average at best. I'm happy, so I belt out the Beatles' "Birthday" as I roll around the couch.

My singing is cut short when our doorman calls, alerting me that Brance is on his way up. Throwing open the door, I stare, fascinated. Brance is hauling three large garment bags and is accompanied by a girl covered in tattoos. She has pink hair and follows him, pulling a makeup bag on wheels.

"Brance, what the hell have you done? It's just us!"

He pushes some metallic streamers out of the way and kisses me on the lips. "No arguing with me, Tess. It's your birthday! Claire is going to need all of my attention." He huffs. "Tess, this is Tilly." He wraps an arm around Tilly's shoulder. "This woman is mind-blowing in the art of makeup. Between the two of us, I am confident we can tape up your mother's eye. Where is she?" His chocolate eyes roam the room and he no doubt takes in the ridiculous explosion of party decorations, paper lanterns, streamers, and tinsel dangling from the ceiling. "Thank God, is that coffee I smell?" He veers toward the kitchen.

Laughing, I say, "What would I do without you?"

I turn to the girl with pink hair. "Hello, welcome to the insane asylum." I wave my hands like I'm Vanna White. She looks around in awe.

"Can I get you a cup of coffee?" I offer, having no idea where Brance found Tilly. She is clearly much older than we are.

"That would be awesome. Wow... I always wondered who actually lives in places like this."

"Yeah, don't hold it against Tess. She can't help that she's rich and some decorator puked glitter all over her apartment for her big day."

My eyes widen. "Excuse me, what are you?"

He ignores me as he opens the fridge.

"Oh my God!" Tilly has her hands over her mouth. "*That* is your refrigerator? It looks like a cabinet!"

Brance and I glance at it, both of us numb to such extravagant things. She walks over to it, her hands touching how it all blends in with the wooden cabinets. "So cool."

Smiling, I say, "Two coffees, coming up. Tilly? Do you like anything in yours?" I'm already scooping two large spoonfuls of sugar into Brance's cup.

"Just a little crème if you have it."

"Of course." I hand them both their cups.

All of us turn as we hear the door open. Maria and her sister Letty bustle in carrying all kinds of bags filled with food and alcohol.

"Hola." I skip over to them. I have grown up with these two women and love them like family. My mother is not an easy woman to work for, so I always make sure they know how much I appreciate them.

"Hola. Happy Birthday, my beautiful girl." Maria drops the bags on the counter, pulling me into a warm hug.

"Thank you." Turning, I hug Letty, who hands me a small wrapped present.

I'm touched. "You two shouldn't have," and I mean that. I have more than any fifteen-year-old could ever want or need. But this little gift means they care. My eyes well with tears.

"It isn't much, but we love you and it's a special day." Maria winks at me.

A loud gasp fills the room, "Oh... *mi amor*, these are so magnificent. From Mr. Reed, yes?" Letty praises my flowers, her fingers fluttering over the roses. She *loves* Reed.

"Yes, Letty, from Reed." It's impossible to stop my goofy smile.

"Jesus," Tilly breathes out. "I don't think I have ever seen anything that spectacular. Your boyfriend sent you these?"

Starting to feel self-conscious, I wonder, what must this woman think?

"He likes to spoil me."

"Uh, yeah, he does. They smell amazing." Her whole face is almost engulfed in them.

Brance chokes on his coffee. "Spoil is a nice way of saying her boyfriend is obsessed, lucky bitch!" He pinches my butt as he walks by, and I squeal. "Come on, my beauties. Let's go find Momma Bear."

I smirk at him as he walks by. "You're fantastic, you know that, right?"

"Undoubtedly. Wait until you see the dress I've picked for you tonight. As soon as Reed sees you, he will fall at your feet and pledge his undying love for you." Placing his hand on his heart, he drops it and dryly demands for me to go take a shower.

"Thank God, I had the good sense to make you get waxed a couple of days ago," he mumbles.

"Yes, master, or should I call you sir?"

His eyes twinkle. "Oh, I think master is fine. Have you had breakfast yet?"

"Here it is." Posing, I hold up my cup as if it's a gourmet meal.

"That will never do." Pulling out his phone, he starts ordering tons of pastries from the bakery down the street. He knows it's my favorite. I happily follow Brance into my bedroom, letting him take charge. He hangs up and sighs, hands on his hips as he studies me. "Music, please!"

Four hours later, I stare at my mom, and I'm not exaggerating—I might fall to my knees and pledge my undying devotion to Brance and Tilly. They have taken a skinny woman who looks as though she had a stroke and somehow magically taped up her eye so that she looks normal. Tilly's makeup skills are brag worthy. She went with pretty pastels. My mom appears softer, younger. Brance has straightened her bleached-blond hair stick straight and parted it in the middle.

The last piece of putting my mother together is getting her into the dress.

Brance unzips the garment bag and pulls out a lavender ruffled, skintight ball gown, with a full-length train.

My phone rings. Glancing at my mother, I reach for it. It's my father calling. I haven't heard from him in a week or so. Last time we talked, he promised to make it to my party. Then he and my mom had a horrible fight, so I haven't been holding my breath.

"I will be right back to help you guys," I say. "Put her in that." I motion to the couture gown.

"We've got it." Tilly nods. "She does better with us anyway." It's the truth. I wince at her easy acceptance of it. A complete stranger has our relationship figured out, right down to the way my mother's mood swings seesaw up and down when she's with me.

"Hello," I say back into the phone, shutting my bedroom door and stepping into the gold hallway. Yes, my mother heard gold was going to be this year's fall color. Also, she thinks it means royalty. So, gold it is.

"Tess, it's your father." His voice is curt, with no affection at all. My heart hurts talking to him.

"Hi, Daddy." My tone matches his. God. It's painful dealing with my parents.

"I'm not going to make it tonight... wait hold on a second, Tess." He starts talking to someone else. Unbelievable! Why do I even care? I have the most self-absorbed parents alive. Staring down at my nails, the urge to start picking at my polish is great. But a quick thought of Brance's horror squashes that.

I have no idea why my dad keeps up this charade of calling me once a week.

He left! And, obviously he's not coming back. I used to be close with him—he was my hero. Now I see his number and groan. He hates Reed, and frankly it's started to wear me out. Ignoring him is so much easier. His negative views about my looks, style, manners, and intelligence are endless. Not to mention his OCD is frightful. The thought that he could have passed that on to me haunts me.

"Tess? Tess, are you there?" His voice makes me respond automatically.

"Don't worry about my birthday..."

"Well, that is why I'm calling. I'm sorry, but I'm involved in a big case, and with your mother being difficult"—he sighs—"it's complicated."

"I said it was fine. I need to go. We're getting ready," I snip.

Silence. "Who is coming tonight?"

"Just some friends. You're not missing anything." I can't help the disappointment from seeping out of me. "I'll talk to you soon."

"So, Reed?" His disapproval carries through the phone.

"Tess, I'm exhausted and the last thing I want to do is fight with you on your birthday."

"Why are you so against Reed? Yes, he is going to be here tonight. He's my boyfriend! He also wants to be around me especially on my birthday. *He* thinks I'm worth it." I know I'm behaving like a child. I mean if he was home, it would be difficult for Reed to stay over. I should be happy instead of upset. Again, I'm greeted with silence, and I almost hang up.

"Happy Birthday, Tess."

The line goes dead. No wonder he has gotten filthy rich as a lawyer. He's a master liar.

Blinking back my stupid tears, which are making my vision blurry, I try to even out my breathing. Why do I let him bother me? It's not like he does anything when he is home. But that kind of a lie? I miss him. He's strict, but at least he tries to stay invested in my life. More so than my mother. When I enter my room, I look at her. She's been drinking Cristal since she woke up. I should persuade her to eat a scone or drink some coffee. I can't see the full glory of her dress because she is sitting.

"Okay, Momma Bear," Brance coos at her, removing the champagne from her hand. "Sit here and let your makeup set. Drink some coffee. I have to get Tess ready."

My mom looks at him. "I think that's a wonderful idea." She sways slightly.

"Perfect. I'll send Maria in with a fresh pot. And my feelings are going to be hurt if you don't try one of these pastries." He raises his dark eyebrows at her.

She hiccups. "Brance, you know I don't eat carbs, but for you I'll make an exception."

I have to look away. She's so worthless. I never realized how lost she truly is. She's only twenty-two years older than me, not yet forty but so broken.

Straightening my shoulders, I make up my mind. *I will never let myself become her.* She shouldn't have been a mother. She's far too self- absorbed.

Even on *my* birthday, we have spent hours getting her ready. I feel like a footnote.

"Sit down, Pretty Girl." Brance and I stare at each other in the mirror.

We don't talk; his eyes tell me everything—he knows how I feel. Brance gets me. Gets my sadness and the painful truth that my mother and father never truly wanted me. He starts to blow out my hair as Tilly accesses my face for makeup.

The warm heat from the hairdryer gives me a false sense of calm. The conversation with my dad has made me remember that I was completely unwanted by them. My mom got pregnant to trap my dad. Even with all my beauty on the outside, they still don't want me, not really. My dad married my mom, stating it was his duty, and they have both been miserable since.

Today, on my birthday, I'm seeing firsthand how tragic she is. I guess when all you do all day is live in extravagant regret, you start to lose what little sense you have of yourself.

"I don't think I will ever have children, Brance. Do you think Reed will be upset?" I say it loud enough for him to hear but not my mom.

Closing my eyes, I don't need to wait for his answer. *Of course he will be upset.*

Turning off the blow dryer, he taps me on the shoulder and I open my eyes. He frowns as he squats down, unplugging the hair dryer and plugging in the styling iron. Crossing his arms, he looks at me through the mirror, his dark eyes filled with understanding. "I think... you're getting too deep on your birthday."

"No, I disagree. This is the perfect time to embrace the truths about myself." Crossing my legs, I continue. "I won't end up like her." I motion at my mother with my eyes. "I don't want children. I'm going to stop the insanity with me. As long as I have Reed, Jax, and you, I will be fine."

Brance looks at Tilly. "Can you give us a moment?"

She looks relieved. "I think I might get myself a glass of Cristal."

We watch her walk over to my mother, who is drinking coffee and champagne—*nice!* Although, she does seem to be nibbling on a couple strawberries. Tilly sits next to her and my mother happily pours her a glass.

Brance tilts my head up. "Tess, I refuse to let you do this on your birthday. I have worked too hard to hear this shit. We are fifteen! You don't want kids? Use birth control!" Taking a piece of my hair, he starts pulling the iron through it. My head jerks. He's not being gentle, frustration oozing out of him. *For a skinny, delicate guy, his hands are awfully strong.* My lips twitch at his passion. He is like my fierce dragon, ready to breathe fire on anyone who dares to hurt me.

"Brance?"

He raises his dark eyebrows. "What?"

"I'm so happy that guy beat you up." His grumpy frown starts to twitch.

"Damn right, baby." He breaks into a smile. The last yellowish blackness around his eye is almost gone. Since that is how we found each other, we're now thankful for that guy.

"Wait until you see your birthday gown! And wait until you see my tux." With a hand on his hip, he gives me a sassy pose.

"You're crazy."

Leaning over, he kisses me on the lips. "Tilly? Turn up the music! And don't even think about getting smashed until all makeup has been applied. That includes me. I want you to highlight my eyes tonight."

chapter 10

REED

Past – fourteen years old

Glancing over at Jax, I start to laugh. He gives me the evil eye. "Don't fucking start." He grabs at his tie as if it's strangling him.

"Screw this." He yanks it loose, unbuttoning the first two buttons on his starched white shirt.

"You read the invitation, man. *Black tie!*" I say.

"Nah, I love Tess, but she's yours. That means *you* have to look good. All I have to do is show up."

Scowling at him, I'm pissed because he's right. Also, I made a deal and I plan on cashing in on it. Jax looks good enough. We're in Tom Ford black suits for fuck's sake.

As I glance out the window, I am at one with New York City and its animal energy; it's alive and breathing as the sun starts to descend. I had wanted to be at Tess's earlier, but Jax wouldn't get off the phone with "that girl." Apparently he's still hooking up with the redhead from Zack's crappy party.

I should have said screw it and hailed a cab, but for reasons I can't even verbalize, I need my twin tonight.

Jay is driving us. We decided to take the Maybach. Sometimes it's easier to get around in it. I know that sounds arrogant and pretentious, but people always give you room when you've got a driver. Rubbing my neck, I interrupt Jax and his texting.

"What'd you get Tess?" I have way too much nervous energy. Jax doesn't even look up from his phone, though his mouth twitches, which aggravates me.

"Another thing, Tess wants you to be super nice to her mother and Brance." I slip this in casually. His eyes slowly go from his phone to me. Raising an eyebrow, he stretches his long legs out, crowding mine. If I didn't need him to help me tonight, I would kick his legs to the side. Instead, I lean forward, nervously cracking my knuckles.

Jax's eyes laser in on my hands "Really? Why would she worry about me? I'm ten times nicer to Claire than you are." He pockets his phone.

"Just be on your best behavior is all," I grumble. His knowing smirk makes me want to punch him in the gut. Suddenly, Jay slams on his breaks. Sliding his window down he curses out a cab driver who cut us off. I bump my head on the back of the driver's seat, but Jax barely registers the car's movement.

"Why? Tess promise you a blow job?"

"None of your business, man, but act right, okay?"

He snorts. "Whatever you need, brother."

Our midnight blue Maybach glides up to the parking area of Tess's building. My heart starts pumping faster. The anticipation of seeing my girl makes me smile. Jay is cursing away at the tight fit of her garage.

"Dude, let us off here, and you can take your time parking," I tell him.

Waiting for the elevator, Jax leans over, putting his annoying face in front of mine. "I got her a giant crystal ball."

"What?" With a blank stare, I shove him backward. "Get your face out of mine!"

He laughs, then acts like he's doing sign language. "I... got... her... a... crystal... ball! For her birthday present." Dropping his hands, he puts them in his pockets and shrugs. "It's a rare crystal, and it's huge. Cost me a fortune. They told me if you hold it, it's supposed to calm and heal you. I think Tess will love it." Knowing he kicked ass on her present, he smiles broadly.

"Yeah, that's right up her alley," I say, taking a quick glance at my reflection in the mirrored elevator.

I look good tonight. The black suit is tailored to a tee. I also allowed my barber to cut my hair, though I did leave some curls. Tess likes them. I catch Jax staring at me, one eyebrow raised.

Rubbing my hands on my pants, I admit it. "I'm nervous."

He starts laughing. "Why? Because you know she is going to like my gift better?" He waggles his eyebrows.

"Why are you being a dick tonight?" No way am I admitting that is exactly what I was thinking.

Jax doesn't answer but keeps that smug smile on his face all the way to her apartment. Glaring at him, I pound on the door. Brance opens it, and I almost take a step back. He's wearing a shiny silver tuxedo! And is that eye makeup on him?

"Hey, hey, hey. Welcome, you gorgeous men." He waves us in.

"Brance, tone the gayness down a notch or two," I snarl.

"Hmm, Tess, *said* you were going to be prince charming tonight." He shrugs, dismissing me and leaving us to enter alone.

"SexyBack," by Timberlake is blasting. With a deep breath, I take in the scene around the apartment. *What the fuck?* I feel like I'm in the Twilight Zone. The apartment has been completely refurbished and repainted in reds and golds. Velvet couches with mixed with metallic gold pillows line two walls. And that's in addition to the ridiculous number of Chinese lanterns, silver and gold streamers, and metallic balloons drifting from the ceiling.

Looking at Jax, I point around the room. "The whole place is changed. Did Tess mention *this* to you?"

He shakes his head. "Wow, Claire might actually be losing it. I can't wait to see Robert's face when he comes home after months of being gone and finds his multimillion-dollar apartment is a gay man's dream." Jax snorts.

"Jesus, I think that's insulting to most gay guys," I say. "It's more like Liberace's wet dream."

Leaving Jax speechless at the décor, I head straight for the kitchen where I know I'll find Maria and Letty.

Their dark heads are close together, and they speak in hushed Spanish, checking to make sure the appetizers are warm.

Their eyes light up when they see me. Grabbing and kissing me, they make me feel instantly welcome.

"What has happened to this place?" They both smile and shrug, a knowing look in their eyes.

"What? You don't like it, Mr. Reed?" Letty acts shocked.

Rolling my eyes, I grab a bacon-wrapped date before Maria can stick a toothpick in it. I pop it in my mouth, almost groaning out loud as it burns my tongue, bursting with goat cheese and the bacon's salty sweetness.

"Holy God, that's so good." Kissing Maria's forehead, I reach for another.

She slaps my hand. "No more, Mr. Reed. You have to wait for everyone."

"Just one more. I need to make sure the bacon is fully cooked."

She eyes me up and down. "One more, and don't get any on your suit."

Hugging her, I ask, "So what's the story with Claire and Robert? Are they getting divorced? Because if they're not, they will be when he comes home."

Both giggle at my joke. Unfortunately, I'm kind of serious. "Is he going to be here tonight?" Tess hasn't mentioned it, but I know she wants her dad to be here for her birthday party.

Maria looks at the doorway, then lowers her voice. "We have not seen Mr. Robert in months. Mrs. Claire was fighting with him on the phone a couple days ago, though." She shakes her head disapprovingly and bites her lip with worry. "I don't think he is going to show tonight."

"Asshole." Robert has never liked me, so I'm not a fan. In the last year, I think I've seen him twice.

The doorbell rings, breaking up our gossiping. Assuming it's my parents, I allow Jax to let them in.

Putting my arms around Maria and Letty, I squeeze them tight. "I'm going to go find Tess. I'll see you two later." When I wink at them, they laugh, then chastise me for stealing another hors d'oeuvre.

"Jesus." Shaking my head at the gaudy gold hallway, I make my way to Tess's room.

When I stop at the door, I'm almost scared of what I'm going to find. Not bothering to knock, I open it. I can't get a good look because Tess, some tattooed girl with pink hair, and Olive Oyl are all screaming at me. I start laughing at the stupidity of it all. Brance appears and shoos me out, shutting the door behind us.

"What the hell has happened to this place?"

He stares at me, arms crossed.

"We need to talk," I say, motioning with my head for him to follow. This conversation is long overdue. Especially, with his decorating and how it seems he is becoming Claire's life coach.

He keeps up with me. His dark eyes show no fear. If anything, he seems to be trying to decide if I'm good enough to bother with.

Snorting at his smugness, I enter the library slash billiard room: meaning it is surrounded with books and in the middle of the room is an ornate wooden pool table. This is one of Tess's and my favorite rooms for numerous reasons. Brance moves to a love seat in the corner. He glances around, taking in the hunter-green walls and dark wooden bookshelves as if he can't wait to get his hands on it.

"Touch anything in this room and you lose a testicle. I'm serious, Brance. Consider this *my* room, and I like it the way it is."

He snickers. "Reed, I can't wait to hear what you have dragged me in here to tell me, or are you only going to threaten me?"

The guy's got balls, I'll give him that. No one talks to me like that except maybe Jax.

Sitting down across from him, I place my elbows on my knees and lean forward. "Look, Tess needs a friend. She has decided that's *you*. You fill some void in her life." Sitting back, I add, "But, I need you to know that I always come first."

Silence fills the room. Brance maintains eye contact with me. Slowly he smirks. "Of course Tess loves you. I would never dream of coming before you." He crosses his leg. "Unless you do something where I have to step in and be first."

I raise an eyebrow. "What does that mean?" My voice is low.

He shrugs. "Nothing, Reed." He stands. "Now, I need to finish Tess's hair."

"Wait, what?" I'm confused at this guy's gall. "I need to talk to Tess for a second."

Brance smooths out his jacket with his hand. "Yeah... *no*. It's bad luck."

"What are you talking about? This isn't our wedding day."

He sighs dramatically. "Reed, Reed, you can't rush beauty. Why don't you go wait in the main room and have some more appetizers? I can smell the bacon on you."

He shuts the door on me, and I stand there staring at the closed door for a moment, replaying what just happened. Brance may play the flamboyant gay guy, but I'm starting to think the real Brance is somewhat sinister.

Taking my time going back, I try to shake off my unease. Tess is mine, and I have nothing to worry about.

I'm expecting to see my parents, but instead, I see Jax talking to a tall, skinny blond girl in a tight black dress. At first glance, I confuse her with Olive Oyl. As soon as I take a closer look, I realize my mistake. Grabbing a crab tart from the round bistro table, I shove the whole cake into my mouth. God, I love Maria's cooking. The caviar and crème on top are mind-blowing.

"Hey." I nod at the girl, turning my attention to Jax. "I really need you to be enthusiastic. Brance is going all out—"

"Dude! What is wrong with you? I'm here all dressed up. Being charming, *having manners*! Did you even realize there is another person here? Or are you so far up Tess's ass you can't even comprehend that you rudely interrupted us?" He motions at us with his hands.

I look at the girl, who shyly looks at her feet.

"Shit, sorry. I'm Reed, and I have no excuse for that. My brother's right."

"That's okay. I get it." Her voice is soft. I take a closer look at her. She has long blond hair and bangs. The bangs cover most of her eyes. Or maybe it seems that way because she hasn't looked away from her feet. She's tall, and I think I can detect small pink lips.

"This is Lexi. Her father is in business with ours. Apparently, she'll be starting school with us." Jax looks around the room bored. "I think that's the door. Excuse me," he says, leaving me with her.

Perfect, *asshole*! Staring at the girl, I have no idea why she won't look at me. She seemed fine with Jax, but if she wants to not talk, that's great with me. I'm about to use the same weak excuse Jax did when she decides to lift her head.

"I hope it's all right that I came tonight?"

I was right—she has small bow-shaped lips and blue eyes. She's quite pretty, if you like blonds. I happen to dislike them.

They always remind me of Claire. She's thin, with delicate bones and pretty much no boobs. But with all my mother's friends having fake breasts, I kind of hope she's one of the few who will let herself be. Clearly, if her father is doing business with my father, she comes from money. More than likely, as soon as she turns eighteen, she'll run to the nearest plastic surgeon.

I smile at her, and she exhales. Wow, this is almost painful. Is she terrified of me or dumb?

Lowering my voice, I try to be reassuring. "I'm sure Tess will be thrilled to have another friend. You guys just moved here, right?"

My mind is already elsewhere, completely tuning this girl out. How the fuck did Brance redecorate this whole apartment so fast? I was here only two weeks ago! At least I like this room. It's got a sophisticated, pleasing feel to it. The dark putty-colored walls have been replaced with crisp white ones, accenting the tall ceilings. A couple of large gray round rugs have been added. And a large gold spiky chandelier hangs in the middle. A little too upscale for me, but at least it's an improvement, unlike the other rooms.

"Yes," she answers, jolting my attention back to her weirdness.

Shit! What was I even talking to her about? Thankfully I'm rescued.

My mom breezes in wearing a green ball gown, with my dad following in a black tuxedo.

"Fucking Brance." I shake my head.

"Pardon?" She bats her eyes at me.

Chuckling, I say, "Nothing. My girlfriend's best friend is... unique, that's all." She looks confused.

"It was his idea to have us all dress up." She nods—that's all she gives me.

Suddenly I cringe almost like someone has dragged their fingernails across a blackboard. Unfortunately, it's Claire's high-pitched, annoying laugh piercing the large room, making me want to duck and run.

Of course I can't. "Excuse me, I have some ass kissing to do." She opens her mouth; however, I walk away. I know its rude, but I did my duty and Jax can step up again.

"Reed!" My mother's face is flushed. Clearly this isn't her first glass of champagne. "Come here." She waves me over, animated.

Looking at the tall couple standing in front of me, I extend my hand to what must be Lexi's father. "Nice to meet you, sir. I'm Reed."

"Oh, such lovely boys." The tall, plastic blond woman gushes.

"Yes, Dimitri and Anna, this is our other son Reed." My mom beams at me.

"I just met your daughter." It's all I can think of saying. Looking over their shoulders, I notice Olive Oyl is whispering something to Maria. I almost rub my eyes in disbelief. She looks like a real person. Her makeup is soft and her dress is... awesome.

Breaking away from my parents and Dimitri and Anna, I reach for her elbow. "Claire, you look beautiful."

She looks so happy her eyes mist up. I almost feel guilty about all the things I say about her. *Almost.*

"Reed." Her bony hands grab my arms. She must see I'm truly being sincere because she throws herself into my arms.

There goes feeling sorry for her. Stiffly I pat her back.

"I can't cry. Brance will never forgive me. And it would mess up Tilly's taping of my eye." She blinks, and her tears instantly evaporate. I can't help but chuckle at her dramatics.

I want to whisper that she probably doesn't want everyone to know that she has a fucked-up eye because of Botox. Instead, I grab her hand and kiss it. A bit over the top, but the room seems to love it besides Jax, who snorts loudly.

"I'm being honest—you are a vision tonight, Claire."

"Reed, you charmer." I know she loves that I'm giving her my attention since I never do.

"Mother," I say turning toward my mom, "looking lovely as always." I kiss her cheek. She smells like peppermint. Must have been drinking her favorite coffee drink—the main ingredient is peppermint schnapps.

"Oh, sweetheart, you look so handsome tonight. You're not a little boy anymore." She strokes my cheek with her hand.

"Brad?" Her voice is loud. "What are we going to do? Our babies are growing up so fast." Clutching his jacket, she looks a little unsteady.

"Dad, how much has she had?" I ask, arching my brow.

He laughs. "Don't worry about your mother, Reed. I've got her." He winks at me.

Frowning at him, I turn away. The last thing I need is a visual of my parents.

"Holy shit." Jax exhales as he stares at the double doors that have been painted a silvery blue. Following his eyes, Brance stands to the side, allowing me the most stunning view I will ever need.

Tess.

My heart is thudding so hard, I don't even hear the classical music playing anymore. I'm so fucked! So ruined. I'm unable to move, even speak. Vaguely, I hear my brother say something. Holding up my hand to shut him up, my eyes sweep her form, seeking her eyes.

Like a magnet, she moves toward me. God, that fucking walk of hers gets me every time. My hand goes to my chest. It hurts to look at her.

She wears a red chiffon dress—well, I think it's chiffon; I have no fucking clue. All I know is that it's tight around her breasts, making them almost spill out and the waist is covered with what looks like small pearls. Layer after layer, the rest of the dress makes her look like a princess.

Tess's body always drives me crazy, but in this dress...

Brance is whispering like a proud father, something about Dior. All I see is the most exquisite girl in the world.

Her dark brown hair is straight and shiny, parted in the middle. Her eyes are smoky, and her puffy lips are red, matching her dress.

She stops when she gets close to me and twirls. Time slows, and everyone fades into the freshly painted white walls. It's only us. As she twirls, the dress expands, like a butterfly, and I inhale again. Her face looks so happy. Like a flawless angel, she throws her head back and laughs. My eyes latch on to her long neck. And the pulse—I swear I can hear it from here.

"Reed? You okay, son?" Swallowing, I sense the room is once again invaded by unwanted family and friends. My dad is chuckling with Brance and Jax. I don't even care if they think I'm crazy, *because... are you kidding me?*

Grabbing Tess by the waist, pulling her close, I lean into her, the scent of vanilla filling me up.

"How are you going to top this when you marry me, Kitten? I can't use enough adjectives to describe how stunning you are," I whisper in her ear.

"Reed!" my mom says. "Let Tess breathe." Smiling, she widens her eyes at us in warning.

Yet I ignore her. Right now, the whole world could end, and I would be fine.

"I told you, you would be happy with the wait," Brance gloats.

"You are right once again, Brance," I say, not taking my eyes away from Tess's.

Interrupting my Tess high, Anna, the Russian woman, blurts, "Oh, they are serious, huh?" Disapproval drips from her.

Tess glances over, looking as aggravated as I am. A small frown appears. I almost kiss it, but that would lead to more inappropriate displays of affection. Obviously, no one thought to give the birthday girl a heads-up that strangers were crashing her party.

"Kitten, this is..." Christ, I'm so caught up in her web, I can't even remember my own name much less theirs.

"Oh, right... Tess." Claire steps forward. "I forgot to mention that Brad and Caroline brought some friends." Waving her hand at Dimitri and Anna, she kind of stumbles over to the blond girl. "And, this is their daughter, Lexi, right?" She looks to my mother for confirmation.

"Lexi is going to start school on Monday with you guys." She smiles, and the big balls of collagen in her lips look like they might pop out. "We thought it would be nice for her to have some friends. What better way to get to know each other than at a party." She sings the last part.

"Christ," I mumble. Tess is stiff throughout all of her mother's ramblings.

My mom smiles and walks over to Lexi, gently bringing the girl forward. "You guys go have fun." Like we're children. She reaches for another glass of champagne.

Lexi stares right at Tess. She's taller. Standing next to my jewel, everything about her screams average.

Tess cocks her head and extends her hand. Lexi hesitates, then peeks at me as she shakes it.

An awkward and weird silence fills our small circle. Thankfully Jax grabs Tess, swinging her around. She screams, trying to grab on to a white cushion on one of the couches. The bad energy evaporates as my twin twirls her faster. She squeals as one of her high heels almost knocks over a large glass vase.

"Jaxton Bradley Ian Saddington, knock it off," my mom yells.

I'm sick of it too. Jax is way too affectionate with Tess. It was fine when we were young, but now, this shit needs to stop.

Claire isn't even fazed. She must be drunk. How else is she not seeing this? She claps her hands and announces that dinner is being served.

"Jax!" I hiss. "Put her down." He grins at me, gives her one last tight squeeze, then lets her go. "Reed, lighten up."

"Then don't touch Tess."

Reaching for her, I tuck her into my arms, kissing her forehead, inhaling the fresh scent of her hair. "Why won't everyone leave us alone?" I grumble in her ear.

"Because it's my birthday." Her delicate fingers run through my hair. "I missed you today. It scares me how much I need you." Her raspy voice hypnotizes me for a moment.

Lifting her finger, I lightly bite it. "I don't want you to be scared. I want you to always need me."

Hearing her exhale, I flash her a grin. She pokes her finger in one of my dimples—she has a thing for them. "So bad."

Jax makes a gagging noise, then turns to talk to Brance.

That's when I make my move. Taking Tess's hand, I maneuver her around the corner and into the gold hallway. Pinning her up against the wall, I can't help myself. My nose goes straight for her throat. That seems to be my weak spot today. Every day it's a different part of her. I wasn't going to do anything other than tell her I love her, but now that we're alone and the loud laughter is in the next room...

My mouth attacks her neck. She groans. The sound makes my dick hard—well, harder. She inhales, taking my breath with her. I feel that rush of love, energy, chemistry. It zings through my body, making me invincible. I kiss the side of her mouth, loving the way her lips feel like velvety softness.

My tongue wants in. "Kiss me, Kitten," I whisper into her mouth. Her sapphire eyes narrow as she parts her lips. My head feels light as I dissolve into her, claiming her perfect mouth.

"Tess..." My erection is rapidly taking control of my brain. Reaching for her glossy brown hair, I tighten my fist around it. Tight enough that she's mine. My prisoner. I want her like this always. She doesn't stop me—if anything, her breathing gets harsher.

"You look so hot like this. So beautiful and helpless." Swooping down on her, I wonder if this feels as good to her as it does to me.

Tess is the only girl I've kissed. But I think I'm a natural because she seems as hungry as I am. Our mouths tangle, teeth clash, and for a split second, it's the most simple, primal feeling. It feels too powerful. Almost like the world has stopped spinning and only our tongues and breath are keeping everyone alive.

Her hands are touching my neck, pulling me closer. My dick is so hard it's painful. Letting go of her hair, I reach for her right leg, raising it. This dress is nothing but layers of gauze making it easy to press my throbbing shaft against her. Holding her hip, I start to move on her, rubbing back and forth against her pussy.

"Oh God, Reed," she moans in my ear. Suddenly my name is all she can say. I pull back, so that I can see her bewitching face.

"Kitten," I whisper, kissing her neck again, my tongue licking up and down. Like a vampire who needs blood to survive, I desperately want to sink my teeth into her creamy neck, marking her as mine. I'm rubbing her hard, wanting to explode, to take us to a place I have never been with her. I drag a shaky breath in. Somehow this has spiraled out of control. Lifting my head, my voice is gravel. "We have to stop."

"Don't stop."

I need to be strong and pull away. Instead, I move my tongue so that I can lick the bottom part of her lips. She groans loudly; I cover it with my mouth. Grabbing her hips tightly, I give one more rub because I can't help myself. Tess makes me weak, which scares me enough to stop.

"Tess, we have to stop before you come." *Jesus, I'm panting!*

Her eyes darken. "This feels... Reed, I want you to do this to me tonight. All of it. Please!"

At least she's panting too. Her hands frantically pull at me like she's possessed. She tries to rub herself on me again. I feel like a god. *Would it be that bad to give in?*

Then, she groans loudly. Covering her mouth with mine, I smile. "Shh... I can't wait to make you come but not right now."

"Why not?" she whines.

"Because you're too loud."

That stops her, and she lifts her head. "I am not!" Her cheeks turn pinker. "Stop it, Reed. I hate that arrogant grin."

"You are." I laugh. Her face glows. Her love, her hopes, her heart, all of it mine. Her nails dig into my arms, clinging to me. Her chest flushes, and there's an almost desperate look in her eyes.

"Kitten, have you ever come before?"

She looks horrified and somewhat angry. "Of course not! You told me all our firsts would be together!"

I puff out some air I was holding because I might just jet off in my pants. Having Tess tell me that might push me over the edge. All I want is to take her over my shoulders and lock us in her room forever.

Grinning at my caveman thoughts, I stroke her straightened hair. "I did say that, but come on, I wouldn't have been upset if you had gotten yourself off." Rubbing my nose on her cheek, I move toward her ear.

"But now that I know"—I shake my head—"I can't wait to watch you come on my mouth." She shivers.

"Wait... how do you know how to... do that?" Her eyes narrow.

I can't help but laugh at her cuteness. "Porn, baby. Hours of it. I can't wait to try everything."

Big eyes stare at me. I take her hand and place it on my erection. She squeezes, gently tracing the outline of my penis in fascination. I moan, wondering why I'm torturing myself. I should take her into the dining room and wait until later. I should, but my hand seems to have a life of its own as I reach for her breast. It's her turn to moan. Her head falls back with a small thud. Leaning into her so that her warm hand is tight on my aching cock, I fondle her breast. Tess's nipples are so hard, they poke through her gauzy dress.

"That feels really good." She moves her other hand to cup and explore my throbbing dick.

"Yeah, that's it," I say, turning to kiss her neck.

I freeze.

Lexi is standing in the hallway like a creeper staring at us. Tess raises her head, sensing the change in me. Her hands stop rubbing, and I cover her scream with my mouth. She wiggles, then pulls away.

"What the hell?" she hisses, horror all over her face.

Lexi looks at her. A glimmer of something I can't explain flashes then is gone. *Wow*, this girl is a serious freak.

"I was wondering where the bathroom is?"

Tess's nails are latched into my forearm. I reach for her hand and gently try to detach them. Taking a step back, I motion in the other direction. "That way."

My hand rubs Tess's back. I don't need this shit tonight— dealing with our parents is bad enough. Now we have some weird voyeur chick messing with my plans.

"Come on, breathe. She didn't see anything." I help straighten her dress, smooth my hair, and lead her away and into the dining room, hoping we don't look as messed up as this feels.

"How long was she there?"

"Not long," I assure her, although I have no clue how long it was. I couldn't care less if that girl gets her kicks from watching people. If it upsets Tess, then I have a problem.

For a small group, we are quite loud. I think it's safe to say all the adults minus Maria and Letty, are shit-faced. Dinner is delicious. Maria and Letty made salmon and prime rib, both with mouthwatering sauces, along with a creamy spinach and cacio e pepe as the pasta. I'm distracted, which sucks because I love Maria's cooking. But my body won't cooperate. I'm still hard. If I was sure Tess wouldn't scream, I would take her hand under the table. A few strokes are all I need.

The older crowd seems to be getting along famously like the phonies they are. Unfortunately, Jax is the only one out of us who looks like he's enjoying himself. He is seated next to Dimitri. Both of them seem to be having a wonderful time talking about the latest software Dimitri is launching.

Brance is on Jax's other side. He and Tess have spent a large portion of dinner whispering.

Pulling her chair closer to me, I say, "Tess, you need to let this go."

She gives me a dirty look, then stands. "Excuse me, I need to fix my makeup. Brance are you coming?"

Fucking great. Leaning back, I throw my napkin on the table.

Now that Tess and Brance are gone, Lexi is the closest one sitting on my other side. I'm forced to turn to her.

"Did you find the restroom?" I wait to see how she reacts.

"I don't think your girlfriend and Brance like me." She sits demurely, but her voice is snippy.

Wow, not even an ounce of remorse. *Interesting.* Picking up Tess's knife, I spin it on the table. "Don't take offense. Brance is obsessed with Tess."

"What about you?" She takes a sip from her water glass, her gaze on the silver knife spinning, which is annoying since she seems to have no problem looking at anyone else.

"Look at me," I snap. Her eyes instantly respond, and a strange sense of power surges through me. I clear my throat. "Sorry, it's been a long day. Tess is mine—has been from the moment I saw her."

I have no idea why I'm telling a weird girl this. Except that she seems fixated on me, and I need to let her know that I'm not an option. Grabbing the knife, I set it back in its spot.

"Yours? As in, you think you own her?" This time she does look at me.

Taking a sip of my water, I leave her hanging, not giving her anything.

"So, I guess, we can't be friends then? She doesn't seem like she wants to share."

"No, she's as possessive as I am." I'm getting sick of her and this conversation.

"And yet you are fine with her relationship with Jax and Brance?" she snaps back.

There's a darkness in this girl. She makes me uncomfortable, guilty. It's an unusual feeling for me. Tess is the one who loves to indulge in blameworthiness.

I scan the lavish table for help. Everyone is happily talking over each other. Pushing my chair back, I stand.

"I think we're getting ready for cake and gifts," I say, starting to get pissed at this whole night. Lexi slowly rises, but my stare freezes her and she sits.

"Jax?" I raise my voice to my brother who is still having a heart-to-heart with Dimitri and his bottle of Russian vodka.

"I'm going to get Tess. Can you keep Lexi company?"

He motions for her to come to him. "Sure, come on over here, Lex. Tell me all your hopes and dreams." He laughs as he takes another shot of vodka. Not caring what she does, I go to retrieve my kitten.

On my way to Tess's bedroom, I'm distracted by Lexi's creepy energy and the gold walls in the hallways and the endless supply of bouncing balloons. I hear Brance and Tess's conversation easily, and I'm not even at her door yet.

"She's after your man, Tess." I hear his voice. "Do not engage with her without me."

"She's a freak! Who watches people?" she hisses.

"You keep saying that! What exactly did she see?" His voice sounds impatient.

"What do you think, Brance? Reed was kissing me... and doing things..."

God, I love her. She's stuttering, and I can't help but smile. Leaning my arm in the doorway, I watch them quietly. Brance is now attacking her hair with a brush. The dark tresses look like shiny brown silk.

"So, she was watching you with Reed?" He waits. "Tess! Why are you getting shy? It's me! What was Reed doing? Details." He snaps his fingers.

"Okay... Calm down." She turns to him.

"He was... you know... rubbing himself on me and touching my boobs and... Oh God, I'm mortified." She covers her face.

He shakes his head pointing the silver hairbrush at her. "*Fuuuck*, I told you she is into dark shit. Did you see how submissive she is with Reed?"

"*What?*" She drops her hands. "You're freaking me out. I can't deal with this on my birthday. What does that even mean 'dark shit'?"

"What do you think it means?" Brance is getting worked up. "She's a bad egg, fucked in the head." He waves the brush around wildly. "I'm sure she likes whips and chains. I have seen plenty of them with my father. We need to shut her down before she does any damage." His voice is tight as he slams the brush down on Tess's vanity.

O-kay, Brance is plotting, slamming, and upsetting Tess. Time to step in. The last thing I need is more drama tonight. I enter the room, moving past the frilly bed loaded with stuffed animals and pillows.

"What are you two doing?" They both jump. I take in Tess's room. I'm guessing she politely declined Brance's decorating skills, or he's been too busy. Whatever, her room is still the same cheery yellow it always has been since we were little.

"Reed! I hate when you do that," Tess screams, putting her hand to her chest.

Brance gets in my space. "I'm explaining that some people are just bad!" Jerking his head, he glowers at me. "And that girl is fucked in the head!"

Again, I'm surprised at him.

I mean, he's right, there is something wrong with Lexi, but invading my space is only permissible with Tess. Pushing him away, I rub her arms soothingly.

"Calm down and stop scaring her, Brance." I glare a warning at him. Snorting, he lifts an eyebrow at me.

Kissing her forehead, I say, "You know you have nothing to worry about, right?"

Tess licks her lips.

"Tess?" I frown at her lack of response.

"What on earth is going on?" Claire stumbles in, literally. "We have to cut the cake."

Tess jumps again.

"Relax, Kitten." Great, Brance has completely freaked her out.

"Hello?" Claire snaps her fingers, only they don't snap.

"God," Tess groans, watching Claire grab hold of the dresser for support. If it wasn't so pathetic, I would give her credit. It takes skill to get fucked up and walk in five-inch heels. I can't believe she's still standing.

Tess sighs. "Maybe you should eat something, Mom, or have a glass of water." She wrinkles her nose at her mother's unsteady form.

Her mom waves her hand. "I'm fine." She nearly trips over her train as she turns.

"Here, let me help, Momma Bear." Brance takes her arm, steadying her. As he guides her, she clutches him as though he is her lifeline.

"Claire? Why gold in the hallways?" I have to ask as we trail behind them.

"Gold is the color of royalty, Reed." Her voice is snippy.

"Um, you might want to research that one. I'm pretty sure it's purple." Snickering, I can't help myself.

She stops, and without Brance supporting her, she would have face-planted. "Wait, what?"

"Claire, Reed is just aggravating you. You like gold. Don't worry about what other people say." His voice is soft like he's talking to a baby.

"But..." She doesn't get any more out since my mother is waiting with Tess's cake.

"There you all are." My mom practically dumps the cake into Claire's hands, who still looks confused about my purple comment. Thankfully, my dad scurries over to help them with the cake.

They set it down and we all admire it. It's large and silver with some sort of glittery shit on it.

"Shall we?" Claire asks, motioning for Letty to light the candles. Maria turns down the lights, the candles casting a pleasant yellow glow.

As I hold Tess from behind, we all sing "Happy Birthday," then wait for Tess to make her wish. Here's the thing: Tess takes forever making her wishes. From the time she was a child, she would sit with her eyes closed. Jax and I used to love to make fun of her. Finally, her eyes open and she blows out all her candles.

"Gift time!" I clap my hands, and everyone looks at me while I steer her into the main room. The sooner we get this over with, the sooner we can kick everyone out.

"Reed!" My mom sounds appalled.

"What?" I snap.

"Son, we need to eat the cake?" My dad chuckles.

I look around the room and run my hand through my hair. I completely forgot about eating the cake. "Sorry, of course, cake."

Letty has turned on the lights and the music is back on. Maria is happily cutting the cake. Reluctantly I take a piece.

"God," Jax moans, "this is fantastic." He has a serious sweet tooth and he's a bona fide chocolate fanatic. Looking down at my cake, I realize I got a piece with a T on it. With a smile, I take a bite. Jax is right—the cake is amazing. The chocolate is dark and not too sweet, so I eat it.

"Wait." Claire stands up. "Before we open gifts, I would like to make a toast."

"Christ," I say under my breath.

"Letty?" Claire calls for her. She comes out with a silver platter, filled with champagne flutes apparently for all of us.

I glance at Maria, who shrugs and rolls her eyes.

"Now, I know that *some* of you are not old enough to drink, but a little champagne never hurt anyone." She giggles.

"In Russia, you are raised on this stuff. Come, Claire, make the toast to your beautiful daughter," Dimitri chimes in. His bloodshot eyes are a good indication he should probably not accept a glass.

Brance finds his way to Claire's side. She raises one of her skinny arms. "To my baby... Happy sweet fifteen." She dabs at her eyes; the fucked-up one is starting to droop again.

"I know it's been a rough year for us, what with your lying, cheating bastard of a father gone—"

"Whoa, Claire." Brance leans over and whispers something in her ear.

Tess turns to stare at me, her eyes wide but her lips twitching.

"Anyway... I love you and hope that you have a better life than me." She starts crying, clutching Brance.

"Jesus Christ, Claire," I say.

"Reed, language," my mom responds, reaching for Claire. She hugs her, stroking her hair.

Brance steps back and takes a glass of champagne. Shaking his head, he raises his glass.

"To Tess. Happy Birthday, Pretty Girl! I wish you nothing but joy and happiness."

chapter 11

TESS

Everyone is cheering at Brance's toast. Well, everyone besides my drunk mother and the psycho chick. Again, resentment wiggles inside me like a worm inserting itself into the dirt. I hate that in some ways she is right. My dad isn't here, and the reminder of my father's stupid phone call gets me fired up. Quite frankly, my feet hurt and I'm sick of 90 percent of the people in this room.

Reed touches my chin, forcing our eyes to meet. "Let it go, Kitten. You know it's the alcohol." He knows me so well, and I smile, already feeling better. "Finish your cake. I want to give you your present and get everyone out of here."

Not even bothering to whisper, I say, "My mom makes me sick. She's a complete waste of oxygen."

"Yeah, she's on a roll."

I shake my head. Her speech about my dad hit a nerve. Nothing like airing our dirty laundry in front of the Russians. Does she always have to humiliate me?

My eyes shift over to Lexi, her weird smile making me uneasy. *I don't like her.* I've never felt such an instant repulsion for someone. She reminds me of a black widow, waiting quietly in the dark.

"Reed?" My hand clutches his forearm.

"Yes?"

"I'm ready for presents." Moving my eyes away and back in Lexi's direction, an odd anxiety engulfs me—that sense of unease that you can't explain, but you want it to go away.

"You okay?" Reed's turquoise eyes take me in.

"I'm ready to be alone with you."

He nods, turning to the drunken messes we call our parents.

"It's gift time." His strong voice makes everyone respond. He sits me down in a large, soft gray leather chair.

I check to see if my mom has stopped her drunk crying. She hasn't.

Jax hands me a large silver box, plopping it onto my lap.

"Mine first." He flashes me those identical Saddington dimples.

"I love it already!" I touch the white ribbon on it.

"Open it, Tess." With his large hands, he starts to help me unwrap it.

"You're the best, Jax." He's so excited, I can't help but giggle with him. "What did you get me?"

Opening the top, he rolls it out of the box and onto my lap. My eyes go wide. It's an incredibly large crystal ball, the size of a soccer ball. "Holy God, this is heavy."

Reed helps me hold it, so I can show everyone. Not that anyone but Brance and creepy girl are paying attention.

"It's heavy because it's a real crystal ball. It will protect and calm you, sis."

My eyes fill up with tears. "I can't believe how much I love this." I hand it to Reed, so I can hug Jax tightly. "Love you."

"Love you too," he whispers back.

As I sit back down, Brance disentangles his hands from my mom, who clutches at Caroline as he moves away. Gross. I mean, come the fuck on!

My eyes narrow as he places the pretty pink box in my lap. "What is wrong with you?"

He smiles and winks.

"Somehow I think I know what this is." Ripping open the paper, I hold up the firm beige box with the white Christian Louboutin Paris logo on top.

Brance and I were drooling over them the other day, but I walked away after I saw the price. "You're crazy—the dress and now these shoes?" I shake the black heels for effect. "What are you, the son of a billionaire or something?" I tease.

"Only for you, Pretty Girl." A wave of emotion bubbles up out of nowhere. I truly am lucky. I might have crappy parents, but I'm loved.

"Thank you," I whisper. He squeezes my shoulder.

Dimitri and Anna hand me an envelope, which I'm sure is full of cash. I choke out a thank-you and hear my mother mumbling to Caroline about their gift. Rolling my eyes, I glare at her and cringe. All the work Tilly and Brance did taping up her eye has vanished, and she looks like an emaciated stroke patient again. Only she's wearing a couture gown.

Caroline pats her shoulder, taking a slim box from my mom. "It's from your mother and me."

"Thank you, *Caroline*," I say, hoping my mother hears my jab. She's still sniffling loudly.

Untying the pink bow, I see an itinerary for Fashion Week in Paris in September.

"Wow." The fake smile is firmly plastered on my face. I so do not want to go. "Um, thank you, Caroline and Mom."

Caroline hugs me. "We'll take the private jet: you, me, Claire, and Brance! We are going to have so much fun!"

Clapping her hands with joy, her eyes suddenly fall on Lexi. "Oh my goodness, would you like to go, Lexi?" She grabs at my arm like she's a genius or getting ready to pass out. Either way, I want to scream.

"Tess?" I must not be breathing because Reed has to instruct me.

"She did not just do that!" I whisper as I take a breath. Reed's hands massage my bare shoulders. The room is silent, I guess because I can't form words. My manners have completely left me.

Reed clears his throat. "Mom, you can talk about all that later. It's my turn." His eyes darken.

He squats down to me and I have never been more grateful or turned on. His turquoise eyes and long black lashes make me warm in all sorts of places. His full lips spread into a grin as he hands me a small box. Excitement makes my hands shake as I unwrap it. Sucking in my breath, I take in the bright red box and sparkly gold letters. They tease me.

"Cartier. Nice, Reed," Brance murmurs.

"Reed!" I exhale.

"Open it." His eyes are gentle.

He reaches into the red velvet case and pulls out the white gold Diamond-Paved Love bracelet.

Unlatching it, I blink back the tears as I gaze at the sparkling, precious bangle in my hands. "Oh my God, Reed. It's... it's magnificent." My eyes lock with his, and for a moment, I don't know what else to say. "I love you," I say at last, throwing myself into his arms and crying.

He kisses me. "I love you too," he whispers into my ear.

"Tess!" My mom's screech makes me jump. "He did not give you that for your birthday. You have to put that in our safe." Leave it to Cartier diamonds to revive her.

"Claire." Reed turns to her. "I had this made the exact size for her tiny wrist. When I put it on, it stays."

He pushes it on. It's tight over my knuckles, but once it's on, it dangles perfectly.

Brance is dabbing at his eyes.

"Stop it—you're going to make me lose it." I slap at him.

"I want Reed," he whines dramatically then starts laughing at himself.

"You're crazy." I can't help my own laughter from slipping out.

I look over and give Lexi a fuck-you stare. The girl looks me right in the eyes and smirks. *Smirks! What the hell? I'm done.* I want Reed alone. I smile sweetly and clear my throat.

"Everyone, thank you all for the beautiful gifts and sharing my birthday with me. I love you all so much." I look at everyone except the Russians.

Caroline and my mom stumble into my arms. Reed helps steady me so that I can steady them.

"It's been a long day, so I'm going to—"

"Come on, Tess, don't kick us out," Jax says. I throw him my "I'm going to kill you" stare. He chuckles but shuts up.

"You look tired, Jax." Sarcasm drips from my voice.

"Whatever..." He rolls his eyes at Reed and me.

"Mom, Dad, I guess I'm heading home." He gives Dimitri a salute and winks at Lexi. I almost kick him.

"Wait up." Reed holds up a hand. "I'm just going to say good night to Tess and then I'll join you. I'm beat too." He kisses my nose. "Brance?" he calls over his shoulder. "Why don't you help Claire to her room."

I almost start laughing. We're so completely obvious. Thank God they're drunk.

chapter 12

REED

Dimitri and Anna eventually take the hint and say their goodbyes.
I give a quick nod to creepy Lexi, who is back to staring at her
feet. "Nice to meet you," is all I can think to say.

"Yes," she whispers. Not having time for her kind of crazy, I
move on, a man on a mission. After kissing my mom, I give my
dad a bro hug and stride into the kitchen, looking for Letty or
Maria.

I find Maria, putting the mountain of leftovers into the
refrigerator. Trying not to startle her, as she has earbuds in and
is humming away, I tap her shoulder. She whirls around, hand
on her chest.

"Mr. Reed! You scared me."

"Sorry, Maria. Listen, I'm going to see everyone out. Can
you do me a favor and not lock the side door?" I give her my
puppy eyes—they always get the job done. She hesitates then
smiles and pats my cheek.

"Thanks, Maria. I owe you one."

"Yeah, yeah, go be a good boy and let me finish. I'm tired."

"I will be on my best behavior."

I make a big show of saying good night to Tess. I'm not an
actor and if all the adults in the room were not drunk, it would
be painfully obvious that we are up to something.

Jax and I take the elevator down. My pulse is racing. In ten minutes or less, I am going to be with Tess. I can't decide what I want to do first—go down on her or finger her. I'll do both...

"Reed! Hello." Jax is waving his stupid hand in my face.

"Knock it off," I snarl, pushing it away.

"Dude, have you heard anything I said?" I must give him a blank look because he sighs dramatically.

"Do not take her virginity tonight! She's not ready."

"You're drunk, Jax." My eyes meet his and I speak tersely. "I have no intention of doing that."

"I'm serious, Reed. You should wait a little longer. It's my job as her future brother to take care of her," he says, pushing himself off the elevator wall as it opens to the parking garage.

"I'm a little insulted you think I would ever do anything to hurt Tess."

"Just don't, Reed." He points at me and weaves slightly as he moves forward.

"What the hell happened to him?" Jay yells, helping him into the car.

"The Russians." As if that explains it all. Stepping back into the elevator, I hear Jax plead with Jay to take him to one of his buddies' strip clubs while the doors are closing.

Leaning my head back, I'm way too excited. My dick is already hard as a rock. Entering through the side, I hear my mom and dad. They are still talking with Dimitri and Anna. Thankfully, Claire's obnoxious voice is absent. Brance must have been successful in putting her to bed. Avoiding that side of the apartment, I head straight to Tess's room, enter, and lock it.

Tess is sitting on a black-and-white-striped ottoman at the end of her bed, talking on her cell, still in her dress and heels.

"Brance, you just left here..." At my entrance, her face lights up with relief.

"Absolutely, I'll support you one hundred percent." Her sapphire eyes take in my appearance as she eyes me up and down. She mouths Brance, like I don't know who she's talking to.

Rolling my eyes, I drop to my knees. My hands start at her ankles and travel upward. Her breathing changes as she watches.

I grab the back of her knees and pull her forward. She squeals.

"Maybe, you should say good night to Brance now, Kitten." Glancing up, I take in the tiny little lights that she has strung up all over the wall.

She bites her lip, then bolts up. "Shit, Brance! Sorry." She almost drops the phone. "Look, Ree... I mean Brance, God... I have to go. I'll call you tomorrow."

Hanging up, she turns toward me. "Reed!" She pushes against my chest.

"What? I'm here now, and when I'm with you, it's only you and me." My hands explore her long legs. "I love how soft you are."

Leaning forward, I grab her right leg and lift it over my shoulder.

"I'm nervous," she whispers.

That stops me. Placing her leg down, I crawl over her so that I can look at her. "It's just us, Kitten." I reach for her neck and trace my thumb over her racing pulse. I love being Tess's everything. Yes, I know I sound like an ass, but it turns me on. "We're doing this together." My hand gently caresses her breasts. Long dark chocolatey hair spills over the end of the ottoman. My cock jumps with excitement. "Tess..." A small groan escapes me. All I can focus on is her. Her scent, her lips.

Dropping back to my knees, I slide my hands up her legs, not stopping until I reach my goal. "Fuck, your panties are wet." It comes out harsh, but I'm two seconds away from coming in my pants. I need to focus on my task. Willing my mind to stay calm, I pull her underwear down and over her heels. *Jesus.* I swallow and slowly pull her legs open. She hasn't spoken, and her big eyes remain focused on me as her body responds to my touch.

"You okay, Kitten? We don't have to do anything you don't—"

Before I get to finish, she snaps, "If you stop, I will kill you." Raising an eyebrow, I grin. "Just checking." I stop talking. My fingers have found her pussy and it's wet and slick. "Tess..." Laying my head on her stomach, I gently explore her with my fingers, fascinated by her wet folds, her scent, the way my fingers touch certain areas and she almost screams.

"Does it feel good?" My voice doesn't even sound like me.

"Unbelievably good..." Her eyes flutter shut.

That's it. My patience is wearing thin, and I pull my fingers away. She sits up, her brows drawn together.

"We need to get you out of this dress so that I can see this. Otherwise, I think I might rip it off you. And I don't want to deal with Brance bitching at me. Stand up."

I help her up as she wraps her hands on the wood of her canopy bed.

"Clips, Reed don't forget the clips," she croaks.

"What the hell? How do I... Tess, I swear to God." My hands are shaking. What clips are she talking about? Where's the zipper? Why isn't the dress off?

"Reed, there are little hooks on the top and bottom."

Looking closer, I finally see them, and she helps by straightening her back. Groaning, I'm harder, if that's possible, because the action pushes her breasts out. But it makes it easy for me to unhook the neck. The dress falls off her shoulders quickly, and I unhook the one at the waist too. *Thank Jesus.* Pulling it down, I slide it over her waist and it spills like silk, pooling in a giant pile of chiffon mess. I have lost all patience and make a mental note: Tess should never wear a contraption that requires this much work!

Lifting her in my arms, I carry her naked to her princess bed. With a frown, I look at the frills and stuffed animals and fluff. I used to get a kick out of it, and she always looked so pretty lying there. Now it's a weird reminder that we are still young but way too old to be in this pink, floral bed.

Setting her down, I step back. "Don't move," I whisper.

She doesn't even try to cover herself. Tess knows she's beautiful and completely owns it. All her insecurities are locked deep inside her. She has no problem letting my eyes feast on her. So I do, starting with her flushed face. Her lips are swollen red and her eyes look like midnight blue glittering pools.

My bracelet sparkles on her wrist. But what makes me want to unzip my pants and stroke myself is my name tattooed on her side.

The need to claim her overwhelms me, and I'm almost confused at how my body seems to have a life of its own.

"Tess." It comes out way harsher than I intended.

"Yes?" Her eyes search my face.

"I'm going to touch you, but you have to be quiet, Kitten. We can't afford to get caught."

"I'll try." She doesn't sound very confident, which makes me smile. Her eyes are half-mast—she wants this as badly as I do.

As I lie down next to her, she instantly pulls off my jacket, tossing it to the floor, followed by my shirt. She is much better at undressing me than I was of her. I'll have to work on that. When her hands reach for my belt, I grab them and pull them above her head. "Probably better if we leave the pants on," I hiss.

"But..." I stop her with my mouth, kissing her deeply, roughly, our tongues touching and tasting. A loud moan escapes her.

With reluctance, I pull back. "Tess you have to do better. No noise. The last thing I want to deal with is your mom going crazy."

"Sorry," she whispers, an evil grin on her face.

Reaching for her lips again, this time I hear a slight whimper when our tongues touch. She tastes like chocolate and Tess. Not staying on her puffy lips, I need her throat. I'm obsessed with it. I want so badly to bite it and suck it, but that would mark her. She's wiggling, trying to get me to let go of her hands.

"Stop, Kitten. I'll let go in a minute. I like you like this." She cocks her head, but she's still. Her chest expands as she breathes.

I'm like a starved beast, and her body is my feast. Lowering my head to take one of her hard, pink nipples into my mouth, I lick it and hear myself groan. A small victory smile touches her lips, and I laugh.

"We're so fucked. Thankfully your mom is smashed."

She nods. "I don't think she would care anyway." She moans it out. As I bite her nipple, a hiss comes out of her lips. Remorse fills me. What the hell is wrong with me?

"Kitten, I'm sorry..." She's panting and grinding herself on me, shoving her breast farther into my mouth.

"Don't be sorry—just do it again."

For a moment I freeze, not sure I heard her correctly. Then I smirk at her. "I should have known: whatever I like, you like."

"You should." Her chest goes up and down, mirroring her excitement. "I love you, and I trust you. Please, make me come, Reed." She sounds frantic.

Taking the other nipple in my mouth. I start to suck it, letting go of her wrists, so that I can use that hand to rub and pinch the first nipple. Her hands seem to be fluttering around trying to find something to grab hold of. I grind on her, and she groans, encouraging me. My hand grabs the post of her canopy so that I can rub her pussy hard. It feels unbelievable. Thank God my pants are soft. Before I even realize it, I'm pulsing and shaking. I fucking come in my thousand-dollar Tom Ford pants.

I sit up shocked. Tess sits up, her eyes filled with wonder. "Reed?"

"I can't believe... that just happened."

She reaches for my cock and starts to rub, feeling all the wetness. "Oh, Reed, um... it's okay..."

Cutting her off, the last thing I need is for Tess to try to make me feel better. "I need to get out of these, take a shower, and then we will continue."

"But... I want you to keep doing what you were doing now!" She pouts.

I'm already stripping out of my slacks and boxers, shaking my head. Turning on the water in her shower, I step into the freezing water. I'm beyond caring as the cold water pierces my skin like little knives. In a way, it feels good. I need a moment to process the fact that I came in my pants. I have lost complete control and hate that. I reach for the soap and take a fast rinse-off. Wrapping a towel around my waist, I go back to Tess. She's removed her heels and is under the covers.

We look at each other.

"I love you so much. Promise me it will always be us—only us."

I nod as my hand instinctively rubs my tattoo. "I promise." Dropping the towel, I'm starting to get hard again. Tess breathes roughly, and her eyes are huge and staring at my cock. Leaning over, she grabs for one of those frilly pillows to shield herself, I guess from my penis.

"Reed, that"—she points at my penis—"looks huge. He's big, right?" she whispers the last part as she licks her lips.

Yep, I was right. She's scared of my dick. I should be modest. *But, fuck that.* I have been blessed with a big, thick cock. And since this is the only one she's ever going to see, I answer truthfully. "Yeah, it's impressive, huh?" Slowly stroking it, I feel it harden and bob past my belly button.

She watches me almost like she is taking notes, then raises her head. "I want to suck it."

"No way, I'm sucking on you tonight. Lie back," I demand. My need to do everything is starting to fuck with me. I'm like a boy in a candy shop. All I want to do is taste her, eat her, suck her, the way I've seen it done on the videos. Taking a calming breath, I pull the sheet away from her. I don't even try to kiss her. I'm on a mission, and since I'm rock hard again, I need to get started. Inching down, I grab her hips. Her legs open for me and I blink. She's pink and glistening and so perfect. I don't move and simply stare at her pretty wet pussy.

"Reed!" She snaps in a whisper. "What are you doing?" She goes to close her legs.

"Don't even think about closing those legs. Kitten, I'm never going to be the same again." Lowering my head, I lick the nub that is throbbing and glistening. She lies back and sobs out my name, her head, turning into her frilly pillow. And then I feast— literally feast on her. Starting with her clit and moving all over— it's sloppy and wet and I'm covered in her juices. She clutches the sheets tightly, her head thrashing from side to side. I stop tonguing her so that I can explore her. As I open her pink folds, my mouth waters at the thought of tasting her again. But I want to watch her as I finger her. Slowly I rub my thumb over her wet clit.

She moans loudly. "Shh, Tess, put a pillow over your head or something." She grabs the lacy thing and covers her face.

"No, take it off. I need to see your face." I throw it across the room. Slowly I take my middle finger and sink into her soft wonderfulness, pumping in and out. Her body is so beautiful as she grabs for my wrist. I lower my head again and suck on her clit hard.

"Holy shit... Reed, I think I'm going to... Yes!" She pulses and clenches on my tongue. Her hands rip at my hair as she convulses. And I'm fucking king of the world. I just gave Tess her first orgasm and experienced the hottest thing imaginable.

Jesus, there is nothing better. Climbing up, I gaze into her perfect face.

"I love you so much. You and me, we're going to experience everything together." Kissing her nose, her eyes, her wet cheeks, I am undone. I can't put into words the depth of what I feel for her. Obsession! She cries softly as she reaches for my face. Her fingertips trace my bottom lip.

"We will always be together, right? I can't live without you."

I stare at her, my finger rubbing her side where my name permanently marks her. Reaching for the hand that has my bracelet on it, I bring it to my tattoo, on my heart.

"Always." Moving my hand and placing it on her heart, which is still pumping fast, I whisper, "This never lies—at least not with us."

She sighs as she turns to spoon. I pull her snug in my embrace, knowing I won't go to sleep because I still have a raging hard-on. I should probably take another shower and take care of it. But the thought of letting Tess go is not an option. Closing my eyes, I wait to hear her even breathing.

chapter 13

TESS

"Tess? Sweetheart?" My door handle rattles.

"Tess?" Someone is tapping on it now.

I bolt up.

"Reed?" I shake him. "Shit, Reed wake up." He groans and tries to pull me back to him. I squirm out of his clutches.

"Tess Rose Gallagher open this door immediately!" My dad's voice booms into my room making the walls shake.

Holy shit! My heart pounds. "Daddy? Is that you?" Kicking at Reed, whose eyes have blinked open, my pulse races.

"Of course it's me. I decided the case can wait a few days, and I can work from home. I'm sorry I missed your party." My door handle jiggles again. "I'm home now. At least, I think this is my apartment." He sighs, annoyed.

I look over at Reed who is now fully awake and pulling on his slacks. He shouldn't be wearing them. The discharge spot has dried, but it's stiff and obvious.

"Um, Daddy can you give me a moment? I'm just waking up..."

Tripping over Reed's jacket, I catch myself on my dresser. It rattles, with all my perfumes.

"Tess? What's going on? Are you all right?"

Pulling my drawer open, I grab the top shirt. It's pink and tight. I need a bra, but I'm too frazzled to deal with that.

"Will you relax? It's going to be okay." Reed has his hands up trying to calm me. All it's doing is reminding me that he is in my room and it's morning.

"He called me yesterday and said he wasn't coming," I whisper, slightly hysterical at the glaring reality that my dad is home.

Reed looks around my room and at me, running his hands through his dark curls.

"Tess, what has happened to my apartment?"

I jump up and down, shaking my hands like a crazy person until Reed stops me. "Pull it together, Kitten," he whispers in my ear.

Taking a deep breath, I respond, "Um... Well, Mom... and a friend of mine have been redecorating. Where is Mom?" Trying my best to distract him, I'm still hoping for a miracle.

I get down on my knees to pull Reed's shirt out from under my bed. "Here." I almost throw it at him.

Thankfully, he is holding it together better than I am. He shakes his head at me and slips his arm into a sleeve. I'm completely losing it. Obviously, stressful situations are not my strong suit.

"Your degenerate mother is passed out. What the fuck has she done to herself? She looks like a truck smashed into her face. Open this door. I need to speak with you."

Shit, shit, shit. I spin around freaking out. Again, I search my large room. The morning sunlight is slowly poking through the clouds, its light seeping in through my one big window. And for the first time, I hate that my room has such an open floor plan. There is nowhere for someone as big as Reed to hide. And with his feet firmly planted on my plush carpet, something tells me he is not in the mood to hide in my walk-in closet or bathroom.

"Oh my God, Reed! He is going to freak!" I mumble, shaking my hands again as if they are asleep.

My dad is known to be a major fit thrower if he doesn't get his way. Also, he has certain ideas that he thinks are right. One is me. He expects perfect grades, so I don't end up miserable like him. In other words, he does not want me getting pregnant and trapping Reed like my mom did to him.

Reed grabs my hands, stilling them. "Just step aside, Tess." He sounds aggravated, then tosses me my black yoga pants that were draped on the edge of my chair. I look at his crumpled white dress shirt from last night, and yes, thankfully it's covering his stain. My eyes go wide, grabbing his bicep. "Are you crazy?" I hiss. "Try to get under my bed."

He rolls his eyes. "Fuck this, Tess. I'm not hiding under your princess bed."

"Tess? Open this door *now*. Is Reed in there with you?" My dad pounds; the pictures on my wall move with the force.

"Screw this!"

I watch in slow-motion horror as Reed unlocks my door. Before I can even grasp what is happening, I'm looking at my father's face. He looks good for a guy who has been traveling nine hours.

My dad is a handsome man. I look a lot like the girl version of him. Right now, he looks like he is going to attack Reed.

"Daddy, this isn't what you think." I hold up my hands.

His fists clench and unclench as he throws the door open and stalks into my room, straight for my wrinkled pink sheets.

My mind spins with excuses, but nothing comes out of my mouth. Reaching for the sheet he rips it back, tossing the pillows across the room, inspecting the bed. My face must be bright red because I feel like I'm on fire. He turns to me, his eyes wild, looking at my appearance.

"Pack a bag, we're leaving," he spits out.

I grab for Reed. "What?" His arm tightens on me.

"Pack. Your. Bag." His voice is like ice.

I'm clutching Reed's hand as if it can somehow merge me with him.

"Daddy, please..." I almost sink to my knees. Instead I face him head-on.

He's furious and his cheek is twitching as he looks around my room.

"Mom?" I scream. Suddenly she seems like the best person in the world. I let go of Reed and run down the hall to her room.

Bursting open her door, I almost take a step back. It's like a tomb. As my eyes try to adjust to the darkness, I cringe at her appearance. Dad's right. She looks like shit! Worse than yesterday if that is possible. It doesn't help that her makeup is still smeared on her face and pillow. Her Botox eye is still sporting the look of someone who's had a stroke.

"Mom?" I jump on the mattress, shaking her. "Wake up! Dad's home." She sits up and grabs her head.

"Tess, please," she snaps, lying back down. Suddenly we both jump.

"Don't bother getting up, Claire. I'm not staying." My dad walks into his large walk-in closet and pulls out a fresh suit.

"Robert?" My mom holds up her hands, kind of reminding me of a vampire trying to keep the morning light from burning her up.

"Christ." His eyes move around his bedroom. Besides the walls being painted a deep rose color, she also got rid of the dark wooden bedroom furniture, replacing it with white.

"You're a fucking disgrace!" He snarls down at her. "If I had any sense, I would divorce your drunk ass. Look at you." He nearly spits in her face. Grabbing my arm, he shakes me slightly. "I just caught our fifteen-year-old daughter locked in her room with Reed! Who the fuck lets her daughter fuck her boyfriend in the room next to hers?" He waits as if my mom is smart enough to spar with him. She only stares at him with her one eye, looking dazed.

"I'm taking Tess with me. You can sit here and drown in vodka for all I care. I'm done." With that he releases me and steps away, walking into the bathroom.

Scrambling over to her, I grab her cold hand. "Mom? This can't happen! You need to get yourself together and tell him no, okay?"

This is it. My moment of truth with her. Her time to be a real mother. "Please." My voice is raspy as I beg. "I need you! Don't let him take me." I'm borderline possessed, and I guess crying because everything is blurry.

Backing off the bed, I scream, "You're going to let him take me, aren't you?" I shake my head at the pain and betrayal. She stares at me then at the closed bathroom door.

"If you let him do this, I will never forgive you."

"Tess." I turn to Reed's voice. He stands in the doorway looking at my disgusting mother.

"Come here. No one is taking you away." Running to him I leap into his arms, crawling on him like a monkey. He wraps strong arms around my legs and I bury my face in his neck as he carries me back to my room and sits on my bed.

"She's not going to stand up to him." I clutch at his neck. "This is bad, Reed." My throat is getting tight, that feeling like something is stuck in it, making me panic. My eyes dart around my childhood room. It's my sanctuary. I love it. I can't leave it.

"Reed... I can't breathe."

"Come on, baby. Breathe with me slowly... in and out." Taking my hand, he puts it on his heart. "Take it, Tess. It's yours. Take it and keep it." Air fills my lungs and brain; my throat opens up.

"That's it... like that. It's almost over. Breathe with me."

I'm sweating, but at least I can breathe. Sagging into his chest, I lean back as he holds me tight.

"Better?" His turquoise eyes, search my face. "We have to stay calm, Tess. It's going to be all right."

My father walks into my room smelling fresh from his shower and cologne. His blue eyes narrow on us.

"Tess, if you have anything that you can't live without, I suggest you pack it. We will be leaving within the hour." His eyes sweep my room. "Actually, just take some clothes. Svetlana, can help you pick out your room."

I spot my mom in her robe, crying. "Do something," I plead, my eyes boring into her. She looks horrible. Her good eye is so puffy from crying, you almost wouldn't notice the other.

"Robert... Please don't leave me. We can work this out." Her skinny arms reach for him.

"Don't touch me, Claire. The mood I'm in... for your own safety stay the fuck away."

"You have been gone so long. I thought it would be fun redecorating. If you hate it, we can change it back."

It's as though I've been stabbed. She's talking about redecorating?

He swings around to her. "You have absolutely no motherly instincts, do you? Your daughter is sleeping with Reed!" If he wasn't taking me away from Reed, I would be cheering him on. At least he's interested in me.

"Jesus Christ, Claire. She needs guidance, discipline, something you know nothing about. It's not in you. You're worthless and you look like a monster." My mom flinches as though he hit her.

Stalking toward her, he points at her. "*I will not* have a teenage daughter pregnant. I did not go through sixteen years of my life with your repulsive ass to watch her become a whore," he roars.

Reed steps forward. "Watch it, Robert."

"You sorry-ass punk, that's Mr. Gallagher to you."

"Tess and I are not having sex." My dad's face reddens even more. I can practically see the steam coming out of his ears.

"You have nothing to be worried about. I understand that you are upset." Reed's calm voice sounds menacing against all our screaming.

My dad cuts him off. "You have no idea what I'm going through Reed! You are not a father. Maybe one day, when you have your own daughter, you will understand. But it won't be with *my* daughter! I'm taking her away from you."

My mom picks that time to interrupt. "Robert, please... I'm begging you, do not divorce me. Think of the scandal. I will tell everything. I will tell everyone about your *new* whore." She sobs.

My attention slams to her and I almost slap her. "Mom, you are unbelievable! Dad is threatening to take me away, and all you are concerned about is that he's divorcing you. You are so *selfish*." Now I'm screaming. Tears run down my cheeks. I don't bother to wipe them away.

My dad shakes his head, repulsion all over his handsome face. "Take a good look, Tess." He motions at her. "This is your mother. Do yourself a favor and don't have kids. You don't have good genes." And that truth will stay with me forever.

"Everyone stop!" Reed yells, turning on my dad. "Robert, Tess is not leaving. She has school. If you care about her, you will walk away." I'm clutching his hand, my legs shaking, my room vibrating with angry energy.

Slowly my dad faces us. "I don't give a shit what you think. She has exactly ten minutes to grab her things because we are leaving."

"No!" I scream. "Daddy, please... I can't leave Reed! Please, I promise he will not stay over ever again. Just *don't do this to me*." I'm hysterical. It's my last stand.

"Get her ready, Reed. Ten minutes. Make sure she has her antianxiety pills. This is happening, and there is nothing you can do to stop it, so man the fuck up."

Moving toward my door, he stops. "You will thank me someday, *trust me.* You're not going to want to be with the same woman forever. I take Tess out of the picture, and you're free. Be young, have fun, screw around. Only never forget, you're not good enough for my little girl, you spoiled, entitled shit."

"This can't be happening," I whisper.

"Ten minutes. Get her together, Reed." This time he does leave my room, with my shitty mother following him, begging for a second chance.

The silence in my room is overwhelming. I sink into Reed's arms. He sits on my bed and plants me on his lap.

"Tess." He pets my hair. "It's going to be all right. Go with him. I'll make my dad call him. You'll be back in a week." He kisses my wet cheeks. "We can do a week. You have to stop crying, babe. You're going to make yourself sick."

I try, I really do, but I can't. The tears won't stop. "I... I can't, Reed. I'm scared." I hiccup.

"You will be fine." He gets up and goes into the closet and grabs my luggage. "Pack, Kitten. I need to call my dad." I watch numbly as he goes into my bathroom and gets my Valium. "Here." He hands me two.

I don't even drink water and instead chew them like a robot. I throw random things into my bag. Reed goes back into the bathroom and packs up my makeup and perfumes. He's on his phone, I guess with Brad.

My dad appears in the doorway. "Let's go, Tess. Say goodbye to Reed." He grabs my luggage. I take one last look at my cheery yellow room. My twinkling lights are still on from last night. This can't be happening. I have to be in a nightmare, right? My sadness almost cripples me.

My mother is nowhere to be found. Reed practically drags me to the waiting car, the driver standing like a statue with the door open. I almost want to plead for his help.

Reed turns me to him, his big hands holding my face, his eyes locking with mine.

"This is only a vacation, Kitten. You will be home sooner than you know." Then he kisses me, but it's short and I grab his shirt. His tongue fills my mouth, and I can't stop crying. I kiss him like my life depends on it, and at the moment, it does. As I sob into his mouth, this feels like goodbye—like forever. He pulls back as my father grabs my arm. I look at Reed one more time; his beautiful eyes have tears.

"What the hell, Robert? Just wait... can we talk about this? *Please*, I need her."

My dad stops and puts a hand through his hair. Sighing he looks around the garage. At anything but me and Reed.

"You will be fine. Talk to me in ten years, Reed. Something tells me you'll be with someone else living a completely different life. This is infatuation, kids, and it does not last."

He pulls me into the car, and I sink into the soft black leather seats. All the fight that I thought I would have is gone. I get on my knees and look out the back window. My heart hurts so bad, the burn is almost unbearable. Reed must feel the same way, for his hand comes up and rubs his chest, right on his heart and on my name.

I can't do anything but stare. My father slams the door shut himself not even waiting for the driver, and I close my eyes, hot tears flowing, burning my face.

"Tess, stop crying." He's rubbing his forehead. "You're my little girl. What did you expect me to do? Hand you over to Reed at fifteen? Your mother is not capable of taking care of you. I guess I'll give it a try."

"How long?" I hiss. Not even trying to disguise my dislike of him, I gaze out the window as my neighborhood and Reed get farther away.

"What?" He sounds distracted.

"How long do you plan on keeping me?"

"You will stay with me until college."

"What?" I scream "*No fucking way, Dad!* If you think to keep me prisoner, you are crazy." I must look wild because he frowns.

"Are you insane? Do you need help in the head? Because, if you think that any normal parent would allow their only daughter to have sex in her *own* bedroom and not do something about it, you need help. Should I have a doctor check you?" He waits. I'm so aghast at his lack of compassion and the question I stare mutely.

"I will tell you right now, little girl, if you're pregnant, you will have an abortion!"

I gasp. He looks like a rabid dog. And he's asking if I'm insane? All the air in the vehicle seems to be sucked into the black leather seats. My throat is closing up on me again. And, I don't have Reed. Without his voice telling me to breathe, without him touching me, how will I control it?

"I'm not having sex, Dad! Although, I wish I had." I try to swallow a gasp of air.

He must believe me, or he is done engaging with me because he pulls out his cell phone and starts texting.

I concentrate on the sounds of my breathing. Otherwise, it's too quiet. The car is so insulated, the noises from outside are gone.

Not even looking up from his texting, he says, "I don't intend on explaining myself to you, but you should know I have a girlfriend. Her name is Svetlana Volkov, and I expect you to treat her with respect."

"I'm sorry, did you just tell me you are living with another woman?"

"Yes, Tess, I am." He glances up for a second, looking like he wants to say more, but he doesn't.

"Why would you bring me with you? You have a whole other life going on." The first glimmer of hope fills me. Surely my dad is not going to want me to stay long if he has a girlfriend.

He shrugs. "Svetlana is perfect, Tess. You could learn from her. All this weakness is your mother. Svetlana will teach you how to fight. Trust me, you're going to need it."

"Why, Daddy?" I whisper, wiping my cheeks.

"You're my child. I know you're angry with me right now, but it's my job to protect you. I had hoped your mother would rise to the occasion, but she's let the booze and her own insecurities take over. You don't need to be around that. Stop crying. It's done." He holds the phone to his ear, dismissing me.

The Valium must be working. Either that or I'm numb, maybe both. The car pulls up to the tarmac. I vaguely feel my dad's arm guide me into his private jet. I walk into the bedroom, shut the door, and sleep the entire flight.

TESS
Present day – twenty-five years old

I stand and wait for the three beeps alerting me my coffee has finished brewing. My pink manicured nails drum the granite counter, the need to feed my one addiction wiping away all my earlier patience.

Fuck it. When I grab the pot, steam blows out the top of the coffee maker. Quickly I fill my mug. *I'm a rule breaker, right?*

Taking a deep sip, I grimace as the hot liquid singes my tongue. The burn is over too quickly. I'm left with the same despair I've been plagued with for hours.

I'm sluggish and my eyes hurt as though I have a fever or someone has thrown sand in them. Hopefully I have eye drops. My overtaxed mind wanders to the contents of my medicine cabinet.

"God, you're pathetic," I mumble, blinking back the tears. A soft wet nose nudges my hand. I look down and start crying. Kind, trusting brown eyes stare up at me, a white tail curled over his back wagging away. The coffee maker hisses. I smell burned coffee coming from the bottom of the carafe, the symbolism not lost on me.

Burned. Dark. Guilty. Remorseful!

Sliding down my cabinet, I sit on the floor. A fluffy white bundle of goodness jumps into my lap.

"I'm okay, buddy. I'm going to be gone for a while. Will you be okay with Uncle Logan?" He cocks his face, and I swear he smiles at me. Like a sleepwalker, I sit on my hardwood floor petting his soft, fluffy fur, confessing all my sins. He doesn't judge me. In fact, he loves me, which makes me cry harder. I rehearse to my Samoyed why I did what I did. His head lies on my thigh and he listens, making me feel ten times better.

"If only I could bring you on the jet. You'd distract everyone, wouldn't you?"

The doorbell rings. Knowing it's Brance, I don't even bother getting up. He has a key. Pushing my dark tangled hair behind my ears, I stay seated. Pudding happily leaves me to greet Brance.

"Tess? Baby Girl? Buddy?" Brance calls.

I groan as I stand up. Turning the corner, I run smack into Brance's lean shoulder as he and Pudding come barreling in. He reaches for me, his beautiful dark eyes full of concern.

"Jesus, are you all right?"

"Of course," I snap, pulling out of his grip. *I refuse to be a victim. What a lie—I'm nothing but a victim.*

He sighs heavily, pulling me into a tight hug. "It's going to be okay," he whispers soothingly. "You knew this day was coming."

My tears fall again. I'm so sick of the tears. As I nod my head against his lean chest, I say, "I know, I mean I thought I knew, but now that it's happening, I'm not ready."

Pulling away, I look at him. "I don't think I can do it." With the lump in my throat, I'm barely able to choke it out.

"I know, Pretty Girl." His strong hands stroke my tangled hair. Three loud beeps fill the quietness in the room. Brance's eyes shift toward the kitchen.

"Coffee's ready." He smiles. I laugh and sob at the same time.

He throws his arm around my shoulder. "How much time do we have?"

"Jax said they are sending the G5 Jet." I stare at Pudding who has made himself at home, sitting in one of my chairs looking out the window.

Brance pulls out his phone. "I called Ken Paves Salon and talked to Stacey. She said she can fit you in at noon."

I snort, reaching for the pot and pour myself a fresh cup.

"I'm getting on that jet because I have no choice!" I blink rapidly as I look up at my ceiling then back at his worried face. "Why are we even trying to be optimistic? This is so bad, beyond bad," I yell, jerking open my kitchen cabinet. "It doesn't matter what my face and hair look like, Brance."

Grabbing a mug for him, I slam the cabinet shut, the sound ricocheting around the room. Pudding jumps off the chair and runs over to me.

"Shit." I brace my hands on the counter.

"Why don't you sit down."

"You need coffee," I say, jerking the pot out. My hands are shaking so badly, I spill brown liquid all over the counter. "Goddamn it!" This time Pudding runs away.

"Tess, just *sit*! God, you're even scaring Pudding." He guides me to the kitchen nook, and I sink into the chair Pudding has just left. It's still warm.

Brance shakes his head as he calmly pours himself some coffee.

Turning away in disgust, I open one of the bay windows. A cool breeze blows on my fevered cheeks. I might be losing it, but as much as I want to, I can't. I have reasons to get myself together. Vaguely, I hear the hum of a gardener's lawn mower and some birds. Birds are good, right?

Brance snaps his fingers in front of my face. "Tess, get your shit together. We don't have time for the dramatics! We have to get organized."

My eyes shoot over to his. "You don't have to be a jerk."

Leaning his hip on the counter, he sips his coffee. "Have you called Scott and explained what's going on?"

Stiffening at Scott's name, I wipe some crumbs off the table. "Why would I do that? This is none of his business," I say, daring him to make it a big deal.

"Tess, you are seeing this man. You need to at least let him know you're going out of town." His disapproval aggravates me. He's only been like this since he married Logan. The old Brance wouldn't have even mentioned Scott.

"We don't have that sort of relationship, and you know it," I snap.

Brance stares at me, then pushes off the counter to sit.

"If I call him, he will want to help, and that is not an option. It's better this way. Scott is way too good for me."

"You think so, huh?"

I stare at him. "Don't act like you don't." Rubbing my fingers on my temples, I contemplate what I'm going to do. He's right. Scott deserves the common courtesy of a phone call. At least let him know we will be out of town.

"God!" I say, briefly dropping my head in my hands. "When have I ever done the right thing? Add it to the list of shitty things I can feel guilty about."

"You're becoming quite the little martyr, aren't you?" I glance up but don't acknowledge the comment. Rolling his eyes, he adds, "Whatever, Tess. Do you want Logan to stay here with Pudding?"

"No, bring him to your house since I don't know how long we'll be gone."

Standing up, he dumps his coffee in the sink. "I'm coming with you. I would never allow you to face this alone." He shrugs. "Besides, I'm not exactly innocent in this fiasco."

Hope surges inside me. "You're coming with me?" I'm so pathetic, but I truly need Brance. "Logan won't want you to go," I remind him.

"He already knows. He hates it, but he has accepted it."

Guilt rears its ugly head. I carry enough, and I don't need to add this. Shaking my head, I say, "No, you should be here with your husband. I'm a big girl. He can't hurt me anymore."

He arches a dark brow. "Tess, we don't know how he is going to react. All we can do is make sure that you look as good as you possibly can." He says this completely deadpan. I blink at him and burst out laughing. Slapping his arm, I laugh. "You're ridiculous. You know that, right?"

His mouth twitches. "I'm being serious. He's always had a weak spot when it comes to your looks."

"I think I'm going to need more than that this time."

"Agreed, but we have to work with what we have. So... even though your lips look spectacular when you're hysterical, your eyes look like shit!"

My mind flashes back to Reed, his smile making my heart ache, calling me beautiful, exquisite, so many compliments, always making me feel like a goddess that he worshiped.

A vibrating cell phone makes both of us look down. Logan's picture stares up at us. Getting up, I go to my refrigerator, pulling out some cut pineapple. "You better answer. He's only going to keep calling." I motion to his phone on the table.

Sighing dramatically, he sits down and answers. "Yes, Logan?"

I can hear Brance's husband going off, and that's saying something because Logan does not yell. He is like a Zen god.

Brance holds the phone away from his ear, and Logan keeps lecturing a good minute before there's silence. Brance pushes the speaker button.

"Feel better?"

"Not really"

"I have you on speaker. I'm at Tess's."

"Of course you are." A tortured sigh comes through the phone. "Hello, Tess." His voice is laced with anxiety.

"Hi, Logan. I'm so sorry to drag you into my mess again."

Guilt!

"Well, Tess, I would love to blame you." He snips, "Let's be honest, Brance is making this decision even though I have told him repeatedly it's not healthy for either one of you. He can't continue to fight all your battles."

I flinch at the harsh truth, and Brance instantly grabs the phone, taking it off speaker. "Logan, I love you, and I know you truly do mean the best, but you need to be careful. This trip is something that has to happen, and you know it." His beautiful chocolate eyes watch me as he listens.

"Without a doubt, it's going to be nothing but a bundle of negative energy. Unlike you, Tess and I are used to that—we thrive on it. I won't allow you to make me feel guilty, Logan."

A leaf blower roars to life outside. I turn, glancing out my window. My neighbor's gardener is blowing dust and leaves into my yard. If I wasn't in such a state, I would go outside and say something, but at this point in my life, dirt and leaves are not a priority.

"Yes, Logan, I'll remind her you told us so. Does that make you feel good? Because it just pisses me off!" Taking my hand, he absently looks at my nails.

"I get that, Logan, but I'm not leaving her to the wolves. Look... I'm trying to have patience." Brance frowns, leaning forward.

"Un-fucking believable!" Turning to me, he says, "You see this asshole blowing shit on your yard?" He points out the window.

I roll my eyes. "It's the last thing we should be worrying about."

"Logan, I need to go, her next-door neighbors..."

Shaking my head, I say, "Brance, it doesn't matter. I'm going to go take a shower. Tell Logan... I guess, thank you is appropriate." Hot tears threaten to spill again. I have come to love Logan. He is one of the kindest, most practical people I have ever met. I think that is what pushed Brance to make the ultimate commitment to marry him.

Logan is truly our opposite. Brance needed his innocence. He grabbed it and has become a much different person.

But ultimately, deep down inside, we are what we are. Logan won't allow himself to accept us. He can't, even when he reluctantly witnessed the decision we made. That one secret that changed all of our lives. The decision that is going to bring my past crashing down around me, like placing the last domino piece and watching everything you have built fall. I don't blame Logan, but I do envy him. His endless chakra cleansing is just that: endless. Brance is still Brance and I'm, well, me. Leaning down, I kiss his forehead as he argues with his husband. Because no matter what, Brance does have a point. I need all my ammunition if I'm going to try to convince *him* that I'm not the vilest person in the world.

REED

Past – sixteen years old

"Dude, did you see that new girl in first period?" Andrew, my latest partner in crime asks.

"The redhead?" Jax responds, in between sets. Jay is torturing us today with his workout.

"Boys, boys, if all you pansies are going to do is chit chat about your schoolgirl crushes, why am I wasting my time?" He taunts us as usual. I want to tell him to go fuck himself, but since he's taking his personal time to train us, and we all have doubled in size the last couple of years, I hold back.

He grabs some barbells and starts doing curls himself.

"No, Jay dog, this girl is beyond hot. Am I right, Reed? Come on. If the almighty Reed Saddington thinks she's hot, you know she is."

Jay stops lifting and looks at me. "Well?"

"She's hot. I'd do her. Do you have her number? We should invite her to Blake's tonight," Jax answers for me as he wipes his face with a towel.

Jay looks at me in the mirror. "I'm still waiting for Reed's thoughts." He eyes me, challenging.

I shake my head. I have been into boxing lately. I had my dad take a portion of our gym and put in a small ring. I look him in the eyes. No way am I backing down.

"I don't particularly find redheads hot, but you would, Jay." Because it's true. I have seen the women Jay likes. He definitely has a type. Unfortunately, it seems to be my type too. I was not about to admit that Gia, the new girl, was too sexy for her own good. That would give Jay an excuse to give me shit about my commitment to Tess.

Just the thought of her hurts me. I start shadowboxing again. I'm so sick of feeling like this. The pain that I have been through this year and a half has been the worst thing I have yet endured. I duck out of the ring and pound the punching bag. Jay walks over and holds it as I take out all my angst. Finally, when my arms feel like Jell-O and my lungs are on fire, I look up. Andrew, Jax, and Jay are all staring at me.

"What?" I growl.

Andrew holds up his hands. "Nothing man." Then he looks at Jax. "I posted Blake's address on Facebook, so I'm gonna roll."

"Later, Drew." Jax snickers.

I nod at him. He grabs his workout bag, stopping beside me. "You know, Reed, maybe you should think about showing some interest in something besides your body or drinking away your sorrows." He slings the bag over his shoulder. "The rumor is she wants you, man." He points at me as he pushes the button for our elevator to take him to the ground floor.

Jay is picking up his stuff. "So, you guys need a ride tonight or cabbing it?"

"You want the night off?" Jax asks.

"No, I'll take the extra hours if you need me to drive."

"Cool, then let's leave around seven."

He nods and steps into the elevator.

I'm still punching the bag—I want relief even if it's short-lived. It's been over a year since she left me. I know she didn't have a choice, but that's not exactly true. Claire, albeit not mother of the year, is still her mother. She has rights to Tess as much as Robert does. He hasn't even allowed her to visit, let alone for me to visit her. I have been supportive, and I know she needs his approval, but I never dreamed she would pick him over me. Wiping the sweat off my forehead, I continue to pound the bag. My breathing is loud, and my arms and chest are burning. I take a breath. It's almost over. She has promised she'll be back as soon as school is out. Unfortunately, the longer she stays away, the more the poison inside me grows. I give the bag one last punch and fall to the ground. Jax walks over and slumps down next to me.

"How's our girl doing?"

I snort a bitter laugh. "How the hell do I know?" I know I sound like an ass, but that's pretty much how I feel since she's been gone. Lonely, lost, joyless—the list of adjectives goes on.

"Well, you two talk all the time via text, Facebook, or Skype." He gets in my face. "I get you miss her. I miss her too, but you have been a miserable shit for over a year now! If you can't wait this out, then maybe you need to cut Tess loose. Because you can't be making her happy, and you're sure as shit miserable here."

I want to punch him, but my arms are like rubber and I think he would punch me back and probably win. "Stay out of it, Jax. I will never get over it. She's destroying me, don't you get it? I only want her, but she's in London. So, what do I do?" I yell.

"I guess, you either love her and wait, or you break up and get laid. Either way, commit. Living like this is not living, brother." He gets up, leaving me in a pile of self-pity and sweat. I don't know how long I sit in our gym alone. At last, it dawns on me: Jax is right. I have been partying way too much. I gave up on school. Thankfully it comes easy to me. Although I'm pretty sure if my dad wasn't who he was, my teachers would not be giving me the grades I'm getting. I can't remember the last time I laughed or had an actual good time. I keep making excuses for her, but the truth is that I'm fucking livid with Tess. I guess it's time I tell her. Standing up, I go to my room and grab my laptop. I Skype her number. It rings and rings. I'm ready to hang up and try again when I hear that fucking raspy voice that haunts me, and I groan.

She must be asleep because it's dark. "Turn on a light," I snap. "I want to see you."

"Reed? What time is it?" Suddenly I see her beautiful face. At first, it's just her dark hair as she moves into the screen after turning on her light. Then her eyes blink a couple of times and she runs her tongue over her lips. I feel myself getting hard, fueling my anger.

"Take off your nightie," I demand, needing to see all of her. I know this is not going to end well. I should tell her I'm struggling and frustrated. But my dick is not listening. She cocks her head at me, her eyes searching for something. Biting her lip, she pulls her black silk nightgown over her head. *Christ, she's beautiful!*

"Sit back and spread your legs." I'm growling like a caged beast.

"Reed? What's going on?" Her hands are touching the screen as if that would let her touch me.

"*I said spread your legs!*" She hesitates and looks at what I assume is her bedroom door, then scoots back, props a couple pillows behind her, and puts the computer between her legs. She opens them slowly. I hiss out something as I see her perfect pink sex glistening at me.

"Happy?" She breathes out.

I look at her flat stomach, her unbelievable breasts, and I almost start crying.

"Jesus." I shake my head. "You have ruined me, Kitten. I'm so sick of wanting you, needing you. Do you have any idea what you have done to us?" My voice doesn't even sound like me, I'm so goddamn broken. She looks sad, and I almost take back what I said, but I'm hurting and want her to know it.

"I want you to touch yourself, Kitten." Needing to control her, it's like a sickness inside me.

"And, I want you to do exactly what I say. Don't you dare come until I say so." She looks at me, and I feel her blue eyes zeroing in on me, almost like she has lasers in them. Like they are slicing my heart in two.

"Take your middle finger and slowly shove it deep inside that warm hole of yours. I can see it glistening already." I pull down my gym shorts.

She does what I tell her, and she arches her back, so her hand and pussy are all I see.

"That's so hot, Tess. Now pump that finger deep inside. Find your G-spot and rub it." I watch, mesmerized.

"Reed." She's all breathless. "You know I never can find it."

I want so badly for my finger to be inside her, stroking her. "That's okay, Kitten. When you're home, I'll find it."

She moans. "Reed... this feels so, so good."

I smile. I love when Tess lets go. She's magnificent. "Let's make it feel even better. Pull that wet finger out and rub that delicious clit." She obeys me, her breath ragged. She's starting to get a little loud with her moaning. I should quiet her, but I hate Robert, so I let her be as enthusiastic as she wants.

The louder she moans, the harder I get. Reaching for my cock, I start to stroke myself. She instantly looks up at the screen.

"Take off your shirt, Reed. I need to see you." Her voice sounds so excited, I moan. Teasing her with a hint of my dimples, I hear her curse about putting her tongue on them. Letting go of my dick, I pull my sweaty shirt off. She puffs out some air. Her fingers haven't stopped rubbing her clit. I praise her, even when I'm upset with her. I can't help but give her my approval. She loves it, needs it.

"That's it, Tess. Does that feel good, Kitten? Do you wish those were my fingers?" I reach for my hard cock again.

"Reed," she whimpers, "I do, *I really do*." She's getting close. I can see her clit starting to pulse and we've only started.

"Don't you dare come, Tess," I scold her harshly. "*Stop* touching yourself." She groans in frustration, giving me the kill stare.

"Tess," I say harshly.

She stops, although she does one last rub over her pink, swollen clit.

I smile, because, she's so goddamn sexy and naughty. She keeps her legs open, so my eyes can feast on that swollen nub.

"Now, I want you to take one hand and spread those lips, No touching yourself, Kitten! Go on..." She opens her slick lips at my command and smiles mischievously.

Now I do give her my dimples. "Since you can't control yourself from coming, you have to wait and watch me stroke my cock."

Her eyes are half-mast, making her look like a goddess. I stroke myself slowly. Her breasts are flushed and her nipples are tight and hard.

"Take your other hand and squeeze those hard nipples. Yeah... Kitten, look at my cock—it's leaking for you." I take my precum and spread it all over the tip. I lean back and spread my legs, giving her a better view.

"God, Reed, I want to touch myself again." She's whimpering.

"Tell me what I want to hear, Tess."

"I love you, I'm yours," she pants.

"Fuck, that's it, Tess. I'm close, baby. You keep those lips open and take those fingers and work them all over that pretty wet cunt." She gasps at my crudeness, but I don't care because I'm close to coming. And for the first time in a while, I feel good and connected to her.

She does what I say. Her two fingers go to town on herself. She puts them inside and pumps herself only to bring them out and rub herself frantically and hard, so hard. I'm jerking myself off rough and fast as our eyes lock.

"Rub that clit hard. I want you coming. Rub, baby." Her eyes darken; her body starts to jerk. "*Yeah...* Just. Like. That. Kitten."

Her fingers stop as her clit clenches and pulses. That's all I need as I jet off all over my stomach and vaguely feel some land on my neck. We're both breathing harshly. There's a small smile on her flushed face. I sit up, pulling my shorts up. Grabbing a bunch of Kleenex, I do a quick wipe off. Now that we both have calmed down, I look at her. She sighs and makes me feel like I'm all she needs. But that's a lie and just like that, the incredible feeling fades. And the truth that we still have to get through four more months makes me frown.

"What's wrong, Reed?" Her voice makes my dick twitch again.

"I'm sick of this. I hate this fucking screen." I lean forward, resting my elbows on my knees. "I don't want to do this anymore."

She sits up and grabs for her black slip nightie. "What are you talking about?"

"I'm saying it's time you come back to me. It's been a year and a half. You're miserable, and I can barely function." My eyes sting. I clear my voice. "This isn't working for me, Tess. I'm either the most important thing to you, like you are for me, or we need to rethink what we mean to each other."

"What do you want me to do?" Her voice cracks and she looks toward her door again. "*He* won't let me come back."

"Just *leave*, Tess. Claire's not perfect, but she's still your mother. How long are you going to let him control you?" She's silent.

"Tess? Is there something you're not telling me?" I'm starting to sweat. After all, the plan was for her to finish the school year, then come back.

I sigh, rubbing my hands up and down my face. "Look, Tess, I'm sorry. I'm impatient. We've made it this long—what's a couple more months."

Tears form in her sapphire eyes. Dread slithers up my spine and into my head. And I know, without a doubt, this is it. Our moment of truth.

"What?" I snap.

Her eyes are huge, and her breathing is elevated. "Reed." It comes out as a whisper.

"I... I don't think I will be coming back until I graduate." Her voice is strangely flat. I stare at her, stunned and confused.

"What are you talking about? I thought you were coming back at the end of this year. You promised me."

A sob escapes her. "I tried, Reed, but he threatened to disinherit me. And my mom is not fighting for my return at all! I'm all alone, Reed. You have no idea what I'm living through!" Her voice is on edge, almost accusing.

"Like hell I don't!" I yell. "Who the fuck do you think has been doing this with you? Who has had to deal with your panic attacks through a goddamn screen? *Who*? If I don't know what you have been going through, then you need some serious help, Tess."

"Stop it, Reed." She pulls her nightie back on. "I can't handle this right now!" She sniffs. "You know, Reed, I see everybody's Facebook posts. You know what I see?"

"No, Tess, what? What do you see?"

"I see *my boyfriend* drinking, laughing, one party after another! How about what all the girls post on you? You know like my *friend Lexi*! She loves posting all kinds of interesting stuff. So, excuse me if I don't weep for you. You have everyone, Reed. You know who I have? My fucking dad's twenty-seven-year-old Russian girlfriend! That's my only friend, Reed!"

"That's bullshit, Tess. You have me, Jax, and Brance. Christ, Brance comes to visit all the time. You want more friends? Get your skinny ass up and make some. But you won't because you know I'm all you need!" She's flushed, and we're both breathing heavily.

"Now, are you going to come home like you promised?" I grit my teeth.

"Reed, you are being so—"

"It is a yes or no question, Tess. Are. You. Coming. *Home*?"

She's silent; then she looks down and my heart breaks. I sit back and rub my chest.

"When were you going to tell me? Or were you going to do what you've been doing since the day you left *and lie*?"

That snaps her head up. "I never lied," she whispers.

"Really? First it was 'I will be home before school starts.' Then, 'I will be home in the summer.' Then it was Christmas. And now we are into March and you are not coming back for another year and a half?" I run my hands through my hair.

"Do you even care that we haven't touched each other forever? Does that even bother you?"

"Yes, of course it does, but what do you expect me to do? I'm not an adult."

"I expect you to come back. I *need* you!" I throw my hands at her almost pleading.

"Reed, he threatened to disinherit me!"

"So what? I have more money than anyone should. You will never want for anything."

She snorts. "Perfect. What happens if you leave me?"

I nearly see red. "You are kidding me, right?" I'm barely able to catch my breath. "You did not just ask *me* if I would leave you, did you? Since I've known from the moment I saw you that you were *mine*." I'm so angry I can barely talk.

"It's not something I can chance." She swallows. "If I allowed you to support me, and you left me, I would have nothing." Her hands are flying around in her agitation.

She has literally knocked the wind out of me. I look at her exquisite face and for the first time, I don't want to talk to her. For the first time, *I hate her*! And I want to hurt her. I want her pain! I don't want to hear any more of her lies. *I'm done*!

"Reed?" Her voice is pleading. "I didn't mean that. I'm confused. I—"

"Tess, I have given you my whole heart. And you have pretty much destroyed it. So before you take my entire soul, I'm going to stop. You do what you need to do, but I'm done." I don't listen to her hysterical pleading. I end the call, turn off my computer, and get into the shower.

Jax is lying on my bed as I come out of the bathroom. Wrapping a towel around my waist, I notice he is dressed for the party but on his phone, clearly trying to calm Tess down. I'm so fucking demolished, I grab his cell from him.

"Tess!"

"Reed? Thank God. Don't do this to us. I'm sorry. I'll do anything." She's crying so hard I can barely understand her.

My first instinct is to calm her, but I don't. "You coming home?" I demand.

She is literally hysterical, but I hear her words loud and clear. "I can't! Reed, you have to understand. Please, this isn't you. We love each other!"

"Tess, this *is* me, I don't want to hear from you. I don't want my brother hearing from you."

"No." She wails. "You don't mean that."

"*You're not listening, Tess*! I'm done! Leave my family and me alone. You're not mine. And, I don't want to be yours anymore." I can barely choke out the words, but I know these words will hurt her more than anything. And right now, I want her to burn.

I hang up and toss my twin his phone. I don't look at him because I can feel him, so what's the point of seeing his pain.

"Reed, you have to calm down. You can't be serious—"

I hold up my hand. "She had her chance to come back. *She* is choosing to stay with her father." I jerk on a pair of jeans, not bothering with underwear. "She's not *our* Tess anymore. That girl"—I nod to his phone—"I don't even know her. She's not mine. And I would appreciate it if you would back me up. As my twin, and my other half, *please!*" My heart pounds in my temple. Jax is pale, but he nods.

"Whatever you need."

"I need you not to talk to her. I need you not to mention her name. I'm done! She's dead to us!"

"Just take a moment and think, Reed. She sounds bad. I... I want to try to help fix this for you two." His face has never looked more sincere.

"If you want to help me, then don't judge me when I fuck someone tonight. Because I have every intention of doing that."

Jax takes a breath. His eyes, like mine, are filled with tears.

"Are you sure? This is Tess we're talking about. She's your soul mate. She's all your firsts," he croaks.

I rub my tattoo, his words nearly bringing me to my knees. I look at him. "*She* got all my firsts! My heart, my soul and she destroyed my very being, Jax. I gave her all of me!" I shrug. "Everything now is just semantics."

"I won't say her name." I turn away because he is pressing his palms into his eyes, and I have to stay strong, angry. I haven't stopped rubbing my damn tattoo, as if that is somehow going to fix me.

"Let's go." I drop my hand, pull on a navy T-shirt, and rake a hand through my wet hair.

Jax brings his hands down. "Okay, who's it going to be, Reed?"

"Gia." I breathe. "I want Gia and then I'll go from there."

chapter 16

TESS

Past – sixteen years old
London, England

I haven't left my room since Reed hung up on me on Jax's phone.

I can't eat; I barely sleep. I have called and left so many messages that Reed's and Jax's mailboxes are full. All I want to do is crawl and beg for him to take me back. I tried to take a shower, but leaving my bed forced me to realize that he is gone and I'm alone. My body reacted by breaking out into a cold sweat. After that, the shaking should have alarmed me. Since I was twitching so much, I barely made it back to the bed and the warmth of my down comforter. I may be having a breakdown, but I'm too sad to care.

The door of my bedroom, or prison, depending on how you want to look at it, swings open.

My father's leggy girlfriend strides in and opens my curtains. The day spills into the room causing me to blink in surprise as she pulls the covers off me.

"What the hell, Lana? I don't invade your personal space," I wail, clutching the edge of the comforter. It's become my security blanket.

"Enough! You will get up. Take a shower and eat, or I *will* tell your father!" She taps her manicured nails on my dresser. "Also, Brance says your phone is dead." She marches out of my room, high heels clicking.

"God." Massaging my aching head, I pull myself into a sitting position and search for my phone. I find it under my bed. Some of the worst things that have happened to me have happened on that phone. I know it's crazy, but I refuse to touch it.

Wrapping the comforter around me, I drag myself to the bathroom. The entire room, including the sink, is white marble. No wonder I freak out every time I come in here—it's like being inside a museum.

Taking a steadying breath, I don't want to take the chance that Lana might tell my dad anything. He would probably have me committed to the looney bin. Unfortunately, with the way I look and feel, they'd probably keep me.

I force myself to drop the comforter and shower, brush my teeth, and moisturize my poor, neglected face.

Once, I've survived all that without having another panic attack, I search for something to wear. As I walk through my large bedroom, it reminds me of a hotel room. Celery-green walls and silky brown Berber carpet grace this room. It's so different from my old room. Espresso wooden cabinets surround the wall that faces my large bed. A pang of homesickness washes over me. I slip on a pale blue dress because it requires less energy than having to go through pulling on pants.

Like an old woman, I enter the upscale kitchen. It's smaller than what I'm used to.

My dad bought this loft years ago. He never stayed here, as he was still living with my mom and me in Manhattan. To be honest, I'm sure my greedy mother has no idea it exists. Probably why he seems to love it. He and Lana have had it completely refurbished.

Svetlana, or Lana as I affectionately call her, is sitting with a magazine, happily drinking her coffee.

She smiles at me. "So much better, right?"

Rolling my puffy eyes at her, I proceed to melt down.

"Reed has broken up with me." I hiccup, trying to tell her everything from masturbating on Skype, to Reed giving me an ultimatum. It's all coming out fast and garbled. It doesn't even make sense to me, but Svetlana is holding me, murmuring encouraging things and letting me sob all over her Chanel dress.

When I have nothing left to say, she wipes my eyes, sits me on the stool next to her, and pours me some coffee.

Fixing her Rolex, she crosses her long legs. "Well, your boy is definitely very naughty. And so domineering already." She lifts my face. "You sure that's what you want? He is only going to get worse as a man."

"He's not mine anymore, so I guess it doesn't matter." I grab her hand as it dawns on me he's truly left me.

"Oh my God. What am I going to do?" I look around the kitchen as if it can help me.

Lana slaps the wooden island, making me jump. "You are going to thrive, my beauty. And don't be so dramatic. He wants you! It's all right to grieve. Then you need to take your power back. Did you call Brance?"

I blink at her, not understanding what she said, but I am feeling slightly better. I shake my head. "I can't touch that phone."

Her eyes narrow on me as if that's the most normal thing to say, and she nods. "Fine. We need to get you a new one." Her slight Russian accent emerges. "Use mine." She hands it to me. "And eat this." She forces a banana into my hand.

After a deep breath, I press Brance's number, taking a small bite of banana as I wait for him to answer.

"Lana?"

"No, it's me." I barely choke out the words, my tears hot and stinging.

He sighs. "Pretty Girl, it's going to be okay."

I nod then realize he can't see me. "Yes... I need my power back."

"Um, yes this is true. I see Lana has started without me. Listen, I'm flying in on Friday, staying until Tuesday."

"Good," is all I can utter.

"I have to fly commercial." The annoyance in his voice is clear.

"Brance, my life is falling apart. Please don't complain about first class!" I look at the ceiling trying to get control of myself.

He's silent. I can almost see him pouting as I try to take a small sip of coffee. "I'm getting a new phone." My voice is shaky at best.

"Good, that's a good first step and when I get there, Lana and I will have you wondering why you ever shed a tear for that arrogant prick."

I start crying again. Did he have to mention him? "He's my soul mate, Brance, and now he's gone. I've lost my soul!" I clap my hand over my mouth, trying not to completely lose it again.

"Goddamn it, Tess, he is a domineering, spoiled fuck! Can't you look at this as maybe a blessing in disguise?"

"No, he's *mine*!" Yet he isn't anymore. He could be sleeping, kissing, touching another girl as I sit here. A torturous vision of Reed doing all those things almost makes me lean over the sink and vomit.

"Tess? You still there?"

Clutching the phone so tightly my fingers are numb, I answer, "Brance, you have to find out what's going on. You have to spy. I need to know everything Reed is doing."

Jesus, I sound like a lunatic. But I don't care. This is what I've become. If he has moved on, I need to know. "Please," I beg, knowing I sound pathetic.

"Don't ask this of me. I want to cut off his dick—not spy!"

That makes me giggle. Unfortunately it turns into sobbing.

"Don't cry, Tess. You're killing me. He's not worth this fucking agony."

"Please, Brance... I need to know."

"Fine," he snaps. "Put Lana on. I'll see you in a week."

"You will? You will spy for me?"

"Jesus, Tess, don't make me repeat it."

If I had any pride left, I would try to pretend. But I'm a shell of my former self. And having Brance spy makes me feel better.

"Love you, Brance."

"Love you too, Pretty Girl."

I put the phone in Lana's outstretched hand. She spins on her heels and walks into another room.

Taking a deep breath, I pour out my cold coffee and get myself a fresh one. I fish around for the Advil, locating it behind the sugar. I take three, wondering if I should take a Valium too. Lana walks back into the kitchen, eyeing me as if I'm an unknown species.

"So, first stop, phone. Then lunch, then shopping?" She claps her hands.

I snort. "Lana, I love you, and I appreciate everything you have done for me. But there is no way I'm leaving the flat today," I say, pulling my wet hair on top of my head in a messy bun.

She looks at me from top to bottom. "You're right."

Surprised, I drop my hands.

She smiles. "First phone, then spa, then lunch or dinner depending on how much time we need to put you back together."

Sighing, I'm relieved. The thought of letting someone else make all my decisions always appeals to me, especially today.

"Finish your coffee. I'll get us appointments. Meet you in ten."

I shake my head at her. "Whatever. I don't have the energy to fight you."

"I know." She gives me a sassy look.

I can't help but admire slash be jealous of Lana. From the moment my dad introduced us, she seemed more like a sister than my dad's girlfriend. I remember being so angry at my father that horrible day. And completely dumbfounded at Svetlana. She was cooking stir fry in her five-inch heels and wearing Versace. I wanted to hate her; after all, she should be my enemy. But she smiled at my father with true affection, then turned the full force of herself on me. Her charm and strength are like catnip to a cat. With her height and killer legs, she's everything my mother dreamed of being. Not to mention she is a natural blonde and stick skinny. Sure, she pumps up her lips, and her breasts are fake, but she wears it well. Everything about Lana screams classy. She's my best friend—I mean best girlfriend. Brance will always hold the spot as true bestie. I don't know how I would have survived the last year and a half without her.

Apparently, Svetlana feels the same way about me. She is my biggest advocate with everyone, including my dad. It doesn't matter that we came from completely different worlds. She's the first to own her past. Not embarrassed of it at all. Her parents are dirt poor from Moscow. She used her looks and long legs, to catch the eye of one of the head mafia leaders, becoming his girlfriend at sixteen. Although, she is a little fuzzy on how she ended up with my dad. All she says is she wanted him and so far, she seems to have gotten him.

Looking at my reflection in the glass cabinet door, I don't recognize the girl staring back at me. I close my eyes, shutting her out. This girl doesn't belong to Reed Saddington. How will I ever survive? I guess I'm going to have to find out who this Tess Gallagher is. The tears want to come. Instead I walk out the door and make my way to our private car. New phone for a new Tess. Maybe I'm not as weak as I think.

REED

Past – seventeen years old
New York, NY

"Christ," I groan, rolling over. My eyes try to focus. The room is slightly spinning. Lying on my back, I look over at the naked brunette.

Rubbing my hands over my face, I feel my cock start to wake up. With the amount of alcohol and coke, my mouth feels like a dead rat slunk through it.

Sitting up, I swing my legs over. I'm in a hotel, a suite. It all comes flooding back to me like a nightmare.

Jax and I celebrated Andrew's eighteenth birthday and his dad thought it would be fun for us to have a suite at the Four Seasons. I glance around the room. The only ones here are the brunette and me. I make my way into the bathroom and pull on my jeans as I go. When I glance in the mirror as I piss, the reflection staring back at me is barely recognizable. *Jesus,* I look like crap. Leaning in closer, I look at my eyes—they're bloodshot and swollen. I need to get myself together and dry out. Huh... my hair is sticking up. It's an interesting look.

The water is ice cold, and as I splash it on my face, I hope it stings. My head is pounding. I need a bump, I think, steadying myself. That's how hungover I am. Lurching over to the love seat, I grab the vial from last night and take a quick snort. Closing my eyes as I feel the rush, my heart starts pumping and my whole body wakes up.

"Fuck, yes!" I hiss glancing over at the woman in my bed. I think her name was Christy, Roxy, something with a Y. She was new and did not disappoint.

I usually make a point of avoiding brunettes and prefer blondes. But last night I was fucked up enough not to care.

Andrew's dad supplied the girls. A blonde, a redhead, and a brunette. It was his welcome-to-manhood gift. I guess everyone forgets that Jax and I are only seventeen. We still have another six months before we're legal.

I feel better! Looking down at the tent in my jeans, I have to admit, I love to fuck on cocaine. I wonder if I should wake her up and take her from behind or see if Andrew or even Jax wants to trade. This chick's dark hair is a reminder that I don't need this morning. I reach for my tattoo and give it a rub, my heart beating fast. Yep, the coke is working. Leaning forward, I take another snort, deciding not to wake the brunette. I'll persuade Jax to give up his redhead.

Opening the door to the living room, I'm greeted with the sight of my twin passed out on the massive L-shaped couch, the naked redhead lying on top of him.

The TV is on, but muted. A porn flick is playing. I should take her, if only to piss him off. Jax is completely stingy when it comes to women. He does not like to share. Which makes no sense. It's not like he gets attached to any of them. Again, everyone thinks I'm the dominant one, but my brother takes the whole caveman thing to another level. He's not into the kinky stuff though. One on one is his thing. I, on the other hand, couldn't care less. I love one on one, threesomes, whatever. Andrew and I have that in common. We've indulged in a lot of it lately. As long as it feels good and it's a female in the middle, I have no problem sharing. There was only one person I wouldn't share. Rubbing the back of my neck, I close my eyes as if that is going to block her out, but she's already invaded me, claiming my shame.

Her face always haunts me, teases me. Everyone said it would get easier, that soon, I wouldn't even remember what she looks like. I clung to that thought like a half-drowned sailor on a raft. She is the first thing I see and the last, her breathtaking visage as clear as the moment we met.

I hate her! I hate that every day I go through this. Rubbing my hands over my face, I glance again at Jax's ginger friend and my cock comes alive. I need to fuck; my erection is becoming painful.

Adjusting myself, I lean over and push the girl's hair away, giving me access to her breast. I don't try to make excuses for my demons. I know my parents are worried and that my dad must know about my addiction to hooker sex. How could he not—they cost a fortune! I guess, he figures it take's my mind off...

After that day long ago when Jax said he would never mention her name, no one has spoken it—it's the proverbial elephant in the room. My mom tried once, and it was the worst fight we've ever had. After that, she kept quiet although recently she mustered her courage hinting that I might want to try seeing some girls from school. The look I shot her froze her in her tracks. I'm not boyfriend material. Never will be, so why torture a girl?

I feed my sex addiction with beautiful pros, like this pretty redhead. No strings and they always make me forget.

I kick at my brother. "Dude, you need to put some clothes on or go to your room."

"Screw you, Reed." He rolls over, pulling the girl with him.

"Actually, I was wondering if you wouldn't mind if I traded you?" The redhead is waking up. Stretching, she shoves her very large fake breasts in my brother's face.

He opens an eye. "Are you trying to piss me off this early?" His mouth latches on to her nipple.

I start laughing. "Go to your room, man, or let's swap." He stops sucking and pats her ass for her to get up. Having no desire to see his morning hard-on, I walk to the bar. "You want a Bloody Mary?"

Jax reaches for his jeans, pulling them on, then leans back on the couch, eyeing me. "What's going on, Reed?"

"Hey, call room service. Have them bring some Worcestershire, Bloody Mary mix, and some olives."

"Starting off with a bang, huh?" He lifts a dark eyebrow at me. Standing up, he reaches for the phone dialing room service as he buttons his pants. The redhead, who has put on some panties, walks over to me.

"So, I never had identical twins before. You and your brother into that? No extra charge." I grin at her and reach for her large breast, rubbing her nipple. She growls, and I pinch it, making her gasp. Her eyes darken.

"That's not up to me. You have to talk to my brother."

"No!" Jax yells and goes back to ordering room service. It sounds like he is ordering way more than Bloody Mary mix. He hangs up and walks over to the redhead, pulling her back to him and biting her neck.

"We all got a girl. You should have picked her last night." His large hands massage her breasts. I turn to the picture window and stare blankly down at Manhattan. "Maybe I'll see if Andrew is up."

Jax stares at me, then whispers something into the redhead's ear. She nods and walks into my room.

"What the fuck, Reed?" I'm not responding to him. My high is wearing off and I want to put my fist through the wall.

"I think I'm going to make myself a Stevie Ray Vaughan Bloody Mary. Want one?"

Jax grabs my arm. "What's going on?" His eyes are full of concern.

"She's a brunette," I blurt out.

He rubs his face. "Goddamn it, Reed, why are you doing this? How much longer am I going to have to watch this? Fucking do us all a favor and call her."

"Watch it, Jax."

He looks at my chest. I'm rubbing my tattoo. I freeze, wondering how long I've been doing that.

"I didn't say her name," he hisses, "but this shit has to stop. The cocaine and girls are getting out of hand. Even Jay is getting concerned, and he's the one who started all this." He motions to the girls and drugs.

We both turn as we hear room service knock. Neither of us moves, our eyes doing silent battle. Finally, Jax steps around me to open the door.

The girls come out of my room, laughing and wanting to party. I pour the vodka, a little Worcestershire, and Bloody Mary mix into the glasses, then sprinkle some cocaine on top and plop in a couple olives.

"Here you go, girls. Jax, you sure you don't want one?"

He shakes his head. "I'm going to take a shower. Enjoy."

"Holy shit, I have always wanted to try this." The brunette laughs and jumps up and down, her tits bouncing.

I look at her and chastise myself for being such a pussy. She looks absolutely nothing like her. Starting with her tits that are boomeranging in my face. They're fake and look like two large balloons on her thin body. *Her* breasts are real and perky, fitting perfectly in my hands. I stop myself. *Jesus!* I chug my morning cocktail, needing a quick high to fill my emptiness.

"So, you two want to fuck?"

Their eyes are dilated. "Yeah, we want to," the redhead purrs.

"I want to fuck you in the ass," I tell her, "while your friend sits on your face." When did I become this monster? It's getting like I need more and more of everything to get off lately.

"How much extra for that?" I say, the welcome numbness starting to take effect.

Both smile and take my hand, pulling me into the bedroom.

"We won't tell, if you won't tell." The redhead shuts the door and peels off her panties.

Turning to the brunette, I say, "Why don't you girls start, and I'll join in."

She smiles and reaches for her friend, peeking up at me. "Are we still role playing?"

Confused I ask, "What?" but the hair on my forearm is standing up.

"Like last night? Do you still want me to be Tess?"

The room starts to spin.

"Holy shit, are you okay?" The redhead reaches for me.

"Shit! Raquel, go get his brother. I think he's overdosing." She extends her hand, trying to get me to sit.

"Get off of me!" I cringe at her touch.

Sweat pours out of me, drenching my shirt. Last night slaps me in the face as I remember.

"I need you to be Tess. I can't get off without it."

"I'll be whoever you want. Is Tess sweet, or a bitch? Soft or hard? Tell me what she is, and you won't even remember my name."

"She's my soul: innocent, fragile, yet way stronger than she knows. She's my heart."

"Reed... Close your eyes... I don't want you to fuck me. I need you to make love to me."

"Tess... I will do anything you want, Kitten."

Holy fucking shit! My feet back away from them.

I did! I made love to her last night. I can't breathe. Maybe I am overdosing. That might be better than the truth.

"I'm going to be sick." Stumbling past their shocked faces, I barely make it to the toilet when my whole stomach unloads. I retch and heave for what feels like hours until it stops. Miserable, that's what I've become. Leaning back, I shiver by the toilet, resting my head on my knees.

"Reed? You okay?" Jax's voice is next to me, his hand helping me up.

I look at him, his face so like mine, except that it's not anymore. His eyes still have joy, where mine are filled with darkness.

"I need to get away from here," I whisper.

"Can you walk? Do you need to go to the hospital?" His voice scares me.

"No, no hospital. Just get me out of here." Pushing away from him, I find Andrew and the girls standing outside the bathroom.

"Dude! You okay? You scared the girls." Andrew's brows are knit with concern.

The girls stand there, all three in a state of undress, curiosity on their faces rather than fear. Obviously, I'm not the first customer to freak on them.

I'm completely undone.

My voice sounds far away. "They seem okay. You two, on the other hand, can relax. I feel better. It must have been something I ate." I run a hand through my wild hair.

Andrew exhales. "Christ, Reed, you've aged me." He chuckles, his hands shaking as he puts his phone in his pocket.

I move past them. "I've got to go. Happy Birthday, man. I'll call you later." Jax is right behind me.

"Thanks, Reed, you sure you're okay?"

"Yeah, I just have to get out of here," I snap. I know he's concerned about being a good friend, but if I don't get out of this suite, I might implode.

"Let me grab our stuff, Reed."

"Hurry the fuck up," I say, taking a shaky breath as my eyes scan the hotel room. It's trashed but not overly so. Picking up my jacket, I avoid looking at the girls.

"Let's go." Jax pulls me back to the present, his voice calm.

"I'm fine. I need some air."

"Whatever—this has to stop." He pushes me out the door, his arm guiding me outside. "How much coke did you do?"

"It's not the coke—or fuck, maybe it is. I don't know." My cheeks are cool and wet. *Am I crying?* Strong arms hug me. My brother, my best friend, my other half, tries to put me back together, and he starts with a hug.

"What's going on? I need you to look at me. Otherwise, I'm taking you to the emergency room."

Putting my head back, I close my stinging eyes. New York is crackling with energy. Horns blaring, garbage trucks rumbling. And I feel better because I'm not alone. As long as I have him, I can make it. I mumble it like a mantra as I pull away and we head home.

chapter 18

REED

The fresh air and the walk have helped. I still feel like shit, but at least Jax is not threatening to take me to the ER. The penthouse is silent as we enter. My heart sinks. Call it intuition, but whenever it's quiet, something is going down and it's usually bad.

I'm beelining it straight to my room. Jax must sense it too because he is heading for his. I need Advil, a gallon of water, and sleep.

"Reed!" My dad is leaning in the doorway waiting for me. *Shit.*

"Unless someone's dead, not today." I try to move around him, but he grabs hold of my bicep.

I stop, more from disbelief than from him actually stopping me. I surpassed my dad on height and bulk a year ago. I look at him, and his green eyes bore into me. "I would like a word with you."

"Dad, I'm not in any condition to talk rationally."

"We will get to that, Reed, but first, this." He holds up some letters. I look around desperately for Jax.

"Your brother can't help you. You're going to have to stand on your own two feet."

"Perfect." I drop into one of my mother's ridiculously expensive chairs. He sits opposite me and lays out the letters on the table. They are all addressed to Jax.

"Reed? Do you have any idea what these are?" He points to the envelopes.

My head is throbbing, and my patience is about zero. I want to walk out of the room, but I can't, so I sit and rub the back of my neck.

"Um, no, Dad I don't." Leaning forward I say, "I can tell you that I feel like crap and would be more agreeable if I had a nap."

He laughs. "Really? My *son* is in a bad mood again?" His sarcastic voice makes me want to punch something. Instead I take a breath and look him straight in the eyes.

"I wish I had some sympathy, Reed, but watching you self-destruct on whores and God knows what else, it needs to stop."

I sit up, ready to do battle. He holds up his hand. "No, you're going to listen, Reed. I was young. I know what you've been going through. Which is why I have been allowing your expensive hobby. And by hobby I'm talking about the girls, not the drugs."

I blink a few times. My eyes are killing me, and I don't have any desire to look at my father's face.

"Why didn't you come to me, Reed? Talk to me? You never reached out to me at all when you and Tess broke up. Did you think I didn't know how much you loved and needed her?"

My eyes are stinging with tears. "I... can't talk about her, Dad."

He nods. "Well, son, I've done pretty much everything. Nothing you can say would shock me or make me feel differently about you."

I rub the back of my head before I look at him. "I'm lost, Dad, and I'm embarrassed to admit it because *I hate it!*" I spit it out. "I lost my soul mate and it hurts more every day." I say the words that have been stuck in my throat for a year and a half.

He leans back and crosses his arms. "What will you do if she comes back? Can you forgive her?"

I shake my head because as much as I love her, I hate her too.

"I think it's too late. I will always resent her. Resent that she picked her father over me."

I feel his hand on my shoulder. "Let's take it slowly, Reed. First, the drugs need to stop."

"I agree." And I honestly do. The reminder of what just happened still makes bile rise in the back of my throat.

"Second, the prostitute situation. You are using condoms, right?"

"Always." I snort. "You think I wouldn't wrap it up? I have never gone bare with anyone."

"Are you with these girls because you like older women? Or because they are the opposite of Tess?" I wince.

"Both, I guess. Also, I have nothing in common with high school girls. They want relationships and I'm incapable of having one."

"Fine." He stands up, hands in his pockets as he walks to the French doors, lost in thought. I'm almost ready to stand, thinking he's done.

"I'm familiar with the madam that you and Jax are paying."

I must look horrified and disgusted because he instantly justifies himself.

"Hold your judgment. I got the call because you two are minors even with your fake IDs. She called to get my permission and a lot of money to overlook your ages," he mumbles.

"Whatever." My head is pounding. He shakes his head at me, clearly annoyed as he sits down across from me.

"Fine, let's go back to this." He points to the table.

"Yeah, Dad, I had a rough night. I've agreed to everything. Can I go? Those letters are to Jax anyway."

179

"Yes, Reed, these are letters to Jax. What I'm wondering is why you have not received any." I glance around the room. Floral displays are everywhere. Absently I wonder if my mom calls the florist or if she has them delivered and displayed daily.

"Reed?" my dad says. My mind returns to him.

"Dad, I never applied," I say at last, leaning my head back to rest as I close my tired eyes. "Tess wanted us to go to Columbia. I never cared about college."

His nostrils flare. "Are you telling me that my son, who tests borderline genius, has no desire to get a degree?"

"Exactly. That was all Jax and Tess." I stand up.

"Huh," he murmurs and sits there, his brows furrowed.

"Are we done?" I glance at the grandfather clock. It's already afternoon.

"No, not yet. These letters are from MIT, Harvard, and Stanford! They are all to Jax, congratulating him and welcoming him to their campus."

I stretch my sore muscles. "Good for Jax because he's actually a *genius*."

"No, Reed, you both tested about the same. If you're not going to college, what are you planning on doing?"

I shrug. "I was thinking about traveling."

He frowns. "Traveling?" It comes out slowly. Then he starts laughing.

"Glad I can amuse you. Are we done?"

He scoops up the acceptance letters. "Far from it. You have no idea what the hell you want. So, I have decided you are going to get your college degree." He says this, and he's absolutely serious.

I stiffen then start laughing. "Perfect! What do you want me to say? Thank you? We're fucking *rich*! Excuse me for not having a huge amount of drive right now. I need to go find myself."

He stands up and pours himself a drink. I raise my eyebrow at him.

"Your grandfather and I have decided for you to take over a huge part of the family business. But you need to have a degree, Reed."

I puff out air. "Why me?" I rub my hands over my face.

"Because Jax wants to do what Jax wants to do. And he's earned that. I'm sure he'll be taking some part in the business too. But he has his own interests. *You do not.* As your father, I've decided to help you thrive not fail."

Dropping my hands, I stare at him as though he's insane. "So, you and Grandpa Ian are deciding *my* life for me?" I laugh bitterly. "I'm not in any condition to take over."

"Trust me, you're not taking over, Reed. You will be supervising a portion. Shipping, hotels, and so on. Whatever you like. But you need a degree. Pick where you want to go."

I sigh tiredly. "Like I give a shit. You have my whole life planned out. Just pick and let me know where and what time. I'll try to show up."

He smiles and stands. "Columbia it is then. I agree with Tess—it's perfect for you. I have connections with people on the board. Also, Jordan is an alumnus. He can pull strings. Thank God your grades and test scores are impeccable. They should be able to overlook your tardiness." Standing up, he pats me on the back. "Get some rest, son. You look like hell." He leaves, and I wonder if it's possible to feel any worse.

chapter 19

TESS

Past – eighteen years old
London England

"I guess we should circle around again. I don't see him," I tell Steven our driver today.

This is our fourth time around Heathrow airport. We're picking up Brance. He's flying in to help me pack.

New York, here I come! Never in a million years did I think I would miss her loud, crowded, dirty streets and stinky smells.

"We are going straight for lunch. Your father told me to call when we are at the restaurant. He might stop by," Lana says, taking out her compact and lipstick from her red Chanel purse. At the mere mention of my father, poor Lana feels she has to primp.

I groan, "Really?"

Things have been strained with my dad ever since I informed him that I had been accepted to Columbia University and was moving back to New York. No congratulations. Nothing. He simply turned and walked out of the room.

"I'm so ready to go back to the States. He's probably jealous."

She laughs. "You're probably right. I know I'm jealous. You need to get your own place fast. I don't think your mother would like me visiting." She smirks.

"I rarely talk to my mother. Brance says she's hitting the vodka hard. She won't want me cramping her style." The thought of having to move back with my mother and staying in my childhood bedroom after she betrayed me in the worst way? I can't do it.

"I have to convince Brance to stay in Manhattan. I'll live with him. He's still insisting on moving to LA now that he's graduated." I sound desperate, but I kind of am. Unless my dad gives me control of my money, I'm at his mercy. And I'm sure he would make me live with my mom if only to punish me for returning.

"Why don't you just go to Stanford?" Lana checks her teeth for lipstick.

"Stanford is not in LA. Besides, I have always dreamed about going to Columbia. Wait... pull over, Steven... there he is!" I squeal.

Steven mutters something but manages to fight his way to the curb.

I throw the door open, and Brance saunters over, a mischievous grin on his face. He hands Steven his bags and slides in.

"You look fabulous. I love your hair," Lana gushes as they air kiss.

"You think it's too light?" With his dark Columbian skin and his dark eyes, his light hair makes his face striking. Somehow my skinny pretty boy has grown up into a sexy lean man.

"Knock it off, Brance. You look like a model and you know it." He winks at me, kissing my forehead.

"Christ, I won't miss that flight. I think I have my father almost caving so that we can use one of his planes for the trip back. I'm so sick of commercial. Anything over five hours should always be in a private plane." Stretching his long legs, he grins, no doubt knowing he sounds ridiculous.

Rolling my eyes, I say, "Whatever, Brance, are you hungry?"

"Famished."

Lana claps her hands. "I know the perfect place." Leaning between us, she tells the driver, not even waiting for our response.

Settling back, she clasps her fingers in her lap. "Now that Brance is here, he has something he needs to tell you."

"Jesus, Lana, can't we even get to the restaurant?" Brance grabs my hand and holds it. Looking from one to the other, I suddenly want to scream for Steven to pull over and let me out. The crowded streets would be better than whatever secret Brance has.

"What?" I dig my nails into his hand.

"Tess! It's not that bad. *Stop* clawing me." My eyes dart down to his tan hand, which I have indeed made bleed with my nails.

"Oh God, Brance, I'm so sorry." I try to erase my craziness with my thumb.

"If it's bad, I don't want to hear it." And I kind of mean that, my mind drifting off to all the work I've done on myself. Every morning, I run at least three miles. Graduated at the top of my class. Got myself into Columbia. And, I did all this *without Reed*. I didn't collapse like I wanted to. I didn't let him completely destroy me. He broke my heart, severed my soul, but I'm still fighting. Brance already told me about the prostitutes and drugs. How much worse can it be?

"Tess!" Lana is annoyingly waving a hand in my face.

"Stop it." I slap it away.

"Well, you're scaring me. You're pale and your eyes are glazed over like you're in another world."

"Lana, back off. She'll be fine. Maybe we should wait." Brance looks at me then out the window.

"No, she needs to know. Maybe that will open her eyes."

Turning so I can see Brance, his chocolate eyes search my face for answers. I curl my hands into a fist and try to breathe.

Whatever is torturing him must be bad because his body is radiating nervous energy. I look away, unsure I want to put myself through anything else. I've managed to lock my feelings away. Do I honestly want them to escape?

The driver clears his throat forcing me to focus. "Excuse me, Ms. Volkov, we're here. Do you want me to drop you off at the door, or do you want me to circle around again?"

She looks at me. "Are you going to make a scene?"

I straighten my shoulders. "Don't be stupid, Lana. I'm fine. Nothing Brance can say can hurt me." Well, that's a lie, but she doesn't need to know that I'm getting ready to snap. Plastering on my prettiest smile, I face Brance. "Is anyone dead?"

"No."

"See... there you have it. Problem solved. Drop us off, Steven."

He pulls over, and we exit. Walking up to the colorful restaurant, we see a red sign and green wooden windows welcoming us.

Lana's phone goes off. I can tell she is talking to my father because her voice drops a notch.

I roll my eyes.

"Stop it," Brance chastises me.

"What? Oh, you mean the eye roll at watching Lana humiliate herself for my father?" I want to say more but she hangs up flustered.

Exhaling, she says, "So, your father is going to join us. Let's go in and get a table."

The restaurant is busy for lunch, and we have to sit in the middle at a long thin table with pretty lilies set in the center. I can't help but snicker, knowing my dad will hate this table. He can't stand people invading his space. The kitchen is open, and it has a big wood-burning oven. White-jacketed chefs remove bubbling pizza and fresh-baked bread from it.

Lana is all business, and our eight-year age difference goes right out the window. She transforms into everything my father wishes her to be: a sophisticated woman emerges.

"I'm going to freshen up." She eyes me like I should follow. I smile. "Fantastic. We'll be waiting."

She hesitates, then looks at her watch and leaves us.

I order some sparkling and plain water and bread. Placing the white cloth napkin on my lap, I face Brance. "Tell me," I hiss, not looking up.

He lightly touches my cheek, forcing me to make eye contact. "You know I just want you to be happy. I have debated saying anything because I'm not sure you need to hear it."

I bite my lip and take a sip of cool water, knowing whatever he's about to say is going to change me.

"Do your worst."

Then he does, butchering me with four words. "Reed is with Lexi."

Lexi. Her blond hair and ugly body swim before me. I never allow myself to think about her since she is everything I find evil. She has been stalking Reed for years. He hates her as much as I do.

"Take another sip of water." Brance holds up the crystal glass to me; the ice cubes swirl and sparkle.

Shaking my head, I say, "I don't believe it!" My voice is getting loud.

Brance simply stares. I look around, not caring what people think about me. But no one seems to notice. Their happy smiles and laughter make me want to throw something to shut them up.

"Tess, look at me." I do, then wish I hadn't because it's all there on my best friend's face. His pain is real, and he is feeling it for me. "I confronted him because I couldn't believe it. He didn't deny it."

I stand up. "No! Not with her—he wouldn't!"

Brance gently pulls me down into my chair.

"He did, Pretty Girl. It's time for you to move on too. I need you to think about this, Tess. Maybe we should move to LA and start over together."

Blinking at him a couple times, I try to get my mind to work. The pain and betrayal are about to make me scream and I might never stop. My eyes dart around the restaurant, looking for a safe corner to curl up in and vanish.

I grab my water, spilling it all over my shirt, the wetness cold and not unnoticeable, but I'm beyond caring.

Brance rubs my back. When Lana slinks into the chair next to me, her freshly applied makeup looks perfect.

"So, he told you what a piece of shit your boyfriend is." She flags the waiter to order a chardonnay.

I clear my throat. "He's not my boyfriend." I stare at them dumbly.

Brance reaches for my chin and holds my face tight. "Tess, you are the most important person to me. You're going to be okay, and just so you know, I have decided not to move yet, so you will be staying with me." He's so good and confident, I wish I could crawl inside him.

Tears sting my eyes. "Brance..." I want to say more, but my father's tall build fills up the small walkway.

"Do you think you could have gotten a worse table?" he grumbles at me and turns to Brance. "And you... are you sure you're gay? I think I have been hustled into thinking you were safe to be around my daughter." He chuckles at himself.

"Daddy! That's not funny. You're being rude."

He ignores me and holds out his hand to Brance who stands.

"Mr. Gallagher, good to see you again."

My father's attention returns to me, and he gives me a disapproving stare. Obviously, I don't rank on his perfection scale. Lana does though. His eyes light up with approval. "Svetlana." He leans down to tenderly kiss her.

That's it. I push my chair back. "Excuse me, I need to use the ladies' room."

I'm going to puke. I can feel it coming up, burning my esophagus. My legs move as fast as they can. Bursting into the restroom, I lean over the toilet, waiting for my body to purge itself. I heave, but nothing comes out. As the agonizing seconds tick by, my mouth stops watering and I lean back resting against the side of the stall.

Reed is with Lexi!

Closing my eyes, I try to calm my manic mind, but the stupid childhood song plays in my fuzzy brain. *Reed and Lexi sitting in a tree, K-I-S-S-I-N-G.* I almost start laughing at the betrayal and that this might be my tipping point.

"Unbelievable!" I kick the door, and it snaps open and shut like a boomerang. This is the ultimate nail in our coffin. He wanted to send me a direct message? Mission accomplished.

Hands go up to my face, and I want to hide. My life is a joke—a sad waste of a pretty face.

"Tess?"

I push open the stall door. Brance stands with his arms crossed.

"You're going to get us thrown out."

"Maybe." We stare at each other. He nods, knowing what I'm going through.

"This one hurts the most." Tears swim in my eyes.

"Christ, you should have let me castrate him." He runs a hand through his hair and sighs. "Come here, Pretty Girl." The tips of our fingers touch as he reels me in to his warmth. The thought of Reed's dick, thick and proud, pulsing in my hand, is enough to make me wail, especially if I had allowed Brance to cut it off.

"Jesus Christ, Tess! You're shaking. Please stop crying. You're killing me."

Lifting my chin, he stares at me. "You know what, screw that! Let it go. Fucking freak out if you want." He crushes me to his warm chest, rocking me back and forth, then opens the bathroom door, pulling me with him around a corner and through a side exit.

"You know that door is for the employees."

"You need some air."

We're in the alley, but I can still see the quaint street we came in on. It's alive with twentysomethings mingling and shopping.

"I want to feel like them," I say, motioning to the carefree girls who are laughing at something on one of their phones.

"I hate him, Brance. And I hate my father. They stole that from me."

Brance glances at the giggling teenagers. I notice my mascara has stained his pale pink button-down shirt.

"If it makes you feel better, I hate him too. Reed, not your father."

I snort, then wipe at his shirt. "I think I got snot on you."

He shrugs. "Doesn't matter. But you have to let him go if you're ever going to feel like them." He tilts his head toward the giggling girls.

I nod because it's true. It's time to bury Reed Saddington.

"I need your help."

He smiles, his pretty white teeth, distracting me. "Anything."

"Good." A siren goes by. "I want to dye my hair blond," I yell over the sound.

He frowns. "Blond?"

"Uh-huh... and I want to pump my lips with collagen."

He blinks at me. "Excuse me?" He grabs my elbow, moving us away from the dumpster and the rancid smells inside it.

"You heard me," I say, wiping my eyes. This is going to take some manipulation.

"No way. No lips. You want to dye your hair, fine. No lips. You'll look like one of the Simpsons."

Rubbing my nose, I say, "Brance, I love you, but I'm going to do this, so you can either support me or go home."

Hurt darkens his eyes. "Really?"

"Yeah, I'm done being nice."

"Apparently."

"Whatever, I can tell you think I'm being dramatic... and immature."

"You are."

We stare at each other in silence. Until I feel a slight drizzle on my eyelashes.

Brance shakes his head. "Congratulations, Tess. Way to let Reed drag you down again."

"I want to be blond and have big fat lips. Just once, I want to tell everyone to fuck off."

"You already have big fat lips," he snarls.

"Bigger. You know what I mean. I want to do something that Reed would hate. I need to be everything he despises. Call it closure."

Brance looks baffled, but then his lips start to twitch.

"Don't you dare laugh!" I say, my lips starting to twitch also.

Looking down at the wet pavement, he responds at last. "Well, I guess you're going to be a blonde then. I will, of course, be there to hold your hand and make sure you don't look like shit." His voice is uncharacteristically weary, like he knows I'm lying about wanting closure.

"I hate you changing anything on yourself. You're perfect and you know it."

"That's exactly why I need to do this—because I'm not perfect. No one is. I'm desperately flawed. But I'm okay with that, and I need for others to see that too."

"Whatever you need, Pretty Girl." Suddenly the door opens, and a waiter steps out, lighting a cigarette. Brance smiles as his foot stops the door from shutting. "After you."

"Thank you," I say, walking toward my father's dark head and Lana's light.

chapter 20

TESS

I stare at myself in the mirror. I don't believe I did this. *Holy shit!*

My long brown hair has been bleached blond and not like dishwater blond. We're talking Marilyn Monroe blond. Leaning forward, I darken my eyelids and smear on some dark plum lip gloss.

Transformation complete.

Lana's plastic surgeon kicked ass. He did my lips as a favor. I guess he doesn't sully himself with collagen anymore. The bickering between Brance and Lana over how much collagen I needed was rather amusing. The poor surgeon had to play referee.

I can't help but smile at my reflection. I love them! Slightly puffy, completely kissable lips. Gone is my darkness.

My albatrosses are gone at last. As I sat in the doctor's chair, my mind replayed the last three years. The sting of the needle going into my bottom lip is nothing compared to the pain of losing Reed. That and the pathetic relationship with my father. I had hoped throughout all the heartache I have endured, I would come away with his love. But he kept that locked up, like he does everything else with me. The humiliation still burns through me at his complete lack of compassion. I thought I would die with shame being dragged into a gynecologist to be put on birth control. Even when I swore I wasn't having sex. Not to mention the constant disapproval of my clothes and that he seems to believe I loved Reed simply to mock him.

"I refuse to be that girl anymore," I say, nodding at my reflection.

Grabbing my new tan, suede three-quarter-length jacket, I slip it on. My eyes scan my room as I make sure I have everything I need. I won't be coming back. All my other bags are already on Brance's dad's private plane.

"Well, I guess I'm off," I yell, nearly skipping down the stairs.

"We're in here," Lana says.

Pushing open my dad's study door, I'm greeted with Lana crying, holding on to my dad who is rubbing her shoulder. She pulls away and looks at me from top to bottom.

"God, you look hot!" I look down at my outfit. I'm dressed in a tight black shirt and skintight black skinny jeans with high-heeled black boots. My tan jacket and my hair are the only lightness on me.

"Well, black is my favorite color." A pang of guilt slithers through me. Lana is going to be alone. My dad works all the time, and she is going to miss me. Cocking my head, I give her a half smile. "Don't you dare make me cry, Lana! You promised."

She nods, but tears leak from her eyes. She snuggles closer to my dad.

I simply stand there. Do I try to hug her with my dad's arm around her?

Moving my Marc Jacobs bag to my other shoulder, I glance at my father. He is genuinely comforting Lana, his large hands caressing her hair while he whispers in her ear. Brushing my blond tresses back off my shoulders, I refuse to admit that his behavior is hurting me.

I clear my throat. "I guess I will see you both when you come visit."

Lana breaks away at last and launches her tall body into mine.

"I can't believe you're leaving me," she whispers.

"I have to."

Her eyes glisten with tears as she nods. "I know."

"Tess, can I speak with you?" My dad's voice interrupts our moment. I almost say no, but I don't want Lana to see that.

"Sure." We break apart.

"I'm going to go to my room. I can't stand goodbyes." Her high heels click on the marble.

He sighs. "You and Lana got close. She is going to miss you."

"What about you?" He freezes, then walks over to his desk, his hand straightening some papers.

"What about me, Tess? I hope that you have finally grown up. That I have instilled in you some common sense."

I can't help but feel tears. That's all he can give me. I look down at my boots. I won't ever allow him to see how his words hurt me.

"Why the transformation?" His question surprises me enough to answer truthfully.

"I needed to change."

"I hate it."

I snort. "I did it for me, not you."

He looks out his window, almost like it pains him to look at me. "Tess..." His fists clench, then unclench. "I know I haven't been the father you wanted and that you blame me for your breakup with Reed."

"Well, you di—"

He holds up his hand. "Let me finish. I may not express myself the way you want. But I did what I believe is best for you. You are my child, like it or not."

My eyes search his. Blue on blue, a flicker of something. A moment paces between us. Then it's gone.

He coughs and straightens himself. "I can't tell you what to do, but I do control your money. So, behave the way I expect, and you will be a very rich woman."

I must look stunned because he pours himself a drink.

"Do you want one?" He holds up his glass.

I open my mouth and close it. *Is he threatening me with my inheritance again?*

"Yes."

He pours the brown liquor into a tumbler and hands it to me. I look down at it, the smoky, spicy aroma making my nose twitch.

"Can I ask you something?"

His eyes narrow. "Sure."

"Why did you bring me here? You and Mom have made it painfully obvious that I'm nothing but a mistake."

The amber liquid that I find so fascinating must do the same to him because he won't look at me. Instead he downs it and pours himself another.

The silence is unbearable. All I want is to get out of his presence and be free. He is never going to be what I need, much like I can't be the daughter he wants. Reed's turquoise eyes appear, his face so beautiful. His wild dark curls fall over his forehead. And he smiles at me with his delicious full lips. Slamming the drink, the bourbon burns and stings down my throat. I need to numb myself. The last thing I need to do is start thinking about Reed more than I do.

"Thanks, Daddy. I'm sure everything you did you did because you love me, right?" Picking up my bag, I start for the door.

"I liked the old you, Tess." I stop but don't turn around.

"You don't have to change to make someone like Reed Saddington love you. Trust me on that." His voice is almost tender.

Shaking my head, I say, "I didn't do this for Reed, Daddy. I did it for me, for a new start." That's a lie, but I'm not telling him that.

"Tess, I watched that boy claim you the day he set eyes on you. I thought it was weird then, and I think his obsession is even weirder now. Stay away from him. Let him have the Russian girl." I stiffen at that last jab.

He runs a hand through his perfect hair. "You can have anyone you want. With your looks, the world is yours. It would be a shame to waste it on an entitled shit." Again, I'm speechless. I have never understood why my father hates Reed so much.

Turning toward him, desperately needing him to answer this, I ask, "Why do you hate him so much? He's a genius, rich, and he loved me."

He looks at his shoes, then straight into my eyes. "I guess I hate him because he just takes. And has no intention of giving back. An eight-year-old boy stole you from me and has never let you go. He made you weak, needy, and I hated him for that. I want so badly to look into those beautiful eyes of yours and see you. Not someone who belongs to Reed Saddington."

I can't let him get away with this. If anyone makes me weak, it's him and my mother. Reed knew me and accepted me. I will always belong to him.

"You're wrong!" Walking straight in front of him, close enough to smell his spicy aftershave, I continue. "Reed is my soul mate! But that doesn't mean that our souls are destined to be together."

He shakes his head and looks up at the ceiling. "Tess... stand on your own two feet. You don't need blond hair and puffy lips to do that." Then he smiles, and I think I gasp. I don't remember the last time I got a real smile from him.

I want to throw myself into his strong arms. I want him to stroke my hair like he does Lana. *I'm so pathetic.* That small smile was all I needed to make my heart swell. *No wonder I have issues!*

Fuck this. He doesn't get to make me feel like shit anymore.

Straightening my shoulders, I speak to him one last time. "Bye, Daddy." I don't look back.

REED

Past – eighteen years old
The Hamptons

I sit by the pool in the Hamptons on one of those days where you hear the seagulls and smell the salt in the air. It's Lexi's family's summer home. She decided it would be fun to throw Jax and me a birthday party. *Eighteen,* and I'm bored. Bored with my friends, bored with drinking, and bored with Lexi! I don't know why I let my mom guilt me into trying a relationship with her. I knew she was a stalker. A complete head case. I should have acted like a man instead of an angry child. And now, everyone thinks we're together—including her.

Raising my face to the warm sun, I dangle my legs in the saltwater pool and try to figure out what I want. How should I pull myself out of this funk? My eyes pop open and I rub my hands over my face, begging my brain not to conjure her up.

I shouldn't be like this. I'm still obsessed. I need her probably more today than I needed her a year ago. Laughter and squealing bring me back to the present.

"Hey, Reed?" Andrew throws a volleyball at me. It misses, but he manages to get me wet.

"Where's Lexi? We're almost out of ice."

"How the hell do I know where she is?" I snap. "Try the house."

"Dude, do us all a favor and have a shot."

I want to yell that I'm unhappy. That I hate Lexi. That if I was free of her, I would be better, but I'm not sure that's true. There is only one person who can make me better, and she is ten hours away. Whatever. I am over being Lexi's boyfriend. Standing up, I stretch. Everyone looks like they are having fun. Maybe Andrew's right and some alcohol will do the trick.

"Baby?" Gritting my teeth, I find my patience is at an all-time low today. I can't stand her calling me that. It must be pretty obvious because she puts her hands on her hips.

"Can you at least pretend to be happy? It's your birthday!" Turning toward Lexi, I take in her appearance. She's wearing the smallest string bikini I've ever seen. Thankfully she doesn't have much of a chest because the bikini is nothing but a lot of straps that cross all around her. Staring at the straps I know she wore this bikini to give me the hint: she wants me to tie her up.

I have to get rid of her.

All her submissive shit was interesting for about a week. I got excited at the thought of completely controlling someone. Unfortunately, having someone need you to pick out her clothes, decide what she eats, and when she goes to bed gets old fast. Maybe I should have my mom's therapist talk to her. What she needs me to do is nowhere near healthy. I dominate her, and she gets off on it. I don't even fuck her.

That's how low I've sunk. I'm probably depressed. Lexi's flowery perfume makes me take a step back almost gagging.

"Andrew says the bar needs more ice." My nose twitches.

"Then have the help do it. Why are you telling me? And are you hiding from me?"

Sighing, I run a hand through my hair. "Lexi, I have a headache."

"Poor baby." Her skinny, oiled-up arms snake around my neck. "Why didn't you say so? Do you need me to massage your neck?" Her sharp nails dig into my skin as she tries to rub me.

"Thanks, I'm fine. Just tired." I remove her hands from me. Great, now I smell like her! I have to end this today.

I know my mom is going to be disappointed. Both she and my dad will think I'm going back to prostitutes. But Lexi's darkness is starting to rub off on me, making me even more miserable.

"Lexi!" Andrew yells. "Get your sweet ass in the pool. Tell your dickhead boyfriend to get us some ice."

"Get it yourself," I snarl.

He heaves himself out of the pool laughing, shaking his head like a dog, spraying us with wet drops. Lexi squeals and hides behind my back. Andrew charges at me, humming the *Jaws* tune. I push him back in the pool and watch him flail around, begging Lexi to save him. I almost push her in to get away from her.

Yesterday, I got the keys to my penthouse. I thought that would make me feel excited... something!

But I bought it with the hope that one day *she* would return.

Aggravated by my thoughts, I must have some secret need to torture myself. The entire place is built for her. The master bath alone was worth the millions I spent on it.

I'm even grateful my dad made the phone calls to get me into Columbia. Lexi is going to Yale. The bigger distance apart can only be beneficial.

I rub the back of my neck. It's hot and humid. I've been sitting by the pool for hours, the sun baking my skin. My head is pounding. Disgusted with myself, I look around. Where the hell is my twin?

It's our birthday. I hate half the people here. The least Jax could do is rescue me. Jamaican music is playing loudly. I need to snap out of this. I have everything going for me, so why do I want to throw myself in the ocean and swim away from it all?

"Baby? I have a surprise for you." I jump, lost in my thoughts. Family friend or not, I need to put an end to this farce of a relationship.

She grabs my hand, her downcast eyes signaling she's going submissive. I'm too tired to question what the fuck is wrong with her. Or even where she's taking me. Truthfully, I don't care. Maybe we'll be alone, and I can break up with her. My pulse quickens at the thought.

Lexi pushes my chest into one of the numerous bathrooms and locks the door. I take in the pale blue walls, only because seashells are everywhere. On the walls. The soap. Even the rug is shaped like one.

"Lexi, I told you I have a headache." *Christ,* I sound like a girl.

"Shh." She pokes my lip with her long pointy nail.

"Ow... what the hell?"

"Look, Reed." She peels down her bikini bottoms and turns around.

My eyes drop to her ass as she puts both hands on the sink and leans forward—giving me a complete view of a glittery gold butt plug.

"I thought you might enjoy this tonight, or right now if you want." My cock does a small jerk. *Thank God!* She's gone to a lot of trouble. If I didn't feel anything, I would worry about myself.

"Lexi." Suddenly I feel sorry for her and reach down to pull her bottoms up.

"Come on, Reed, fuck me!" Her voice is shrill, desperate, as if she knows I'm going to break up with her.

Taking a step back, I hold up my hands. "You don't want me to do that."

"Yes... Yes, I do." She sounds breathless.

"I don't have a condom." Again lame, but whatever.

"I'm on the pill, or you could... you know" She shakes her ass.

"No, Lexi." Her neediness is like a bucket of cold water being thrown on me. My cock subsides. I'm on edge today. Fucking would help. But whatever dark shit is festering inside her, I don't want it inside me. That's why I have to cut her loose.

"Listen, Lexi..." As I rub my forehead, it's now full-on pounding, like someone is hitting me with a bat on each temple.

"Reed?" she interrupts. "I... thought you would like this. I was hoping to please you. That we would actually... you know, have sex finally."

Christ, I'm an asshole. I don't want to hurt her, and she looks hurt. Lexi's been a constant presence since *she* left.

"It's the sun, Lexi." I make the same stupid excuse.

"Should I get you some Advil? What can I do to make you happy, Reed?"

Be Tess! It almost slips out. Fear worms its way into my brain. What if I'm like this forever?

"Advil would be nice." I don't trust myself to say more.

"Be right back." She gently shuts the door behind her.

I can't lock the door fast enough. Looking at my reflection, I hate the guy staring back at me. Not because I look like shit. Just the opposite—my looks have always caused people to comment about how handsome I am. But all I cared about was whether Tess liked the way I looked. I have a trust fund that's in the millions. But the person I thought I was going to be and the person I have become are two very different men. And this shit with Lexi is not helping me. Closing my eyes, I wonder, When was the last time I was happy? Visions of puffy lips and sapphire eyes swirl in my mind. My eyes snap open. I'm pissed at myself. Pissed at her. She is the cause of all my anger. Staring at my tattoo, I snort in disgust. I should get it removed. Even so, my hand reaches to rub it, needing it.

Finally, I grow some balls and leave the bathroom. Someone has changed the music from Jamaican to techno. Taking a breath, I wander through the large house, trying to find Jax.

Spying Andrew in the living room, he's in the corner with two girls I recognize from the pool. All three are snorting coke.

"Andrew, you see Jax?" The air conditioner hums on. Cool air blows down on me, making me grateful for modern technology.

Andrew finishes snorting, then gives me a peculiar look.

"What?" I can't say my tone is pleasant, and the girls look at me nervously. He snorts and wipes his nose.

"Um... Yeah, I think I saw him over by the tiki bar talking to a blonde."

"Cool..." He's giving me a weird vibe and I frown. "What man? Is something wrong?"

"Um... I'm not sure." Andrew looks uncomfortable, like he wants to say something, but he can't."

"What the fuck, Drew? Spit it out."

He shrugs and rolls his neck. "I'll go with you."

Holding up my hand, I stop him, my sarcasm thick. "I think I can make it alone. I'm a grown-up now."

"Still, you might need me."

"Drew, my head is killing me."

"Yeah, it might really start hurting... once you see Jax."

My eyes narrow on him, then roll. He's on coke, I remind myself.

It's been over a month since I have done anything besides drink. But with my head throbbing, coke sounds like the perfect thing to help.

"Fuck it, give me some of your blow." I motion with my hand for his vial.

He cocks his head. "You told me to say no if you ask, remember?" We stare at each other. Andrew sighs, unbuttoning his obnoxious Hawaiian shirt pocket. "Fine, I'm only giving you this because you might truly need it."

He tosses the brown vial at me.

I catch it. "Maybe I should hold on to the this. You're acting paranoid."

"Fuck off, Saddington."

I don't even bother to hide and turn around and snort some into each nostril. With the rush, my head is instantly better. In fact, I haven't felt this good in months.

"Jesus... that helps. Thanks, brother"

Suddenly, I'm okay. Better than okay, I'm fucking great. I find myself laughing with Andrew as I see Jax's dark head. We've been distant lately. I know he doesn't understand the whole Lexi thing. Also, he's been gone a lot. I've been meaning to ask if he's seeing someone. I guess my question is answered. He's standing with his arm around a blonde with long killer legs. I have to hold myself back from throwing my brother's arm off her shoulder. Taking a steadying breath, I'm surprised at my aggression.

Jax doesn't notice me. He seems to be enthralled by the blonde. His smile is filled with genuine affection. Which stops me like a knife has pierced me. Shaking my head, I give myself a mental lecture about wanting my brother to be happy even if I'm miserable.

The blonde moves but not much. Just a slender arm, a toss of her long blond hair, and I freeze. I wonder for a moment if I snorted bad coke. Because that girl moves like the one person I can't escape. The one person who has haunted me for twenty-four hours a day for three years.

"*TESS!*"

chapter 22

TESS

Jax is forcing me to come to his birthday party. I'm not hiding, but I'm not sure I want to see Reed yet. Brance and I have been in New York for almost a month. Even though I still love to hate New York, I'm happy to be here. The city I used to dread welcomed me back like an old friend. The yellow cabs and rude people only make me smile. I almost hugged a girl in Starbucks when she cursed me out for taking the last croissant. The weather is hot and sticky. The smell of garbage is worse than I remember, and I saw a rat in a bar that Jax and I were watching football in. Yet I'm happy.

Brance and I do yoga in the morning at a little studio down the street. We're a family—that includes Jax.

I called him as soon as we landed. He has been practically living with us. I even convinced him to take a beginner's yoga class.

I love that I walk down the crowded sidewalks and women do double takes. With Brance's model face, and Jax being a full-on hottie, I'm like a celebrity.

I'm not joking. Jax looks like a tall dark god with turquoise eyes.

Sighing, I'm forced to come back to reality, which sucks because Brance has conveniently gotten the flu. He doesn't feel good enough for the drive to the Hamptons and Jax and Reed's party.

Traitor!

He truly is sick though. I feel a little guilty about leaving him, but he assures me he's fine and that I must seek and conquer my revenge, whatever that means. I guess he wants Reed to combust when he sees me.

We decide on a red bikini with cute bows on each side and one in between my breasts. Plus a black cotton tube dress and black high-heeled Prada sandals.

I'm wearing my blond hair down and blown out straight. Although with the humidity, it will curl. And, of course, some light makeup. All right, full makeup—after all, I need to look amazing. I twirl in front of Brance and Jax, and they both simply stare. Brance smirks in his silk robe and slippers. Jax looks like he might have forgotten that he calls me sis.

I laugh. "That good?"

"Oh, Pretty Girl… that good and then some!"

Winking at him, I throw Brance a kiss, which he dramatically grabs and brings to his heart.

"Now, please don't forget the Advil and vitamin C packs. And if the fever comes back, call me," I say, picking up my black Audrey Hepburn Chanel sunglasses and bag.

"Shall we go, birthday boy?"

"Um… yeah if my feet can move. Please tell me you are wearing a one piece under that dress?" he hisses, guiding me through the concrete parking garage.

I wave at Carlos, who whistles after me and giggle as Jax shoots him a warning glare. Even though Jax is probably a good five inches taller, Brance's bodyguard's nickname is *Asesino*. Translation: killer.

"Don't be absurd." I smirk, waiting as he opens the door to his new black Ferrari. Apparently, Reed got a matching blue one.

"You're spoiled!" I shake my head.

"What? Don't all boys get Ferraris for their birthdays?" He grins, and his dimples appear. For a moment, I can't move. My hand clutches the black leather steering wheel. It's like he gut punched me.

Tess? You okay?" He eyes me.

Taking a breath, I let go of the steering wheel. "God, sorry, I just... sometimes you look so much like Reed." He gives me a sympathetic smile and winks.

I roll my eyes. "Never mind."

He laughs. "Come on, Tess, it's my birthday! I'm finally eighteen. We are definitely going to have fun."

"About that... are you sure I should come today? I want you to have a great birthday. And something tells me Reed is not going to be as happy to see me as you were."

He raises an eyebrow as he starts the car, then smirks, his eyes alive with mischief. The Ferrari purrs.

"You hear that?" He presses on the gas. The car sounds as if it's alive. As it roars with each acceleration, I shiver with anticipation.

"You cold?" He taps the air conditioner button.

"No, I'm fine, just nervous."

"Look, Tess, Reed is going to freak! He made his bed and he'll have to lie in it. Besides, you've been hiding long enough. My mom and dad are going to be there, and they are dying to see you."

Needing to change the subject, I say, "So... Harvard? Premed—impressive. I mean, technically you don't have to work."

"Yeah, I do. Since Reed lost his mind, thanks to you. My dad and Grandfather Ian are giving him the business."

"You're not serious."

"Very."

"Wow." I'm stunned. Reed is going to take over the Saddington empire?

"And stop saying I made him go crazy. *He* broke up with me. I can't even begin to explain the pain I have been through." Snapping at him, I try to watch the road. But Jax is gunning it, and the scenery is all a blur.

"Whatever, Tess. All I know is that I had a happy brother. Then I didn't."

A small smile escapes my lips. Unfortunately, Jax catches it.

He shakes his head. "You're happy he's in pain. That he's made all sorts of fucked-up decisions because of you. You know you broke him, right?"

I think for a moment. Am I happy Reed is miserable?

Yes. Yes, I am.

"You two truly are perfect for each other." He chuckles, tapping his fingers on the steering wheel. "Well, close your eyes and rest up, Tess. I have a feeling you're going to need it."

Reaching for one of his strong hands, I tell him, "I'm not scared anymore, Jax. I know I can make it."

He snorts. "You're as screwed up as he is, only you're hiding it better."

Glaring at him, I snatch my hand back. "You know what, Jax? I have worked hard to get myself together! I exercise and... well, I exercise and that helps."

A huge grin appears. "Calm down. I didn't mean to fire you up." He smirks. "Poor Reed."

Not being able to help myself, I blurt out, "Is he honestly with Lexi?"

"I don't know what he's doing."

"Bullshit, Jax. You always know. Are they together?" I don't know why I'm pressing this, knowing I'm going to hate the answer.

"He hasn't told me anything lately. I do know that our parents have been pressuring him to at least try."

Crossing my arms, I'm hurt. Caroline and Brad were more like my parents than my mom and dad. "I can't believe Brad and Caroline would like her!"

He looks at me sheepishly. "They want him to stop sleeping with hookers. And not do blow or ecstasy. If she can keep him away from those distractions, then they're happy."

"So, you guys started having sex with prostitutes as soon as he dumped me?" I can't help the stinging accusation in my tone.

"*You* dumped him, Tess. He waited for you for almost two years, and you never came back! So, yes after seeing my brother unhappy for two years, I absolutely wanted him to get laid and move on."

I can't look at him, so I look at my nails.

Jax reaches for my hand again. "He needed to try to forget you. Unfortunately, it backfired."

Looking over at him, I ask, "What does that mean?"

He sighs. "It's only that... he's different now."

"Because he's into sleeping with high-priced whores?"

"Take it easy."

"Jax, he was the love of my life. He swore to me every day that I was his one and only! And now you say he's 'different.' He does drugs and sleeps with anything that walks. I'd say he's a little different."

Jax turns up the air conditioner. "Think about how experienced he is now." He waggles his eyebrows.

"I don't find that funny." I frown at him.

"You're right. It's not funny. I'm sorry. It was a dark time for us. We both got caught up in that lifestyle."

My imagination is starting to run away. Reed kissing older, beautiful women. His strong tan hands touching them. Making them cry out with pleasure. My face burns with humiliation and something else. "Have you guys been tested?"

He smiles and pats my knee. "Yes, Mom, we've been tested."

"Stop it. This isn't anything to make light of. Just the other day I was reading an article about Super G." Looking out the window, I'm hurt that Jax seems to be on Reed's side.

"Super G? What are you talking about?"

"It's a new strain of gonorrhea that antibiotics don't work on. You suffer until you die or your dick falls off." I made that last part up, but it's still scary.

"Well, rest assured, Tess. The women we paid for were not street hookers." He keeps his eyes on the road. "They charge thousands of dollars for their pussies. And they get tested constantly. We got tested too. You have to with these women. And to reassure you even more that we don't have Super G, Reed and I always use condoms."

"I don't want to hear any more." I hold up my hand. "I... I never thought we would be talking about this." It's impossible to stop the sting of pain and tears. "Can you turn on some music, please?"

"It's okay to be angry. But if it makes you feel better, he's still in love with you. Still obsessed. Are you ready for that? Because as soon as he sees you, he is going to claim you and this time, you're both adults."

I can't acknowledge that his words have made my belly flutter and my heart beat faster. Shrugging I say, "It doesn't matter anymore. He lied to me, and he committed the ultimate betrayal by sleeping with Lexi. She is worse than any prostitute."

"We don't know if he's fucking her."

I roll my eyes at him. "I would never take him back."

"Right." The smirk returns to his face.

"Are you kidding me? Even if I could forgive him for sleeping with half of Manhattan, I can't ever forgive him for Lexi!"

"Well, that's a bit dramatic considering you two are not even together."

Leaning my head back, I absently think this might be the most comfortable seat ever. I stare up at the top of the Ferrari. "Let's not talk. It makes me want to kick you."

He bursts out laughing, and I have to turn my head. It hurts how much they look alike.

We sit in silence for a moment, and I feel Jax's warm hand on my leg. Looking over at him, he is still grinning. I have to fight myself not to smile back.

"How long you going to make Reed grovel before you gift him with your golden cherry?"

"Jax!" I fling his hand off my leg. "I have no idea what you are talking about," I snip.

He's full-on laughing now. "Come on, Tess. This is *me* you're talking to."

Glaring at him, I say, "You're going to get a ticket. I'm pretty sure the speed limit isn't one hundred and three miles per hour."

"Shit." He lets up on the accelerator and the car purrs as she slows down.

Now that everything is not flashing by, I'm able to admire the view outside my window. The green trees and tall grass sway with the breeze. It's like seeing an old friend again. If we weren't going to Lexi's family's home, I would be excited. There is something magical about the water and the Hamptons in general.

"Don't try to change the subject."

When I look over at him, his eyes are full of mischief. He is obviously not going to give up until I give him something. "What makes you think I haven't already given up my cherry?" I ask, trying to sound confident.

"*Golden* cherry, Tess. Don't sell yourself short."

I shake my head at him. "You're absurd,.." Looking out the window again, I stay that way before he can see my smile.

"It's in your eyes, Tess."

"Whatever, Jax." I bite my lip.

"Also, I know you. You would never give your virginity to anyone but Reed. He'll be all your firsts. The good and the tragic."

My eyes snap to his. What a telling thing to say. Is that what Reed and I are? Good and tragic? I reach to turn the radio on. U2's "With or Without You" fills the silence. Turning away from Jax, I mumble, "Wake me up when we get there."

chapter 23

TESS

The party is a hit. I mean, it's crowded and loud. Lots of girls in bikinis and boys without shirts. And alcohol, lots of it. There's even a DJ over by the drink cabana pumping out his own kind of dance-rap mix.

Smiling as I take in the crowd, I scan the area for the familiar dark curls. I'm even drinking beer, which I despise, but I'm choking it down because I'm with Jax and it's his birthday. And if I'm honest, I'm having fun. Maybe all my worrying is for naught. I mean with the size of this place, there's a good chance I will never even see Reed.

"Oh my God! Tess? Is that you?" Glancing over Jax's shoulder, I notice Tiffany as she stumbles toward us. Clearly, she's intoxicated and not very graceful. Grabbing ahold of Jax's shoulder to stabilize herself, she laughs as if not being able to walk is hilarious.

I groan into my plastic cup and take a quick sip of warm beer.

"Tiffany! How great to see you," I gush, then want to gag. Maybe it's the stale beer or I'm making myself sick at my phoniness. Her eyes sweep me from top to bottom. Unfortunately,

213

it seems Tiffany has not found a new muse. Her brown hair is still cut exactly like mine three years ago. Her hand stays on Jax's shoulder as if she needs him to stand.

"Wow, you're a blonde." Her voice is wistful. "I was thinking about going blond too."

"Jesus Christ." Jax pulls her hand off him. "Pull it together, Tiffany."

She frowns, then gets distracted by a drone someone is flying. It hovers right in front of us buzzing away in our faces.

"Hey," she screams. "It's my turn to fly that thing." She marches toward the guy, who turns and runs, taking the drone with him.

Jax wraps an arm around me. "See, same old shit. You do know Tiffany will be blond tomorrow."

I laugh. "Only if she can remember today."

"That reminds me—I need to remember today." He pulls out his phone and positions us for a selfie. We make stupid faces. I turn and take the phone to check the picture. I'm still surprised when I see myself. Clearly the blond hair still hasn't sunk in.

With a shake of my head, I say, "I used to pour over Instagram and Facebook, wishing I was at one of these parties. I was a complete stalker you know." When I look up at him, the sun is in my eyes, so all I see are dark dots, but I feel him tap my nose.

"If you weren't stalking us, I would have been worried." He takes back his phone.

"*Tess*?"

My heart starts beating so hard and fast I'm sure *He* can hear it. A wave of pure adrenaline and terror snakes up my spine. *Why?* Why did I think I could face him? I can't turn around. *Shit, shit, shit.* I look around for an escape. God, why do I do this to myself? Suddenly, I hate Brance for not being here.

The smell of chlorine reminds me—I could jump into the pool. It's right there. I could swim away from him, show him I'm done and free of him. It's tempting, but instead I reach for Jax. Maybe I'm hearing things. After all, I have blond hair and my back is to him.

"What the fuck is going on, Jax?" he snarls.

Nope, not hearing things. My hands are shaking, and I'd give anything for some water. My tongue feels like it's stuck to the roof of my mouth.

"I know it's you, Tess. You might as well turn around." His voice is deep and strong.

Taking a breath, I look at Jax's handsome face, his turquoise eyes, full of challenge.

This is ridiculous. I'm not that girl who lets Reed control me. I'm completely different. Flipping my hair, I turn and face him.

Jesus! He can't be standing in front of me with no shirt, his tan six-pack teasing me. He looks so good, I almost stomp my foot. He's supposed to look like a skinny drug addict drowning in despair and nothingness! I feast on his face. He has the five-o'clock shadow thing going on, and his incredible eyes are latched on to mine. And. I. Literally. Can't. Breathe.

He doesn't seem to be breathing either and I feel slightly better. He's taller and way more muscular. Obviously, he is still working out. His dark hair is, as always, longer than Jax's. I can't help but be happy to see he still has his curls. So cute! My heart flutters in my chest. I chastise myself for staring. So, he's hot. That's nothing new. That doesn't excuse his deserting me. Breaking me, tearing my heart out, so that I had to fight and claw my way back.

"Stay away from me, Reed." I haven't uttered his name out loud in so long, the pain of speaking it slices through me.

He's bad for me and he hasn't stopped staring. His eyes caress my face, hair, body as if he wants to memorize it over and over again. He moves closer and I step back into Jax's strong chest.

"Jax can't save you, Kitten."

Anger awakens me. "Don't call me that! Don't ever call me that." I'm almost screaming. He's like a beautiful predator stalking me.

"I don't need Jax to save me." I look into those pretty eyes. "You should probably go find your girlfriend." The need to punish him is still alive and breathing inside me.

If it wouldn't be weird, I would kiss Jax. But it would, so I do the next best thing. I pull my dress up slowly over my hips. Suddenly the DJ and his loud music are gone. Jax and the group of friends vanish. I only hear his breathing. I only watch his eyes. His stiff muscles flex as he clenches his hands. His jaw ticks. He looks at me like I'm his kryptonite. I want him to look at me this way. I hope it hurts him, fucking tortures him. It's spilling out of me, like a volcano exploding her ash.

His eyes darken, lingering on my breasts. As I whip the dress off, I smirk. Yes, I look good. Brance picked this red bikini so I could get this very reaction from Reed.

Jax leans into my ear, breaking the spell. "Tess, you should probably put the dress back on."

Slowly I turn from Reed, knowing everybody is staring. "That would be silly. After all, we're at a pool party," I say, dropping my dress next to my bag.

Reed reaches down and grabs it. "Put it on, Tess," he commands.

Rolling my eyes, I smile at the guy behind him. "Hey, Andrew."

"Tess, damn..." He shakes his head, his eyes staring at my breasts. "Sorry, I didn't recognize you at first. I mean, I thought it was you, but with the hair and all." His eyes go up and down the length of my body. He moves to hug me.

Reed grabs his arm. "Touch her and you lose a limb."

"Dude, relax! I was only trying to welcome her back." He holds up his hands, backing away.

Before I can comprehend what's happening, Reed has me, pulling me toward the house.

"Reed! Fuck..." Jax moves to stop him.

"*What?*" he yells, getting in his face. "You knew she was back, and you said nothing?"

Jax winces. "Everyone is watching, man. Think of Lexi."

He snorts. "Right! Lexi. Like you give a shit about Lexi! Back off, Jax. I'm warning you." His voice is tinged with desperation.

"Reed, let go of me this instant." I try to jerk away. "You have got some nerve." Looking around at the curious faces, staring at us, I thank God for the loud music. All Reed does is pull me closer.

"Jesus, Reed! It's our birthdays! You're making a scene." Jax is speaking so low only the three of us can hear.

"I don't care what any of these people think," he snarls, waving his arm.

"I want answers, and I'm going to get them." He starts to drag me again, getting sand in my high-heeled platforms.

"Jesus Christ, you can be a dick sometimes," Jax mumbles. "Watch yourself."

Reed stops. "What did you say?" His body is ready to attack. "Jax, you're my brother. And I love you, but don't *ever* think you can tell me what to do especially with Tess!"

Sucking in a breath, I jump when Reed's fingers singe my arm. Butterflies explode inside my stomach.

"Reed," I plead. But I sound excited rather than pissed off. Why is he my weak spot?

"Just remember, she's not yours anymore."

"What the hell, Jax?"

Both are so beautiful, powerful. Jax breaks the stare turning to me. "I'll be over by the pool if you need me."

I nod, then exhale. The last thing I need to do is pass out.

"She won't," Reed spits out, pulling me toward the house.

I wiggle, but it's stupid. Reed's fingers are locked onto me like a pit bull with a new bone.

Jax is right. He's changed. He's not the same boy I knew. And, I'm not talking about his five-o'clock shadow and body that have matured. It's in his eyes. His whole vibe is different, harder, distant.

I want so badly for it to repulse me. Instead, I might as well be panting. Looking up at the mansion, I have to bite my tongue not to comment on what a fabulous place it is.

White pillars stand proud circling the house. Brick covers the side part of the mansion. It also showcases three brick chimneys. There's a large balcony off the master suite. Chairs and a table face the water and sandy beach. If I owned this house, I would have breakfast out here every day, drinking coffee as I watch the sunrise and the waves roll in.

I stumble and realize that Reed is almost dragging me. "Stop it, Reed," I say, slightly out of breath. "I'm in heels. Who the hell do you think you are?"

He grunts, looking down at me, then back at my eyes. And it seems like we've gone back in time, where a tall, dark-haired boy laughed at a sad little girl's gold shoes. Closing my eyes, I block out the painful memories—so many memories threatening to make me weak. Reed must feel the same because he's frowning and has slowed down. His grip on my arm has softened though. At least I can walk up the brick stairs. The numerous French doors are open allowing a nice breeze in.

"Tess?" My skin pebbles as Lexi emerges from inside.

"Perfect." I'm somewhat taken aback at her bikini. She's so skinny, I think she might give my mom a run for her money. And flat as a board. I know I'm being catty but what the hell? She looks like a long, skinny lizard. Even her tongue darts out to lick her pink lips. *Gross!*

"I had no idea you were back in town. How long are you staying?"

Should I engage? I want to, but that would also mean giving her the upper hand. I may turn to putty with Reed. But girls like Lexi? I don't think so. Channeling my inner bitch, I look her straight in her beady blue eyes.

"I'm back for good."

Reed inhales, his hard body pressing against my back. Ignoring how his mere warmth reminds me how united we always were, I try to put some distance between us and step toward her.

"I hope you don't mind, but Jax insisted I come today."

"Tess." Reed's voice is way too close.

Tossing my hair back, I say, "I wanted to wish you guys the best. I heard that you two are together."

Reed mumbles a curse as I try to twist my arm away.

Lexi smiles, but her eyes dart to Reed's hand. "Yes, we're very happy."

I almost gag. So, I lower myself to her level. Her strong flowery perfume invades my nose. God, how can Reed possibly be with her?

"Tell me, Lexi, it doesn't bother you that he has fucked half of Manhattan?" It's mean and immature, but I never claimed to be perfect.

Reed's grip tightens even more. I'm almost positive I'm going to have a bruise. "Enough, Kitten," he growls in my ear.

Lexi looks like she's been slapped. Either I hit my mark, or Reed calling me Kitten is about to do her in.

Narrowing her eyes, she almost looks like she wants to attack me. My mouth twitches. She's nothing to me. And since Reed has put his dick in her, he's nothing to me. Maybe I truly am getting closure?

Lexi shakes the Advil bottle. The pills jingle like spare change.

"Reed, baby... I got you the ibuprofen you wanted."

Baby! She calls him baby? I would start laughing if this wasn't so traumatizing.

"He has a headache, and I know exactly how to take care of him."

I need to walk away while I'm ahead and never come back. Maybe Brance is right. California might be the best place for us.

Holding my shoulders back, I can practically feel my mouth watering at the thought of telling them both to fuck off.

Instead I smile. "Good luck." I pray I'm getting what Brance has because I'm not feeling so good. More than likely, it's Lexi and her repulsive perfume. That and the visual of Reed's dick inside her.

"Let go, Reed," I hiss. I'm done. And if he doesn't let me go, I may give in to my stomach issue and vomit on them both.

"Love your hair, by the way, Tess," Lexi interrupts my attempt at freeing myself. "We could be twins, right, Reed?"

Please God, no, she is not going there! I look up at the blue sky, praying for divine intervention. I would even take an alien abduction over this.

Lexi pins me with her reptilian eyes.

I can't help it. I back into Reed's chest instinctively needing him. He wraps his other arm around my stomach from behind.

Lexi's eyes narrow on us, and she taps the Advil bottle on her lips. I have to look away, willing myself to focus on the green lawn. Even the couple making out in the middle of it is better than her.

"Is that what you want, Reed?" She points at me. "You must have heard how he likes threesomes," she sneers.

"Jesus, Lexi, what's wrong with you?" Reed snaps into action. Lacing our fingers, he pulls me around the she lizard.

"I just want to please you. Don't tell me you wouldn't love it." I can't see his face, but she can, and she smiles at me.

"Look at her. She will never be able to keep up with you sexually."

Reed turns around to her. "How would you even know what I need sexually?" His voice is cruel.

I can't help but wonder if she is not right. I have no idea who this new Reed is or what his needs are. And suddenly I don't want to know.

"Reed." This time I do manage to free my arm. He goes to reach for me and I back away, hands up. "Don't you dare touch me! I *will* make a scene none of us will live down." Pointing at Lexi, I say, "This is your world. I neither want it nor fit into it. You said we needed to talk. Well, here it is... You are not the same boy I loved. And I need you to stay away from me."

He steps back like I've stabbed him. And maybe I have if the pain in my heart is any indication of how he feels. His hand goes to his tattoo, and tears form in my eyes. I don't know why. I can't stand him. Everything he has become is not something I want.

"Go back to Jax. I need to talk to Lexi." His hand drops. She slithers after him. I should feel victorious. Until I realize that my hand is touching my tattoo.

chapter 24

REED

I can't stop myself from turning around to look at her. Tess is still so fucking beautiful, my chest burns. My eyes follow her incredible ass in that bikini, which I will definitely be throwing away. The vanilla smell that is hers lingers, clinging to my skin. I vaguely hear Lexi talking to me. But I can't look away from Tess. Hating myself even more for letting Tess go, I take a step after her, then stop. I have to get my shit together. The need to go to her, grab her, lock her in my room, and mate is overwhelming.

Tess is back!

And we are old enough so that nobody can dictate our lives. Like a stalker, I watch her cling to my twin. Like a sleeping lion, my anger awakens. I don't care if she lies to herself. She can claim it's over as much as she wants. Her words float in my brain: *You're not the same boy I loved!*

Well, that may be true. But she's changed too. My little kitten has grown some claws. *Mine!* I want to roar.

"Fuck me." I run my hands through my hair.

What the hell was Jax thinking keeping Tess from me? I thought I was going to beat the shit out of him. Jax and I are evenly matched. But I have rage on my side, so that would give me an edge. Tess will be mine until one of us takes our last breath.

I'm all off and wish I'd never snorted that coke. I want to go caveman on Tess. Those fucking eyes of hers, like glittering sapphires. Shaking my head at her ridiculous lips, I smirk. Only Tess can get away with pumping shit into her lips and still looking hot. My cock's getting hard. *Great!* Now, all I can think of is how unbelievable her lips will feel wrapped around my shaft. Shifting uncomfortably, I'm in board shorts, so being this hard with my size is not something you can hide. Turning, I walk into the house, needing to splash water on my face and put on some jeans and a shirt. Maybe I should take a shower.

"What are you doing?" Lexi's voice jolts me back to the present, her skinny body following me.

"Christ." I had forgotten about her.

My obsession with Tess was steamrolling over me. Speed walking into the guest room where I left my stuff, I say, "Listen, Lexi, I'm sorry."

I go to tell her it's over, but she is staring at her feet.

Gritting my teeth, I continue. "I'm going to take a shower and then we'll talk."

She shakes her head. "There is nothing to talk about. I'll wait." She moves toward the door.

Grabbing her arm, I stop her. "Lexi," I say gently because she's not getting it. "I know you saw us going somewhere. But the truth is even had Tess not come back, it never would have worked." I let her digest what I'm saying. I don't owe her any more than that.

"Will you still be my master?" Her voice sounds scared, eyes still downcast. I have to take a breath. Now is not the time to lose my patience.

"Excuse me?"

"It's what you are. We don't have to stop. We haven't been having sex anyway. I will let you dominate me."

Taking a step back, letting go of her arm, I'm stunned. I wonder again if Andrew had bad coke because *What the hell?*

"Lexi, come here." My tone is demanding. I pat for her to sit next to me.

Instead she kneels. Like I'm a fucking king or something. "Look at me."

When she looks up, her eyes are full of tears.

Sighing, I say, "I'm sorry, I'm not what you need or what you want. We are not the same. You want a master. That's not me." My thoughts stray to Tess. Did she put her dress back on? Is Jax making sure no one talks to her?

"Why?" Lexi's thin shoulders shake.

"Hey... come on, Lex." I almost lift her onto my lap. I want to comfort her. But how do I do that without giving her false hope?

"I'm not what you need, Lexi, and you know it."

"You're wrong." Her eyes light up. "You could be great. I knew it from the moment I laid eyes on you."

Shaking my head, I push on. "I'm trying hard not to make this unpleasant. We were friends before. Let's go back to that." I'm done talking, so I stand.

"Do you honestly think she is going to forgive and forget, Reed?" she spits.

"She will," I say, grabbing my Fairtex boxing bag that has my clean clothes in it.

"I'll wait for you, Reed." Her voice cracks.

That stops me. "Why? Why would you even want that?" I have to bite my tongue not to tell her to get therapy.

"Lexi." I use my commanding voice since that seems to be the only way she listens. "I'm never letting her go. I never have."

Suddenly I realize it's true. I've been waiting for her, never letting her go in my heart. And now she's back with blond hair and puffy lips. With a fire in her that I know will feed my addiction.

Lexi looks at me. "She's going to hurt you, Reed. Break you because she can. When that happens, when she does something you can't forgive, you will need to get control back and I will be there for you. You are my master. Whether it's now or ten years from now." Her voice is eerily calm.

I'm done with her crazy shit. "Lexi, go find someone who is like you and be happy. It's not me. Now, I'm going to take a shower." Gently I push her out, locking the door.

I'm smiling. It's done. And Tess is back. I need her to forgive me. The enormous void that has been present is gone. I want to breathe her light, her sweetness, her innocence. I have to convince her to trust me again. I promised all her firsts would be my firsts. I've ruined that one. But I'll never stray again. She is my lifeline. My soul.

Stripping off my board shorts, entering the shower, I let the hot water cascade over my tight muscles. My mind replays the day. As I hang my head, the water massages my neck and back. And her beautiful face comes to me. This time I don't fight it and lean my head back, and there she is, lips parted, her naked body slick with water. Groaning, I reach for the soap. My hand fists my thick cock, stroking it up and down. Closing my eyes, I kiss Tess. She tastes like she always does. Sweet like candy. I suck on her fleshy bottom lips, and then my tongue fills her mouth. I hear her sigh and moan. My hand quickens, my breathing harsh.

As I stroke myself, her face shows she is ready to come. She tells me she loves me. Forgives me for not sharing our first time.

My eyes snap open, "*Shit!*" I'm so close, I jerk myself harder, trying to block out that I desperately want to be her first. I want it so badly. The damage is done, and my vision of Tess is gone. Closing my eyes, pumping myself roughly, all I see is her beautiful face, laughing with someone else. Her long legs wrapped around another guy. Her swollen lips sucking another's dick. Tess's head thrown back as she comes.

"Fuck." I hit the tile, feeling the burn in my hand. When I bring my fist up, it's puffy and red. The pain reminds me of the last three years. Tilting my head back, I grab my throbbing cock with my sore hand and jerk it hard until my balls tighten. The searing pain causes me to explode; thick ropes of semen shoot out. I lean my forehead on the cool tile and let the water soothe me and calm my breathing. Turning off the water, I open the large glass doors and step out.

That will go down as the worst masturbation session in history. I'm angry again. *How am I going to get her back?*

Lexi's right. How am I going to get her to forgive and forget about the other women? And if she is not a virgin, which is a strong possibility, how do I forgive her? Fucking someone else. Giving a stranger *my first*!

Yeah, that hurts!

I reach for my heart and massage my tattoo. Grabbing a fluffy towel, I do a quick dry off and toss it in the corner. I throw on my clothes, not wanting to waste another second without her. Even if she hates me, I will win her back. I'm done waiting.

Once I've packed all my shit in my bag, I head out.

Looking over, I see Lexi's door open. I stop and stick my head in to tell her I'm out.

"Lexi, I'm leaving." Yet what I see makes me drop my bag.

She's on the floor, her back to me, her skinny body slightly convulsing. I grab my phone and dial 911.

"*SHIT!*"

Turning her over, I notice her lips are blueish. "Come on, Lexi. What the *fuck*!"

I slap her, and she responds slightly, yellow liquid dripping from her mouth and onto her white carpet.

I tell the operator the address and pick her up and bring her downstairs. Dimitri and Anna are dancing. In his loud voice, he sings in Russian. A few of our classmates are drinking shots of his favorite Russian vodka. Cans of Beluga caviar are strewn across the table, sitting open. "My God, Lexi!" Anna screams, breaking away from a stunned Dimitri.

"What happened to my baby?" She is clinging to her, almost bringing us both to our knees.

"Anna, it's okay. The ambulance is on the way."

If she understands, she doesn't let on. Her wailing is alarming. As I look around the large room, faces crowd in, everyone whispering or crying. Some even have their phones out.

I make my way to the large couch by the window and gently lay Lexi down on her side. Fluid comes out of her mouth again. People scream in disgust.

I hear my dad's voice behind me. "That's it, son. Keep her on her side. We don't want her to choke. Is she breathing?" His calm voice is soothing; it wraps around me like a security blanket. "What happened?"

A siren pierces the air. My body almost collapses in relief at the welcome sound of the ambulance arriving.

"I have no idea. Maybe she took something."

Dimitri is wild, his anger and grief causing him to trash his living room. He's throwing glasses at the pale blue walls. Liquid trickles down them like rain. The table with the vodka and caviar has been thrown on its side. I feel like I'm in a dream. Everything is somewhat slowed down.

I look over at the open doorway. Jax is talking to one of the paramedics. Somehow, hands are pulling me back. Someone gives her an injection and her eyes open.

I glance over at Anna and Dimitri. They are kneeling and praying. At least I assume they are praying since I don't speak Russian. Suddenly a gurney lifts Lexi and they rush her inside the ambulance. Poor Dimitri and Anna trail behind trying to talk to the paramedics.

Guests with stunned faces are talking to me. I only need one though, and I don't see her. My mom wraps her arm around me. "Reed? Sweetheart, I'm so sorry. Are you all right?"

I look down at her worried face and nod.

Dimitri and Anna get into the ambulance, and sirens blast from the driveway.

"Jesus, I have no idea what she was thinking." I stare at my parents.

"I'm sure she will be fine. Come on, son, we should follow and meet them at the hospital."

I look at Jax. "Tess?"

"She went home about an hour ago."

"Good, let's go."

"Is there a Reed Saddington here?" I open my eyes. Trying to focus on sitting up, I look around. All of my family is sitting or sleeping in the uncomfortable chairs. We are in the waiting room at the nearest hospital.

Clearing my voice, I answer, "That's me," and I stand, towering over the shorter man. He smiles and introduces himself as Lexi's doctor.

"Is she okay?" I ask.

"Yes, thanks to you. She said you saved her."

I look around the waiting area. A little couple probably in their eighties sit in the corner, holding each other's hands.

"I happened to be there at the right time. What's wrong with her?"

"She OD'd on cocaine, which caused a seizure. If you hadn't found her and called 911, she probably wouldn't be with us." I let out a puff of air.

"I wanted to let you know that she is stable, and we will be releasing her in the morning." He smiles, his brown eyes tired but kind.

He turns to my parents. "You must be very proud of your son. I only wish my daughter's boyfriend was like him," he says, patting my dad on the back.

"Reed, if you want to see her, you can. Visiting hours are almost over, so you should make it quick."

He nods at all of us and goes to the nurses' station.

I slink down in the slippery hospital chair. My parents along with Jax sit next to me. I'm tired and hungry.

"You want some coffee? Before you go see her?" my dad asks.

"I'm not seeing her." My parents look at me and frown.

"Reed, I think you should at least stop by."

"No." I stand up.

"Son, I know this is awkward, but she's your girlfriend."

"No, she's not. She never really was, Dad." Tired, I rub my hands across my face.

"Truth is, I had just broken up with her. That's why I was at her room to say goodbye. I'm not the good guy." Leaning back, I close my weary eyes.

"For all I know, she planned it."

"That's a little harsh, Reed," my dad says with a sigh. "Since we are all here, let's talk."

I snort. "You're kidding, right?"

"Reed, even if this was a cry for help, attention... whatever, she's still a human being. And you were spending time with her."

"Dad, I'm tired. I don't want to talk about my personal life."

"Okay, I can respect that, but if you broke up with her because of Tess..."

"Did you know she was back?" I look at my parents. My mom nods yes.

"So... my whole family knew that Tess was back. And not one of you thought I should know?"

"Honey, we didn't want you to be upset. You know how you are with her—look at what happened today."

Suddenly exhausted, I stare at my mother. "Mom, Tess had nothing to do with Lexi being a nut job!"

"Shh, lower your voice. Someone could hear you. I'm not saying *that*. It's only I wanted you to be happy. And if I had told you Tess was back..." Her voice trails off.

"We were waiting for her to contact us before we said anything." My dad takes my mom's hand.

"What?" Looking at all three of their guilty faces. "You seriously thought Tess would not come back to me?"

Jax sighs. "Reed, it was more than—"

"Shut up, Jax." I stand up. "I'm tired. I need some sleep."

My mom looks as if she's going to cry.

Taking a breath, I try to get ahold of my anger. "Don't worry. I'm not a complete ass. I'll stop by and check on Lexi later. Hopefully she will get some help."

"I didn't know she was that bad. Should I talk to Dimitri?" My dad looks genuinely surprised.

"I think, when this happens, they *make* you get help. But yeah, she could use some." Feeling slightly guilty about ratting her out, I look away for a moment and turn back to him. He frowns but nods.

"Reed?" My mom goes to hug me. "Please don't be upset. We were trying to protect both of you. I thought you were trying to have a relationship with Lexi. I... I should have told you about Tess. I see that now."

"I'm over it, Mom. Getting upset is pointless now." I give her a hug and nod at my dad and Jax as I jog out the hospital doors.

Starting my new Ferrari, I command my car to call Brance. It rings and goes to voice mail. Slamming my fist on the steering wheel, I wince at the sting in my right hand where I punched the tile in the bathroom. I hang up and try again.

"Goddamn it, Brance, answer." Listening to the phone ring, I reach over to disconnect right when Brance answers.

"Reed! You do know I'm under no obligation to answer to you!" Brance sniffs into the phone.

With a sharp exhale, I grip the steering wheel tightly and start to back out of the hospital's garage.

"You sound like shit. Is Tess staying with you?"

"Nice, thanks for your good energy. Why would I ever tell you anything about Tess, you *entitled dick*?" He blows his nose into the phone.

"What the fuck, Brance?" I say, weaving in and out of traffic.

"I'm sick. And going to bed. Goodbye."

"Don't you dare, man. I have had a shit day and shittier three years. I'm on my way to your place. Let your guards know."

He sighs, then starts coughing. *Christ!*

"It's late. My phone has been blowing up with everyone texting and posting about your girlfriend trying to kill herself. Trust me when I tell you this: talk to Tess tomorrow."

I don't answer him because I hadn't even thought about that. But of course, everybody at the party would be posting all kinds of shit.

"Hello?" I can almost see the smirk on his face at my drama.

"Feeling guilty, Reed?"

I start laughing partly because I've missed Brance. He's an asshole, but he loves Tess.

"You're a piece of work, Brance. You know Lexi was never my girlfriend, and—"

"Excuse me?" he says. "I personally asked you if you two were together, and your answer was yes! I'm sick and don't have any patience. Go home. Get some sleep. See Tess tomorrow. Trust me—you will thank me for this." The line beeps off.

"Motherfucker." I go to redial then hang up. Maybe he's right. I've been up for two days. I need to make this right with Tess. I can't get anywhere near her tonight. Without Brance's help, I'll never get in. His security is as good as the president's. Turning my car around, I head to a hotel close by. I'll start fresh in the morning.

chapter 25

TESS

Something awakens me, and I sit up and glance at my phone. It's 6:00 a.m. I hate when I wake up this early. Flopping back onto my fluffy down comforter, it's all I can do not to scream.

"Jesus, Reed! You scared the shit out of me." I blink at him. He's sitting in my chair in the corner.

The morning peeks in, casting a soft light on his handsome face. His hair looks wet. One long leg is resting on his knee, and he looks like a king on his throne. I back up, pulling the comforter with me.

"How did you get in?"

Hoping to quiet my heart rate, I try to ignore the butterflies in my stomach. He doesn't talk but keeps staring at me as though he hasn't decided what his next move is. Either that or maybe he knows and is torturing me.

I square my shoulders back and cross my legs. Taking my rubber band from my wrist, I pull my hair into a messy bun and shoot him a glare.

"Shouldn't you be at the hospital?"

The latest wound is still too fresh for me to say more. Dropping my hands with a dramatic slap, I look out my window, mind spinning. After I convinced Jax it would be better for everyone if I left the party, I had barely made it into the apartment when Brance shoved his phone in my face. There I was with Reed and Lexi. Posts and videos all over Instagram, Facebook, even Twitter. Then the pictures started coming in of Lexi overdosing, Reed by her side looking every bit the concerned boyfriend.

Frowning, I glance down at my floral comforter. "You two deserve each other. You can do drugs and have threesomes." My voice cracks. I sound like a child but can't stop myself.

He sits there, unmoving. His gaze makes me shiver. It's intense, almost yearning. My fingers ache from gripping the comforter so tightly.

Finally, he stands and like old times, and my heart skips a beat. *Damn him.* He's at the edge of my bed in seconds, his large form looming over me. With a deep breath, I attempt to steady my breathing.

He reaches for a piece of my hair, rubbing it in between his fingers as if he's testing its softness. Then his strong thumb finds my lips. His touch is not gentle. Back and forth he rubs my lips making them hot, swollen, tingling.

I almost bite him. But he stops as if he can read my mind. I guess this is his subtle way of telling me he disapproves. His strong hand reaches under my chin and jerks my comforter off me.

"Reed!" My voice rises two octaves. "You can't march in here and do this." Pushing him aside, I have to get away from him. Already I'm on the verge of crying.

I bolt out of bed, make my way to the bathroom, and slam the door.

Leaning against it, I try to get ahold of my emotions. I'm so weak around him. In less than two minutes, he has me hiding in my bathroom.

"Jesus, pull it together!" I snap at my reflection in the mirror. Swollen red lips and giant blue eyes stare back at me.

Angrily, I grab my toothbrush and slather toothpaste all over it. I will not allow him to do this to me. He has a girlfriend. Who OD'd last night! Spitting out the foaming toothpaste in the sink, I pee and wash my face quickly. The last thing I want is for him to think I'm hiding, so I open the door and march out. An empty room greets me.

"Reed?"

Quickly, I throw on some sleep shorts and make my way to the smell of coffee. The kitchen is deserted and dark, which is unusual. Someone is always around. Grabbing a mug, I pour myself some liquid energy. I make my way into the main room and slow down to watch him.

He's lost in thought. Staring out at the magnificent view of Manhattan in her morning glory. *Why does he have to be so beautiful? Why does he still have so much power over me?*

He must sense me because he turns and his eyes take hold of mine. Exhaling, I wait for him to make his move. Instead he turns and looks back out the window.

"I would like answers." His deep voice is smooth, calm. It carries across the room.

"Okay." I hear a slight echo as I sit on the leather couch. The heat clicks on. Even though it's summer, Brance's building gets cold in the morning.

"Why are you back? And don't say college."

My head lowers. I stare, fascinated at the steam swirling up from my coffee.

"That is why I'm back."

He doesn't respond but keeps staring out the window. A garbage truck faintly beeps its presence.

Clearing my voice, I ask, "Can I get you a cup of coffee?" I don't know why I'm being nice. Maybe because he's actually acting mature, making my earlier outburst seem juvenile.

"I would like that, Tess." His voice is rough, raising goose bumps on my arms.

Swiftly I stand, relieved to have a task. I'm already needing him far too much, and he is not mine to need anymore. I pour him a cup, leaving it black. That's how we both used to drink it. Granted that was three years ago.

When I return, he has moved and now sits on the couch, elbows resting on his knees, fingers clasped together. Not hesitating, I invade his space, forcing him to lean back. He reaches for the cup. Our fingers touch. A zing of electricity hits me.

Pulling away like I've been burned by scorching water, I almost spill the coffee.

He arches a dark eyebrow. "Thanks, Kitten." Both of us freeze at the endearment. He recovers first, taking the coffee from me with both hands.

"I didn't put anything in it. I don't know how you like it now." *Wow, if that's not the truth.* I'm flustered, which aggravates me. I sit, turning slightly so I can see him. He leans over again looking down at his coffee.

"I'm all fucked up, Tess. I have been since you left."

Oh God, stay strong, I chant to myself.

"I want to say I'm sorry. But I think we both are so..." He looks at me, his eyes so blue and open. For a moment, I'm back three years ago, when his honesty was pure and no darkness haunted him. Time stands still as we evolve into each other.

"What do you want me to say?" I whisper.

"I want you to tell me the truth. How you feel about me... us?" He runs a hand through his exquisite curls. "I need to find a way back to you."

I exhale. Even when I fantasized about Reed begging for forgiveness, it was never this. Sitting up straight, I look directly at him. "I don't see how that can ever be possible." Breaking eye contact, I sip my coffee.

"Why?" His voice sounds strangled.

My anger returns, and I look back at him, slamming the mug down. The loud crash almost makes me jump.

"You're kidding me, right?" I puff out air. "If you don't know, then you're not as smart as I thought." Jumping up, I pace back and forth.

"Humor me, Tess."

My face heats up. Anger drives me to be honest with him. "*I loved you*. And you gave away all your firsts!" My hands are clenched in front of me. I need him to hear me... to know that his actions are why we are in the place we are today. "You betrayed me. By giving it to prostitutes and Lexi!"

"Tess... Christ." His eyes are filled with tears. "I... you had all my firsts."

Reed's words bring me down. My legs give out, and I sink to the couch. I avoid looking at him and focus on the coffee table. If I see his pain, I won't be able to stop my tears. Frantically, I reach for my coffee. I can barely swallow the mouthful with the lump in my throat.

"Go on. I want it all, Tess. Let it out."

I blink a couple of times at the ceiling, trying to reel in my emotions.

"Cry, Kitten. Then we'll put us back together." His strong hands reach for me.

I twist away. "You're with *her* now. What does it matter?"

"It matters. We'll get to Lexi later. Talk to me!" He stands up.

I follow, not allowing him to intimidate me. "What should I tell you? That I can forgive you? Or forget that you used to be a different person?" In need of a barrier, I scurry around the couch.

He crosses his arms. "I *begged you*, Tess. Literally begged you to come back to me. And what did you do?"

"Stop." I wish I could put my hands against my ears.

"*What?*" he yells. I jump at his anger.

"You killed me," he says. "You took my heart and ripped it out. So yeah, you're right. I turned into a different person."

"I can't do this. You shouldn't be here." My eyes scan the room.

"Relax, Tess." His voice is strong and reassuring like a warm blanket. "This is the only place I should be." He stalks toward me, graceful, like a dark, sleek panther.

Run! flashes like a neon sign in my brain. I back away until I hit a wall.

His warm breath is at my ear. "What do I need to do to get you back?"

My breathing is harsh. Again, he robs me of thinking clearly. He's too close. His fresh Reed smell makes me almost groan with want.

"Kitten?" It sounds like a caress. I want to tell him he is not allowed to call me that anymore, but what's the point? Instead I nod my head yes.

"When Robert showed up that morning, I didn't panic because I was positive my father would send one of his planes and you would be back. When that didn't happen, it all spiraled out of control for me."

He looms over me, forcing me to look at him.

"I was like a drug addict without his fix. You were my drug." His thumb rubs my lips, his eyes fixated on them.

"I had Jax, but you are my soul, my life," he murmurs so close I can smell his minty breath.

Then he pulls back, his arms caging me in. "Your father wouldn't let me visit you. Every time you told me that you were coming back, I believed you. When you started lying, the pain was something I never want to go through again. It broke me, Tess."

I prepare to defend myself, but his eyes stop me. "No. You did and by the time you told me the truth, it was like you took that piece of my soul I had given only to you and sliced it out of me."

"Reed please..." I don't even know what I'm asking for.

"Let me finish. I was not mature enough to understand or believe that you would come back."

A sob escapes me. This time I do cover my ears. He's making me the bad guy. *I can't be the villain.* He grabs my wrists tightly, pinning them on top of my head.

Twisting in his grip, I say, "Let me go, Reed. I had *no choice!*" I'm frantic. If he touches me, I'm doomed.

"No choice?" His eyes pierce mine. "You had a choice. I told you I would take care of you. All you had to do was come back to your mother. But after two years of listening to your pathetic excuses, I gave you an ultimatum. And you chose your fucking father!" He's so close, his full lips almost touch mine. "Why, Tess?" His grip punishes my wrists. "Why didn't you come back to me?" His voice is pleading, almost hoarse.

"You never gave me a chance to explain. I called you, wrote to you. But you never even called back," I whisper, chest heaving.

His eyes examine my face then move to my breasts. The room that was so large a moment ago has shrunk. The intense attraction that has always been with us has been unleashed at last.

He leans his forehead against mine. "What would have been the point? To make myself suffer even more? Just keep dragging it out?"

"You're hurting me! And you're a liar!" I spit out.

He pulls back slightly, then drops my wrist and runs his hand through his curls. "Fine, Tess. I'm the asshole." He grabs my chin "You're not a victim. Don't tell me you're still pure! I might have betrayed us first, but I'm positive you are no saint." He sneers.

I'm stunned. Slowly my mind begins to process his words. "You shit!" I push him back hard. But he's like a tank, barely even moving.

He arches a dark brow at me. Not even stopping to think, I slap him. His head snaps back. I go to hit him again, but he grabs my wrists.

"Watch it, Kitten." He grits his teeth.

"You selfish ass," I say, trying not to think about my stinging hand, which he's holding way too tight. "You don't deserve to know about my personal life. Get out. Don't make me call Carlos—he's not a nice man." How dare he make himself feel better about betraying me! I should tell him. Watch his smug face crumble with my truth.

Narrowing my eyes on him, I hiss, "*Let me go.*"

"No, I think I like you like this. I have you right where I need you."

"Fuck you, Reed. No matter how you twist it, you did this. You didn't want to wait for me." I try to free myself, causing his fingers to tighten. "God, you're such an asshole!" I try to wrestle my hand away. "Admit that you wanted to fuck other girls. That you can't be faithful! I deserve better."

That seems to do the trick. He releases my wrist like I've got a disease. "You do deserve better. But I can't let you go. You're mine." His voice sounds tortured. Or maybe that's only what I want to hear.

Suddenly I'm tired. The stress and pain have worn me out. I want to crawl into my soft bed, pull the covers over my head, and cry.

"Why are you doing this? It's pointless. You're with Lexi." My voice is cracking, probably because the bile in my stomach is churning at the thought of it.

He looks out the window as if it has some magical information. The way his eyes are downturned and the edges of his mouth tug down makes him look sad, almost guilty. Finally, he looks straight into my eyes. "I'm not with Lexi. It was a mistake."

"Oh, right." A crazy laugh escapes me. "I heard you broke up with her, and she tried to kill herself."

Suddenly, he's in my face. "She a very sick girl. But she was someone who put me first. So, keep your judgment to yourself."

Turning away from me as if he doesn't trust himself, he says, "Goddamn it, Tess." He scrubs his hands up and down his face. "Just so we're clear, I never fucked her."

It's as if I've been slapped. Saying nasty things about someone who almost died is beneath me. And he knows it. I want to bolt, hide, anything but stay here. He must sense it because he grabs my hand, pulling me behind him as we enter my bedroom.

"I'm not leaving, Tess. We can fight, scream for days, but I'm not going anywhere." He locks the door. My stomach flutters in excitement, which horrifies me a little.

Shaking my head, I tell him, "You're a slut and a liar."

He doesn't try to defend himself. Instead he reaches for me and in one swift move, lifts me onto my dresser. Spreading my legs, he pushes in between them, pulling me close. His large hand wraps around my neck, his thumb rubbing my pulse.

"I did a lot of things I wish I could take back. I'm sure you feel the same. I can forgive you." He presses gently on my racing pulse. I swallow.

"You need to let the past go. Let's finish this now." He pulls me tight against him, pressing my pussy against his erection.

"But I..."

He dips his head to my neck as his tongue licks me.

"Your pulse is racing. Are you scared?" A shiver goes down my spine, and he smiles as though he felt it.

"I'm not scared." I raise my chin, noticing us in the mirror. My blond hair and flushed face stare back at me. Reed's dark head and broad shoulders are sexy as always.

"I can't breathe, Reed. Let go of me." My voice is soft, sounding the opposite of what I'm saying.

His lips and nose are in my neck. "You can breathe," he coaxes, then lifts his head to cup my cheeks, forcing me to see him.

"I love you."

I blink at him not knowing if I want to kick him or scream for joy. I should kick him. But doing what I should do has only brought me pain. He owns my heart—always has.

"Why are you looking surprised? I told you I'm not playing games. You're mine. And I'm done being without you."

My nipples harden at his arrogance. His self-confidence has always been the biggest turn-on for me.

"Tell me you want me," he demands before his lips travel to my neck. I close my eyes, wondering at what point do I admit that this was my plan all along? That maybe I have more control than I give myself credit for. Because if Reed makes me weak, I bring him to his knees.

"Kiss me, Kitten... Let's see if it feels as good as we remember." His mouth takes mine. It's sweet and stinging all in one and I lose whatever battle I was having. I open to him. He groans, and his tongue thrusts and tangles with mine. Desire and power slither up my body. He's giving it to me, so I take it, moaning into his cinnamon coffee kiss.

"I need to be inside you. I wanted to go slow, to prove myself. But maybe this is exactly what we need." Picking me up, he sets me on my silky sheets. His eyes are electric, blue and fiery.

"Reed, I have to tell you something." My nails are latched on to his forearms.

He cocks his head stroking my hair out of my face. "Okay— what is it?"

"Um."

He grins. Leaning in to pepper kisses on my eyes, he uses his tongue to trace a path down to my mouth. Jesus, how can

I think when he does that? How did I forget the incredible feel of his lips? Our tongues twist and suck as we drink each other's nectar. It makes me want things I shouldn't.

I need to tell him. But I'm scared he'll stop, so I close my eyes and let him take control, submitting to his experienced hand and magical mouth. He pulls back, lifting himself off the bed. Somewhat mesmerized, I watch as he pulls the T-shirt off in one jerk and unbuttons his jeans, making me squirm in anticipation. My core clenches and my thin night shorts are wet with my excitement.

He looks at me as he eases the jeans down, allowing me to worship the six-pack and V of muscles. His body has matured. He's no longer a boy. The years of boxing and training with Jay have paid off.

I suck in some much-needed oxygen as he lets them slide down his legs and kicks them off. His thick, long cock juts up to his belly button almost as if it's searching for me.

"Reed..." I swallow, trying to help my dry mouth. His eyes are so dark now; desire oozes from him.

"I have never wanted anything but you my whole life. I promise I will slow down next time. I need to be inside you," he growls out.

This is the Reed I remember. I don't know what is going to happen later, but right now I'm staring at *my* Reed.

It's now or never. Maybe I should go along and let him do it fast and hard.

He grabs my chin. "After today, it's only us, Tess. I hope you know that."

I whimper. He pulls back. "What's wrong?"

"I... I..." *What is wrong with me?*

"Sit up." I do.

He pulls my thin nightshirt over my head and pushes me back down. His mouth attacks my hard nipple. He sucks it into his mouth and desire flares all the way down to my core. His teeth softly roll it with his tongue. Then he bites me. I groan not knowing how much I wanted that. His eyes shoot up to mine.

"I want to fuck you. Claim you so that you never leave me again."

I almost remind him that he left me. But fuck it. The wetness between my legs is making me almost self-conscious. He hasn't even touched me down there yet.

"God, these nipples have haunted me." He rolls one roughly with his fingers, then lowers his head to my stomach and makes his way to my tattoo. His tongue licks the arrow all the way to my heart, and he sucks the spot the arrow is supposed to pierce. I arch into him, my body starting to move against his.

"Reed..." But he takes my mouth again, stealing my breath.

"No more talking, Tess. You're not making sense, anyway." He pulls down my shorts and I feel cold without his hot touch.

"So fucking beautiful," he says, his voice gravelly. "I love you. I know I'm pushing you, but I can't stop saying it."

And I can't think straight. I want him. So, I give in, knowing this is what I came back for. This is why I never let any other guys get close. I have always been his and I always will.

His strong legs nudge my thighs open. Suddenly I panic sitting up.

"What's wrong, Tess?" This time he is demanding not asking. "Kitten? Tell me."

My breathing is harsh. I must tell him. He is going to know somehow, and that will be worse.

Gasping, I try to take a breath. His large tan hands caress my breast, then move to my neck gently guiding me back.

"You need to talk to me. Or let's talk after. Just feel, Tess. Feel how fucking good it is." Taking my hand, he wraps it around his thick dick.

A moan escapes me as I stroke him. Then I blurt it out. "I'm still a virgin!"

He stops thrusting his cock in my hand. His eyes fly to mine, and his body goes still.

I let go of him. "I should have told you, but you were so sure I had. I didn't know we would be doing this." I'm speaking fast.

"Stop," he groans, lowering his head onto my forehead as he closes his eyes. His body is stiff. Gently, I touch him.

"Reed?"

He grabs my hands and holds them on top of my head.

"Tess..." His voice is raspy, almost harsh. Then his blue eyes look at me. And I almost melt into a puddle. His face is full of triumph.

Keeping my hands pinned, he says, "Open your legs." I obey his command.

"We're going to go slow." His voice shakes with excitement. I nod.

"Good, now I'm going to eat this pretty, wet pussy of yours."

He doesn't wait for a response. Which is good because I can't talk. All I can do is try to breathe as his tongue licks me from top to bottom.

"Reed." It comes out in a groan. He spreads my pussy, making me smile. He always loved to look at it.

He places a light kiss right on it. "So pink, tight, delicious, and mine."

His dark eyelashes are so long, I can't see his eyes. But his strong hand glides over my flat belly, holding me tight. "Lie back—I want you screaming."

I fall back as he pulls my legs closer, opening me up as he lowers his dark head. His tongue starts circling and he sucks on my clit, the pleasure so shocking that I grab his hair and pull. We only got to do this once. He's improved. I'm ready to come already and try not to think about how he got so good at oral sex. He looks up at me as if he knows I have drifted away from him.

Frowning, he says, "I want your eyes on me as I eat you." My wetness covers his lips. They glisten. He's so nasty. I want to say

I hate it, but the truth is it turns me on. I open my legs wider and arch up to his waiting mouth.

He smiles and lowers his head straight to my sensitive clit. Back and forth he roughly rubs against it, his scruff adding to my pleasure.

"Holy shit, Reed." My hands frantically reach for something to hold on to as my body starts to pulse.

"Tell me you want me." Inserting his middle finger deep inside me, he causes me to gasp. He crawls up to kiss me. I'm throbbing, my core clenched around his finger.

His voice is calming but strong. "Tell me, Kitten, and I'll let you come." His thumb starts circling my wet swollen clit. He never takes his eyes off me.

"You already know," I moan into my pillow.

"I need to hear it," he whispers as his finger pumps into me faster.

My hands find my comforter. It's hard to breathe because I'm losing it. I'm climbing with wave after wave of pleasure.

"Please..." My head thrashes back and forth as I beg.

"Good enough." Lowering his head to suck my throbbing clit, he pumps his finger faster.

"Reed, I'm going to come." My body goes off. I'm soaring, quivering. The pulsing pleasure makes me jerk in his mouth.

"Yeah... that's it, Kitten. Come all over my face."

I think I told him I love him, but I don't care as he moves his finger higher and touches a spot I never can find. My body goes off again. His hand is on my stomach and he praises me as I climax on his finger.

I'm shattered and vulnerable. Closing my eyes, I'm not ready for him to see how much I need him.

"Open your eyes, Kitten. We're doing this together." His voice is harsh but his face is full of love. Blinking my eyes open, I watch as he leans down and softly kisses me. His tongue tastes like me.

I can't talk because I'm afraid I will say something mean or something nice. Either way, I'm way too emotional, so I nod yes. He moves his body on top of mine.

"I want your eyes on me the whole time." Taking his hard cock, he rubs my clit with the tip until it pulses, leaving us moaning.

"I want to go slow, but it will be easier if I don't."

His breathing is rough, and a sheen of sweat covers him. His hot tip slides into me.

"Christ," he groans, leaning his forehead on mine, ecstasy all over his face.

Then his mouth is at my ear. "Kitten? You feel me?"

I don't say anything because how can I not feel him? He's huge and he's barely in. I tighten around him and he breathes out.

"Fuck, you're hot... and tight." He pulls out and circles my clit with his dick again. "Relax, Tess."

He takes my mouth with his, his tongue seeking mine, sucking and circling, so deep and intense I'm sure my lips and chin will be chafed.

He thrusts in deeper. I try to relax, but it's starting to burn and stretch.

"Reed you're too big. I didn't think... I mean this hurts." I whimper, tightening up on him.

He caresses my check. "Let me inside you, Kitten. It's me." I'm caught off guard at his declaration. Suddenly, I don't care how much it hurts—I trust him. All I want is for us to be one and his body inside mine.

I'm so wet, it drips down my ass.

"That's it... so fucking good, keep relaxing." I feel full, still burning, but Reed is inside me, so I don't care.

"Reed, I... I need you."

He moans. "Grab ahold of me, Kitten."

I do and in one thrust he pushes past that barrier and is completely inside me.

I scream, the pain way worse than I imagined. "Reed! That fucking hurt!" Tears sting my eyes.

"I know." His nose caresses my cheek. "Hold on to me. Let yourself take me. I have to train your pussy." I feel him smile. "I'm inside you, Tess. I'm never leaving. You feel so good."

His exquisite face is like nothing I have seen on him: a cross between pleasure and pain. I'm burning and stinging, but my body is adjusting to him.

"Better?" He takes my breath from me, his full lips on mine.

"A little."

"I'm going to move. Breathe. You... have no idea how good you feel. But you will."

He pulls out slightly and pushes in again. It stings, but it's slightly numb, so that helps.

"Breathe, Tess. Wrap those long legs around me." Again, he pulls out and goes back in until he is able to slowly pump himself inside me.

"Kitten... Jesus." His voice is pure gravel. "Talk to me, tell me how you feel." His pace quickens, his biceps huge as he holds himself back.

"It's better but sore." My fingernails are attached to his back.

He reaches in between us; his thumb finds my sensitive clit and he applies pressure.

"Oh... that feels good."

One look at his dimples and I melt. He's moving faster and faster and the pain lessens a bit. My swollen clit is throbbing.

"Yeah, that's it ... Fuck, Kitten, I can't stop. You still on the pill?"

How the hell had I not thought of that?

"Yes." Holding on tight, I watch his beautiful face.

"You want to see me come?" I nod. "Fucking watch me be owned by you."

Holy shit, he is so incredibly hot. His body starts to jerk, and I watch every single twitch of ecstasy on his face. The way his eyes narrow into slits as his jaw clenches down in sync with his rapid thrusts.

"Fuck," he hisses as he slams into me and freezes. His warm seed pulses and spills deep inside me.

Our breathing is harsh. Reed is kissing my face, rubbing his nose on my sweaty neck, slowly pulling out of me.

He rolls over on his side bringing me with him. He looks down to inspect us. I follow his eyes.

"Oh my God, Reed." I sit up and lift my hips. There is bright red blood underneath me. I look at his penis and it glistens with blood too. He grabs me and pulls me up. We both stand together and look at the sheets.

"I had no idea I would bleed like that, did you?" I look at his cocky smile and roll my eyes. "We need to change the bed. I liked these sheets too." Starting to rip them off, I hand them to him.

"Please put them in the garbage, Mr. Smugness."

"No way." He folds them up. "This is my trophy, woman!"

Laughing, I say, "Reed! You are not keeping them."

He pulls me close. "Of course I am. I earned this. It's my treasure. I might even frame it."

"You are not framing it! Stop being a weirdo and give it to me. Obviously, I can't trust you."

He pulls it behind his back. "No, and I will frame it if you aren't a good girl." He puts the sheets on the chair and reaches over and lifts me over his shoulder. I scream and slap his tight ass as he goes to the bathroom and starts a bath.

"You need to soak so I can fuck you again."

Gently he lowers me. Our bodies touch the whole way down. He kisses me then puts me in the tub. I stand there smiling at him because I love him, and I never want this to end.

"You seem very pleased with yourself." I slowly sit and relax back, letting the soothing water cascade over my body. Sighing,

I reach, for the bubble bath and squirt some under the faucet. Reed steps in behind me and pulls my body between his legs. He lightly bites my ear.

"I can't even begin to tell you, how *pleased* I am. For the first time in three years, I can breathe." He rubs my arms, then my breasts. Bubbles are spilling over the tub.

"Think you went overboard on the bubbles." He moves my hair away from my neck and starts to suck on me.

I moan. "Never too many bubbles." My hands latch on to his wrists as he glides them over my breasts, his fingers rubbing my nipples.

"How do you feel?" His warm voice wraps around me, pulling me back to him.

"Hmmm, so good." I lean my head on his shoulder.

His hands stop fondling my breasts and we lace our fingers together.

"You want to talk?"

Sighing, I say, "No. I don't want to ruin how happy I am or get angry. I'm still trying to figure out what's happening with us."

I feel him stiffen. He pushes me off him. The tub is huge, and I turn to the side as he washes himself. I can't help but stare at him—he truly is mouthwatering. My insecurities take over. I should stop this now. All he's going to do is break my heart.

"I love you, Tess. You are it for me. I understand that you have hang-ups about me and the other women. But that is the past."

He scowls at me, then turns on the shower. I gasp as the water hits me and he rinses off. Standing up, I push the drain button and let the bath water out. He steps out of the tub and grabs a towel, leaving me.

I hate myself for looking at his toned butt as he leaves. See, as usual, he is a master at turning things around. Well, I'm not eight anymore. I don't have to do what he wants. I lather my hair and wash myself, mindful of the tenderness between my legs. It's not horrible, and in a way, it feels good—my reminder that Reed was inside me.

Then it all crashes down. Turning off the shower, I jerk open the bathroom door. Barely covering myself with the towel, I emerge to find him standing by the bed fully dressed in his jeans and T-shirt, staring at his phone.

Asshole.

I drop the towel and march over to him placing my hand over his phone. His fingers stop and his mouth twitches. "I guess I'm not giving you enough attention, right, Kitten?"

"I could have an STD or something worse." His eyes look at me from top to bottom. I refuse to be insecure about being naked. My looks are the only thing I have to use on him. I put my hands on my hips letting his eyes travel over me.

"I personally assure you that you have nothing to worry about." He goes back to his phone.

"Unbelievable." I spin away from him, jerk open my dresser, and grab a pink lacy bra and a matching pink thong.

I tug on my panties. "You have admitted that your sexual history has consisted of high-priced whores. And that is supposed to reassure me?"

"Tess, I said you're fine."

I snort.

Shaking his head, he looks down at his phone again. "Fine, I'll call Dr. Miller today. Have him test me for everything."

I put my bra on and glare at him. "You know what, Reed? I need time to think about us. This has been a little overwhelming." Looking around my room, the bed is torn apart and the room smells like Reed and me and sex. I almost inhale but I hate him right now, so I don't.

He laughs, and his eyes narrow on me. "No, Tess."

I want to throw one of my shoes at him. How dare he decide whether or not we are together?

"Get dressed. We're going to see our apartment. If you hate it, I'll get us a different one."

Now it's my turn to laugh. "You are completely delusional. I have no intention of moving in with you." I lower my voice, realizing I'm starting to get a little loud.

He takes my arms and pulls me until we are nose to nose.

"You're moving in with me, beautiful. *We're done being apart.*" His eyes move over my face. I watch in a blink of an eye how fast he changes. His features soften; his thumb caresses my bottom lip.

"You don't have to worry about STDs. I have always worn a condom." He winks. "See you do get all my firsts. Making love with you was the first time I have never not worn one." He lowers his dark head and lightly bites my lip. "And it was fucking mind-blowing." His blue eyes sizzle with sexual energy.

"So, since you're the only one I'm going to be putting my dick inside, you never have to worry." He gives me another kiss. A ding from his phone ruins the moment as he pulls back to answer it.

I stand there staring at him, completely shell-shocked.

He brings the phone to his ear and glances at me. "Get dressed." Turning, he walks away. In my closet, I reach for the pale pink dress Brance bought for me recently. It's short and tight. I turn around and look in the mirror: sexy but still classy. Lana would approve. I slip on some pink ballet flats that wrap around my ankles and return to the bathroom to do my hair and makeup. Dabbing on my French vanilla perfume, I'm so engrossed in my thoughts, it takes a second to notice Reed is gripping the doorframe, silently watching me. The sight makes me ache as I look at his biceps bulging beneath his tight T-shirt along with the tease of his happy trail on display.

Frowning, I bite my lip and try to concentrate on fixing myself. My hair is wild, my lips are puffy, and my cheeks are flushed. Either that or they have razor burn from his five-o'clock shadow.

"I hate your hair." He sounds bored.

Lifting an eyebrow, I say, "Really?" I turn toward him. "That's not what I heard. I did this for you. You know how I live to make you happy." I smile sweetly at him.

His eyes narrow. "Dye your hair back, Tess." He drops his hands and walks back into my bedroom, leaving me alone. I open my mouth, ready to tell him to fuck off but decide against it. What's the point? I hate being a blonde anyway. The maintenance is ridiculous.

Quickly I apply my makeup, and since I'm in pink, I try to go natural. I do darken my eyes. The smoky look always works.

I take one more glance at myself.

Reed will think I look hot. Suddenly I remember my birth control pill. *Shit*, I must get better about taking it. Obviously, Reed is not going to use protection. I can't keep forgetting it. Especially since I'm the one who doesn't want kids. Popping it into my mouth, I go to find Reed.

chapter 26

REED

As I hang up with Dr. Miller, Brance walks straight past me as if I'm not there. Fucking drama queen! I smile. Brance has balls. I've missed him.

He stands at his refrigerator staring at the contents.

"So, Tess making you get your dick checked out, huh?" Obviously, he heard me on the phone.

"Yep, it helps to have money. Dr. Miller is sending someone here to draw my blood. I should have the results by the end of the day. Do you mind letting your guys know not to kill him?"

He snorts but presses the intercom alerting Alejandro.

"I'm doing this for Tess." He eyes me. Going back to the refrigerator, he takes out the orange juice and shuts the door, shaking his head. "I can't have you hurting her, Reed."

"Brance, I'm going to tell you this one time. I love her and we're back together. The rest is none of your business. She adores you and you're her best friend. That makes us stuck with each other."

He slams the container down and little drops of orange juice hit us.

"Fuck off, Reed. If I were against you, I wouldn't have allowed you in here this morning." Pulling a hand through his hair, he goes on. "And you know what? It *is* my business since I'm the one who has to pick her up and put her back together after you destroy her."

"I'm not here to argue with you. I appreciate that you took care of my girl. But I can take it from here." Absently my eyes travel around the kitchen. Brance has stainless steel cabinets. I don't think I've ever seen that before and wonder how they'd look in our penthouse-to-be.

"I'm not going anywhere until you have redeemed yourself." He pours the OJ into a tumbler and takes a huge swig.

My head snaps back to him. "I think you are forgetting *she* is the one who has been gone for *three* years! She's the one who wouldn't come back. What did you expect me to do?"

He rolls his eyes. "Right, it's Tess's fault that you fucked anything that moved."

I grate my teeth, then check for Tess. The last thing I need is for her to hear this conversation.

"It's done... over. I can't change the past. All I can concentrate on is the future. I have a headache and you are making me want to punch something."

He snorts. "Tell me something new. She loves you, Reed. You sure you're ready to be what she needs?"

"Judge me all you want." I scrub my hand over my face. "I love her. Always have. You have been in her life for three years. I have been there forever."

"So? You think because you two were having tea parties together that gives you a get-out-of-jail-free card?"

"You know I love her."

We stare at each other in a silent battle. He raises his glass. "Great! Because you two don't do casual."

He doesn't trust me. But I don't give a shit. As long as I have Tess, I'm willing to put up with a disapproving Brance.

"She's moving in with me starting today!" I blurt.

"Well, I guess that's not moving fast." Brance leans toward me, elbows on the counter. "I don't care that your family is a bunch of billionaires. I come from drug money. I *will* have your penis cut off and shoved down your throat if you hurt her again." He lifts the last of the juice to his mouth.

I can't help but smirk because if Brance is sick enough to think it, he'd probably do it.

"Fair enough, man." Grabbing a banana, I start to peel it.

"Did you even ask her? Or did you tell her she was moving in with you?"

"Does it matter?" Glaring at him, I pop a piece in my mouth.

"Does what matter?" Tess walks into the kitchen.

My pulse leaps. Fuck, she does things to me. My eyes follow her as she drops her bag on one of the stainless steel barstools. I want to grab her, pull up her pink dress, and thrust myself deep inside her. But I refrain. Brance probably wouldn't appreciate it.

The intercom beeps, interrupting my thoughts and alerting us that the guy Dr. Miller sent is on his way up.

Tess walks up to Brance, checking his head with her hand for a temperature I guess.

Jealousy punctures me, and for a moment, it takes my breath. I want her touching me, not Brance.

I reach for her. "So, Kitten, this guy is going to draw my blood and whatever else needs to be done. I will have the results by the end of the day."

"What... already?" Her big blue eyes open wide. She turns and cuddles in my arms. Christ, she feels good. Her vanilla scent wraps around me like an invisible force field.

"Will this make you happy? Relieve your mind?" I pull a piece of hair off her face.

"Of course." Her voice is raspy.

"Then I want it done." Rubbing the back of her neck, I pull her closer to kiss her temple.

Brance interrupts us with his empty glass clanking as he puts it in the sink.

"I love this dress on you. Turn around." He spins his finger. Tess laughs.

Reluctantly I let her go. She twirls and catwalks around the kitchen. Her pretty pink dress accents her thin body and fantastic tits.

"Work it, baby." He grabs her as she passes and twirls.

"What do you think, Reed? It's okay to admit that I'm a master at dressing her."

He winks at me. Then he dips her, they both laugh, and my heart aches. It's been so long since I heard her laugh. I forgot how good it makes me feel.

"My personal Barbie doll." His brown eyes are full of mischief.

A cough causes all three of us to turn. The guy that Dr. Miller has sent is standing in blue scrubs in the doorway, a tall guard with a beard standing behind him.

Brance chuckles. "And on that note, Tess and I will leave you to it."

"Actually, it's important that Tess stays"—I pull her to my side—"in case you have questions."

Knowingly, she narrows her eyes at me. "You're just scared of needles," she whispers. It's the first time I've seen her face genuinely soften since we had sex.

"That too." My lips twitch. "I need you to hold my hand."

"Christ, you two, I think I'm going to be sick again. Although knowing that Reed Saddington is afraid of needles makes my day," Brance calls over his shoulder as he leaves.

I turn to the guy in scrubs. *Shit,* he looks nervous. I smile, trying to calm the guy. I mean he is going to be putting a needle in my arm.

"Can I get you something to drink?" Tess's manners break the awkward moment.

"No... No, I'm fine. He glances around Brance's ridiculous fortress. The white walls make me nervous. I can only imagine what this guy is thinking.

"So, where do you want me?" I want this done. I hate needles. When we were kids, my mom always had to bring Tess whenever I got a shot; otherwise, I caused a scene.

"Uh, well, wherever is comfortable. I need to draw blood. When was the last time you ate or drank anything?"

"I had coffee and a banana."

"That's fine. So, I need a urine sample, and I'll draw your blood. Dr. Miller will get the results and call you in a couple hours." He smiles reassuringly. I fight the urge to laugh because this is so stupid but I guess necessary.

"Wow, that is so quick." Tess caresses my arm as she holds my hand.

"This is my girlfriend Tess."

"Hi." The guy is flustered. He barely looks at her as he writes something on the plastic cup he wants me to pee in.

"And you are?"

"Um, yeah... I'm Steve. Sorry." He looks around like he's sure someone is going to come around the corner and gun him down. Can't say I blame him. If our positions were reversed, I would probably hesitate to give my name too.

"My girlfriend has some questions for you. Tess, fire away."

She smiles at him, obviously trying to put him at ease too.

"So, *if* he is clean, that means I have nothing to worry about?" Her new attitude is different. I love it.

Steve clears his throat. "Well, yeah, if all the tests are negative, you should be fine. If you're worried about it, he can get retested in six months."

Holding up my hand, I say, "We're fine. Let's do this. I'm hungry."

He gets prepared, and Tess watches as he ties the band around my bicep. "You have great veins. Makes my job easy." A nervous laugh escapes him.

I look at Tess who's biting her lip as she looks at me. I'll give Steve credit—he knows what he's doing, and I barely feel the needle prick. Tess moves closer. I lean into her as she runs her hand through my hair.

Steve clears his throat again. I wonder if it's a nervous tick

"So... that's done. Now take this, urinate in it, and I will be out of your way. Unless you have any more questions?"

"No, thank you. You've been great." Tess smiles at him.

He blinks, clears his throat, and looks at his feet for a moment. I can't help but chuckle.

"Steve?" His eyes pop over to me.

"The cup?"

"Oh, geez... I'm sorry. Here." He shoves it at me.

"Thanks." Making my way down the hall, I pee quickly and send him on his way.

I turn to Tess. "Pack some stuff. We can come back for the rest in a couple days."

Surprisingly she doesn't fight me. She walks to her room and returns with a bag. Brance is leaning against the wall as we leave.

"Call me, Pretty Girl."

"Love you."

I roll my eyes as they do their hug thing.

"Christ, you two, enough. I'm not taking her to China. We'll be at the Saint Regis," I say, grabbing her hand and bag.

"Reed," she says with a hiss, "I swear to God, you can't boss me around like that. I'm not Lexi!"

"Don't." The blood pumps in my head. She needs to let this shit go. So I take it out on the poor elevator button.

She doesn't speak, but her energy says it all. We glare at each other in the elevator as it glides down to the concrete hole Brance calls his garage. I wait as she slowly sinks into the seat of my Ferrari.

I'm exhausted. The last three years have caught up with me at last.

My fingers grip the steering wheel. "I want to show you the apartment. How hungry are you?"

"I'm fine, but you're not. We should stop and eat." She's right. Food would help immensely.

I reach for her hand, bringing it to my lips. Neither of us speaks and we let the fact that we're together sink in.

"The apartment has nothing but white walls. I thought maybe you and Brance might enjoy decorating it."

Her eyes light up and she dazzles me with a smile that almost makes me grab my tattoo it hurts so bad.

"I'd like that."

"Good. I want our place to be everything you dreamed about for us."

She swallows and holds my hand as we listen to the Clash.

I park the car in the garage of our new penthouse. Turning off the ignition, I don't budge. My mind is moving faster than my mouth. I want Tess to love this place. This is our beginning and it's important she knows it.

She looks at me as she grabs her purse. "You okay?"

Unbuckling my seat belt, I turn. "I bought this apartment for you."

She blinks at me.

"It's true. I was going to rent, and the realtor brought me here. As soon as I walked in, I knew."

She frowns. "But you didn't know I was back or anything."

"It didn't matter. Or maybe it did. All I know is I walked in and I saw you everywhere. I was willing to pay whatever they were asking."

"You're getting awfully sentimental in your old age."

My hand strokes hers. "Only for you. Come on—not only is the apartment fantastic, there's a coffee house across the street. You'll love it. Great coffee, omelets, pastries, all your favorites. And the best part about this restaurant is it's delicious and quick." I'm mentally calculating the minutes it will take us to order and eat, obsessing on how my body wants to mate with her. I'm like a barbarian. I want sex in every single room, on the counters and the floors.

Holding the door open, I admire her as she walks in. Tess has grown into a woman who turns heads from both genders. She has always been stunning, but now she seems to embrace it.

The coffee house has bright turquoise walls with large chalkboards dangling from chains. Their daily specials and menu are printed in neat handwriting. It's loud and crowded. The dark wooden tables are almost all taken. Standing behind her as we wait to order, I pull her back, settling her in my arms. She fits like a glove. I rest my chin on the top of her head. As she checks out the menu my nose goes into her neck, breathing in that wonderful Tess smell.

Vanilla. I almost back away. The fierce emotions terrify me for a moment.

"What are you going to have, Kitten?"

"Coffee."

I move closer, wanting to rub my hard cock on her ass. "Of course. Anything else, skinny?"

Her lips twitch. "Yes, how about a bacon, avocado, cheddar omelet with sourdough toast."

"Love it. Can I copy?"

Raising a dark brow at me, she says, "Well I hope so. Otherwise, I'm losing my touch."

"You're definitely not losing your touch." Taking her hand, I casually place it on my erection. She stiffens and looks around. Everyone is too preoccupied with each other or on their phones

She goes to pull away, and I tighten my hold on her wrist. "Just rub it, Tess. No one can see you."

"Reed," she hisses, but she starts to slowly rub and I nearly moan out loud.

I move back and lace my fingers with hers. "That was a bad idea."

She laughs. "You're crazy."

My heart aches. "I love you happy. We're going to eat and then your lessons begin."

Rubbing her shoulders, I smile as she leans into me. "Really? What if I'm a bad student? Are you going to spank me?" she jabs.

I clench my teeth together. "You have got to let this Lexi thing go."

"Trust me, I'm trying, but when you get all domineering on me it's hard," she whispers loudly.

Thankfully the guy ahead of us moves away and it's our turn to order.

We find a table in the corner. Tess crosses her legs looking satisfied with herself. Clearly winning her back might take some time. She's given me her body, but her trust might need some work. Which is okay. I've got nothing but time to make her trust me again. After all, if the situation were switched, I don't know how I would act.

"I'll get our coffee." I walk back up to the counter.

When I return and set down our coffee mugs, Tess is staring at my vibrating phone.

"It's Dr. Miller."

"I see that. You could have answered."

"I can't handle any bad news." She reaches for the napkin holder; it's funky and made of a tin can.

"You know I don't have anything."

A ding alerts us that there's a message on my phone. The arrival of our omelets stops me from listening. I wait for the meal to be delivered before I pick up my phone, watching her eyes follow my hands. Her cheeks turn slightly pink.

I tap my fingers on the table. "So, when I get a clean bill of health, we're done with all the past, right, Tess? We can start building our lives together?"

She caresses the handle on her mug. "I don't want what we used to have. I want better. You're mine and I'm yours. But I need you to trust me."

She looks around the coffee shop then straight into my eyes. "If you get a clean bill of health, I'm all yours."

I got a clean bill of health. And now I'm nervous about showing Tess the penthouse. Even though it spoke to me, that doesn't mean she'll love it. Fuck it, if she hates the place, we'll find another. I hate second guessing myself. I'm like an actor needing people to tell me I'm good. But instead of a whole group of people, I only need Tess.

I glance at her. Her big cat eyes are wandering around the posh lobby. It's the standard millionaire's building. High ceilings with marbled floors. Chrome elevators with a large wall of water next to our private one. I nod at the doorman and concierge who are engrossed with their phones. Both straighten as we pass.

"Why the penthouse?" She turns to me.

"What do you mean?" I touch her hair for a moment, pushing it off her shoulder.

"I don't know, sometimes I wonder what it would be like to be a regular person." Her sapphire eyes connect with mine. Our elevator opens silently to the apartment.

"What's going on?" I ask, pulling her into my arms.

She shrugs. "I'm sick of being controlled by money. I spent three years without you because I was scared of my dad disinheriting me. Sometimes, I wonder if I might not be happier without it."

I cup her cheeks. "You amaze me." Rubbing my nose on hers, I ask, "Do you want me to donate all my millions to charity?" I lean over to kiss her puffy lips.

She sighs dramatically. "No, because you would just get more. It's your curse to be rich, Reed Saddington. But, no doubt, you should donate to some to new charities."

I swoop her up in my arms. "What are you doing?" she squeals.

"I'm carrying you over the threshold. What else would I be doing?" I plant kisses on her nose.

"I'm pretty sure you only do that if you're married." Her laughter makes me feel like I've won the lottery.

Setting her down, I say, "Not me. I do it when the woman I'm going to spend the rest of my life with is seeing her first home."

Tess twirls around. "You're crazy, you know that, right?"

"Only for you." I slap her ass and she shrieks, a big, stupid smile on my face.

She runs one finger across the white walls as she looks around.

The ceilings are tall. Windows stretch from one side of the apartment to the other. It's what first attracted me to it. All the lights and city being seen yet not heard. Tess hates to be alone. Living in this penthouse, we'll be surrounded with light and life.

"Come here"—I take her hand—"I need to show you something."

Pulling her behind me, I approach the ornate staircase, taking the stairs two at a time.

"Why are we hurrying?" She puffs.

"I'm excited." After I open our bedroom door, she steps inside and her eyes take in the giant suite.

"This isn't what I wanted to show you. Although I like it too."

Smirking, I pull her into the master bath. She gasps, covering her mouth as she looks around.

"Oh my God... This is spectacular." She jumps into my arms. Chuckling, I hold her as she clings to me, planting small kisses all over my face.

"When the realtor brought me in here, I saw this tub overlooking Manhattan. All I could see was you in it. I bought the place that second. I don't think I even saw the rest of the apartment."

"This is... I mean, come on, this tub and..." She slides out of my arms to peek inside the shower.

"Well, it's got enough buttons. And we can fit six of us in here."

"As long as you and I fit, that's all I care about." Crossing my arms, I watch her.

She spins around, her hands behind her back. "I'm putting a couch and a chair over there."

"You do whatever your heart desires. This is all for you. I want you so spoiled no one but me can stand you."

She tilts her head and laughs. "Careful what you wish for."

Caging her in with my body, I reach for her neck and stroke it with my thumb. "I don't have to be careful. I already have my heart's desire."

"Reed... the windows." She frowns.

"The glass is tinted. I'm not into anyone seeing what's mine." I rub my nose along her cheek. "Are you sore?"

She bites her bottom lip lightly. "A little, but it kind of feels good."

I lift her up, and she wraps her legs around me as I walk us over to the elaborate toilet seat. Sitting on it, I let her stand, so I can reach up and pull her panties down.

In one swift move, I grab her leg and throw it over my shoulder, bringing her honey straight to my mouth.

"Wait. Here?" She looks around.

"Here." I grin then pull her onto my mouth. Sucking her clit causes her to fall forward and she grasps the gold towel rack. She's wet and I drink and suck her hard. She pants, saying my name. One hand holds the rack; the other holds my hair. "Mmm, you're lucky you taste so good. I can't decide if I want you to come on my dick or in my mouth." Torturing her, I add a finger and push up to rub that velvet spot and watch her face.

"Reed..." Her fingers tighten on my hair as I pump my finger into her. Her pussy clenches onto it. One more rub.

"Let go, Kitten." And she does. I hold her tight as her whole body spasms. I can't help myself. My greedy mouth latches on to her clit as she pulses in my mouth. With one hand, I unbutton my pants and tug them down. My swollen cock juts out. Her eyes are huge as she swallows.

"I want to suck..." I stop her as I grab her waist and guide her pussy to my waiting cock.

"Not right now. I need this," I say, lowering her wet sex onto me.

"Jesus." My head falls back as she moans against my neck. The tightness of her pussy is almost a religious experience.

"Fuck me, Kitten. You're in charge." Lifting her up, I thrust her down on me, then grab her neck and crush her lips on mine. My tongue needs hers like I need water. Her hands find the towel rack again. Her hot pussy tightly clenches my cock with every thrust, and the pleasure is intense.

"I need your tits in my mouth." Her dress comes off with a quick tug and I unsnap her bra. As I suck her tight nipple into my mouth, a growl escapes me. Or maybe it's her.

"That's it, Tess." My eyes remain fixated on her as she rides me. Have I ever loved her more? My stomach muscles tighten as she grinds herself on me.

"Rub your clit on me." I jerk her up and down on my cock. "Christ, I'm ready to come. You're too tight."

She's on her tip toes. I maneuver myself so deep I can sense her start to tremble and clench.

"Come on, Tess." Snarling, I bite her nipple. "I want to hear you scream."

She does. Her body responds to me. Her pussy is pulsing and clenching like a vise around my thick cock, almost like she's milking the come out of me. She lets go of the towel rack and reaches for my neck as she attacks my tongue with hers.

"Reed... Reed, I'm... Fuck, I'm coming." Her body jerks and convulses on my cock, setting me off. I pull her twitching pussy tight as I shoot my release inside her.

When I pull her hair back, she looks down at me.

"I had no idea. I love this... I mean, it feels good, doesn't it?" Her beautiful eyes try to focus on me.

Looking at her as we both catch our breaths, I cup her cheeks. "I have never felt this ever." Tears spill from her eyes and I gently rub them away.

"I love you," she whispers. "I love you so much."

Grabbing her neck, I kiss her hard. We break apart only to catch our breaths. Then slowly I lift her off my semihard cock, steadying her as she stands.

Her legs are shaking. "Maybe I need to let you rest." I grab some toilet paper. "Let's get you cleaned up." My eyes scan her body as I gently wipe her down. When I arrive at her waxed pussy, my thumb dips into her wetness to rub her clit.

"Why are you waxed?"

She looks dazed as a moan escapes from her. "What?" she whimpers.

I pull my thumb away. Her eyes narrow and I feel her nails bite into my shoulders as she pulls away. Standing up, I run my hand through my hair. Unwanted jealousy creeps into me.

"Seriously, Tess, why?"

She grabs her panties from the floor, stepping into them gracefully, her tall thin body glistening. I should shut up. I sound like a lunatic.

"Um, because I like it."

"What does that mean? It's not like you were having sex. So, who were you waxing for?"

Not even looking at me, she pulls her pink dress on, straightens it over her hips, then walks right up to me.

"Reed, you asked me to let the past go. So, your behavior right now is sending mixed messages. You want me to shut up and forget about the last couple of years. Well, then I deserve the same."

She's right, but visions of guys being anywhere near her pussy make me sick. The irony is not lost on me. She stands in front of me, head held high, hands on hips. Like a queen. I don't deserve her, but that never stops me.

She sighs. "Stop thinking! I can see your mind whirling. How can you feel threatened when you know you were my first?"

Closing my eyes, I unclench my hands.

"Reed! I started getting waxed years ago with Mom. And I've kept it up. It's like shaving my legs. I just do it."

Rubbing my hands across my face, I smell her on them. *What am I doing?*

"I'm sorry. I know you started waxing before you left. I guess I thought..." I shake my head. "Clearly, I'm not rational when it comes to you. I'll work on it," I say, kissing her eyes and nose.

She looks up at me. "I think you need sleep if these black circles are any indication." She lightly traces my eyes.

I nod. "Let's go check in. You can see the rest tomorrow."

chapter 27

TESS

I wake with Reed's body draped over half of me and the windows dripping with rain outside. Snuggling in tighter, I've forgotten this sense of security. I turn my head, bury my nose in his strong neck, and inhale his fresh Reed scent and my own. We checked into a suite at the Saint Regis and collapsed into bed. I woke to Reed's head in between my legs at around 4:00 a.m. He wasn't joking when he said he can go all night. I don't remember when we ultimately drifted back to sleep, but if I can walk today, it will be a miracle.

"You okay? You look far away. What are you thinking about?" His rough morning voice makes my eyes connect with his. I smile up at him.

"Us. Last night." I bury my head in his warm chest.

He chuckles "I keep telling myself to let you rest. You're sore, aren't you?" His full lips kiss my head.

"I'll be lucky if I can walk! I can feel a pulse down there."

He rolls on top of me laughing. "Your body will get used to it. I'll let you rest today. I have plans anyway. Get up and let's shower. We're going out."

I look out the window. The rain seems to have let up, but it's wet and likely muggy.

"Maybe we should stay in and order room service and watch a movie today." With a yawn, I snuggle back into his warm spot.

He slaps my ass. "Up! We're roughing it today." He chuckles, his dimples teasing me.

"What does that mean?" I say, sitting up. Pushing my hair out of my eyes, I take in the full beauty that is Reed.

"Well, we're on a budget. That is, after we get a bed." He stretches, and I can't help but blush at his thick hard cock. He grabs my face for a kiss.

"I love your blushing. You were never shy with me. What's changed?"

I want to say everything's changed. That I'm all in. That if he leaves me, I might shrivel up and die. Instead I pull my knees up.

"I guess I'm not used to being happy." Not a lie—I've been sleepwalking for three years.

He pulls me up as though I weigh nothing. "I know that feeling well. I meant what I said yesterday. This is us, our new life. I'm not going anywhere." With his full lips, he tries to kiss me, but I turn my head away. "I haven't brushed my teeth."

He smiles. "You're too beautiful to have bad breath. Now kiss me."

I laugh. "Now I really can't. That's way too much pressure."

Reed kicks open the door to the lavish bathroom and lets me slide down his hard body. He turns on the water for the shower. Completely uncomfortable, I look around. Should I get in with him, or wait?

"Tess? What's wrong?" There's amusement in his turquoise eyes.

Glancing at my reflection, my blond hair's a tangled, wild mess. My blue eyes look so big. Absently I think I look like a Disney princess. You know, the ones whose eyes take up too much of their face.

"Talk to me. What's going on in that stunning head of yours?"

Sighing I straighten my shoulders, causing his eyes to drop to my chest.

"I... I never thought it would be like this."

His hand cups my cheek as steam starts to fill up the large bathroom.

"I mean, I have always loved you, but now... it's... there's this closeness that I never knew existed." I cover my face with my hands. "I'm being silly. It's hard to explain."

He gently removes my hands and tilts my head up. "It's not silly. I feel it too." His thumb traces my lips.

"Yes, but you've had sex, so you're used to this sensation." His hand tightens on my chin.

"What does sex have to do with the way we feel?" He says, his voice low and gravelly.

"I... I don't know. I only assumed..."

"Don't assume. It has nothing to do with it! I could have fucked a thousand women and never felt the way I do when I'm inside you."

My heart thuds, and I look away. His words are too powerful, giving me hope when I still need to be cautious.

"Look at me." He grabs my chin. "Those women meant nothing." He laughs bitterly. "I don't think I even kissed them. I used to have to fantasize it was you. I tried so hard not to, but you always haunted me." He drops his hands. We stare at each other until he finally shakes his head and enters the shower, leaving me to digest his confession.

What the hell? Pulling open the shower door, I find his magnificent body so distracting, I almost forget how to talk.

"Are you trying to tell me that you thought about me when you fucked other women?" I'm whispering, which is stupid—it's only us and the shower.

He opens his eyes, and I watch transfixed as he washes himself. Feeling myself get wet and that pulse between my legs, my core starts to throb.

"Yes. Does that make you happy? I couldn't come without calling your name." He reaches for me, dragging me into the hot shower.

"I'm done, Tess. I don't want to fight. You're feeling vulnerable. Fine, that's expected. It's hard to trust me after what we've been through. But come on, you have to know that what we have is powerful." I blink back the water drops.

"We need to be careful, Kitten. Otherwise these emotions could hurt us. Do you understand?" He brings his wet lips close to mine. "I love you and you love me. Always have. Call it destiny, soul mates, whatever you want. It controls us both." I stare at him, his face serious, the shower pitter-pattering around us.

Then he turns and steps out of the shower. "Do you want me to order room service before we start roughing it?"

Slightly dazed, I shake my head.

"Just let us be us, and I swear you will be happy." Wrapping the towel around his waist, he leaves me. I let the hot water beat down on me for a moment, trying to get a handle on my spinning emotions. Reaching for the shower gel, I squeeze some on my palm, watching as the gel bubbles and foams to life. As I wash myself, the sweet lavender smell calms me, and I suddenly get it. Or maybe I accept it. Reed is right. We are destined to love each other, and it's okay to feel vulnerable. I mean what I feel for him is not rational or even controllable. It's pure and right and I want him more than I have wanted anything. When did he get so wise? Or maybe he truly is done playing games. If that's the case, I need to do the same.

Turning off the shower, I reach for a towel. As I stare down at my feet, I inhale deeply and take one step forward.

We spend the rest of the day walking the streets. The crowded sidewalks seem unnecessary as we hold hands talking, laughing, being together. It's as though I'm almost high or reborn. As though I've shed my old skin—the anxiety that's been my life—in the shower and watched it flow down the drain.

"Do you want anything else on this?" the guy holding up my hot dog asks.

"Nope, I think that will do it." I laugh as Reed rolls his eyes, trying to hand me the oozing chili cheese dog.

"Sixteen dollars." He pulls a twenty out of his pocket, paying the guy.

"Keep the change." Reed wraps his arm around my shoulders as we walk and eat our hot dogs. It's slightly raining again, but I don't even feel it. Seriously, someone could shoot me, and I wouldn't know it. I'm walking on a cloud.

"So, that was our last twenty dollars. Since we're broke, what should we do?" Reed stops us to sit on an empty bench.

This has been our ongoing joke today. Since I wanted to know if we would be happier without money, he left his wallet in the safe at the hotel. We have wandered the streets with only fifty dollars.

"We could go to a museum." I play along.

"Nope, too expensive." He puts the last of his hot dog in his mouth and throws the aluminum foil in the trash can across from us.

"Isn't this fun? I mean who knew how much fun you can have in Manhattan without money."

Pulling me close, he gifts me a smile so beautiful, my heart skips a beat.

"God, I love you." He kisses my nose.

I finish chewing and try to swallow the hot dog that is stuck in my throat. Reed takes what's left of it out of my hand, then pulls me onto his lap. The drizzle has started to pick up and I raise my flushed face to the dark skies. Wetness cools my cheeks and I blink at him as our lips touch. I taste the chili and mustard on his lips and lean into him, allowing him to deepen the kiss. His strong tongue twists with mine. The drops are getting fat and the splatter of wetness makes me moan and seek his warm tongue even more. This moment is perfect.

I feel like Holly Golightly in *Breakfast at Tiffany's*. I know this man will either be my savior or my destruction. No matter what, my future is sealed.

chapter 28

REED

Present day – twenty-five years old

My stomach growls, waking me. Looking around, I try to figure out where I am. When I close my eyes, it reluctantly comes flooding back to me. Sitting up, I run my hands over my face. I'm in our private jet on my way home.

Home. Is it even that anymore? Four years doesn't sound that long. Yet with what I've been through, it seems like forever. The shock of Jax's phone call has gradually worn off. I'm grieving for so many things. My grandfather dying is the tip of the iceberg.

With a sigh, I glance around and note this is one of our newer planes, the luxury abundant, almost reeking excess. Leaning forward, I reach for my phone. The leather chair glides with me, so soft it's like a downy bed. Dark wooden tables sport vases with red roses. I guess they go with the bright red carpet. I notice the couch is white with red throw pillows. My mind drifts back to the last time I flew commercial, then shuts down. That's a wound that never needs to be reopened. A low commotion brings my eyes to the large flat screen. Hockey is on and a player has been shoved into the boards. The fans seem to have taken offense, hence the commotion. The player gets up and spits blood on the ice. Even with the volume low, I can sense the anger and excitement coming from the arena. I've become immune to that life—a life where you go and drink beer and cheer for a team. A life that has meaning, even if it's only to be a fan. Somewhere I lost that. My grandfather dying is the first real emotion I've had in a while. I want to thank him for that and so much more. Pain rushes over me like waves in the ocean. For one split second, I was distracted enough not to remember. I pride myself on control, which means regret isn't part of my vocabulary. But today, I allow myself to feel something even if it's a simple longing for a game. Sadness that my hero is gone. But not regret. He wouldn't allow it, nor will I.

"Good morning." The flight attendant smiles. She's petite and pretty in a nerdy girl way. Black-rimmed glasses sit on her face and small purple lips smile at me.

"Mr. Saddington, can I get you something to drink?" Her tight white silk shirt is ironed and tucked into a black pencil skirt. Dishwater-blond hair is twisted up in a bun.

"Yes, coffee black, please."

"Of course." She turns and I watch the blatant swing of her ass.

"How much longer until we land?" I say, stopping her before she goes into the kitchen area.

"About two more hours. I hope you brought a jacket. It's supposed to be raining." She smiles, causing me to notice a gap between her front teeth. I nod.

Rain. That's something I'm used to. As I glance out the window, the morning sun peeks through. The moment I land, I need to make sure Michael, my second in command in London, is apprised of the situation. Somehow this trip seems final.

"Sir, your coffee." The woman sets it on the table along with some pineapple and mango.

"I'm sorry for your loss. If you need anything at all, I'm here for you." She looks down at my cock, her hand casually brushing my leg. Her attempt to be professional when sending me signals to fuck her is rather humorous.

Unfortunately, I can still smell Victoria's flowery perfume on me. Poor Victoria. Her disappointed face and desperate need to please make her somewhat pathetic. She should count herself lucky if she never sees me again. I hope I was clear that we are over. It hasn't even been twenty-four hours, but I can barely remember.

I smile at the woman. "Thanks. I won't be needing anything but breakfast." She looks disappointed.

"And would you like that now?"

I arch an eyebrow at her. Any other time, her aggressive nature would spark at least enough interest to bend her over the table and take her from behind.

Taking a sip of the dark coffee, I swivel the chair around facing her.

"Do you have any hot dogs?" Her look of shock almost rivals mine. The recurring dream I've been having lately hits me in the gut. *Shit, that's what woke me up.* I was dreaming about eating hot dogs in the rain...

Bringing the coffee to my mouth, I drink deeply, allowing the hot, bitter liquid to slide down my throat. It gives me a moment to compose my thoughts. My hands start to sweat. Since moving to London, I've been having this dream. It started one night after I worked for hours. I was tired and cold when I got back to my flat and fell into a restless sleep. I woke in terror, my screams echoing off my empty walls. It soon became recurrent. Sometimes they are good. Most of the time I wake up with my heart racing, my fingers clutched around my scarred-up chest, her scent embedded in my brain. She's always laughing, kissing me. Then she's gone, and I can't find her. I search and search. Usually my brain makes me wake up there. Other times the nightmare goes on until I collapse at different places, crawling in the rain looking for her, the taste of her lips burned into my memory.

I have trained my mind not to think about her. But she haunts me in my dreams and elsewhere.

"Sir?" The flight attendant clears her voice. My eyes snap over to hers.

"We do. In the freezer. Would you like me to heat one up?" Blinking at her, I stand and try to calm my racing heart.

"Yes. Give me twenty minutes. I'm going to take a shower first. I don't suppose you have chili?"

She cocks her head confused. "No, we have eggs benedict and asparagus with multigrain toast."

"Hmm. Yes, that's one of my favorites. Bring me two hot dogs with mustard and ketchup." I walk away with my cup of coffee.

"My name is Willow," she calls after me and I turn briefly, "in case you change your mind and need me." She licks her lips.

I don't bother responding and keep moving toward the shower. My earlier rejection should have been enough. Shutting the door, I peel off my suit jacket, the need to remove all traces of Victoria and London suddenly strong. My hands move frantically as they jerk off my clothes. I'm not quite certain what I think this shower is going to solve. Will it wash away my shame of my torn relationship with my brother? My endless lack of consideration for my parents' feelings? My sadness and pain at my grandfather dying? It won't. It never has, but I get in anyway.

TESS

Past – eighteen years old
New York, NY

"Pretty Girl, we need to talk about this." Brance sits in my fully decorated and kickass kitchen.

"Why are you doing this to me?" I frown. "You know I need you."

He stares at me, forcing me to smile at my antics. "I waited for you to get your life back together with Reed. You two are basically married. You've been going strong for four months. I need to make the move for myself. I'm done with New York." He reaches for a couple of the grapes in a bowl sitting in the middle of my island.

"I want to visit my family in Colombia. Have a heart-to-heart with my father. Hope he doesn't disown me." He checks his watch as I hand him an omelet that I learned how to make watching the Food Network channel.

"Wow!" He turns the plate. "Can I be seeing things? Did you make me something to eat?" He waves his hand up from the plate to his nose. "It smells like real food."

"Knock it off. I have decided to learn to cook." Using a sponge to clean the counter, I continue. "I mean, look at my kitchen. It would be a shame not to use it."

Sometimes I want to pinch myself to make sure I'm not dreaming. It took Brance and me a month of furniture shopping and the efforts of a team of painters we hired, but we turned it into a masterpiece. To be honest, we could have been done earlier, but Brance discovered this place that installs old railroad ties as floors. Outrageously expensive but so worth it. Then he decided to have a brick wall installed, so that took time. But the finished product speaks for itself. Yellow and French blue were our main colors, adding a warmth that most places lack. Secretly I think it looks better than Caroline's, and that's saying something.

Rinsing my hand under the water, I ask, "Don't you think a phone call would work equally as well? Isn't it dangerous for you to go to Colombia?"

"No doubt, but I'm long overdue to see my family. My middle brother is recovering from a gunshot wound. I told you he almost died, right?"

"Yes." I chew my bottom lip. "That's what I'm talking about. I can't stand the thought of anything happening to you."

He smiles, showing off his pretty white teeth. "My dad will take care of security. Believe me, he will have me so heavily guarded, I will be fine."

"I guess." I glance down at my nails.

"Also, it's only fair to tell my father in person that I'm still gay and moving to West Hollywood." Brance sprinkles some salt on the omelet from my cute little rooster salt caddy.

"I hate it. What am I going to do without you?"

"You have Reed, Pretty Girl. And school and obviously cooking." He holds up a forkful. "I'm not lying. This is delicious."

Smiling, I grin. I love to cook. "I made lasagna last night for Reed. He said it was so good I could open my own restaurant."

Brance's lips twitch. "Of course he did. Well, he would know."

"I'm being serious. Reed loves when I cook for him."

"Reed loves anything you do. Which is why I can safely leave you in his hands."

I stare at Brance, my mind scrambling to find a way to make him stay. He has been my one constant for the last three years. Sighing, I've known from the beginning that he was going to eventually move to California.

"I'm being selfish and spoiled. I want you to be happy. I guess this means as soon as we graduate, we'll move to Los Angeles. I hate New York anyway," I say, popping a grape into my mouth.

"Says the girl who won't leave it." His snarky voice makes me stick out my tongue.

"You know I have a love-hate thing with New York. I guess it symbolizes security because of Reed."

"Whatever." He takes another bite. "Holy God, Tess Rose Gallagher, this is fantastic. I'm extremely impressed."

I smirk. "I told you I was getting domestic."

"You weren't kidding. Next thing, you'll be barefoot and pregnant."

I glare at him. "What?"

He arches an eyebrow at me. "It was a joke. God, you're sensitive today."

"I wonder why that is. Hmm, could it be because my best friend is being a jerk?" When I glance out the window, gray skies stare back at me. "You know I don't find the baby thing funny. I don't even like you joking about it!"

"Lighten up, Tess. Reed cares about two things: you and him. If you don't want kids, believe me, the man will be more than happy not to share you," he says in between bites.

"You think so?" My voice betrays my insecurities.

Brance stares at me like I'm insane. "Are you eating or not?"

"I can't eat." I reach for some grapes. "Do you want me to fit into that gown you have me wearing tonight?"

He appraises me up and down again. "You're right. Coffee and fruit for you."

"So..." Taking a breath, I try to prepare him. "I need you to rethink your negative vibes about Reed's grandfather's party tonight. Lana is going to need you." I'm trying my best to guilt him.

He snorts, forking in the last of the omelet and pushing back the plate. "There is nothing negative about me not going to that party tonight. It's positive all around."

"No, it's not." The thought of my mom and my dad being at the same place nearly makes my chest break out in a rash.

"Please... I need you! So does Lana. She is going to be humiliated. And I can't be in two places at once." Sliding close to him, I clutch tightly to his shirt.

"Tess? Let go of my shirt. I'm not Reed, so stop whining." He cups my face. "I'm trying to get away from the one percenters. The Saddingtons are old money. It goes against everything I'm striving not to become. I mean, come on, wasn't Reed's great-great-great-grandfather a duke or something?"

"Fine." I pull away from him, grabbing my rubber band from my wrist to tie up my hair. "Just let me have to handle everything." Dramatically, I wave my hands. "You know my mom is going to go insane when my dad walks in with Lana. It's going to be a complete slap in the face for her. Not that I'm her biggest fan, but even I have to say it's humiliating." I open the refrigerator for a bottle of water.

"This is not our problem. Lana needs to tell Robert to fuck off. I told her that too." Taking the bottle from me to open it, he looks at his watch again. I almost kick him.

"Stop looking at your watch. We have plenty of time before we have to meet her."

Brance sits back down. "The truth is they are going to eat her up. I have no desire to see a bunch of entitled fat fucks humiliate her or your mother."

"Exactly, Brance." I slap the counter. "That's what they're going to do to her. My dad is being a dick all around. I know he wants my mom to sign the divorce papers. But bringing his mistress to this party? This could be awful."

He's silent, then looks at the ceiling, closing his eyes.

"Goddamn it, Tess." He shakes his head and throws his hands up. "Fine, I'll go! For you and Lana. It's going to be a shitstorm."

Squealing, I throw myself into his arms, kissing his face.

"Now what's happening?" Reed startles us with an amused glare. He's back from working out in the custom gym he had built downstairs. My eyes greedily sweep over his sweaty, shirtless body, his gym shorts low on his hips, his six-pack pumped after two hours of punching the bag. He walks up behind and pulls me tightly to his chest.

"Reed, you're all sweaty," I say, twisting around.

"You like me sweaty. I was hoping we would be alone." He arches a dark eyebrow at Brance, starting to pull the tape off his hands, keeping me locked in his hot embrace.

"Sorry, Pumpkin." Brance smiles. "Tess has somehow manipulated me into going to your grandfather's birthday party tonight."

Reed looks at me, then back at Brance. He nods approvingly. "Actually, you probably should come." He roughly throws the tape away, not saying anything else.

Brance rubs his temples. "Fine, but both of you owe me. Please put a shirt on your chest—it's distracting me," he snips.

Reed laughs. "I'll do better than that. I will remove myself from your view. I need Tess for a moment."

Brance's eyes get big. "Is that your subtle way of telling me you're going to have sex with Tess? Classy, Reed," he says dryly.

"He doesn't mean that," I yell because Reed is literally dragging me upstairs to our bedroom.

"No, Brance, that's exactly what I mean."

"We have hair and makeup appointments," Brance hollers up at us.

"Reed, have you gone insane?"

"It's only Brance, Kitten. I've been hard all morning waiting patiently." His voice husky, he puts my hand on his erection.

"See... I need you." He shuts our bathroom door and instantly pulls down his basketball shorts. His beautiful thick cock stands at attention.

"Reed, I have to go to the salon, get my hair done, then makeup and nails. I don't have time for this." It's impossible to keep my eyes on his face because I'm sorry, his dick is spectacular.

"My cock is going to be in your pussy in exactly one minute." He reaches down and starts pumping himself. Watching, I love when he masturbates in front of me. He knows it too. Despite my protests, my traitorous body is getting excited.

"If you like that cute little dress, I'd take it off." Reaching down, he pulls me forward, claiming my lips. Before I can explain that I don't have time, I moan and our tongues suck and bruise each other's lips. And like that, all my scheduling and Brance seem to fade away.

It's only Reed and me. My desire for him takes over like a drug because I have become a junkie. He growls in my mouth. "Tess, clothes."

Quickly, I pull my dress over my head, tossing it onto our antique couch. Reed is waiting with the shower door open. His strong hands wrap around my arm, and he pushes me against the tile wall. His turquoise eyes search my face as the water sprays us from different angles.

"Don't worry, Kitten. I'm going to fuck you hard and fast." His full lips latch on to my neck.

I moan loudly; it echoes off the walls.

"Yeah, that's it." Two strong fingers enter me, reaching to rub my magical spot. "Fuck, Reed…" Throwing my head back, I feel myself thrust against him and my body is already pulsing.

"Come, baby." Gasping, I feel him bite down on my neck, his fingers stroking hard and fast. My pussy quivers with bliss then gushes with pulse after pulse of exquisite pleasure. Thankfully he is holding me because his lips are all over my face praising me for coming so hard.

"Fuck, you drive me crazy." His head drops to my breast and he sucks my nipple hard. He wasn't kidding when he said he was going to be rough. Not being able to help it, I moan my pleasure loudly.

Reed lifts his head and gazes at me, his eyes hot with desire. "I need to be inside you, Tess," he demands, somewhat frantic. I run my hands through his wet hair.

"I need that too," I groan as something close to liquid fire pulses in my veins. Reed lifts me up easily. I wrap my legs around his waist as he thrusts into me hard.

"Oh my God, Reed, I love you, love this…" My back is against the tile and he fucks hard and fast, his strong hands holding me as his thick cock plows into me over and over.

"Christ, Kitten." Our bodies are so in tune. At some point, I realize we're loud and frantic. My nails claw his back as he praises my pussy. My head is in his neck and I can't help but suck it.

"Reed," I whimper getting ready to come, my pussy vibrating with need. As I grab ahold of his shoulders and neck, he thrusts higher. I scream his name as he continues to impale me deep and hard.

"Reed… I can't." Still pulsing and clenching him like a vise, I grab his forearms and he throws back his head, his beautiful body jerking as his warm seed fills me. Slowly, I come back to earth hearing our harsh breathing and the water.

"That was incredible." I try to catch my breath, and Reed gently lowers my legs. He hasn't pulled out yet and his face is buried in my neck.

"Reed?" He looks at me, his eyes filled with love, the beast in him satisfied.

"Jesus, you okay? I wasn't too rough, was I?" He holds me, kissing my eyes and lips. As he sets me down, his hands stay on my hips almost knowing I need a second, seeing as my legs are shaking again.

Grabbing his forearms again I say, "Reed I'm going to be wearing five-inch heels in a couple hours." I glare at him.

He laughs and happily starts lathering up his hands, then reaches for me, soaping my body quickly. And because he's Reed, he starts to stroke my pussy."

I grab his hand and hold it tightly. "Don't even think about it."

"Oh, I'm going to make you come again. So lean back in my arms and relax. The quicker you come, the faster you can go do your stuff."

His hand dips inside my wet core, the other gently holding my leg up.

"Please, Reed... I..." My mind is latched on to the pleasure, so I stop pleading. His slick fingers are so gentle, rubbing my clit lovingly. His tongue is in my ear, my neck, sucking and licking. Doing what he says, I lean back, resting my head on his hard chest.

"Look at this beautiful pussy respond to me," he grunts in my ear, causing me to shiver. My breath is ragged and harsh sounding as the water pelts my neck and stomach. He rubs me harder, dipping in and out, circling my clit.

"This pussy is mine, Tess. I love it.... let go, Kitten. I want to feel you strangle my finger and come on my hand." His dirty words send me over. My body convulses as wave after wave of pleasure courses through me. Reed holds me tight, and his fingers stay inside me.

Slowly I stop jerking. "Why? Why couldn't I have left the first round. Now I can barely move!" My head is on his shoulder. His hands caress my breast.

"I have to go... Lana and Brance are waiting."

"Go. Have fun. Spend lots of money."

I smile at him. Opening the shower door, I step out, wrapping a red fluffy towel around me.

Looking at my Tag Heuer watch, I groan. "Reed! Lana is going to kill Brance and me! We're going to be so late. This is all your fault." I reach for my dress and force my legs to work since I need to grab fresh panties from the bedroom. I don't bother with makeup. Reed's still in the shower, so I peek my head in.

"I'm going. I love you."

He lifts his head, and blue eyes like the clearest oceans greet me. His full lips grin. "I love you too."

God, he's hard to leave. Racing down the stairs, I scream for Brance. Silence greets me. I pull out my phone tapping my foot like a crazy person.

"This is Brance."

"Where are you?" I grab my purse in a bit of a frenzy.

"Downstairs in the garage."

"I'm coming. We are so late. Lana's called like a dozen times." I hang up on him. For once, I'm happy to have my own elevator.

I spot Brance laughing and talking to Jay and run over to them. "Thank God. Let's go. She's going to kill us."

"Relax, Tess. Get in. I'll drive you guys." Jay chuckles and opens the door of the Range Rover. I hop in, sliding to the right so Brance can get in. Looking over my shoulder, he's simply standing, texting on his stupid phone.

"Will you get in? Lana is going to freak about us being late."
He arches a dark brow at me as he sits. "Now, Tess... whose fault
is it that we're late?"

"Reed's!" I snap. Laughter fills the SUV.

"Stop laughing, you two! Just drop us off at the salon."
Ignoring them, I push on Lana's number. It rings once. "Where
are you two?"

It's noisy in the background. Feeling crappy, I figure it's
clear she's already at the salon.

"Sorry... traffic is awful."

"Knock it off, Tess," she snaps. "I already talked to Brance."

"Well, I guess we'll be there in ten."

"Fine." The line goes dead.

I throw my phone in my purse disgusted as I lean back.

I glare at Brance. "Don't even."

"Wouldn't dream of it." Biting his lip, he looks out the
window. "I'm assuming since you have a huge hickey, you will
be wearing your hair down tonight?"

Horrified, I reach for my bag, trying to find my compact
with a mirror. "What? No, no, no." I gasp. Sure enough, there is
a bright red hickey on my neck.

"Unbelievable!" Pulling my long, wet hair down, I shiver as
I toss my compact back in the bag and cross my arms.

"Let's not blame all of this on Reed. I had no idea you were
so vocal." His lips twitch. "I figured Reed would fuck like a
champ, but my sweet, darling Tess..."

I cover his mouth with my hand. "Brance!"

He sticks out his tongue. I jerk my hand away. Both he and
Jay start laughing again.

"Shh. I'm mortified. I had no idea you could hear us."

He snorts. "Why do you think I was outside?"

Jay chuckles again. "Come on, Tess." My eyes jerk to his in
the mirror. "We're just having fun. Don't get upset. Your face is
turning red." He pulls over to the curb.

I put my hands to my cheeks. "I don't want to talk about it! Thank God we're here. I think I'd rather face Lana than you two." I pull on the handle before Jay can even open it.

Lana is pacing on the side patio of the salon. Aluminum foil pieces cover her hair. A cigarette dangles from her fingers.

I stop, causing Brance to bump into me. Reaching for his arm, I say, "Oh God. She's smoking."

Lana glances over at us, and I wave enthusiastically. She glares and turns her back.

Brance chuckles. "Still want her over Jay and me?" I throw him a dirty look but grab his hand for support.

Taking out his phone, he starts typing. "I'm having a couple bottles of Cristal delivered. I don't think we can make it through this day without it."

I want to argue, but he might be right. Lana is going to be hysterical because of my mom. That and my dad coming out publicly that she is his mistress.

"Good thinking," I whisper as we approach the reception girl to check in.

"Hi, sorry we're late. Tess and Brance for Brigitte and Sal."

She looks at her screen. "Of course. Can I get you two anything?" We look at each other.

"No, thanks. If a Hispanic man asks for me, please send him my way." Brance flashes her his killer smile. The poor girl blushes and stutters a yes.

Brance extends his arm for me to go first. "Let's make Reed happy and turn you back into a brunette."

Five hours later, Jay drops Brance and me off at the penthouse entrance. I'm exhausted and slightly tipsy. The day took forever. Getting my hair back to its original color was a challenge. Brigitte had to take a good three inches off my length to keep it healthy.

I'm pretty sure Reed is going to hate it. Twirling a silky piece of it in my hand as we ride the elevator, I try to imagine his reaction. Brance has gone from being a happy drunk with Lana to full-on having no filter. Which sucked earlier—Tilly had just finished her makeup when Brance informed Lana how bad it was going to be tonight, causing her to burst into tears.

I eye him as we ride the elevator. His head is resting on the mirror, his eyes closed. "Are you going to be okay tonight? We have to leave soon."

He opens one pretty brown eye, reaching for me. "Come here, Pretty Girl." I'm facing the bright light of the elevator as he inspects my face.

"Tilly did a fantastic job on you. Is it possible you have grown more exotic?"

"God, Brance you're drunk! Please pull yourself together. I need your help tonight."

I drag him out of the elevator into our lobby, which is not easy because we also have large shopping bags in our hands.

The Sex Pistols engulf us. Johnny Rotten's screeching is so loud, the windows look like they are moving with the beat. Reed had some elaborate sound system put in. I can never figure it out. Besides, I like silence when I'm home—or opera.

"Reed! We're home," I yell.

"Christ, Tess, make it stop!" Brance covers his ears with his hands. "I'm going to get dressed."

Unfortunately, the whole apartment is wired so he's not going to get any relief when he shuts himself in the guest room.

I grab the remote from our coffee table and start pushing buttons like an idiot. The flat screen bursts to life.

"What the hell? Reed!"

"Off." The screeching and TV blink off. Reed's commanding voice swings me toward him.

"It's voice activated, remember, Kitten?"

He's leaning in the doorway clad in a black tuxedo, and I want to drop to my knees and blow him, he's that hot. He must read it in my eyes because the cocky smirk is back. "We don't have time for that. You need to get dressed. It's getting late."

"Sorry." I shake myself back to the present. "It took us forever today. Some of us have to work at making ourselves look fabulous." I nervously pull my hands through my hair.

He cocks his head at me but says nothing. I hate when he does this. It's a control thing. Obviously, he hates my hair. I open my mouth to explain, but he puts his finger to my lips, then slides his hands down my arms, lacing our fingers together as he takes me upstairs.

Why isn't he saying anything? I can't stand it any longer. "You hate my hair! It's still long. I had to have her cut some length. It was fried from the bleaching."

"I love it." He grins. "You have never been more breathtakingly beautiful." He kisses the tip of my nose. "Let's get you into your dress. It's already five, and we need to leave soon."

Nodding, I enter my large walk-in closet and pull out the gown. It's a Valentino with beige, skin-toned flowers in gauze.

I shimmy into it and turn around to look at myself in the full-length mirror.

Reed steps up behind me and zips the dress. After stepping into my obnoxious, expensive Jimmy Choo pumps, I turn and look at myself. The dress clings to my curves. My breasts are pushed high. It reminds me of Marilyn Monroe's dress when she sang "Happy Birthday, Mr. President." Except I have gauzy flowers instead of sequins. It doesn't matter—it's a gorgeous dress and works perfectly with my new dark hair and kickass makeup. I can honestly say Reed is right: I'm breathtaking. My gaze follows him. Like a dark panther, he walks to his dresser and pulls out a turquoise box. My heart does a little flip.

"With all my spare time today, I decided to shop for you."

The excitement makes me shiver and I puff out some air as he opens the box. "Shit! That's a lot of big diamonds." My eyes search his.

His full lips break into a smile. "Yes, there are a lot of big diamonds." He turns me, sweeping my hair out of the way, his nose fitting right in the spot where my neck ends and shoulder begins. He breathes in and latches it on.

"Stunning."

My fingers sweep over the large diamonds.

"I love it." My voice is raspy.

The necklace is cold and heavy. His hands sink into my thick, straightened hair, pulling me tightly to his chest.

"I love the way you smell, Kitten. Have I ever told you that?"

I laugh. "All the time."

"Then have I told you how much I love spoiling you?" He spins me around so that I can look at myself in the mirror. My eyes widen at our reflections. My dark blue eyes find his light blue. It's almost as if I can see inside him. Reed takes his finger and traces what is now the purple bite mark he gave me earlier. I decided not to cover it up. If anyone sees it, they will know who I belong to.

He murmurs in my ear as his eyes stare at me in the mirror.

"I should get my grandfather to open up the family vault." I watch as his hand tightens around my neck, bringing my back flat against his chest. He whispers, "That vault holds a lot of secrets. Journals, art, and family jewels. Hundreds and hundreds of years of jewelry and gems. Some are priceless, given to my ancestors by kings and queens." He licks my ear. "Are you impressed?"

I smile, nodding my head yes. Playful Reed is out tonight.

"You want to hear a family fairy tale, Kitten?"

My excited breathing fills our quiet room. Outside, the sky is dark, and New York has all her welcoming lights glittering in our room

He chuckles. "I see that you do... Once upon a time, my great-great-grandfather fell in love with his best friend—a girl he had known since she was a child. The story goes that she was wild and beautiful but a complete pain in his ass." His eyes never leave mine as we stare at each other in our full-length mirror.

"She was also years younger than him. So, he leaves to seek his fortune in America, and when he returns to England, she's grown up and is engaged to his brother." He chuckles, nipping my neck.

"Hmm, really?" I smirk at him.

"Yes... really! The moment their eyes connected after so many years, he fell so in love with her that he killed his own brother to save her."

"Reed! Is this true?" I twist my head to see his face.

He grins at me through the mirror. "I can't make this shit up. Do you want the story or not?"

I can't help but laugh. "Sorry, proceed." My eyes return to the mirror.

"The brother was older and heir to the dukedom. Apparently, he was insane and obsessed with my great-great-grandmother."

My mouth twitches. "Of course he was."

"So in desperation, he kidnapped her." His voice is dramatic, and he wraps his arms around me tightly as if to protect me from the story.

Gasping at the ridiculousness of this, I play along. "Then what happens?" I start to grind my ass on the hardness in his pants. He straightens, taking hold of my hips as he allows me full access. My breath hitches.

"Well, my great-great-grandfather rescued her." Turning in his arms, I wrap one arm around his neck; the other reaches to rub him through his tuxedo pants. Reed closes his eyes. A slight hiss escapes him, but he continues on.

"He was the one who forfeited his dukedom so that he could permanently move his family to the United States."

"Did they live happily ever after?" I whisper into his mouth.

"Of course. He was rich as fuck. He and his wife both lived to be old... I think."

Sighing, I say, "I loved that story."

He chuckles and rubs his nose against mine. "You're such a girl."

"Reed?"

"Hmm?" His hands caress my ass.

"I love my necklace. Almost as much as I loved your grandparents' love story."

His nostrils flare slightly. "We need to get out of here. Let's get this night over with."

chapter 30

TESS

The ride to Ian Saddington's estate is painful to say the least. Brance is still being bitchy. He sits in the back sulking with his arms crossed, not even bothering to try to put on a good face. His energy is so awful that he brings Reed down to his level. I look at both of them pouting and almost laugh. You'd think we were going to the salt mines instead of one of the most prestigious parties this year. Not to mention it's his grandfather's.

I do my best to lighten the mood, telling silly stories, but after a half hour, I give up and close my eyes. Reed wraps an arm around me as I snuggle into him, the champagne from earlier catching up with me. We took a limo tonight, mostly so that Reed and Brance would have ample leg room. The traffic is flowing, and since the car is quiet, I start to drift.

Soft kisses and dirty words are being whispered in my ear.

"Hmm." I stretch. Instantly lowering my arms and sitting up, I open my eyes to find Reed's amused eyes watching me.

"I was going to warn you. I don't think you ripped it." His eyes are full of mischief.

"God, don't say that too loud or Brance will lose it," I whisper, looking for Brance.

"Why is he sitting with a cocktail in his hand?" I hiss.

"Because I was sick of hearing his loud sighs. So, I poured him a brandy hoping it would lighten him up."

"Great," I mumble, looking down at my skintight gown. I didn't feel anything rip. Reed's lips are all over my face.

"Don't mess up my makeup," I grumble, trying to get my bearings.

He bursts out laughing, opens the door, and steps out. "Come on, sleeping beauty." His tan hand reaches for mine.

"Give me a second." Opening my clutch, I pull out my powder compact, checking my makeup. Satisfied that Reed didn't ruin me, I step out of the limo.

It's been years since I was here last. We used to come here a lot as children. Reed, Jax, and I have played all over these manicured lawns. This was the first place I ever shot a rifle. Grandfather Ian had bought the boys two for their eleventh birthday. They couldn't wait to shoot them. It was one of the few times I ever bested them. Turns out I'm a natural markswoman.

"What are you grinning about?" Reed whispers in my ear.

"Just thinking about the time when I made you and Jax cry. Because I was better at shooting a rifle than both of you."

"That never happened," Reed snips, holding my hand as we walk up the winding brick driveway. Brance trails behind us with his tumbler of brandy. Music and laughter fill the balmy air.

"Ha. I kicked both of your asses." Reed says nothing but reaches down and picks me up, throwing me over his shoulder.

"Reed, put me down," I squeal. "You're causing a scene."

"You're taking too long. Besides, I can't have Brance thinking a little girl like you beat me."

Brance rolls his eyes. "I assure you, Reed, you're all red-blooded man. Please put her down."

Reed sets me down then stares at me. "We brought him—why?"

Ignoring the comment, I take the glass from Brance and hand it to a valet who looks slightly confused but takes it.

Looping my arms with both my men, I say, "We are going to have a good time tonight if it kills us." Brance rolls his eyes again. I roll mine back at him. When I look up at Reed, he chuckles. "Whatever you say. You are my queen. I'm just a lowly servant. Maybe if you're lucky, I might take you to the gazebo where I might be able to service my lady properly." He speaks with a thick but surprisingly good British accent.

"Christ! You two have more sex than anyone should." Brance pouts.

"No such thing," Reed answers still with his accent.

Laughing at him, I lightly punch his arm. "Stop it, Reed."

He laughs too. "Do you think if I did it all night anyone would say anything?" His eyes twinkle.

"I'll give you a hundred dollars if you do it all night," Brance eggs him on.

"Hmm." Reed looks at him. "How about we make a wager of two hundred dollars? Whoever stops speaking with an accent loses."

Pulling my arms free, I say, "O-kay, first, this is not the place. Second, it's rude. Third, you're both millionaires and you're only betting two hundred dollars?" I can barely say it with a straight face.

"My love, you can up the wager," he challenges me.

"Come on, you honestly think no one is going to notice you and Brance are speaking like Henry Higgins? Someone is going to say something."

Reed kisses my forehead. "I don't think anyone has the balls," he says absently then salutes a waiter. "Hello, old chap."

Laughter bursts out of me. Even Brance can't hold it in. "You're crazy!"

"So, my friend, do we have a bet?"

Brance drapes a hand on Reed's shoulder. "We jolly do."

"Oh God." I groan. Brance's accent is awful. He sounds like Antonio Banderas trying to do Shakespeare.

"It looks like your grandpapa went all out." Brance sweeps his hand indicating the setup.

"I don't know either one of you." Preparing to run away, I stop. Unfortunately, in five-inch heels, I have no choice but to stay right with them.

All three of us scan the massive grounds. The colorful dresses and tuxedos look like a giant bowl of jelly beans. The estate is impressive on a regular day. Tonight, it's awe-inspiring. Massive amounts of glittering little lights are all over. Flowers are everywhere. I can't even try to guess how long it took the florists.

Tuxedoed waiters and silver-laméd women carry appetizers and flutes filled with champagne.

"Reed... Tess." Caroline is waving us over. She's in a skintight emerald-green gown. The middle looks like a bow is wrapped around her. Reed's mother always looks fabulous, but tonight she's radiant. Snaking our way through the crowd, I notice some actors and models. Reed nods at a couple of tall guys. I'm assuming they are athletes.

Entering the elegant tent, I spot Caroline talking to a man who must be a Kennedy.

"Hello, Mother, smashing as always." Reed smiles, still using his stupid accent. Caroline frowns, excusing herself from the Kennedy guy.

"Are you drunk?" she whispers as she guides us to a corner.

"No."

My face must show guilt because she puts her hands on her hips. "Reed and Brance made a bet with each other." As if that explains everything. My eyes sweep the massive posh tent. I don't dare look at her expression—I can sense her disapproval already. Instead, I take in the round tables with white tablecloths and gold cutlery and an enormous crystal chandelier in the middle.

"Reed Saddington, you will stop talking like that immediately. And no drinking. All of you are underage." She straightens her diamond bracelets and smiles at me.

"Tess, you look stunning. Where's Brance?"

"He's right—" Turning, he's gone.

Great!

"I'm sure he had to use the loo, Mother." Reed can barely keep a straight face with that comment. Caroline's eyes narrow. "Go wish your grandfather a happy birthday. And please, Reed, this is a stressful night. I'm sure you know that Claire is... not doing well, what with Robert showing up with his girlfriend."

I cringe and take a breath. "How bad? Are they here?" I scan the area, but it's so crowded, I can't see anything.

"I think they left. God, I hope so. He introduced her in front of us all. Even to your mother. I know Robert is your father, but seriously, was this called for?" She's looking at me like it's my fault.

"Mother." Reed's voice holds a warning. "Tess has nothing to do with this."

She sighs, taking my hand. "I know. I'm on edge." She starts to fan herself. "Is it hot in here?"

"Poor Mom." I can't help but feel bad for her.

Reed rolls his eyes. "Drink some water, Mother. We're going to find Jax."

Clasping hands, we head toward the front door. Music fills the fragrant air. A full orchestra plays to the side of the entrance to the mansion.

"Jesus, Reed, my dad really did it. I'm so embarrassed." Glancing at people as we pass, I'm sure they're judging me.

"Fuck everybody." His warm hand tightens on mine. It's as though I'm back in high school and everyone is whispering about me.

The large wooden antique doors stand open, almost beckoning us to come inside. Reed is instantly greeted like a crown prince, bombarded with well-dressed strangers with outstretched hands, all wanting his attention. I smile and nod so much, my lips start to twitch and ache.

"Tess! Thank God you're here."

Wow, is all I can think. She's skinnier, if that's even possible.

"Mom." I let go of Reed's hand and hug her. "We just got here."

"Did you know?" Her blue eyes are glazed, and she appears almost shocked.

Perfect. She's not even trying to hold it together. I wrap my arm around her waist and guide her over to a life-size ice sculpture of Ian Saddington. A waiter walks by, and grabbing a napkin, I load it with shrimp skewers.

"Here." I shove it at her. "Please eat this. Do not make a scene." Her clawlike hand grabs my arm. I smile at people as they walk by us, their eyes filled with contempt.

"Did you know?" she demands.

"Mom, this is not the time or place," I whisper.

"Your father brought his whore to a party where all my friends met *her*! He introduced his slut as his girlfriend to me!" She's loud and not very steady. If a small wind came in, it would probably knock her over.

"Take it easy." This time people aren't even trying to hide their stares.

"He's ruined me. Made me a laughingstock." Tears fill her eyes.

"I'm so sorry. No one should have to go through that." For a moment, I stare up at the tall ceilings and the numerous oil paintings of Reed's ancestors. Some of the men look so much like Reed and Jax it's uncanny. When I return my focus, it's obvious I need to get her out of here, pronto.

"Why? Why would he do this? Does he love her?" Her nails bite into my arm.

"Okay, let's get some fresh air," I say quietly. People are watching and whispering. This time, I'm not being paranoid.

I groan, desperate for Reed or Brance. Even Caroline would do. Scanning the large room, my gaze lands on tables set up with piles of gifts. A huge three-tiered cake sits in the middle.

"He's trying to divorce me. I won't let him. I'll never let him win." She's rambling like a crazy person, and absently, I wonder if this is the final humiliation for her. Has my dad made her insane? A wave of pity floods me as I guide her outside.

The fragrant flowers in the air make my nose twitch. I guide us along the little path that leads to the duck pond.

The gazebo is unoccupied, I note with relief. Little lights are strung up all around it, some mixing in with the climbing pink roses and purple wisteria. In the middle sits a wooden swing. Reed and I have spent hours swinging on this swing. It's old but in perfect condition and looks like it's been freshly painted.

"Here, Mom." I help her sit back in her ridiculous harlot-red velvet gown.

We can barely hear the music although an occasional loud scream or laughter filters through.

We swing in silence until I can't stand it. "Mom?" I turn and look at her. "Why don't you just do it? Sign the divorce papers. You'll be rich. And I have to think happier than you are right now."

"Why would I give him to her? After all these years? Walk away and let some Russian gold digger have him?" She turns so fast her elbow slips off the armrest.

Reaching out, I steady her. I want to defend Lana, but it's pointless.

"He's living in another country," I say, trying to be gentle. "You have to face the fact that he's been with her for years."

She runs her hands through her hair. "He'll come back! He always does."

Shaking my head, I search the dark skies. "What Daddy did tonight was unforgivable and wrong. But he wants out. And what I have learned living with him is that he gets what he wants. So, be proactive, take the money, and move on."

I hate feeling like this. I don't have one thing in common with this woman. She has never once in my life put me first. So, why do I feel so sorry for her or want to help?

The ducks squawk, causing me to turn. Someone has added swans. Their snowy white bodies and necks dip and flutter in the dark water.

"I... I don't know who I am without him." I almost fall off the swing. Did my mom actually say something honest?

Blinking at her, I respond, "That's not true. He's been gone almost four years. And you have survived. You could do anything you want. Think about it, Mom. You're still young. You can find someone who truly likes you and be happy."

"You believe he is not coming back?" Her voice is fragile.

Looking her straight in the eyes, I say, "I know he is not. And I don't want him humiliating you or anyone anymore."

She puts her head in her hands. I stop swinging.

"Mom?" Holy shit did she pass out?

She sits up on the swing and groans in distress.

"I'll think about it. Talk to my lawyer. I'm taking him to the cleaners, just warning you."

I shrug. "Doesn't affect me one way or the other. I simply want it done."

She doesn't respond after that, her face looking lost. I gently rock us, the crickets and ducks making more noise than my mom and me.

"Tess?" Reed's deep voice penetrates the silence.

"We're in the gazebo," I call out.

He walks up the steps, face full of worry. "I've been looking for you. My grandfather is waiting for us." His eyes dart back and forth from my mom to me. "Everything okay?"

"Yes, Reed." She sighs dramatically. "We're having a mother-daughter moment. Or at least we were."

He smirks, leaning over to give her a kiss on the cheek. "Still as entertaining as ever, Claire." Straightening, he likely steals both our breaths with that smile.

"My grandfather is asking for Tess. We should think about..."

I can't help but snort back a giggle. He is completely ridiculous. My mom is so self-absorbed she hasn't even noticed his accent and he is laying it on thick.

"Shall we, my ladies?" He winks at my mom, holding out his arm.

"Reed!" I say.

He lifts an eyebrow. "Yes, my love?"

I jump out of the swing so fast it causes my mother to flop back against the wooden swing with a shriek.

"Sorry, Mom." I lean over to steady her in the swing. "Have you seen Brance or Jax?"

"Brance is here?" My mom's face is suddenly alive. Reed chuckles and helps her to her feet, patting her hand as we walk toward the music.

"Ah yes, Claire, the ever-loyal Brance has decided to make an appearance only for you."

She chatters on happily. I start to wonder if all the booze has permanently messed with her brain. Or is she truly that sad and needy? Minutes ago, she was lost and despondent about my dad. Now she's flirting and clinging to Reed like he's her best friend. Turning the corner, I see Brance laughing with Jax and some man I have never seen.

"Look, Mom, there's Brance." I point at him, having absolutely no guilt since the traitor deserted me.

She gasps and saunters toward him. Confused, I watch her. "Tell me I will never be like that," I say, frowning when she flings herself into Brance's arms.

Reed cups my face. "I can guarantee that will never be you."

"I worry that it's like a hereditary thing. I mean, I think her mom was like her. I don't remember her very well, but my dad said they were carbon copies."

"Let's dance, Kitten." Reed takes my hand in his. Everything about him is strong and warm. He feels like the most magical security cloak. I cling to him as he leads us into the ballroom. It takes at least twenty minutes since we are forced to stop to make idle chitchat, but I don't care. I'm with him and nothing else matters.

At last, he swings me in his arms. The old wood floor gleams as he swirls me around. I laugh out loud. Could I love him any more?

The orchestra has moved to the large balcony. Their exquisite instruments shine under the moonlight as the musicians play the famous "New York, New York" theme. Reed pulls me close, taking my hand and placing it right on his heart as we sway old-fashioned style. My head relaxes on his shoulder and I let him guide me. There are moments, split seconds in my life that I will never forget. The first moment my eyes found Reed's at eight. My fifteenth birthday. Eating hot dogs in the rain, and this moment. The grand ballroom is packed with people, but I see only us. This is what Reed was saying about us having to be careful. I don't know what exact action or word has triggered this strange enlightenment inside me. But it's awake and I can't ever let it go.

The instruments fill my senses. Lifting my head, I look at his handsome face.

"I love you. I truly love you." My voice comes out raspy and fierce.

He grins. "I know."

I laugh at his arrogance. His full lips brush mine. He twirls me, then pulls me into his warmth.

"You make me happy, Tess Rose Gallagher."

My eyes sting with tears as he twirls me one more time. On the last note, he dips me. And I smile knowing he won't let me fall.

chapter 31

TESS
Present day – twenty-five years old
Santa Monica, CA

I'm sitting in my living room, going over my checklist in my mind. Pudding, my Samoyed is at Logan and Brance's house. My hair has been trimmed and styled. My makeup is perfect: smoky eyes, light blush, and nude lips along with matching nails. My Bottega Veneta luggage is next to me along with my phone and wine.

Thank God for the wine. Tilting my head back, I close my eyes, the spellbinding voices of Mirella Freni and Pavarotti weaving their magic through my house. I'm calm, which should alarm me, but after my hysterics this morning, I have given into my fate. I know what I have done is horrible. So wrong, that it doesn't matter anymore. As soon as I land in Manhattan, I will have to atone for my sins.

Lifting my head, I blink at the large living room. *Yellow*, it's my favorite color. It makes everything cheerful and fresh.

I love my house and my neighborhood. It has green lawns, and everyone has a dog, a kid, or both. It's home. So why do I feel like I might not be seeing it for a while? Shaking away my morose thoughts, I stand and take my empty wineglass into the kitchen and rinse it. Looking longingly at the half-empty bottle, I know I need to stop. I have responsibilities, and it's not like I can go ahead and drink the whole bottle and forget. I've tried that, yet somehow I still remember, still crave him, hate him.

The doorbell rings and energy instantly surges through my body. A wave of dizziness seizes me. Slowly, I walk to my front door taking deep, calming breaths. Hesitating a moment, I unlock my two dead bolts and open it.

It's like I have gone back in time. Except Jay is in Santa Monica, California instead of New York. He looks the same. The man must be in his midforties, but he looks the same.

"Jay, thank God they sent you."

The tears sting my eyes. He removes his mirrored aviators, his dark suit looking out of place in my family neighborhood.

"Tess, you get more beautiful every time I see you." His smile is real. Not being able to stop, I throw myself into his arms.

He stiffens at first, then pulls me in for a tight, warm hug.

"I'm sorry," I mumble. "I know this is completely unprofessional." Sniffling, I wish I had a Kleenex.

"I need a friend. Tell me you're on my side. Please, Jay, I need at least one person from their camp on my side." The wine has not helped. If anything, it's making me lose it. I pull away and look at him. He does look good—besides the lines around his eyes, the man looks exactly the way he did when we were teenagers. Realizing that we are standing outside on my brick driveway, I motion for him to come in.

"Can I get you something to drink?" He looks around my house. His eyes zero in on my half-empty bottle of wine.

"I'm over twenty-one now, Jay. You don't have to worry about losing your job," I snip, suddenly feeling like I'm fifteen again.

"I never worried about losing my job." He looks up and down at my décor. "That's what always amused me with you three. So arrogant and sure of yourselves and how your lives were going to turn out."

He puts his hands in his pockets. "Brad hired me to do a job, Tess. That job was to protect his sons and you. I gave them a detailed report every Monday morning at nine a.m. sharp on everything you guys did that week."

"Brad had you spying on us?" I knew Brad was sneaky, but I had no idea he basically planted a mole in our group. Jay went everywhere with us. Jax was sure they had cameras. Instead, it was Jay.

"You ready to go back and face him?"

"Of course!"

"I hope so. Don't show weakness. Otherwise, he will eat you up. And you could lose everything."

I blink at him. His ominous words hang in the air. "He can't hurt me unless I allow him to."

Jay stops eyeing my walls and looks at me. "He can and he might. Wrap your mind around it."

We're both silent, letting his words sink in. Sighing, he stares at his polished shoes. "You did what you did. And now you need to come clean."

I swallow and nod. "That's why I'm going. Is...?" I swallow again, trying to relieve my dry throat. "Is he there?" I croak out.

Jay's eyes assess me. "Picked him up this morning, dropped him off at the estate." He turns away, again inspecting my art on the walls. Any other time I would happily discuss it, but not today, not right now.

"I need to know," I say.

He keeps looking at one of my favorites. "What is it you need to know, Tess? I was told to come get you. Here I am. I was told to make sure you bring everything. I'm assuming you understand what that means and that you are cooperating?" He lifts a dark questioning brow at me.

I turn toward him, "Who said that?"

"Jax."

Panic races up my back, causing goose bumps on my arms.

"Reed's changed. I'm not going to lie and say it's for the better. It's in his eyes. He's seen things that have made him ruthless."

I sink down in my chair and gesture for him to take a seat on the couch.

Turning off the opera music, I murmur, somewhat dazed, "You know Brance is coming with me, right? I need him." The last twenty-four hours seem like a bad dream that I wish I would awaken from.

"Whatever you need." He leans back, stretching his legs out in front of him. I fidget with my watch.

"He wanted to get some of the energy out before getting on the plane. He'll be here soon."

"Relax, Tess. I'm not your enemy."

I cross my legs, looking at my new Louboutin Bianca platform boots. I wasn't going to buy them because I don't usually spend that kind of money on shoes anymore. But Brance wouldn't leave the store until I had them. So, here I sit in my house, waiting, uncomfortable, a nervous wreck, and all I can think about is admiring my boots? *Christ, I really am losing it!*

I clear my throat. "So, Brance and I are going to stay at the Plaza. Did Jax give you any information about when the funeral is?"

Jay looks at me. "I think everyone expects you to stay at the estate."

My cheeks heat up. "What?" I stand and start to pace. "Well, I can't do that!" My breaths come in shallow and fast. "If that is what Jax is thinking, then you might as well turn around and leave because I... I can't do that!" I'm stuttering in full-blown panic.

The room is silent, except for my boots clicking on the hardwood floors. I run my fingers through my straightened hair. Fear like I have never experienced crawls all over my skin.

Jay stands. "I guess I need to make a phone call then."

"Yes, you do. You know what? Screw it. I'll call."

Taking my own phone, I walk into the dining room and push on Jax's name. *Figures, it goes to voice mail!*

My hands shake as I call again. At long last, Jax growls, "What?"

"You didn't honestly think I was going to waltz in there after being gone for years and confess to Reed, did you? Your poor family has just lost your *grandfather*—a man I genuinely loved. For fuck's sake, Jax, he is not even buried yet." I try to stay calm and sound reasonable. The last thing I need is Jax knowing that I'm ready to have a complete breakdown.

"You didn't honestly want me to do all that. Tell me you didn't!"

"Tess, I have been up for almost two days. I'm fucking exhausted. What we did was wrong on so many levels—" I try to talk, but he raises his voice and talks over me. I give up and listen. "Reed made his mistakes, and he is paying for them. It's time he knows, Tess. Get on the jet or I'll tell him *everything*. And you can deal with him alone banging down your door in LA."

I tilt my head up and stare at my white ceiling, taking deep breaths. "Please, I'm going to tell him, I promise. And I appreciate everything you have done and still do for me. *Trust me*, I know Reed. Blindsiding him right now will cause more damage. I won't do it."

Jax is silent. "You will do it. You have to."

"That's not what I mean," I snap, losing patience. After all, I'm the one with the secret eating me from the inside out. "Yes, I'm going to do it! I was hoping to at least get through the funeral first. You know how many people are going to pay their respects to you and your parents? Me showing up is going to be a fucking mess as it is. Telling him the truth as soon as we get to New York is crazy!"

His silence tells me he's thinking. Poor Jax. I love him like a brother. But Jesus, when he gets his mind set on something.

"It's time to tell him. I'm not denying that. But *please* think. This is not the right time. After the funeral, okay?"

He sighs. "Tess what you fail to understand is that we're all involved in this dirty secret. None of our hands are clean. My dad and mom are sick over worrying what Reed is going to do. Literally, we had to sedate my mother earlier. They need this to be over."

My head is throbbing. I lean against my polished wooden dining table. Silence fills the phone.

Finally, I speak. "I can't, Jax. I have to think of what's best for everyone involved. Telling Reed as soon as I land is not going to happen. So, I guess if you can't respect my wishes then you do what you have to do. Also, we will not be staying at your grandfather's estate. You let me know if you can live with that. Otherwise I will send some flowers." I push End on my phone.

Oh God, this is so bad. I don't even have Jax on my side and other than Brance, he's my partner in crime.

Jay's phone rings, and I assume it's Jax, letting him know my fate. I walk into my bedroom, shutting the door, and make my way into the huge bathroom—my one big splurge. I had a contractor come in and knock out a wall so that my bathroom is the size of a bedroom. I love it. It's my safe haven. My gaze absently drifts over my custom bathtub large enough for three. Separate shower, over by the window. I even had special lighting put in, so that when I put on my makeup, it's perfect. An extravagant, gold-striped, antique couch sits in the corner. Like a sleepwalker, I make my way to it and sink down.

Jax is obviously exhausted and not thinking straight. I know what I have done is wrong. But he was there. He supported my decision. In fact, if I remember correctly, he helped make it for me. Or did he? Maybe he protected me because that's what he and Reed have always done. A light tap alerts me that my time is up. Standing, I square my shoulders back and walk out to whatever my future holds.

REED

Past – twenty-one years old
New York, NY

"Nice shot, Kitten." I'm standing behind Tess as she bends over the worn green felt of the pool table.

"Why the hell would you wear this skirt?" Growling, I take in her long tan legs as she straightens up.

With a sassy grin, she ignores my question and starts singing "Take on Me," a shitty eighties song that's playing on the sound system. *Fuck, I love her.* My lips twitch as she throws her arms around me and grinds her hips against me.

"Christ, Tess, I'm serious. I can see your G-string when you bend over." Glancing around the Irish pub, I look to see if anyone is checking out my girl's goods. *Of course they are.* You would have to be dead not to. In her defense, we thought we were meeting up with Jax for breakfast. But as we were walking out the door, he called to say he hadn't even left Harvard yet. So here we are, drunk on shots of Jameson and playing pool at three in the afternoon. Tess pulls my ear to her lips. She smells like vanilla and Jameson. *Is there anything better?*

"Reed?" she tries to whisper.

I grin because she is so goddamn cute when she's fucked up.

"Yeah, Kitten?" I wrap my arm around her.

"I want to take you in the bathroom and suck you off." She's loud, so the couple next to us stares in shock.

I glare at them but pull Tess close and whisper in her ear to keep it down. "Stop it."

Pulling away, she stomps her foot like the brat she is. I can't believe I allowed her out of our apartment in this outfit. Tank top and white Converse complete her gorgeousness.

"I want to be gagging on your thick cock *now*!" Launching herself into my arms again, she rubs herself on me much like a kitten would.

"Jesus, Tess." I can't help but laugh. "I think you're cut off, babe."

She glares at me. "Are we going?" She licks her pink pouty lips. Thank God, they're normal again.

"You want me to get the check? Even though you're actually winning this game?" I tease, knowing exactly what she wants. But a hole-in-the-wall bathroom is not the right place for Tess to give me a blow job.

Her eyes narrow on me. "We're not leaving." Taking my hand, she pulls all six four of me into the small women's bathroom.

Locking the door, I can't help but smirk. She's determined, I'll give her that. I watch with amusement as she takes in the dirty floor. But she surprises me. Grabbing a bunch of paper towels, she drops them on the floor and kneels down. Her hands go straight for my cock, which has been hard the last hour.

I should stop this. After all, we're both drunk and deserve better. But I don't because my balls have been uncomfortable for too long. I almost had a heart attack at the view she presented me with when she leaned over to take that first shot, her tiny black G-string barely covering her pink pussy. Every shot she took on that ratty pool table, I grew harder until I almost picked her up and fucked her on it. But since I'm graduating next month, I'm trying to be good, presentable. Instead, I sent the death stare at every single asshole in the place. Stood behind her like the good boyfriend I am. Guarding what's *mine*. No one gets to see her perfect cunt but me.

She pulls down my basketball shorts and moans with delight when my erection springs free.

"I love your cock...sooo much. I love, love it!" She sucks the tip, sliding her pink tongue around the edge.

"Fuck," I groan, and I'm gone. My head thumps on the bathroom stall. I'm going to allow her to suck me off in a shithole and love it. Her tongue licks my slit and then she takes me all the way to the back of her throat.

"God, Kitten, you are the best." My voice is like gravel.

She smiles up at me. "I ought to be. You're the one who taught me." Her hand grabs at my base and squeezes tight. Then her mouth—that fucking sweet mouth—is sucking my cock hard. With every bob of her head, she tries to take me farther until I'm ready to jet off in her warm mouth. I fist her thick dark hair and guide her head as she makes the hottest sucking noises. Her other hand goes to my tight balls and starts to massage them as her lips suck my cock deep. I lean my head back, banging it against the door, letting Tess use her magic on my dick. In and out she sucks and pumps her hand.

"Yeah... Kitten, that's it, I'm going to come. You ready?"

She moans her want and squeezes my balls tight. And I literally explode in her mouth. Spasm after spasm of ecstasy spurts into the back of her throat.

"Fuck... Tess." I jerk one last time. Pulling her up, my hands under her arms, I kiss her, my tongue going deep inside her mouth. Tasting myself on her tongue, I pull back. "Sorry, that was a lot to swallow, wasn't it?"

Her eyes are half-closed, and she looks so magnificent I rub my heart. Taking her hand, I place it on my tattoo. We don't talk. I lean my forehead on hers. Our moment is broken by a rude pounding and kicking on the door.

"Give us a minute," I yell, and Tess's eyes get wide.

"Reed," she hisses. "You're not allowed in here. I'm the one who does the talking." She grabs some clean paper towels to dry me off, noticing one of the towels she was using as a buffer is stuck to her knee.

"Gross." She tosses it off. "We will... I mean, just a minute." She laughs, moving her hands away. I pull up my shorts and kiss her swollen red lips.

"You're ridiculous." Swatting her ass, I unlock the door. An angry-looking woman, sixtyish with tattoos, pushes past us and slams the door, mumbling about youth. Lacing our fingers together, we walk over to the bar and signal for the check. The bartender takes one look at Tess and smirks as he sets the printed bill down. *Fucker.* I have half a mind to give him a shitty tip, but that's not my style, and again, it's not his fault Tess is drop-dead gorgeous. I leave a couple hundred on the bar and take her out into the warm sunny afternoon.

Blinking as our eyes adjust to the day, we hail a cab back to our apartment. She pretty much passes out. I tuck her in and make myself a sandwich, take a shower, and slip into bed with her. She turns and mumbles how much she loves me. With half her body on top of mine, I fall into a peaceful sleep.

Morning sunlight blinds me. I must have forgotten to shut the blinds last night. Reaching for Tess, my hand feels nothing but a crumpled sheet. I bolt up from our empty bed. As I'm getting ready to search for her, I hear the toilet flush and flop back onto the mattress. I don't know what has spooked me.

"Tess? You okay, Kitten?" She opens the bathroom door, and I chuckle at her appearance. I can honestly say that no matter what Tess does, I always find her beautiful. That being said, this morning her pale face and wild hair have definitely got me wanting to take care of her.

Getting up, I guide her back to bed. "Kitten?" I lay her down and slide in behind her, pulling her tight to my warm chest. I land kisses on her neck. "Did you throw up?"

"Yes, I'm never drinking again!" She groans. "Why did you let me get into that condition?"

Laughing, I say, "I *tried* to stop you, but you kept ordering more shots, then insisted we play pool. Remember that? Your fucking skirt was so short, every time you leaned over the table, I had to stand behind you so that no one saw what belongs to me." I rub her stomach in gentle circles as she moans again.

"I feel like shit, Reed." She snuggles her tight ass on my erection, all whiny and needy the way she always is when she's hungover. I love it.

"I can see that, baby." I kiss and suck her neck, licking her ear, moving my hips to rub my hard cock in between her ass cheeks. "Maybe I can help." Rubbing her stomach, I slide my hand in between her legs. She's already wet.

"Reed," she groans. "I can't. I don't feel good. And I hate you since you're the reason I feel like this." She says all this as her ass is moving to the same rhythm of my hips. Her hands clutch the white sheet.

"I know, Kitten," I whisper. "Let's see if I can redeem myself." Moving my two fingers back and forth, I smile as she becomes wetter.

"Fuck, you're drenched, Tess. You need a release. You need to come hard." She's panting and rubbing herself all over my slick fingers. I let her fuck herself with my fingers any way she wants and dip inside her to stroke that G-spot before I let her go at it again.

317

A loud moan fills the room, the smell of her making me have to taste her, eat her. Her body starts to tense and clench. I roll onto my back and pull her on top of me. Her blue eyes meet mine, her lips downturned. "Reed, I don't want to play games—I want to come," she snarls. I love when she's a bitch. So does my cock, and it's straining for her impatient pussy. I pull her up and place her two knees between my face as I look up at her pink, glistening cunt.

"Sit on my face," I demand. Quickly, she lowers herself onto my waiting mouth and tongue. She must be hungover to be that greedy. I growl my approval as she starts to fuck my face, her hips thrusting hard on my mouth and chin. I grab her ass and take over, rubbing and sucking her until she screams my name, her pussy pulsing and clenching all over my face. Tess is draped on our headboard, her wet center resting on my neck.

"That feel good, baby? You came so hard." I pull her hips down and before she can respond, I shove my hard, throbbing cock inside her. Gasping as I fill her, she arches back, her arms reaching, grabbing my shins as I thrust and guide her hips on me.

"Christ, you are so hot, so wet, I love it."

She sits up and grabs my chest, her nails clawing into me. I moan at the slight burn and watch as she lifts herself almost off me then slams herself back onto me. My breathing is harsh, my blood is pumping, and she keeps impaling herself on my cock. It feels so fucking good I'm seeing spots. My stomach muscles tense, and her sex starts to quiver. With one last thrust, she sits still as we both feel how hot and deep I am inside her.

Lowering her lips to mine, she hisses, "Shit... Reed, I don't want to come yet. You feel so fucking good!" She grinds onto me, rubbing her clit against me.

"Fuck yeah, Kitten. Fuck me hard. Rub your clit on me hard." My cock is deep inside her, easily hitting her spot. Her swollen clit is so tight from doing what I told her that a couple more grinds is all she can take. Her body goes off, pulsing and throbbing in orgasmic bliss... so strong that I can't stop myself exploding into her, spilling my seed over and over deep inside her. She stays on top of me, her vagina clenched around my dick as our breathing returns to normal. At last, she reluctantly lifts off me, collapsing back on the pillows.

"I need a shower." She looks at me, her eyes narrowing. Turning on her side, she props her head on her hand. "Please tell me that I dreamed I pulled you into one of the most disgusting, filthy bathrooms ever yesterday. That I did not kneel on that floor and give you a blow job."

I trace her perfect nose with my finger and can't help but laugh.

"Again, you were full of surprises yesterday. I was going to stop you, but when you put the paper towels on the floor and knelt, my mind left me and my dick took over."

"*Reed!*" She pushes my chest.

"What? You have been insatiable lately. Good thing my life is about pleasing you," I tease.

Rolling over, I get up and pull her with me into our large bathroom.

"Come on, my little nymph, let's get you cleaned up."

I spend the whole day babying her, giving her Advil and orgasms. Besides our shower and answering the door for pizza and wings, we stay in bed naked all day.

It's late now. Tess is on her side, curled up against me, both of us laughing at *Curb Your Enthusiasm*. My fingers stroke her back, and I close my eyes and just be. I hear the TV and Tess's laughter. I hear Manhattan with her horns and ambulances. But all I truly hear is my heart and how much I need her. My soul mate, my lifeline. As I tighten my arms around her slim body, breathing in her scent, my mind plays over and over what

I want to do. Tess will say we are too young. I'm sure everyone will think that, but it doesn't matter. I need her. It's gone beyond obsession—it's become my mission. I want Tess to have my name and legally be bound to me forever. Absently, I hear her switch off the TV. Her contented sigh brings me out of my zone. "Tired?" I whisper, kissing her head.

"So tired, you wore me out." She snuggles her face into my neck. She loves to fall asleep with her nose next to my neck.

"Go to sleep, Kitten. I'm meeting my grandfather for lunch, and then I'll be home. Are you going to your study group tomorrow?"

She sighs. "Mm-hmm, Mr. Gifted. I will be going since I still have a year left. Also, I need to get ahead seeing how we are visiting Brance this weekend."

"You don't have to finish. If you need a break, take it. We can do anything you want us to do."

"Hmm." She rubs her cheek on my chest. "I need to graduate. I know I've been teasing you about graduating a year early, but I'm proud of you." Her voice is sleepy and sexy. She lifts her head, placing a hand under her chin on my chest. "You know that, right? You are brilliant. And I am so in love with you it scares me."

"I want you to be happy. I know you're excited about staying in Italy this summer. If that's something you want to do longer than the summer, we can. We can do anything we want." I tell our dark bedroom this while I imagine her face as she tries to decide.

"Just something to consider." My hand strokes her silky soft skin.

She's silent. "I'll let you know." Her even, soft breathing lulls me to sleep.

chapter 33

REED

I've been summoned by my grandfather. He's asked me to come to his estate for lunch. Since I'm done with school, and Tess is busy most of the day, I accepted. He's going to corner me about taking over some part of our vast businesses. Yet I can't commit until Tess figures out what she wants. Of course, he is not going to want to hear that, but it's the truth. Might as well get it out there.

Pulling up to the massive gates, I punch in the code and use my thumbprint. Silently, they open. I speed up the long stretch of brick driveway to his mansion, turn off the engine, and sit a moment. Tess was the last one to drive the Ferrari, and her scent has been with me the whole trip.

Christ, I've got it bad. Reluctantly, I step out. One of the immense wooden doors opens.

There's a moment of unease. In all my years of coming to visit my grandfather, he has never greeted me. One of his numerous staff always shows me in.

"Hey, old man," I say, taking the brick steps two at a time and giving him a big hug. At eighty-two, my grandfather Ian is tall and surprisingly fit.

His wise green eyes take in my appearance. Obviously approving, he clasps my shoulder as we enter the mansion. He had it completely redone a couple years ago, still keeping the dark ornate carved woods but adding a lot of much-needed upgrades.

I glance at him as we walk, so proud, commanding, intimidating. He has always been a hero to Jax and me. Even with his gray hair, he still gets women my age, and I chuckle at the thought.

"Reed, I'm glad you came. We need to talk."

Wrapping my arm around his broad shoulders, I say, "Well, that's what I'm here for. I've got all day. Tess has a study group lasting until late this afternoon."

He nods. "Good because she is one of the things we need to talk about."

That stops me. "What does that mean?" My blue eyes narrow on his green ones.

"Nothing bad, Reed." He chuckles, making his eyes crinkle and his whole face relax. "So protective." He pats my shoulder with a tight grip. "Such a Saddington." Unmistakable pride oozes from him.

Sighing, I say, "Still working on that."

I relax, running a hand through my hair. "You know how I am with her. Actually, I have something I want to discuss with you too." I take a deep breath. Even after three years of living together, any little remark or some guy looks at her and my temper goes off. "Sorry, Grandfather. Believe it or not, I am working on my... whatever I have concerning Tess."

"I do, Reed. I see an incredible change in you. I have never seen you happier." His eyes sparkle with delight.

He opens the French doors leading out to the west side patio. It's cooler out here, peaceful. Birds are chirping, and I let my mind unwind having left behind the horns and cursing of

Manhattan. We sit down and are instantly served some sort of kale and cranberry salad, with bread that still has steam rising out of it.

Arching an eyebrow, I look at him. "What's up, Grandfather? You hate salad. Where's the steak?"

"Can't an old man try to fit in? I know you and Tess eat this rabbit food. And we're having steak next."

Laughing, I hold up my hands. "I'm not complaining. This looks amazing." Since I'm starving, I dive right in. It's fresh and crisp. He's right—this is one of our favorites.

"So, you going to tell me why you're not at work?"

He grimaces slightly. If I didn't know him so well, I wouldn't have seen it. He's hiding something.

Ignoring my question, he says, "First, I need to tell you how proud I am of you. Graduating a year early. Being with Tess..."

I take a sip of the sweetened ice tea and look at him for a moment.

"What's wrong?" I demand.

He starts to laugh. "Nothing. I'm genuinely happy for you." He looks down at his wedding ring, which he still wears. "And... it's time I step down. Hand everything to your father, your brother, and you."

Putting down my fork, I lean back in my chair. "Why?"

"Because I have been running an empire my entire life. I'm tired and I'd like to enjoy myself. Which is why I pushed so hard for you to go to Columbia. I wanted you to get your degree. I know you don't need it. But you did it, and in record time." His eyes gleam with what looks suspiciously like tears.

I frown. "What aren't you telling me?"

"I'm fine, Reed, but it's time." He motions to someone in the corner.

"Whiskey please, Rebecca. Reed, I assume you're fine with iced tea since you are driving?"

I cross my arms. "That, and it's barely noon."

"*See*, once I retire, I can drink any time of the day." He grins at me.

I shake my head. "Whatever makes you happy, Grandfather."

"You and Jax make me happy." He clears his throat. "Do you want to take over the London office? You and Tess can live overseas for a while."

I reach for the bread, considering if I should tell him. Fuck it—he's being somewhat honest with me. Might as well tell him the truth. "I'm thinking about asking Tess to marry me."

He exhales, staying quiet as he takes a sip of water. Putting it down, he looks me straight in the eye. "Nothing would make me happier."

I'm stunned. I was all ready to defend myself, convinced he was going to say we were too young.

"You have no idea how happy that makes me." I almost reach over and hug him, but I stay seated. "To be honest, I was hoping I could get into the safe. Use one of our grandmothers' rings?"

"You can have whatever you want. Marry her, settle down, have children." Again I see tears in his eyes.

"One step at a time." I laugh. "First, I have to get Tess to agree. She has this idea that we should wait. Worried that people will judge us for being too young."

"That's absurd." He thanks Rebecca as she sets down his highball filled with whiskey.

Taking a sip, he ponders for a moment. "We're too rich for her to worry about that."

"She seems to care." I shrug. "We are going to Los Angeles this weekend. I was thinking about maybe proposing there if the time is right."

He smiles as they bring out our rare Kobe beef fillet with asparagus.

"You weren't kidding, steak for lunch." Taking a bite, I moan. It's that good.

"You don't even need a steak knife to cut this."

Realizing I'm the only one eating, I look at him curiously. He seems satisfied with watching me and enjoying his drink.

"You sure you're okay? I'm not going to lie. You saying you want to retire when you are a workaholic..." I'm pressing the issue because he is behaving differently.

"I'm fine," he says, his voice gruff. I decide to drop it, knowing if he hasn't said anything yet, he's not going to.

"Anyway, I have complete confidence in your father and you to take over. What I want to talk about is Tess."

"Okay..." Hesitating to say anything, I wait to see where he is going with this.

He swirls his glass. "You are young. You need to trust me when I say there is nothing worse than losing your soul mate."

Uncomfortable with his grief, I look away from his tortured eyes. He rarely mentions my grandmother; the few times have always been painful. She died in a car accident before Jax and I were born. He's never fully recovered from the loss.

He looks up at the blue skies. "Let's go back to your future with Tess. I think she would love living overseas. You both can travel, and you can take care of our European market."

I start to eat my lunch again. "That's the thing, Grandfather. I have to wait and see what she wants. As of yesterday, she was adamant about finishing her last year at Columbia."

"Hmm, well, whatever you think is best. You can easily help your father here and we can leave our overseas people alone. We have a good team in place."

"Don't worry. You will be the first to know. I mean, we are spending the whole summer abroad. That could change her mind."

"What about Jax?"

Arching an eyebrow at him, I say, "What about Jax?"

"Well, do you think he wants in on the family business?"

I snort. "Grandfather, Jax seems pretty determined to do what he is doing. He's happy at Harvard." Pushing back my plate, I turn my face to the sun, closing my eyes and letting my food digest.

"I love it like this: warm yet still able to sit outside without the bugs eating you."

"Yes, it's very beautiful... Reed?"

I open my eyes and look at him. "Listen to an old man. Men like us, we love only once."

I swallow, getting that ominous feeling again. "You don't have anything to worry about. I love her. She will be my wife. There is nothing she could do that would make me not love her, *nothing!*"

Silently he nods raising his glass to drink. "Good, because life throws things at you unexpectedly. You need to think before you let the famous Saddington temper get in the way. Take it from an old man who wishes he could have a redo."

"She's my life. It shouldn't be hard. I never lose my temper with Tess."

He laughs, his eyes far away. "You'd be surprised," he says, swallowing a huge sip of his whiskey. "I fight for my family, Reed, always have. We're hotheaded. Just remember to love her. All the other stuff falls into place."

I don't know what to say, so I stand up. "How about you show me the family jewels. I know whose ring I want to give her."

That seems to have lightened his mood. He stands, smiling as he walks us into the house, hand on my shoulder again, and we make our way to the vault.

TESS

I'm running around like an idiot, grabbing way too many clothes for our four-day stay in Los Angeles. We both overslept, and I didn't pack last night after I spent extra time studying.

Reed decided that I can miss a couple of days, and at the time that he mentioned it, I happily agreed. *What was I thinking?* Finals are coming up. I'm not a genius like him. I have to put the work in to get the grades I want. So I was up late finishing a paper and now I'm dead tired.

"Jesus, Tess, we're going for four days. What the hell are you packing?"

Lifting my hand, I say, "Don't start, Reed Saddington. I'm a nervous wreck. Brance is going to be all over me because I look pale and skinny. So, I need a lot of options." I say it like he should know all this.

"In other words, you are making yourself sick, so that you don't upset Brance because you're not tan and fat?"

"*Yes*! I mean, not entirely. We're going to LA. They have the most beautiful people in the world there. I want to... you know, look good."

He laughs at me. "God, I love you." Pulling me in tight, he kisses my neck.

"Even at your worst, you look better than everyone at their best. How many times do I have to tell you that?"

"Reed, let me go. I still need to pack my cosmetic bag." He does but follows me into the bathroom.

Crossing his arms, he says, "Kitten, all kidding aside, we need to get a move on. I have the pilot and staff waiting for us."

Huffing, I turn to him. "I know, so let me do this."

"Tess! We are going to LA, not a third-world country." Closing my bag, he takes my hand. "Anything you need we can buy in Los Angeles. Let's go. You know Brance is going to make you go shopping anyway."

Taking a breath, I stop my preparations. "You're right. I'm excited, that's all. It's been so long since we've seen him. And now he has a boyfriend. I hope it's not going to be... different."

"Well, he sounds serious about this one. I know you aren't used to sharing him, but I think you might have to adjust."

Grabbing my new Marni bag, I push my straightened hair out of my face.

"Don't be ridiculous. I couldn't be more excited about meeting Logan."

And I mean it. I have never heard Brance this into someone *ever*. Reed is right though. I can't help but feel a slight prick of jealousy. After all, Brance has been mine for years now.

He smiles. "Keep telling yourself that, Kitten. Now let's go." I scowl at him while he smirks. Clapping his hands, he guides me to the door.

He motions for the guy waiting for us to grab our bags while we make our way into the elevator.

Squeezing his hand tightly, I whisper, "Do you think we should have flown commercial? After all, Brance says Logan comes from a very middle-class family. I don't want him to think we're rich."

"You're kidding me, right? We never fly commercial. And I don't give a shit what Brance's boyfriend thinks about us. We are what we are. You can't get any more ridiculous than Brance. He's a complete prima donna."

Leaning into him, I breathe in his scent. "You're right. We'll look like regular Joes compared to him."

The elevator opens, and Reed grabs my hand, signaling for the driver to stay put. He reaches for the car door handle and I slip into the back seat.

We make great time. By the time we pull into the private hangar, I have relaxed enough to stop torturing Reed's hand.

"Why don't you go settle in. I need to have a word with the pilot."

"Okay." I climb the steps and look around. This is one of the newer Learjets. I don't think I've ever been in it. It's pretty much all white besides the dark tables and chairs. I'm so excited to see Brance and LA, I'm hoping this will entice Reed to want to move to the West Coast.

Settling into the comfortable chair, I cross my legs and wait for him. I hear the doors close.

Reed pulls me onto his lap. Sighing, I cuddle up in his arms.

A flight attendant stops by to ask us if we need anything. Reed orders some Cristal and strawberries while his strong hand caresses my hair. She smiles at him then leans forward, giving both of us a clear view of her large breasts.

"Will that be all you want?" she purrs at him. I stiffen and lift my head, glaring at her. Yes, my boyfriend is hot and rich, but come the fuck on! In front of me? Seriously?

"No, we're fine," I snap. She nods and goes in the back.

"Unbelievable! That was entirely unprofessional." My eyes narrow on his turquoise ones, his dark hair curling around his ears.

He winks. "I think she likes you, Kitten."

"What? Stop it. She was eye fucking you completely." Hearing the engine roar to life,

I don't bother moving to another chair. Reed reaches down and pulls the seat belt over both of us. As the jet races down the runway and takes to the skies, I sigh into his neck.

When we reach altitude, the flight attendant returns with our champagne and fresh strawberries. Again, I give her the death stare. She is average height with long blond hair. Pretty but nothing special. I relax back into Reed's arms. She ignores me, opens the bottle, then smiles at him again.

Gritting my teeth, I watch as he grins back. "Thanks, Julie. We'll call if we need anything."

"Perfect." As she walks toward the kitchen area, her ass sways so much it's almost comical.

I jump off his lap. "You know her name? Did you fuck her?" I hate when I get like this. Sometimes I have no filter.

"No, Tess. I don't fuck around on you." He sounds pissed.

"I meant years ago." I wave my arms around.

He's silent for a moment and examines my face. "You look tired. Why don't you go into the bedroom and take a nap? I'll join you shortly."

I stand there stunned. Did he order me to bed like a spoiled child?

I march into the bedroom to use the bathroom only. Sitting at the edge of the bed, I kick off my heels, cross my legs, and wait.

Then I sigh dejectedly. What the hell am I doing? This is not a good start to our vacation. So, the skank wants Reed. It's not like this is unusual.

"God." I flop back into the puffy, comfortable pillow. My head pounds, and I shut my stinging eyes and wait for Reed. I'll apologize. It's not his fault he's perfect. I must be getting my period any day now. It's hormones—that's why I've been all over the place. As soon as I start, I'll be back to normal.

"Tess, baby, wake up." I slowly blink, trying to force the fog away.

I focus on dark denim legs. Rolling on my back, I look at Reed. His hair is wet and he smells yummy.

I can't help but smile at him. He leans down, his strong arms caging me in. "You feel okay, Kitten?"

"Tired! How long did I sleep?"

"The whole trip. We're getting ready to land." Giving me a quick kiss, he swats my butt. "Come on. We need to get into our seats."

Stretching, I say, "I need two minutes for a quick shower." Standing up, Reed hands me my shoes. My top looks like it's been left in the rain and a dog rolled on it.

"We're getting ready to land. You can take a shower at the hotel."

"Reed, you can't be serious! You took a shower." I blink at him. "Also, I can't wear this blouse. Look at it." The wrinkled yellow sheer shirt is a sad sight.

The phone rings and Reed motions for me to get ready.

"Hey, Charlie... I know. We'll be right out. Thanks, man." He hangs up. "Come on, Kitten. Your top is fine."

"I can't meet Logan looking like this," I say, motioning to my wrinkled shirt and face. "Tell Charlie to fly around. I'll be quick." I pout.

He pulls me into his arms "Weren't you the one wanting to fly commercial so as not to look rich? Now you want me to tell Charlie to fly around so that you can take a shower. Talk about spoiled. We're already cleared to land. Trust me, Logan is not going to notice."

I glare at him using my own words to his advantage. "Easy for you to say. You're wearing a clean white button-down shirt and dark jeans." Wish I could throw my high heels at him.

Instead, I hold on to his shoulder as I slip into my pumps. Grabbing my bag, I glance around the cabin to make sure we're not forgetting anything.

I expect to see Julie; instead we're alone.

Settling into the chair, I pull out my makeup bag and groan in frustration at my reflection. My mascara has smeared under my right eye.

"I look like Spot the dog."

"You worry too much about your looks, Tess." He pulls out his phone.

I roll my eyes at him. "I don't understand why you didn't wake me earlier."

"I tried, and you didn't move. Obviously, you need sleep."

How can I argue with that? But come on... all my lipstick has been smeared off. And I don't even want to get into my hair.

Crossing my legs, my eyes scan the area for Julie. "What did you do while I slept?" I cringe and wish I could take it back but it's out there.

He cocks his head. "What's going on with you?"

I rummage through my makeup bag not able to look at him or I might start crying. "I'm sorry, I don't know why I asked you that."

Reed stares at me then sighs as he shakes his head. "I talked with Charlie for a bit. Then I wanted to fuck my girlfriend. But she was exhausted, so I sat and watched her sleep for a while. After that, I decided to take a shower. Oh, wait... I also fired poor Julie. She cried if that makes you feel better."

I groan, rubbing under my eye, trying to get the black mascara off. "Maybe I overreacted. I was tired. You can rehire her." I glance around for her so that I can do it myself.

"Tess, I'm joking I didn't fire her. That would be ridiculous. I did ask her to be more professional, and she apologized."

Breathing out, I say, "Thank God," and put all my makeup back into my bag. We're landing and I can't concentrate. Reed reaches for my pinkie finger.

"Relax, I won't let anything bad happen to you."

I look down at our pinkies locked together then up into his incredible eyes.

"I know." Because I do.

Charlie, our pilot, brings the plane down like a pro. And a few moments later, I'm walking down the steps while Reed stops to talk to him.

Los Angeles and all her sunshine does not disappoint. Even on the private tarmac, it's brighter.

Brance and a blond man are waiting for us. I scream and throw myself into Brance's arms. He pulls back and looks me up and down.

"What the hell did he do to you now?"

I laugh. "Well, hello to you too. This time it wasn't Reed. I fell asleep, and this is the finished product."

Gesturing to my face and shirt, I add, "I looked great this morning if that helps."

"Wait. You took a nap?" Pulling me back so that his dark eyes can sweep my face, he says, "Are you sick? You never nap."

"Stop it. I was up super late last night writing a paper, silly." I run my fingers through his thick hair. He must be letting it return to its natural color.

"I've missed you."

"Miss you more. You sure you're all right?" He arches his dark eyebrows.

"Brance! I'm fine."

He doesn't look convinced. Probably because I'm not convinced. The truth is I haven't felt good for the last two weeks or so.

A nervous cough reminds us that we are not alone. We both turn to the man standing next to us. I go to hug him.

"You must be Logan. So wonderful to meet you." He's stiff at first then slowly relaxes enough to return my hug. Slightly shorter than Brance, he has sandy-blond hair with big blue eyes. His face is cute in that boyish, charming way. Brance grabs hold of his waist.

"This the man who has changed me." He pulls him close for a full-on kiss. Logan is beaming.

"I hope he is changing you for the better. He has his work cut out for him." Reed has somehow sneaked up behind me. He wraps a possessive arm around me.

Brance shakes his head. "Logan, this is the infamous Reed Saddington. Reed, Logan."

Reed holds out his hand to shake Logan's.

"Um, yes, nice to meet you."

Brance purses his lips. "Shall we... Tess, my love, would you like me to fix you up in the car?"

"I was hoping you'd say that." Sliding into the Ford Explorer, I ask, "Whose car is this?" I think this is the first time I have ever been in a Ford.

Logan turns before he starts it. "It's both of ours." His tone is chilly. He sounds insulted. *Perfect, he hates me.*

Brance enters on the other side of me and promptly goes to work on my face.

"I'm starving. I hope this place is good."

Logan guns it, merging onto the famous 405 Freeway. I barely get a chance to look out the window with Brance doing my eyes.

"We love Osteria Mozza. Best Italian food in LA. And don't get me started on the desserts. We go so often, we've become friends with the owner and the pastry chef." Brance is happily saying all this as he starts to fix my hair. Logan drives quietly, listening.

We pull up to the valet and shuffle out. I feel better and Brance seems satisfied. We're on the corner of Melrose and

Highland. It's like night and day from Manhattan. The palm trees swaying over my head are a glaring reminder that I'm finally here. I look up to the right and there it is: the famous Hollywood sign welcoming me. That, and the numerous hipsters wearing shorts and flip flops.

I squeak and grab for Reed's arm. "Look, we can see the Hollywood sign." I jump up and down in excitement. "And this weather, it's so beautiful. I never want to leave."

He looks around Melrose, his blues eyes sparkling at my silliness.

Logan holds the large door open. As we all file into the restaurant, I barely notice the teal-green walls and dark wood.

Turning to Brance and Logan, I say, "I'm starving! I want the whole menu."

Brance chuckles. "Good. Something tells me you'll be stuffed when we leave."

He reaches for Logan's hand. "Did I ever tell you that Tess is my personal Barbie?"

Logan looks confused. "Um, no you failed to mention that when talking about her."

"Look at her. Tall, thin, clothes just weep for her to wear them."

Logan clears his throat. Brance glances at him. "What?"

"I'm sorry, this is the first time I'm seeing this side of you."

Reed snorts. "I wish I could say the same." I pinch him.

"Hello." A pretty hostess greets us. Brance steps up, taking charge. We follow as the hostess sits us at a square bar. I notice that it's made out of Carrara Italian marble.

"Fantastic." The smells make my mouth water.

"Yes, it's a very enjoyable experience. This is the Mozzarella Bar," Logan informs us, putting a napkin on his lap.

"You okay?" Brance examines his boyfriend, somewhat confused.

He nods. "Yes, I'm tired. I had a full day of work." Brance places his arm around the back of Logan's barstool.

"Logan recently opened his first of many yoga studios. He's teaching a lot of classes, getting his staff ready."

I look at Reed who is checking out the Mozzarella Bar. A cute curly-haired woman is making what looks like a plate of a big ball of mozzarella and bacon.

"We need to order that." Reed stares at the mouthwatering dish.

I elbow him, bringing his attention back to us.

"Reed, did you hear what Brance said about Logan and his new yoga studio?"

Reed looks over at them. "Congratulations." His eyes move back to the curly-haired woman and her new creation.

Brance laughs. "That's Nancy, the owner. I'll introduce you in a minute. Maybe she'll have time for a glass of wine with us."

The music is loud, and I can't help but gawk at all the pretty people. Not that New York has ugly people—it's just different. There is a lightness in LA that is appealing on so many levels. The bartender introduces himself and sets a couple dishes in front of us.

"Compliments of Nancy." Brance and Logan thank him and request the sommelier to pair our wine with our food.

Then we start. Now, bread is my weak spot. And if I had one last meal on earth, I would ask for bread, or more specifically, this bread. *Oh my God,* it's huge, grilled with olive oil I think. Then the mozzarella arrives with roasted cherry tomatoes. After that, the grilled octopus salad is placed in front of us. Reed takes one bite and promptly orders another.

Halfway through, I'm stuffed and on my way to being drunk.

"I'm in love with this food." I lean in between Reed's legs and he wraps his arms around me. "Wow, it gets busy fast in here, huh?" Looking around the large room, I recognize some big celebrities eating dinner. The vibe is energetic. "Give it Away" by the Red Hot Chili Peppers pulses through the space.

I turn in Reed's arms. "I want to live here," I speak into his full lips.

He chuckles, sipping a glass of red wine. "I know. You've been saying it all night. I thought you wanted to graduate?"

I wave my arms. "Graduate, shmazuate"

He laughs. "You're drunk." He motions the bartender for some water.

Gasping, I respond, "I am not. What comes next?" and glance around for the sommelier.

"Bed I hope." Reed motions for our bartender. "Can we get the check?"

"Absolutely not, Reed! You must have dessert. Is Dahlia here tonight?" Brance asks the bartender. His handsome face is flushed with wine. Actually, his lips are purple. I almost tell him he should switch to white.

"She is. Shall I tell her you guys are here?" Brance nods and fills up his glass with more red wine.

"So, Logan?" I lean over, trying to make him like me. "Brance says you grew up here?" My voice is a little loud. After all, I have to talk over Brance's head and all the other people in here.

He shrugs but keeps his voice low. "My parents live in Tustin, California. They are both teachers. I'm an only child."

"That is so noble. I thought about being a teacher." Reed and Brance look at me like I'm insane.

"What? I did for a moment."

Reed shakes his head, pulling me close so he can kiss me.

"Brance mentioned you were studying Greek classics and French?"

"Um, yes, I'm still figuring out what I want to do."

"Tess is majoring in Reed Saddington." Brance laughs at himself.

Logan frowns and hands him my water. "Here, drink this. How are you going to function in the morning?"

"Logan, lighten up. We are celebrating," Brance snips.

"We need the check." Reed stands up, his arm still locked around my belly. I sway with his every movement.

"Reed, please sit. I have something important to tell you."

My eyes get big. "Oh my God."

"Not that important, Tess." Brance motions for the bartender to refill his wine.

"What is it, man? Tess is fading fast. Drink your water, Kitten." Reed brings the crystal water glass to my mouth.

"So, Logan has been going to Malawi in Africa every year. He helps teach English, builds houses and schools."

Brance takes a breath and smiles scooting closer to Logan. "Now, I know you two are going to think I'm crazy, but being with this incredible man has made me want to be a better person."

"Meaning?" Reed sips his Hendrick's and tonic the bartender brought over a few minutes ago.

"That I have money. I have decided to join Logan. We're going to build houses, schools. They need electricity, clean water, vaccinations. You name it, we are going to do it."

Both Reed and I must look shocked because Logan puts his hand on Brance's as if for support.

"I'm sorry, did you say you are going to one of the poorest areas in the world to help?" Reed looks at Brance like he has horns growing out of his head.

He lifts his glass to drink, setting it down with a dramatic flair. "I know it's hard to believe, but I'm actually excited." He and Logan share a tender glance. I almost don't recognize him.

"But you hate dirt. And being dirty and—"

Reed cuts me off. "He needs your support, not pointing out his dislikes," he whispers in my ear.

"That is amazing, man. Tess and I want to donate. Let me know how much and it's yours." Reed sounds genuinely happy even if I'm struggling.

Logan has tears in his eyes. "You have no idea how many lives you will be saving."

I stare, astounded and uncomfortable. *Logan is a saint!* I shift in between Reed's legs suddenly feeling inferior.

"You okay, Pretty Girl?" I look into my best friend's eyes and see complete understanding.

I clear my throat and take a sip of water. "I'm surprised, that's all, and... I feel slightly guilty."

"Yes." Logan sighs dramatically. "This dinner." He indicates with his finger. "This alone could probably feed ten families for a month."

Now I definitely feel guilty. Talk about a buzzkill.

Brance rubs his back. "Easy, Tiger, they only met you a couple hours ago."

An uncomfortable silence falls over the four of us even with the loud music and people laughing on all sides of us.

"Logan is very passionate about saving the world." Brance gives us a tight smile.

Reed's grip on my stomach tightens. "So, we're done. Ready for the check?"

Brance stops the bartender. "Don't be ridiculous. We haven't even had the Butterscotch Budino.

"Brance, I'm stuffed and slightly drunk. We should be going." My eyes plead with him.

"*No...* I'm not leaving until we have dessert!"

Great, he's drunker than I am and starting to get mean. Glancing up, I notice Reed is silently assessing the situation.

Logan sniffs. "Look, I don't know you people. I'm sorry if the truth hurts. I grew up with pretty much nothing. But people are starving all over the world, including in our own country." He keeps preaching.

Reed's jaw is clenched. "Logan, I have already said we *want* to donate. Do not think because we are wealthy that we are ignorant. Or that we don't care. My mother donates to so many charities, I think even you would be speechless."

Logan sits with his mouth open.

"Reed, you've made your point. Now sit down for fuck's sake. The desserts here will help us all," Brance mumbles, looking into his empty wineglass.

I suddenly feel sorry for the poor pastry chef. Her desserts better be mind-blowing because without a doubt, the night has taken a turn.

"Hello." A petite woman with salt-and-pepper-colored hair and cute glasses walks up to us. She's tiny and looks delicate in her white apron.

Brance jumps up, nearly knocking over a glass of wine to hug her. I want to too; her timing could not have been better. "Tess, Reed, this is the famous Dahlia Narvaez. She is the best pastry chef in the world."

She laughs. "Well, let's not go overboard. You look like you have been enjoying yourselves." Her eyes take in our plates and wineglasses.

Turning to us, she says, "Hi, I'm Dahlia. Welcome to Mozza." She shakes my hand first then Reed's. Now, I don't care if her desserts are crap. The fact that she acknowledged me first instead of my hot billionaire boyfriend makes her my new best friend.

"Thank you," I gush. Even Reed smiles. I can almost feel Brance relax beside me.

"So, what are you guys going to do while you're here?" she asks.

"I think we are going to eat and sleep. Hang out at the pool, maybe do some shopping."

She nods as her crew brings out five different desserts. "Well, that sounds nice. I hope you enjoy your vacation."

She smiles at us, turning to Brance and Logan. "See you two soon. Enjoy."

After she disappears back into the kitchen, I turn to Reed, sighing into his neck. "I love LA." He laughs.

"Oh my God, you have to try this." I snap my head up quickly enough for Brance to spoon some lusciousness into my mouth.

"Holy God, that is divine." My eyes roll back in my head. All of us are feasting and sharing, even Logan. When the check comes, Reed grabs it. Logan thankfully averts his eyes as Reed pulls out his American Express Black card and pays.

The temperature has slightly dropped to a beautiful 78 degrees.

Reed takes my hand. "You two go ahead. We're going to get an Uber."

"Don't be a dick," Brance slurs. "We are driving you two to the Four Seasons."

It's been awhile since I have seen Brance drink that much. He rarely lets himself get into this condition.

Logan is silent, and the drive is thankfully short because again, the only sound we hear is some strange instrumental music. Reed and I can barely get out fast enough.

"What the hell? You believe that guy? I love how he is funding his save-the-world campaign on Brance's money." He rips off his shirt once we're upstairs.

"Reed, he's different all right?" Although even I was surprised at his disdain for us. As I strip off my clothes, his blue eyes darken. "I'm drunk and tired, not to mention in desperate need of a shower. I don't want to gossip about Logan right now."

Marching into the spacious and classy bathroom, I turn on the shower and don't wait to see if Reed will join me. All I want is to be clean and go to sleep. It's not even eleven yet and I'm tired.

I try to make myself feel better by saying it's the time change, but I napped on the plane. Finishing my shower, I brush my teeth and pad out into the enormous bedroom suite. Reed is already in bed. He lifts the covers and I happily slide in, sighing at their clean coolness against my warm skin.

"Feel better?" He kisses my forehead, snuggling into me.

"So much better. My head is only spinning a slight bit." I throw a leg over his, resting my hand on his chest, feeling his strong heartbeat.

"Just breathe." He holds me tighter. "I love you, Tess. We're truly lucky." His voice is raspy with emotion.

I open my eyes then close them because it's pitch dark in here. "Yes, we are."

chapter 35

REED

My head is pounding. Tess is sprawled on top of me. We drank way too much wine and gin last night. Thankfully, we ate a ton, otherwise Kitten would be spending all day in bed recovering.

Slowly, I disconnect myself from her and make my way into the bathroom. After I pee and splash some water on my face, I start to think about last night. Shaking my head, I've got to give it to Brance. Only he would find a boyfriend who would want to save the world and be a dick about it. Whatever, as long as Brance is happy. Hopefully this guy is as good as Brance believes since he's changing for him and footing the bill.

Visions of Brance in Africa trying to build a house then crying when he gets a splinter make me snicker. Honestly though, I admire him. He wanted to leave and start over and he did it. Now he'll tackle saving the world. More power to him. I wasn't joking when I said I would help. Maybe I should call Richard, one of our accountants, and have him wire Brance a couple million.

I open up Tess's boat anchor, or what she calls her purse. I need some Advil this morning. Shaking out three, I grab a couple bottles of water and go back to bed.

Her eyes are fluttering open. She sits up and bolts toward the toilet. I throw the water bottles on the bed so I can hold her hair back as she throws up all of last night's wine.

"You okay?" I ask, stroking her hair as she sits up. Her eyes are still watering, and despite having puked, she's so beautiful, I almost laugh at how bad I have it.

"God... I'm never drinking wine again."

"Kitten, this happened last weekend."

"I know. You know how I hate throwing up."

"I do, baby." I pull her into my arms, and her small frame feels almost fragile. I don't like this. For some reason, unease shivers up my spine.

Kissing her forehead, I say, "I'm going to get you some Advil and order us room service. Then we are relaxing the rest of the trip. I want you to sleep, sunbathe, and get pampered."

She smiles as she grabs her toothbrush.

"That sounds great. Let's start with coffee and lots of bread. Maybe a banana."

Smiling, I dial room service. I get a kick out of Tess's diet. It mostly consists of coffee and bread. If I didn't make her eat vegetables, she never would. I order us some real food—not only bread and a banana. Then I go to get her some Advil.

"Reed? Can you grab my birth control pills? I think I forgot to take one yesterday."

"Of course. Where are they?"

"My purse."

I grab the bag. "Here. The Advil's in there too."

She sits up, pushes her hair out of her face, and starts to look. I open up a bottle of Smartwater for her. She could certainly use the electrolytes.

"Thanks, babe," she says, not looking up. She's found the Advil and takes two, then goes back to digging inside her bag.

"What the hell?" Dropping her bag onto the floor, she marches past me to our suitcase and starts to rip the shit out of it.

"While you are destroying our clothes, can you hand me my sweats? Room service will be here shortly." She throws me my sweats.

"Are you sure they are not in my cosmetics bag?" she says, frowning at me like it's my fault she can't find them.

"Kitten, go check and while you're at it, put on a robe."

There's a knock at the door and I point toward the bathroom. She huffs but obeys. Waiting until she is safely in the bathroom, I open the door. I'm greeted by a friendly server and a frowning Brance standing next to him.

Brance brushes past me. "Not even a hello?" I yell after him.

Signing for the breakfast, I roll the cart into the room myself. I hear Tess and Brance in the bathroom and call out, "What the hell, you two? I know you're gay, but I don't like you in the bathroom with my girl." Opening the door, I find Tess in a robe and all the shit from her cosmetic bag scattered over the bathroom floor.

"What are you doing?"

Her eyes shoot up to mine. "I forgot them, Reed! You rushed me so much, I fucking forgot them. And I already forgot to take them yesterday and the day before I think." She's clearly distressed because she is starting to pace.

"Somehow I knew this would be my fault." I rub the back of my neck.

"Tess, you promised you would be more responsible." Brance scolds. "One of these days you're going to get pregnant, and I don't want to hear any whining."

Tess presses her fingers to her temples. "Brance, I can't deal with you lecturing me right now."

Stepping into the large bathroom, I say, "Okay, relax you two. Tess, you're fine. It's only a couple days. Brance, what crawled up your ass?"

Both of them stare at me. "I need coffee," he grumbles.

I cup Tess's face. "This is not the end of the world. You've been on the pill for years. You're not going to get pregnant." When I rub my nose against hers, she softens and relaxes into me. "Come on. I want to have a good day. Let's eat breakfast."

She holds me tight. "I'm sure you're right."

"That's my girl." Kissing her plump lips, I whisper, "I love you."

"I love you too." She sighs, and I almost bend down on one knee to propose. But I don't, even though I can't wait to slip that ring on her finger. The timing is all wrong. Brance is being a drama queen. Tess is stressed out. So instead, I kiss her again and pull her into the dining area in the suite.

Brance is sitting, drinking coffee, and helping himself to the bacon and eggs along with the pastries I ordered. Thankfully, there is plenty because I'm famished. Tess goes straight for the coffee.

As I load up my plate, I look over at Brance who is still wearing the same clothes as last night. Arching an eyebrow, I can't resist. "In training for Africa?"

He stops midbite. "You're such an entitled ass, Reed. I will have you know that I have been up all night fighting with the man I love about you two." He pulls a shaky hand through his dark hair.

"What?" Tess runs to him, kneeling down so that she can comfort him.

"Tess!" I say. "Get up." I glare at Brance. "What kind of crap are you spouting?" He knows Tess is fragile right now, and he's taking advantage of it.

"Logan wasn't raised with money and he felt intimidated. We live very modestly." Brance looks around our lavish suite, the large glass windows giving us a panoramic view of the Hollywood Hills. His eyes land on the piano in the corner and he groans. "Last night, he saw a version of me that he didn't like."

I stare at him like he's insane "What are you talking about? The version that is *you*," I roar.

"Reed." Tess places her hand on my arm. "Let him speak."

She leaves me and walks to Brance again, sitting next to him, holding his hand.

Snorting at the absurdity, I go back to my food.

"So, he has no idea how much money you have?" she gently asks.

Brance sighs. "No, I've told him about my family. About my dad. But I don't think it registered until he was around you two."

"He didn't like us?" Tess looks crushed. I couldn't give a rat's ass if he likes us. But I know Tess. She will want Logan to love us for Brance's sake.

"Tess, we did nothing wrong." Looking straight into Brance's eyes I say, "I'm sorry, but you never told us we would have to pretend to be something we all three are not. And if that is what this guy wants, then you need to get out now, man. You are what you are, Brance. He can either love that part of you or he can get the fuck out."

Brance shakes his head. "Logan is it for me. I need you both to accept him. He is the best person I know. I can only strive to be the right man for him."

"Wow, he must give great head because I have never heard so much bullshit—even coming from you, Brance." I stand up to make Tess a plate.

"Reed... knock it off." Tess turns to Brance. "What do you want us to do?"

"I already put my foot down about you, Pretty Girl. I told him you always come first. I am serious about going to Africa. I need to do this for my soul. I want to give back. It's going to be a challenge, but at the end of it, I know I will be a better person." He leans back in the silk-backed chair.

Tess nods, taking his hand. "It's a wonderful thing that you guys are doing. Reed is going to donate a huge amount of money. How long are you going to be gone?"

He picks up his coffee and looks out the windows. "Three months and I probably won't be able to contact you either. They have no internet or phones."

"What? Oh God, I forgot about that. We talk every day." Her eyes get teary.

"I know." He puts his forehead on Tess's hand.

"Christ, you two. Brance, pull yourself together. If it makes it easier on you, we will pretend we are poor. We don't have to go to expensive restaurants or shop. Tess needs to rest."

"No, Logan works all day at the yoga studio, so we'll shop while he is working."

I laugh. "Perfect. Anything else we need to lie about?"

Brance glares at me zeroing in on Tess. "I think it would be nice if you guys tried one of his classes. He is an amazing teacher."

"No," I cut him off. "No way! If he owned a boxing gym, yes. Yoga, no."

Tess shoots me a glare. "I would love to go."

"Thanks, Pretty Girl. I'm tired. I need sleep and a shower. I will see you guys later."

"One more thing." I stop Brance at the door. "Don't fight over Tess. She has me, and I take care of what's mine. Concentrate on Logan. He wants to be your number one, let him."

Brance studies my face. "Thanks, Reed, but that is the way I'm wired. I have enough love for both. Tess will always come first if she needs me."

"I release you, man. Go be happy with Logan, helping people. Tess has *me*!"

"We'll see, Reed." His black circles make him look older.

"Brance, go get some sleep." I smell Tess's delicious vanilla scent behind me.

He nods. "Tess." He leans over so they can do their usual kiss-him-on-the-mouth stupidity.

Rolling my eyes, I say, "You two might want to rethink your public displays of affection. Logan doesn't seem to be as understanding as me."

"Logan will come around. He loves me."

After Brance leaves, Tess turns to me, sitting down at the table. "Well, what do you think?" Her big eyes are full of concern.

I sigh. "Fuck if I know, but Brance is in love with this guy. I mean he's changing himself for him."

"That's what concerns me." She scoops a huge amount of cream cheese on her knife and slathers it on a bagel. I pour her some fresh coffee and orange juice.

"That's his problem. I have my own problems." She sets down her orange juice. Her eyes sweep my body, stopping on the erection that tents my sweats.

"Hmmm, does this problem have anything to do with your favorite part of my body?"

Reaching into my pants I pull him out and look down at him. As my eyes lift to hers, she is setting down her coffee.

"Yeah. I'm in desperate need of your help."

She unties the belt of her robe, licking her rosy lips, and stands up.

My eyes feast on her, starting with her stunning face. Rubbing my tattoo, I sense that familiar tightening in my chest. Her eyes darken. For some reason, she gets turned on whenever I touch my tattoo. Biting her plump lower lip, she cocks her head. *Fuck...* she is my everything. My eyes travel down her slender throat, her pulse visibly beating fast and strong. Her full, lush breasts and those goddamn nipples harden as my eyes devour them and move down her toned flat stomach and hairless pussy. I silently move close to her and drop to my knees not touching her, only observing.

"Huh? I seem to remember a couple days ago a landing strip here?" My eyes reluctantly move from her pussy to her face. She's glowing, cheeks flushed, skin soft and creamy.

"I thought I would surprise you. Do you like it?"

"I do. It's fun." Standing up, I take her chin in my hand and lightly kiss her, sucking on that bottom lip. When I pull away, it makes a small pop.

"Let it grow back. I like the landing strip better."

"I was wondering when you were going to mention it."

I flash her a wicked grin. "Let me take a closer look to make sure." Picking her up, I toss her over my shoulder like the caveman I am. "We're spending all day in bed. If I still have this problem, we will spend all night." She laughs as I toss her onto the bed.

"Reed, we're on vacation. We are not staying in bed all day."

"Don't worry, Kitten. You're going to be too busy to care."

Her eyes blaze with want. "Okay."

Leaning down so that we are both breathing each other's air, I whisper, "Such a good girl."

I make love to her all day, and fuck her all night. Life couldn't be better.

chapter 36

TESS

Present day – twenty-five years old
On the way to New York

The G5 Jet dips, and my eyes widen and blink. I look around making sure it didn't disturb my secret. Apparently, I am the only one turbulence seems to bother. I get up and make my rounds, checking on everyone.

Quietly, I open the bathroom door. Leaning my hands on the sink, I try not to remember.

"Turn around, Kitten, hands on the sink, hold tight, this is going to be fast and hard." His beautiful eyes lock with mine, one hand gently around my neck, the other holding my hips as he enters me.

Gulping in some air, I rapidly blink back the tears. I can't mess up my eyes, I can't mess up...

Shaking my head, I give myself a harsh pep talk as I wash my hands. I grab for a towel, glance up at the mirror, and freeze. The woman who stares at me looks perfect, her hair and makeup creating a façade, a crazy illusion.

I'm struggling. I can't hide the sheer terror that my soul seems to be extracting. Leaning my head back, I try to calm my breathing.

"You all right, Pretty Girl?" A light tap on the door makes me jump.

"Be right out." I lean my forehead on the cool door. "Fuck it," I say, swinging the door open, nearly screaming. Brance is standing with his arms crossed, face full of concern.

"Jesus, you scared me." I will my heart to calm down.

"Do I need to worry?" His eyes roam my face.

"Um... Do you need to worry? Wow, that's a loaded question." Rolling my neck, not wanting to make eye contact with him, I shake out my long hair. "It's going to be okay, Brance, for everyone's sake." My eyes stray to the other side of the jet. He doesn't say anything. His worried gaze says it all.

"I want to go straight to the Plaza. We should know more as soon as we land and talk to Jax."

"Good. We need this to happen on our turf, our time," he says.

Nodding, I'm slightly nauseous. "Thank God I have you. I feel like a terrible person for dragging you away from Logan, but I can't do this alone."

"Sit down and meditate. He's not finding out tonight anyway." He stretches out his long legs.

"Exactly," I mumble, looking down at my trembling hands.

Brance gently grabs them, holding them together tightly. "We are going to get through this." Taking my bag, he pulls out my pill case and hands me a Valium.

"Thank you." *I won't cry, I won't cry.* Opening my Fiji water, I swallow the pill.

The jet dips again, and my fingers claw the soft leather armrest. Glancing around, I note this must be a new jet because it is decked out, screaming wealth. Absently I wonder if this is the same one that brought Reed this morning.

Exhausted, I rub my temples, the stress of my sins starting to take its toll. How is this is going to go down? I wonder for the thousandth time as I lean back. Does it matter? With a sigh, I try to slow down my racing pulse. Yes, it matters for them. It matters.

Maybe I should get a lawyer. Maybe he won't care. After all, it's been almost four years. He's never contacted me—he simply moved on. A sob threatens to come out at that thought and I swallow it back. I *need* to remember all of this! He is not innocent in this nightmare that is our lives. He did end up committing the ultimate betrayal. *Right, keep telling yourself that, Tess.* The guilt clearly lies at my feet. Closing my eyes, I wonder what would have happened had I done things differently.

"Oh God." I cover my face, needing to be quiet so I don't wake them. It upsets them when I cry. I hear the small lull of the jet.

And I *can't* help but let my mind drift back. Back to when I never dreamed I would be in this situation. Back when he promised to love me until I died, no matter what.

"Kitten, you feel this?" He places my hand on his heart. "This is all that matters. What I have in here, that's only ever been for you. I need you to trust me. I will always be here for you. I'll take care of you. Forever." His lips claim mine and I feel myself falling so hard for him, my love like a raging fire that can't ever be contained.

"I want to believe you so badly, Reed. But what if I do something you don't like?"

He frowns. "I guess that goes both ways. Are you going to leave me if I do something wrong?"

"Never. I will never leave you. I love you."

"Then you have nothing to worry about. Because there is nothing you could do that I would not be able to forgive." My eyes pop open. I look around, my breathing harsh. Reaching for the water, I take a swig to cool my hot mouth.

"Liar," I whisper.

TESS

Past – twenty-one years old

Flushing the toilet in our penthouse, I grab ahold of the sink and try to rinse my mouth. Slowly the feeling that I'm going to vomit again passes. With an exhale, I reach for my toothbrush, instantly gagging as I taste the minty paste on my tongue. Frustrated, I continue to brush, ignoring my dry heaves. I rinse my mouth and splash some cold water on my face.

The coolness helps. If I had the energy, I would love to soak in the tub. Maybe later after I take a nap. I don't even bother looking at myself in the mirror, too scared at what I'll see.

Slowly I make my way to the kitchen for a bottle of water. I also reach for an electrolyte drink. Maybe a banana would stay down? But I'm tired right now, and all I want is my warm bed.

"Tess? Sweetheart?" Reed gently shakes me.

"No..." I moan. His hand caresses my face.

"Still sick?"

I snuggle into his caress.

"I'm sorry I was gone so long, babe. The meeting with my dad lasted longer than I wanted. I was hoping you were going to be better."

"Me too. It's so weird that I'm still sick. Who knew food poisoning would kill me," I whisper, my eyes still closed. Reed is silent, but I can feel his gaze on me.

"I'm calling Dr. Miller. Two weeks is long enough."

"It hasn't been two weeks." I try to sit up. *It's been three, but who's counting?*

"We need to talk, Kitten."

I groan again. "Not now, Reed. I'm tired. What time is it?" I glance around our dark bedroom.

"It's one in the afternoon. How long have you been asleep? Have you eaten anything?"

"I can't eat!" I snap. "I have the flu."

"This is enough, Tess. I should have done this days ago." He stands with his phone, glaring at me.

I raise an eyebrow. "Why are you scowling at me?"

"Because you are a complete neurotic and yet anytime I suggest we call Dr. Miller, you refuse. You want to tell me why?" He looks so healthy I want to punch him. But I literally have no energy. The thought of sitting up is a chore.

"I... he's always so busy and I truly thought I was getting better," I say, trying to sound convincing.

His blue eyes search my face and he shakes his head. "Whatever."

Turning away from me with his phone, he asks for Dr. Miller, his soothing voice comforting. My eyes close again.

"Tess, honey? Come on, wake up." Reluctantly I open my eyes, and my stomach immediately heaves. It's been so long since I ate anything, I only gag a little.

Blinking in confusion, I look around the room for Reed. "Dr. Miller? What are you doing here?"

"I'm going to take some blood, honey. Then I'm going to give you an IV. You're dehydrated. That's why you can't get your strength back." He pats my hand. "This IV is going to fix you all up." He smiles in that calm, kind way of his.

"Thank you, Dr. Miller." Looking away as he draws my blood, I soon feel the cool fluids enter my veins. My eyes start to clear.

Dr. Miller sits at my side. "Now, Tess, how long has this been going on?" His brown eyes are so kind and understanding. I shouldn't feel shy. After all, I've known Dr. Miller since I was a child.

"Um..." I ease my way into a sitting position. "Oh God, I feel better already... I guess it started about three weeks ago. Reed and I had sushi, and I threw up at the restaurant."

"At the restaurant? Food poisoning takes a few hours, so that couldn't have caused it."

My cheeks heat up for the first time in a while. "Oh." What else can I say?

"Reed says you have been unusually tired for the last couple of weeks and you've been throwing up?"

"I've been so miserable. I thought it was bad fish."

Dr. Miller pats my hand again. "Well, that is why I'm here. Any fever?"

"I don't think so. I guess I should have called you, but I kept thinking I would get better."

I try to smile, but my lips are chapped.

We both turn our heads as Reed walks in carrying a paper bag. He pulls out a box of saltines. "How is she?" His beautiful eyes are full of worry.

I smile at him. "So much better already."

Exhaling, he says, "Thank God. You were scaring me. Did you tell Dr. Miller you have been throwing up off and on for about a month and a half?"

"I have not. It's only been a week."

He arches a brow at me. "What about in California?"

Leaning my head back, I close my eyes. "That was because I drank too much."

"Tess, you have been sick and tired for over a month. It started before California and that was six weeks ago."

Shit. I lift my head. Has it been that long? Forcing my mind to work, I think about my strange exhaustion. Has it been longer than three weeks?

"I'm cold."

Reed sits next to me and brings the comforter up around my neck, careful of the IV. But now that the truth is out in the room, looming over me, I'm not sure it has anything to do with the temperature.

"Okay." Dr. Miller leans over and tests my glands in my throat.

Seeming satisfied, he turns to Reed. "Did you get the test?"

He nods, nervously running his hands through his hair. The IV drip ends with a small beep.

Dr. Miller checks my blood pressure and temperature. Standing up, he gets his stethoscope and listens to my heart. "I think you can use another bag of fluids," he says, disconnecting one and reconnecting a new one.

"Well, I'm definitely getting hydrated. Is it almost done? I need to use the bathroom."

"Almost. I want to make sure we get enough fluids into you." He smiles down at me, then asks me the question. "When was your last period, Tess?"

And there it is. The question that I have buried deep in my subconscious. I can't speak. Nothing comes out as I mentally track how long it's been.

Reed cocks his head at me then turns to Dr. Miller. "She's a little late, probably because she's been sick." I cling to him mute.

"Yes, that can happen. Are you still taking the pill?"

"Yes," I whisper.

"Tess, you look terrified. I'm sure it's exactly what you think." The bag of fluid is done. Dr. Miller takes out the IV.

"I need to use the bathroom."

"Perfect. I took blood and I will have those results in the morning. I think we need to do a pregnancy test now though." The doctor hands me a white stick.

I sway. Reed is beside me, his strong arms wrapped around my waist.

"I'm not pregnant... I can't be. I'm on the pill." My voice sounds weak and far away. I have the oddest sensation, almost like I'm on a rollercoaster, holding my breath, waiting for the first plunge. Reed's strong hands have me sitting on the toilet.

A cool plastic white stick sits in my palm.

"Pee on it, Tess," he demands, so I do.

As I watch, the little result window changes and right away two solid lines appear. Well, that didn't take three minutes. That took five seconds.

Pregnant!

Deep down I knew. Deep down I know that this is the end. A tortured sob escapes me.

Reed holds me. He is murmuring comforting things. Things like it's going to be all right. Like it's meant to be.

Lies!

"Make sure she eats the crackers, applesauce, bread. Bland is the best with morning sickness. Her OB may prescribe her a pill to stop the vomiting. But hopefully, with the fluids we pumped into her she will be able to keep some food down and that won't be necessary."

Dr. Miller smiles down at me. "And I will call in the morning. Congratulations, you two."

My mind is numb. I don't even know how long I've been inspecting my nails. They are chipped. I hate chipped nails. I look up to see Reed staring at me.

"Do you feel up to talking" His blue eyes are guarded, unsure.

"What's to talk about?" I look past his head and out the window. It's getting dark out.

He sighs, running his hands through his hair. "I know this is a shock. Believe me, I'm shocked too. But the more I let it sink in that you are pregnant... with my baby. Kitten, *we* made a baby."

And I think I might die. My heart is being torn in half.

"Reed," I say, clearing my throat. "I can't have this baby!"

I say this because it's the truth. I'm mentally unfit, unstable, and let's not even get into my pathetic body, seeming to be rejecting the whole idea.

He snorts and scoots me over so that he can slip in behind me. His warm, hard body instantly makes mine relax. His large hands pull me close then spread out on my flat stomach.

"Dr. Miller gave me a name of the best OB/GYN in Manhattan. I will get you an appointment tomorrow," he murmurs in my ear. Tears slide down my cheeks.

"Reed!" I turn my head. "You're not hearing me. We can't have this baby!"

He grins. "Well, it's a little late for that, Tess. You'll be fine. Dr. Miller said in a couple of months the throwing up will be over and then smooth sailing."

I turn over, lying on my back, and look at him. This man, who I have loved my whole life, is happy and wants this baby. I knew he would. My heart is racing.

I reach up and trace his full lips. "Please don't make this harder than it needs to be. You can't honestly want to be a father. You're not even twenty-two. Maybe later."

His warm hand caresses my chin, his thumb gently rubbing my bottom lip as he leans over and kisses me. I feel the wet tears, taste the salt as he continues to worship my face.

"You have always sold yourself short. You are going to be the best mother, trust me."

I search his face. Jesus, he believes it. He loves me so much that he has no idea I'm not capable of this. Christ, the alcohol alone could have damaged the baby. Or it could be even crazier than I am. After all, I come from a long line of terrible people.

"Shh, rest. We will talk in the morning. You need your body to recuperate before you say anything you might regret."

I turn to my side, my heart breaking. He's wrong, so very wrong. I'm not going to change my mind. Some people can rise to the occasion. Do things they don't want so they can make someone else happy. And I would do that. For Reed, I would do that. But I won't do that to an innocent baby. No one deserves a mother like me. Both my parents would tell him so if they were here. He knows I suffer terrible anxiety, panic... whatever. I can't pass that on to a child.

I close my eyes, my body and mind hurting. But that is nothing compared to what my heart feels. A hysterical giggle escapes me. I almost remind him I took a Valium last night. How could I even think about going however many months without one? But what's the point? He wants to talk tomorrow. So, I'll put off the inevitable.

REED
Past – The Day

I wake because I feel her gone. Then I hear her small gasps and heaves as she quietly pukes. I smile and stretch, amazed I slept the whole night.

"Tess? You okay?"

I jump up to help her. The sun is shining in our room. Everything feels shiny and fresh. Like my eyes have finally been opened and the world is exciting and new. I wasn't surprised when I saw those two lines. I've suspected she's pregnant for a while. Throwing up every time she had a drink was unusual. Then her exhaustion and lack of period seemed so obvious. Every day I waited for her to mention it. Or take a test. But she was adamant that she had the stomach flu and food poisoning, so I didn't want to push her knowing she needed time to ease into things. Especially this. From day one, Tess has insisted that she's terrified of being a mom. By my calculations, she's about two and half months already. I should be scared or upset. All I can feel is joy. This is everything I have always wanted with her. I have to fight myself not to go to my closet for the ring. She'd kill me if I proposed with all this going on.

Opening the bathroom, I find her clutching the porcelain sink, her knuckles white from holding on so tight. She's staring at herself almost trancelike as she brushes her teeth. She doesn't even react to me.

Frowning, I walk up behind her. "You okay? Do you feel any better?"

She whirls around "Feel better? No, Reed, I feel like fucking death. As a matter of fact, I'm sure I am dying. No one can throw up this much and survive."

I back up only because I don't want her to see my lips twitching at her dramatics.

"Again, this is all part of it. We will get through it. How about I make you some eggs?" She looks at me and I instantly move aside and help her, holding her hair back as she gags into the toilet.

"Oh, Kitten, if I could trade places with you, I would." Scooping her up, I carry her to our bed. One of our phones is ringing, but I ignore it as I tuck her in, caressing her hair.

"I love you."

She turns and looks at me, her eyes shiny with unshed tears. My heart starts to beat faster. The feeling of doom takes ahold of me and twists and turns all over my heart. Suddenly our room isn't so bright.

"What?" My voice sounds unintentionally harsh.

"I can't do this." Four little words that make my heart start to bleed.

"You're doing it. And you will be fine." Looking away, I don't want to see her tortured eyes. The sapphire sparkle is gone. My eyes focus on the clothes in the hamper. Tess usually keeps everything neat for the maids. Since she's been sick, the room could use some help.

"You're delusional!" Her raspy voice forces my eyes back to hers. "Listen to me. I *cannot* have this baby!" She sounds pathetic.

Suddenly I have no patience for her shit. She's pregnant, not dying.

"What the fuck, Tess?" I must get away from her, or I'll say something I shouldn't. I hear her soft sobs and hiccups.

"I'm sorry, Reed. Please understand. I... just... can't."

"What are you saying? You want an abortion?" I spit it out, needing her to deny it.

"Yes."

I stop. Surely I didn't hear her right. "What?"

She cringes, and I take a breath. But it's too late. The time for breathing is over. "You're not that fucking pathetic and weak! Or that *insane* to want to abort it!"

Jesus is she that fucked up? Have I been loving someone who is not real? A made-up version of a little boy's idea of perfection?

"Reed." She sits up, her arms reaching for me. "Don't look at me like that."

I shake my head, trying to get some semblance of rational thinking. My temper has always been my weakest of faults. I can go from calm to seeing red in a moment. But never with Tess.

She launches herself at me. She's crying and I catch her. For one moment I hold her and breathe her in. That wonderful Tess smell circles me like smoke coming out of a campfire. I let my mind pretend that she is not trying to kill my child. That she is crying tears of joy like me. She reaches for my face, her hands ice cold on my cheeks.

Shaking her head, she says, "I told you I don't want children. I only want you."

Her eyes are so hopeful. I start to question myself.

"I'm not fit to be a mother. I've been drinking and let's not forget my Valium."

I grab her wrists tightly. "You. Are. Fine. But if you do this, we won't be."

She pulls away and walks slowly to the window, crossing her arms, almost as if she's protecting her belly. "Reed, it isn't even a person yet."

It's as though she just stabbed me. I can't stand her right now. I back away from her. My ears are burning. I'm losing this battle of controlling my emotions.

"You're in shock." I spit it out, although I'm starting to think I'm in shock.

"Probably."

"You want an abortion." I'm not asking her. I need to hear it so that whatever I have loved about her can finally be free.

She reaches for me. I step away, and for the first time in my life, I don't want her to touch me.

She drops her hands. "I would never make it through a pregnancy. Then having a baby at twenty-two years old it... it's insane! What kind of parents would we be? You think you want this, but you don't. You have no idea what children need. It takes way more than money to be a good parent."

"You've become your father," I whisper, the fury of her betrayal burning a hole inside my heart. "You sound exactly like him."

Her shoulders slump. And I wonder how I ever thought her beautiful.

"Stop looking at me like that!" she screams. "You know deep down inside, I'm right. Admit it! I'm a big enough person to."

My eyes shift to her pale face, the black circles under her eyes. I feel nothing. Sinking to our bed, I put my hands over my face.

"Tess... I'm begging you not to do this. I love this baby already." I'm saying all this like a robot, knowing it's pointless but needing to try. Try for that little boy or girl who is ours.

"I know you don't feel good. And you're scared of becoming Claire and your dad. I know they made you think you can't do this. But you can! You're strong and healthy. The girl that I love would never even think these thoughts." Somehow, I'm searching her face. She's like a zombie. Dead inside. I grab her shoulders and shake her. "What is wrong with you?"

"*Nothing*! I don't want to be a mother! I shouldn't be punished for that!" she screams in my face.

I drop my hands like she has singed them. My stomach cramps and I might be sick.

"I won't bring a child into this world and fuck it up. I want you—that's it. Can't that be enough?"

"If you abort our baby against my wishes, I won't stay. I can't."

She grows even paler if that's possible, her thin frame sinking to the floor.

"You're threatening me?" Her voice is surprisingly calm as she starts to laugh. "Everybody thinks they can control me, threaten me. Well, I'm not going to be bullied into doing something I don't want." She's shaking.

I look down at her. "What are you going to do, Tess?"

For a split second, she must realize what she is doing is crazy. Then she looks down and whispers, "I'm going to find a clinic and put this behind us."

"Jesus Christ." I run my hands through my hair. "I hate you!" It sounds childish, but I want her to know. "You are fucked in the head. Who says that? Like you are going to get your teeth cleaned at the dentist."

I don't trust myself to be around her. I need to leave. Get some air and try to talk to her later.

"You're a liar," I say. "I should never have taken you back when you lied for three years. But I loved you."

"You can call me a lot of things, but I never lied. I'm not mentally capable of taking care of a baby. Maybe when we're older."

My mind can't deal with this. I feel a migraine. Or I'm having a brain aneurysm because this kind of burn can't be described. I stumble into the bathroom.

This isn't pain; this is agony. Death would be easier than having to live through this.

I hear a sound that gives me goose bumps. Makes my skin crawl. It's guttural, primal, and its pure *pain*! And it's coming from me. I can't stop it. Tess is pounding on the door, screaming for me to let her in.

But... it's too late. There is no Tess. She was only an image. A person I thought I loved. A beautiful viper with the face of an angel. A weak, soulless oxygen thief. A murderer—that's the real Tess!

"*Fuck!*" I see myself for a split second in the mirror. Then my fist shatters my image. Looking down, I'm standing in a pool of shattered glass, the mirror splintered all around me. Tiny shards like falling snow surround me. Splintered pieces, with drops of crimson red. My hand is bleeding, but I feel nothing. *Dead!* Dead like my whole fucked-up life. Dead like our baby will soon be. I reach for my heart. My tattoo, it's instinctual, it will calm me. I rub and rub. Blood covers the area where my heart is, where my tattoo is. This is a lie; my fingernails scrape my skin. I should have gotten rid of it a long time ago. I can get rid of it now. My pain isn't because I'm cutting up my tattoo. It's the pain of my heart dying. The pain of Reed dying. Finally, I drop the shard of glass. My chest is in ribbons where the name Tess used to be. *What the fuck am I doing?* Absently figuring out what I've done, I hear nothing, which is strange since New York is never silent. No horns, no screaming, just silence. Opening the door, I face her. Her beautiful ashen face. So beautiful. Her big eyes horrified at my appearance. Her cheeks wet with her tears, her lips red and swollen. Her mouth is moving, but I hear nothing. I push her hands aside, and she frantically latches her nails into my arm. With her other hand, she tries to check my chest.

"Don't touch me," I snarl. She does anyway, her hand crimson.

"I'm leaving."

"Reed, what have you done?" It's like a bullhorn going off in my head and I can hear again. Noises pound at me from all directions. The horns, the yelling, and the sobbing hysterics of the shell of the woman I loved.

"I'm leaving you."

chapter 39

TESS

Present day – twenty-five years old
New York, NY

"Mommy... Mommy? Wake up." My eyes blink open as I stare at my secret. My reason for living, that and my other bundle of trouble.

"Uncie Bwance, sas we here." My soon-to-be three-year-old son climbs onto my lap.

"We're here," I correct him. He turns and snuggles into my neck, taking a deep breath, and sighs.

"Yow smell goowd, Mommy."

He's such a little charmer. "Thanks, baby." I smile. "You smell good too." I ruffle his dark curls. One of his fat cheeks is rosier than the other. He must have slept on it.

"Where's your sister?" I ask, looking around the plane.

"With Uncie Bwance." He smiles, and my heart skips a beat. Out pop two dimples, one on each side, just like his father's.

"Mommy?" I wipe away a tear that escaped despite my rapid blinking.

He places both his chubby hands on my cheeks, his cute nose wrinkled. "Mommy sad?" His eyes fill with big fat tears too.

"No, Mommy's fine." I smile as another tear slides down my cheek.

"Then why are yow cwying?"

"So, smart." I take a calming breath. "Mommy's a little sad about Great-Grandpa Ian passing." I give him a tight hug, my nose stuck in his warm cheek.

"Um... Mommy?"

I pull away and smile. "I love you so much. You be my good boy while we are visiting, okay?" He nods, happily snuggling in my arms and playing with my watch.

"We get to see Gwandma, Gwandpa, and Uncie Jax." I cringe. This is so bad. How are my children ever going to understand this?

I stare at my perfect son, the exact replica of his father. Except that Reed has turquoise eyes. Luke and Lilly, have deep green eyes. Other than that, there is no denying who the father is. At least Lilly looks a little like me. She has my lips and nose.

"Luke...?" Snapping my mouth closed, my mind spins. *What am I going to tell him? I have been keeping you and your sister from your father. He thought I aborted you, so he deserted us?*

He's not even three yet, won't be for another two weeks.

Leaning my head back, Luke snuggles in my lap, my guilt eating at me. I kiss the top of his head, and I almost hear the phone ringing again.

"Hello?"

"Tess, honey, it's Dr. Miller. I've been trying to reach you all morning. Everything all right?" I almost start laughing. I have to bite my tongue not to scream out that Reed has left me because I don't want his baby.

"Tess?"

Clearing my voice, I try to speak. It's hoarse with all the screaming and crying I've been doing. "I'm here."

Silence. "Well... you are indeed pregnant and according to your HCG levels, it's very likely you are carrying twins.

Now, I have made an appointment with the best doctor in Manhattan..."

"Mommy? You seeping?" My eyes bolt open and I blow out some air. That phone call changed everything.

"Mommy!" Lilly, comes hard, charging straight into my arms. She shoves at her brother, trying to push him off my lap. He wraps his arms around my neck.

"No, Luke, I want Mommy." She pushes again.

"Both of you stop. Mommy has two legs, one for each of you." My arms surround both of them tightly.

"Uncle Bwance says you need to get it together." She takes my face with her chubby hands, holding it so that I'm forced to give her my undivided attention. Lilly repeats everything Brance tells her. See, my daughter is almost three but going on thirty and Brance's best confidante.

"He does, huh? I'll do my best." It's impossible to hide my smile.

"Now I need you both to listen. Mommy is really nervous and sad. This is a different visit. We're not coming just to see Grandma and Grandpa. I need you two to stay right with me or Uncle Brance, okay?"

I grab Luke's hand away from his sister's hair. "Luke, stop pulling her hair."

"But Mommy, she won't shware," he says.

"I share," she whines.

"Enough! Stay with me or Brance, all right?" Looking at them, I sense my heart fluttering. They are quite frankly remarkable. The most pure and good thing Reed and I have ever created. He's going to want them. I know it in my gut.

I should hide. Run away. Nothing good is going to come of this. Glancing down, both of them are playing happily with their toys. No matter what I do, he is going to find out, Jax has assured me.

"What are you doing?" I jump at Brance's snippy tone.

"Go and fix your makeup. I see the Bentley. Jax is waiting." He leans over me to stare out the window.

"Brance?" I grab his arm and drag him away from Lilly and Luke.

"I have a bad feeling. Like I know this is going to be horrific!" I'm in a full panic.

He grabs me by the shoulders. "Not now. Not in front of them." He motions to the twins with his eyes. I look over at them. Luke is still blissfully playing while Lilly watches us, too smart for her own good. Her green eyes look away and I snarl at Brance, "Do not take your eyes off them."

"Tess, he is not going to kidnap them. It's his grandfather's funeral."

"You don't know that. We have no idea what he is capable of, *remember*?" I hiss.

He sighs, rubbing the back of his neck.

"You two ready? The doors are opening." We both glance over at Jay. He gives me a nod.

Don't show him weakness. Jay's words replay in my head.

Squaring my shoulders back, I grab my bag. Not even bothering with a mirror, I slather on some lip gloss. "I'm ready."

But I'm not ready. I'll never be ready. "Wait." I look at my children. "Do you need to use the potty?" Lilly has been potty trained since two. Luke got the hang of it last month.

"Nope, I just went," Lilly says as she tries to wiggle her hand in my purse. She pulls out some lip gloss.

"Honey, not today. No lip gloss." She pouts as I take it away. I look at Brance, who is staring at her like she is a genius. "Can you help?"

He chuckles. "Come on, princess. I think I saw Uncle Jax." He takes her hand, helping her put on her glittery unicorn backpack.

"What if he tries to take them away?" I try to breathe as I put on Luke's backpack.

His angry gaze swings to mine. "We can afford lawyers who are at least as good as his. Let him try," he whispers.

The doors open with a smooth swish. Jay exits first, then Brance and Lilly.

Looking down at Luke, I smile reassuringly. "Ready?"

"I have to go pee-pee." He jumps from one foot to the other.

I almost cry; my nerves are completely shot. "Such a good boy, Luke. Let's hurry, though. Your sister is already outside." I quickly pull him into the bathroom, almost unable to pull his pants down fast enough. My mind is in a frenzy. Lilly is with Brance. He would kill for her. She's safe.

"Come on, baby, it's time." Quickly helping him wash his hands, I don't even bother to take time to put his backpack on. I swing it over my shoulder along with my purse and drag Luke down the stairs, needing to get to my daughter.

"Mommy, your face is wet," Luke tells me.

"Mommy's a little tired. We'll get some food when we get to the hotel." I smile.

"Good, I'm hungwy." His dimples peek at me. Glancing away, I focus on finding Lilly.

Jax has her in his arms. Brance is standing next to him, watching.

I sigh with relief. Brance is right—I do have to pull myself together. Taking the last step, I let go of Luke's hand and let him run to his uncle.

Slowly I make my way to them. Jax has both of them in his arms and kneels down so that he is on their level. Lilly is talking nonstop and Luke is crawling on his back.

"Hey, Jax." I give a him a sad smile when he looks up at me. His turquoise eyes look tired.

"Tess." He stands, taking Luke with him on his back and picking up Lilly. She squeals with delight, happily wrapping her arms around his neck. He looks away from me, focusing on Lilly and Luke.

"So..." Brance yells over an airplane taking off. Luke looks up at the plane, his eyes so alive with knowledge.

"Tess and I are going to take Luke and Lilly to the hotel and get checked in," he informs Jax, who ignores him and continues to play with the twins.

Frowning, I say, "Jax?"

And then I know. Dread like a deadly snake slithers up my spine.

Jay opens the back door of the Bentley. Fear takes over my body. I'm frozen. This can't be happening. I'm not ready.

I know why Jax is ignoring me, concentrating only on his niece and nephew.

I don't have to look over to see him. I can feel him. That pull, like a magical string that never fully snapped. My eyes swing to Jax's, my mind still trying to absorb that he is going to know. Frantically I snatch Lilly out of his traitorous arms. But Luke is still on Jax's back.

"Tess... I warned you. Tried to reason with you."

I want to scream. Instead I snarl, "Give me my son, Jax."

"He's fine, Tess. Relax." His voice is completely calm.

"You promised," I hiss. "Now give me my *son*!"

Jax's eyes lock onto mine. "I never promised. It's over, Tess." As he swings Luke around, he hands him to me. I put one on either side of my hips. Along with my bag and their backpacks, I wonder if I'm going to topple over.

"Mommy?" Both Luke and Lilly look scared. For the first time in my life, I don't let fear control me.

Fuck this!

I'm their mother and I will do anything to protect them. "It's okay, babies. Mommy's got you!" I kiss their dark curls, holding them so tight Luke is making a face. I hear Brance swearing; Jax is holding him back.

Turning around to face my enemy, I stand frozen and blink at the face that has haunted me for more than three years.

Reed!

To Be Continued...

If you enjoyed *The Entitled*, please leave a review.
Thank you.

**Reed and Tess conclude in *The Enlightened*
Book 2 of The Entitled Duet
Coming soon**

My secret's out. Reed knows the truth.

The destruction's done. There's no taking it back.

Reed took *all* my firsts like a shiny present. He made promises with silky words I greedily kept as truths. But the moment I faltered, he took away everything.

Now we're both guilty of sins.

As we come together for Grandfather Ian's funeral, it's time to face what I've done—what *we've* done. The boy I've loved since age eight is now a man, his rage palpable, his turquoise eyes piercing me with an intensity that sets me on fire. Each delicious kiss seems to peel away our ugly past—a past we're desperate to escape.

They say forgiveness comes from within. Can I trust him to forgive me? Have we *both* been enlightened?

I used to believe in the fantasy of a happily ever after. Trouble is my life's not a fairy tale.

WEBSITE www.cassandrafayerobbins.com
FACEBOOK www.facebook.com/
cassandrafayerobbins/
INSTAGRAM www.instagram.com/
cassandrafayerobbins/
PINTEREST www.pinterest.com/scarllettt/
TWITTER @CassFayeRobbins
Cassie's Sassy Crew/ Reader group
NEWSLETTER www.cassandrafayerobbins.com

acknowledgements

First, I have to thank my wonderful husband Mark. He has supported and loved me even with all my craziness for years. I'm just so happy I got drunk on margaritas and said yes! To my incredible children who think I'm the best mom in the world. Best kids ever! To my brothers Chris, Duke, and Jake, I'm so lucky to have you guys. To Dahlia Narvaez, my sister-in-law. Not only did you let me read to you constantly, you were my food guru. To my dad, your support and love mean everything to me. I love you all so much.

To my incredible editor, Nikki Busch. Your guidance and ability to smooth out my sentences—and let's not forget removing my commas—is a feat in itself. I loved *The Entitled* from the beginning, and you turned it into something I'm extremely proud of. Thank you. My cover designer, Michele Catalano, you are a true artist. Thank you for creating pure magic and for capturing Tess and Reed so perfectly.

To the Next Step PR Services, all of you are unbelievable. Thank you! Colleen Oppenheim, I can't tell you how much I appreciate everything you do—so lucky I found you. To my best friend Jean and her fantastic husband Richard: Jean, your support, endless patience, and help with all my writing can't be expressed. To Bex Dane, your knowledge astounds me. Not only are you a great author, but your help is unbelievably appreciated. Naomi Springthorp and Auden Dar, your good energy and help were amazing. To my betas—Ann Marie, Regina, Annie, Debbie, and Sarah—I thank all of you from the bottom of my heart. Love you guys.

I want to give a big thanks to our Minnesota family. I couldn't ask for a better cheerleading squad, and it means the world to me. Connor, your videos are fantastic! I can't wait to do more. To all my friends on Facebook and Alessandra Torre Inkers, I literally learned how to self-publish from all of you. To all my friends I didn't get to mention, if you are in my life, you're important. To my mother, Alma. She installed in me the joys of reading and was the greatest woman I know. She was more than my mother; she was my best friend. I miss her every day. I know this book would make her proud. My last thank-you is to you, my readers who bought this book. I hope you enjoyed it. I loved writing it and can't wait to carry on with this duet.

about the author

Cassandra Robbins is a *USA Today*, Amazon Top 100, KDP All-Star, and international bestselling author. She threatened to write a romance novel for years and finally let the voices take over with her debut novel, *The Entitled*. She's a self-proclaimed hopeless romantic driven to create obsessive, angst-filled characters who have to fight for their happily ever after. Cassandra resides in Los Angeles with her hot husband, two beautiful children, and a fluffy Samoyed, Stanley. Her family and friends are her lifeline but writing is her passion.

Made in United States
North Haven, CT
22 August 2022

23063454R00233